OCT - - 2017

CH

the Summer *that* Made Us

ROBYN CARR

the
Summer
that
Made Us

mira

ISBN-13: 978-0-7783-3104-9

The Summer That Made Us

Copyright © 2017 by Robyn Carr

For questions and comments about the quality of this book, please contact us at
CustomerService@Harlequin.com.

www.BookClubbish.com

Printed in U.S.A.

For Margaret O'Neill Marbury,
whose brilliance I greatly admire and whose wit and charm
are extraordinary. Thank you with all my heart!

the Summer *that* Made Us

Chapter One

Charlene Berkey was devastated. Her television career had come to an abrupt end. She should have been better prepared—the ratings had been falling and daytime talk shows were shrinking in popularity, but she thought her show would survive. The suits at the network kept telling her she'd be fine. Then, without warning, they canceled the show. They didn't offer her any options. There wasn't even a position available doing the weather. She was on the street, unemployed and feeling too old to compete at the age of forty-four.

The situation put a terrible strain on her relationship. Michael, typically such a sensitive man, didn't seem to understand what this turn of events did to her self-esteem, her self-image. She felt overwhelmed, terrified and useless. She had no idea what the future held for her.

If all that wasn't bad enough, her sister Megan was only forty-two and fighting stage-four breast cancer. Her most recent procedure to beat the monster was a bone marrow transplant and now all she could do was wait.

Charley made a quick decision. She wanted to use this time she suddenly had to be with her sister. She picked up her phone.

★ ★ ★

"I want to go to the lake house," Meg said. "Like we used to when we were kids. I want to get up on one of those bright summer mornings, sit on the dock and watch the sun rise and the fish jump, and see those old fishermen floating out there with their lines cast, waiting for a catch. I want to spend the summer thinking about the way we were—six little blondes with bodies brown as berries. Half-naked, dirty as dogs, flushed and happy and healthy and strong. Our sleeping bags out on the porch, giggling late into the muggy summer nights."

"While the mosquitoes ate us alive," Charley said.

"I don't remember being upset about mosquitoes as a kid."

"You got it the worst," Charley said. "You looked like you had chicken pox."

"I want to spend the summer at the lake."

"God, no! It's not the place you remember," Charley said. "It must be uninhabitable. It's been years since the family abandoned it. It's old, Meg. Old and neglected. It's dying a slow death, I think."

"That makes two of us," she said.

"Please don't say that," Charley begged.

"John and I snuck up there once," Meg said, speaking of her husband, a pediatrician to whom she'd been married for twelve years. They were like the perfect couple with the exception of a brief separation just a couple of years ago. "It looked kind of tired and it needs some work. But...oh, Charley, it brought back such wonderful memories. The house might've gone to hell like the rest of the family, but the lake is still so pretty, so peaceful."

"It's a long way from your doctor, from the hospital," Charley said.

"Better still. I'm sick of both. I want to rest, have some peace."

"And you think opening up that lake house against Mother's express wishes will bring peace?" Charley asked.

"Guess what? I don't give a shit, how's that? Bunny died twenty-seven years ago. If Mother wants to suffer for the rest of her life, what can I do about it? It's time Louise learned, not everything is about her."

"She's going to be impossible," Charley said.

Megan laughed. "Do you care?"

"I don't have a key," Charley said, refusing to answer the question. "Do you?"

"You don't need a key, Charley. Those windows on the porch aren't even locked. Or the locks rotted away and are useless. We can get in and have the locks replaced."

"She'll have us arrested."

"Her dying daughter? And her unemployed and homeless daughter?"

"You're not dying! And I'm not exactly homeless—I'm just going to rent out my house so I can come and be with you."

"You *are* unemployed…"

"That's just for now," she said. "I'm going to be with you until you turn a corner and start to get better. Stronger. Which you will."

"At the lake," Megan said.

"Aw, jeez…"

"Admit it, you're dying to go back. To the scene of the crime, so to speak. We might figure out a few things…"

"What's there to figure out?" Charlene asked. "It was the perfect storm. Bunny drowned, I was already in trouble even if I didn't know it, Uncle Roy was down to his hundredth second chance and blew town and Mother and Aunt Jo weren't speaking. When they couldn't help each other through the darkness the rest of the family went down like dominoes."

"All precipitated by Bunny's accident?" Meg sounded doubtful. "There was other stuff going on or else Mother would have accepted whatever comfort Aunt Jo could give. They were so close!"

"Jo didn't have much to give just then," Charley said. "Her husband ran off, leaving her penniless and heartbroken. Mother seemed to blame Aunt Jo. Mother has always found a handy person to blame. All of us kids struggled as a result but I've made my peace with it—we were a completely dysfunctional family that, God forbid, should get help."

Charley had often wondered how they could have been saved from such utter disaster. It was obvious what went wrong—poor little Bunny, gone. But it remained a mystery how everything could go as wrong as it had. That was probably why she had been so successful in the talk show business—that search for answers. She'd had a San Francisco–based television talk show for a dozen years and, since she'd studied journalism and psychology, she'd favored guests who had insights into dysfunctional people and relationships. It had been a very popular show.

And it was now canceled. "I want to go back," Meg said. "I want to see if I remember."

There it is, Charley thought. Everyone in the family had their own response to Bunny's sudden death and Megan's was to forget. Most of that last summer at the lake didn't happen in her mind. She had been only fifteen at the time. The doctor called it a nervous breakdown and completely understandable, given the circumstances. They hospitalized and medicated her. She didn't stay in the hospital long, then came home and seemed her old self with one exception—she couldn't remember almost a year of her life. Pieces came back over time but it wasn't talked about.

The Berkey-Hempstead family was very good at *not* talking about things.

"Do you think if you go back to the lake for a while it will all come flooding back, after twenty-seven years?"

"No," Meg said. "I think I'll remember the golden days of summers there. I think I'll remember what a happy childhood we had. For the most part. I think it will be healing. So relaxing and healthy. I want to hear the ducks, the boats on the lake, the children at the camp down the road, the naughty teenagers partying across the lake in that cove. Surely that's still there, the cove."

Charlene remembered partying on the beach at the cove around the bend from the lodge. She had been all of sixteen. "Hopefully someone built a great big house there," she said. "Or a parking lot."

"I hope it's not very changed…"

"That's what you really want?" Charley asked.

"It's all I want."

Charley knew she had no choice because you don't deny your only sister who has cancer anything. "I'll have to go there," she said. "Certainly things will have to be done to make it civilized. I'll have to make sure the house is habitable. I should tell Michael our plans, talk with Eric…"

"Will Michael put up a stink about this?" Meg asked.

"I don't know why he should. Of course I'll have his complete support—he loves you. Maybe he'll even steal a little time and come out for a visit, bring Eric."

"Everything is all right with you and Michael, isn't it?" Megan asked.

"Of course! Why would you ask that?"

"I don't know," Megan said. "You sounded uncomfortable when I asked about him."

Charlene laughed. "Sorry. This is an odd time. I have no job, no place of my own, no idea what's coming next. The only home I have is Michael's house in Palo Alto. It shouldn't be such an adjustment. But it is."

"I bet you feel dependent for the first time in your life," Megan suggested.

"Maybe that's it," she said. But that wasn't it. She and Michael were fighting. They'd had a standoff. About marriage, of all things.

Charley Hempstead met Michael Quincy when she was twenty-two and he was thirty-two. It was supposed to be a rebound fling, not a twenty-two-year love affair. Charley had been through quite a lot by that time in her young life; she'd had a baby out of wedlock at seventeen and had given her up for adoption, was attending college in California—as far away from her mother as she could get—and had been through a string of boyfriends, all useless college boys.

Michael hadn't fared much better. When they met he was separated from his wife of six years and it was a bitter parting, the divorce promising to be quite messy. He was a professor of political science and had just escaped a shallow, loveless, acrimonious marriage. On the one hand, he was relieved there were no children to suffer through the divorce, but on the other, he worried he might never be a father. He had wanted children. His wife had not.

Both of them embarked on their relationship thinking it would probably be a mere comfortable blip on the radar, a placeholder until they could heal and regain their strength. But they were derailed by passion. Michael, the handsome young professor who all the coeds crushed on, fell in love with

THE SUMMER THAT MADE US

Charley. And Charley fell for him. They were living together in a small apartment in Berkeley within a few months. They talked, debated, read and made love constantly. They didn't marry—at first because of the complications of Michael's divorce and later because Michael was a little soured on marriage and didn't want to spoil the relationship they had. Charley, if she was honest with herself, wanted to be different. Modern. And she didn't mind pissing off her mother. The fact that Charley became pregnant accidentally a few years later changed very little. By then, Michael's divorce was final, the settlement done, and he bought a small but fashionable home in Palo Alto, a place for them to raise their child. It was the '90s—people cohabitated and had children together all the time; women even had them alone without suffering much recrimination. So, for Michael, who had feared he might never have a child, and Charley, who had been forced to give one up, the birth of Eric brought much happiness.

Michael did want them to marry one day to establish that their commitment was real, fearless and holy.

"Holy?" she'd asked with a laugh. "When did you get religious?"

"I just mean I'm not afraid to make a lifetime pledge. I want to do that. Someday."

By the time little Eric was four years old, Charley had graduated from Berkeley and been in the workforce for some time, moving up very quickly in the world of television. She used the name Berkey, dropping Hempstead. She said it was better for television, but truthfully, she was still angry with her parents and secretly hoped it would piss them off. Michael was a full professor at Stanford. Charley went from production in the San Francisco affiliate, to weather reporter, then anchorwoman, and it wasn't long before she took over a local morning talk show. The ratings soared and she was picked up by other markets. She bought herself a town house in the city—a very nice town house with a view—which she had used every nickel plus loans to buy. It was not only a great investment but convenient. Even though there were two houses between them, they managed to spend most nights together. If they stayed with her in the city, Eric and Michael would head back to Michael's Palo Alto house and that was where Eric went to school. Charley's house wasn't entirely an indulgence. She reported to the studio at four a.m. and as long as she lived in the city the station sent a car for her.

They'd been together for twenty-two years. They'd had arguments here and there, power struggles over how to raise Eric or how the money should be spent, and conflicting political ideas. They managed well for two people with demanding careers and a child they were devoted to; they made such an exceptional team they were the envy of many long-married friends. The subject of their own marriage hardly ever came up.

Then Charley's world turned on its ear. She had not been prepared for the network to pull her show without warning. She had no backup plan. At almost the same moment Megan was undergoing radical chemo to precede a bone marrow transplant. The doctors gave her a fifty-fifty chance of surviving the cancer, which had spread, and the chemo had already nearly wiped her out. Charley was not prepared to lose another sister.

And she was not prepared to have no career. Her career was her identity; she was proud of it. She had been successful.

"Sounds like a good time for us to get married," Michael said.

She was stunned. "What, in your twisted mind, makes you think this is a good time for me?" she asked, gobsmacked.

"And what, pray, do you think marriage will do to make it good?"

He frowned at her. "You're not working. You don't have anything else going on. You said you weren't prepared to dive into the job search immediately, that you needed a rest and time to think, which is a very good decision. I'm going to Cambridge in the fall for one semester. You should come with me."

"So you're going to rescue me?" she asked.

"I hadn't thought of it exactly like that, but wouldn't it take some of the stress off you?"

"Very sensitive, Michael," she said. "My job loss and my dying sister make it a convenient time for you to drag me to England for six months. How perfectly relaxing."

"If you're going to be irrational, I withdraw my offer."

"You needn't withdraw it," she said. "I decline the very romantic proposal."

"You want romance, Charley? Here's the romance of it! My father died when he was fifty-seven. I'm fifty-four. I'm perfectly comfortable with our relationship except for one thing—Eric. No, that's not all—there are several things actually. If my fate is similar, I'd like to leave a widow, not a girlfriend. I'd like to bypass inheritance issues. Hell, if I'm sick in a hospital I don't want you to be denied being at my bedside because you're not my wife."

"Who's going to bar my way? Our son? Your mother, who adores me? Your sister, who wants to be my best friend? *Girlfriend!* After twenty-two years and a son!"

"You know you're more than a girlfriend," he said.

"But apparently you don't!"

"I didn't think it mattered, being unmarried," he said. "Lately it's started to matter to me. I love you. You love me.

I'd like a legal commitment. I want there to be no doubt how we feel about each other."

"I didn't think there was any doubt," she said. "Apparently you have some doubts if you suddenly need to legalize things."

"It's not doubt," he said. "It's the feeling that something is missing. As I get older that feeling gets stronger."

"And so you decided that this moment, when I'm crushed by suddenly being fired and terrified that my sister could die...*this* would be the best moment for me to make a decision like this?"

"We could have an extended honeymoon in England," he said.

"While *you* work? What is it you expect me to do while you're working?"

"I'm sure you wouldn't be bored. Look, this isn't just for us but also for Eric. For Eric's children. But I don't want to push you into making a commitment you don't feel."

"Eric is eighteen," she rallied. "We have, if nothing else, a common-law marriage."

"Common-law?" he shouted back. "Is that good enough for you? Because it's not good enough for me!"

Of course the argument escalated from there as all of the frustration and fear and disappointment poured out of her.

It ended with her saying she needed to go see Megan and him saying, "Maybe that's a good idea."

She told herself their relationship wasn't falling apart. They bickered but also said "I love you" a lot. She didn't leave Palo Alto angry, but she did leave worried and confused. Why did he doubt her now after all these years? And why, for God's sake, was she refusing to legally marry him? He'd been the only man in her life for twenty-two years! What was wrong with them?

Maybe with time apart she'd figure that out.

★ ★ ★

Charley had been in Minneapolis with Megan and John for a few days, watching as her sister grew a little stronger every day. She'd seen Eric right before she left and had talked to him since she'd arrived. He was a freshman at Stanford, where his tuition was free, one of the perks of having a professor father. He didn't live with his father, however. He agreed to Stanford but he was ready for a little independence. He was in a dorm but he'd pledged a fraternity and in a couple of years he'd live in a frat house, something that made Charley shudder. But she completely understood.

She called Michael. "How are you? I miss you," she said.

"I like the sound of that," he said.

"Are you walking? It sounds like you're walking…"

"To my car. I'm done for the day but I have to go back for a department meeting tonight."

"Have you seen Eric?" she asked.

Michael laughed. "He sees me as little as possible. I have to make an appointment. He texts me. I think he does that to keep me from trying to find him and actually talk to him. He's getting decent grades so I guess he's all right."

"I probably talk to him more than you do," she said. "I responded to one of his texts and told him that was not going to scratch my mother-itch—I had to hear the sound of his voice. So he calls. He's placating us."

"More like playing us. He's keeping us out of his business," Michael said. "He's building his own life."

"Michael, I miss you, but I'm staying here awhile. Meg is getting stronger. That doesn't necessarily mean she's out of the woods, but it's such a relief. She's eating. She's up and about. Reading. She doesn't have a lot of energy but it's better than none."

"I'm glad to hear she's feeling better," he said.

"She wants to go to the lake house for the summer," Charley said. "I'm going to drive up there, see how it looks, maybe do some repairs, see if I can get it ready. And I can't let her go alone."

Michael was quiet for a moment. She heard his car door open, then close. "I understand." Something in his voice said he was disappointed, that he'd rather they spend the summer working out whatever was wrong with them, not being apart.

"I'm going to take care of things like that, then I'll come home to visit, to spend some quality time with you. I can put someone else in charge. Maybe John can take some time off. So, give me a little time to get the lake house straightened out, then we'll talk about your schedule. When you have a little time for me…"

"I'll make time for you," he said. "I miss you, too. I even miss fighting with you."

"We don't fight much," she said. "Do we?"

"We've been fighting too much. Just about that M word. I think you have a deep psychological fuckup that makes you scared of it and you should seek help."

She laughed in spite of herself. "You're probably right. Add that to all my deep psychological fuckups. But I'm going to see you before too long. I'm really no good without you. You're my rock. I love you."

He let out his breath. "That was nice to hear," he said. "I love you, too."

What is wrong with me? she asked herself. Why not just agree to marry him, go to England with him, settle in as a wife, adjust to that new title? It wasn't as though she'd give him up at the point of a gun. Then why not just marry him if that's what he wanted?

Because right now she felt very vulnerable and dependent. She didn't feel whole. Michael hadn't exactly said, "Since you have nothing better to do, we might as well get married," but his presentation left her feeling worthless. And who was going to feel sorry for her? She had twelve years of extremely well-compensated success. People said she should take a year off, clear out the cobwebs, rest and relax.

She felt anything but relaxed. She was stuck with time off because she was canceled and because of Megan's illness, but it didn't feel good. It didn't make her feel strong the way her talk show had. She wanted to feel sturdy and confident again. Marriage after all these years wasn't going to do that for her. Turning her into a wife instead of a television star didn't make her feel stronger; it made her feel even more vulnerable. She wanted to feel equal again.

Charley went to the hospital to see Dr. John Crane, Megan's husband, rather than waiting to talk to him when he got home in the evening. She wanted him to speak frankly with Megan not present. She asked him if he could arrange his schedule to look after Meg for a few days if she wasn't available. John said it was fine; he could be there earlier in the evening and leave later in the morning. He would adjust his schedule to make dinner in the evenings, breakfast in the morning before he went to work, and he would check on her at least once during the day.

"You're such a good team," Charley said. "A couple of years ago when you were separated briefly, you seemed to be as much in love as ever. If you don't mind my asking, what happened?"

"Love was never the problem," John said. "We'll talk about it someday. Right now I just want to get her through the next few weeks. Are you going back to California to see Michael and Eric?"

"No, actually. I'm going up to the lake house to see what

needs to be done to make it habitable. Meg wants to spend the summer there."

John's face split into a huge grin. "So she finally found someone who would take that on. Why am I surprised that it's you?"

"Maybe because if I was still working it wouldn't be. Or if Eric were younger, or many variables. But I'm available and want to see Meg through this recovery. Maybe you should tell me right now—how much care should I plan on for her recovery? Could this get worse?"

"It could, but it shouldn't right now. She doesn't need around-the-clock nursing care. But at the moment she's too weak and tires too easily to look after herself for any length of time. She can't cook, do her own laundry or clean the house, but she'll probably continue to get stronger. At least for now."

"And then?" Charley asked.

"And then stronger still unless…" He shrugged. "Look, the reality is, it could go either way. Quite a while ago she said no more chemo, that it took too great a toll and she wanted to enjoy what time she had left. This last round, prepping her for the transplant was the hardest yet. Four years, Charley. She's had enough." He hung his head slightly, then raised it again. "And that's why. That's the separation, right there."

"Huh?" she said, confused.

"The separation. Our disagreement was all about treatment. I bet you didn't expect that, did you?"

"Wait," she said. "I didn't know you didn't agree on the course of treatment…"

"She doesn't want you to know, Charley. Meg didn't want treatment. I wanted her to do anything and everything. I admit I wouldn't have done it, either, if I was facing stage-four metastatic cancer but I wanted her to. I couldn't let go.

22

I wanted anything that might give her a chance and I would have taken miracles."

"But she's been in remission a couple of times!" Charley said.

"Only for it to come back harder and force her into more torture. She didn't want me to make medical decisions for her if she was unable to do it herself and I'm afraid I brought that on myself. But we made our peace with it—I won't do that to her anymore. I've given her my word—it's up to her. I'll support her. She says this is the last time, and if that's what she wants, so be it." He was quiet for a moment. "Because, no matter what, I love her."

Charley had wondered why John and Megan had been arguing so much, especially when Megan was undergoing chemotherapy and radiation. Then she wondered why John was still around so much if they were supposed to be separated and talking divorce. That was two years ago. Now it all made sense—John wanted Meg to accept radical and even experimental treatment while Megan was saying, "It's not just a waste of time. It's also making me so sick."

Charley knew from her research into various talk show guests that it wasn't always the case with cancer treatment. In fact, most forms of breast cancer were easily treatable and highly survivable. Megan just got herself a rare and aggressive form. And Charley, like John, had always thought, *That means you just fight harder.*

But she knew how much Meg had suffered. And fought. If she wanted this to be her last battle, that was her decision. And Charley vowed to honor it.

It begged the question—did Meg want to go to the lake to rest and recover? Or to die in the last place they were a family?

★ ★ ★

As she drove to the lake house, Charley thought back to all those summers when her family made the same drive. They spent every summer at the house on Lake Waseka. A cabin or house on a lake was almost an institution in Minnesota, the Land of 10,000 Lakes. Lake property was handed down through the generations and people who didn't have a home or cabin had a piece of property they could park a fifth wheel or Airstream on for weekends or vacations. But the Berkeys had a very nice house because Charley's grandfather was a superior court judge. The judge started sending his wife and two daughters to the lake for the summer when his daughters, Josephine and Louise, were nine and ten years old. He'd drive up from the Twin Cities on some weekends and for two weeks in August. Lou and Jo continued the tradition of summer at the lake after they were married and had daughters of their own.

Charley, her sisters and her cousins lived for summer. They looked forward to it all year, started shopping in April and packing in the middle of May. The very day after school let out, off they went, north to Lake Waseka, a two-hour drive. Two moms and six kids packed into Louise's car—first a station wagon and later, as the kids grew, a van. There was no law about seat belts back then—they were merely recommended. The Hempstead girls usually piled into the back on top of each other. They'd take enough luggage to get through a week or two, stacked on top of the car in a luggage rack, and on the weekend Charley's father would bring the rest, thoughtfully packed boxes of linens, clothes, towels, toys and any other items they didn't want to live without for three months.

It was always so meticulously planned.

The judge and Grandma Berkey stopped going to the lake

house by the time there were four granddaughters, being overwhelmed by the noise and clutter of small children. And soon there were six—all little girls—and it was more than the grandparents could take, so they started renting a cabin at the lodge across the lake for their occasional weekends.

Six girls, each born one year after the other. Three for Louise, three for Jo. It seemed perfectly choreographed—Louise, the oldest sister, had Charlene and the following year Jo had Hope. Next Lou had Megan; a year later Jo gave birth to Krista. Then there was a little slip and when Krista was only a year old Jo gave birth to Beverly, who came so fast she was actually born at the lake house. Not to be outdone, Louise then had Mary Verna, who they called Bunny. And then they stopped. Six girls, sisters and cousins, in six years. Stairstep, tow-haired girls, bonded by blood and family and not just a little DNA because sisters Lou and Jo had married brothers Carl and Roy.

The Hempstead girls appeared to have charmed lives and they were happy and carefree during summer. Life back in the Twin Cities the rest of the year had its challenges, like all families. Particularly for Jo and Roy; they struggled with money and issues brought on by that struggle. But summers were different. The lake was a magic place. A haven. All of the problems they might have had through the school year drifted away. Until the summer of '89. That summer everything changed. Charley and Megan's little sister, Bunny, the youngest of the six girls, Louise's baby, drowned accidentally. She was only twelve. Louise, grief-stricken and half-mad with the pain of losing a child, insisted the lake house be closed up. For good.

Charley found that at first sight the house was worn but presentable. She knew her mother paid a local family to keep an eye on the place over the years. The grass was cut and the hedges trimmed. But it was clearly in need of some attention. It was a roomy place—three bedrooms downstairs, two small rooms upstairs in the loft with dormers, two full baths and a half bath in the master. Plus, there was living space over the boathouse and the wide, deep porch was screened. The screen was torn and sagging and there wasn't any outdoor furniture anymore.

She pried open a porch window. Meg was right; it opened easily. Upon getting inside it became obvious she hadn't been the first one to do that. The place was heaped with trash and the beds downstairs looked used. Stained. There were, of course, no linens. But all that aside, she was wildly optimistic—the damage was all cosmetic. She would need new furniture and new appliances. The porch would have to be rescreened. Everything would need a serious scrubbing and fresh paint. There should be new toilets and maybe new tubs.

But first, she'd call an electrician to make sure the wiring was safe. And she'd have to hire someone who would clean the place out and make a trip or two to the dump.

Charley went back outside and sat on a tree stump that had been there since she was a little girl. She pulled out her phone and began making a list in the notes section. The afternoon was sunny but not warm; April in Minnesota, especially on the lake, was chilly. The lake was so calm and quiet. The gentle lapping of the waves at the shore was soothing. She closed her eyes.

Then she began to hear it—the laughter of children. Someone's mother yelling from the porch, *You better not be in the lake without an adult!* She could smell hot dogs and ribs on the grill, smell the campfire, toasted marshmallows; she saw seven sunfish lying on the dock to be cleaned—the largest of the catch. Someone whistling for his dog. A happy squeal and splash. Women laughing. The horn of a speedboat and the whistles of men. The pounding of little feet across the porch, across the dock. Whispers and giggles from the screened-in porch at night; laughter from the moms inside the house. Music from the radio mingled with the laughter. Voices and shouting of a late-night party somewhere on the lake. She recalled it so vividly she could hear it—the sounds of summer.

Maybe Meg was right. Maybe summer at the lake would bring her comfort. It could heal her, Charley thought hopefully. Or give her peace in her last days?

When Meg was going into the hospital for the bone marrow transplant she had said, "This may not work, Charley. But there's one thing I need you to know. It's important that you know. I'm not afraid. Either way, I'm not afraid."

That's when Charley decided. Whatever Megan wanted, if it was within her power, she'd make sure she had it. *And,* Charley thought, *it wouldn't hurt me to make peace with the past.*

Chapter Two

Megan was thrilled to get a call from Charley right away. "Good news, Meg. The house needs work but it looks like it's all cosmetic. It's a wreck—people have definitely broken in and used the place. It's trashed. And of course the furniture is dirty and rotting—but I can buy furniture and appliances in a flash. I'm going to get an electrician out here to check the wiring first. Also someone to haul trash. Those two things have to be done right away before I come back to the city."

"Oh, Charley! We'll repay you every dime!"

"That's the least of my worries," she said. Charley had been a minor star and had earned good money and invested wisely. She gulped back the fear that her earning days were over.

"Is it going to be a huge job?" Meg asked.

"Nope. Soap and water, paint, new furniture and appliances, new screening."

"I wish I could help," Megan said.

"I'm not going to do it myself," Charley said with a laugh. "I'm going to hire people."

"When will it be done? Will it be done soon?"

"It'll be done by June," she said. "It'll probably be done

before June but it's really too cold to stay here right now. We need to wait for summer, Meg. The weather has to be warmer, especially for you. I'll know more after I talk to a few people. I'll be home in a few days."

"Where are you staying?"

"There's a motel just outside Waseka."

"Did you look at the lodge?"

"Uh, no. For some strange reason I don't feel like going to the lodge."

"I promise you won't see a familiar face, Charley!" Meg said.

"Just the same," Charley said. "So, I don't want you doing anything strenuous, but if you're feeling good, you might start making a couple of lists. I haven't looked through the cupboards yet but I'm sure most of the kitchenware is just too old and filthy to work for us. And there are no linens here. None. It looks like most of the pieces of wooden furniture are salvageable after some cleaning and polishing, but the armchairs, sofas and mattresses are out of here."

"Okay!" Meg said. "I'll do that! I'll make lists!"

"Don't get yourself too excited," Charley cautioned. "You're supposed to be resting and meditating and growing healthy cells."

"I will!" she said. "I am! OMG, this is happening!"

"Oh, brother," Charley said. "I hope this wasn't a mistake..."

"It's not! It's happiness! Haven't you heard that joy is good for illness? Joy and laughter and lake houses."

"Take a nap," Charley said, signing off.

Meg immediately started making lists and it filled her with optimism. That had to mean something good, she thought. She'd listed about twenty items when she stopped and instead went to the desk in the den and got out her stationery.

She wanted to write to a lot of people who would probably either ignore her note or laugh and throw it away, but she was hell-bent.

Dear Hope,
In June we're opening the lake house. Charley is doing most of the work and we're going to spend the summer there. As you know, I've been somewhat under the weather.

She stopped long enough to laugh. But she thought it would be impolite to write, "As you know, I'm probably dying…" She pressed on.

I've finished my chemo and bone marrow transplant and the only thing to do now is rest, relax, eat healthy food and heal. The lake is the perfect place to do that. We'd love it if you could join us. Just let me know the dates if you're coming.
Just like old times,
Megan

She sent notes to Hope, Krista and Beverly even though Hope lived in Pennsylvania and hadn't been back to Minnesota in at least five years and the only person Hope really kept in touch with was Grandma Berkey and occasionally Charley. Hope was a snob and loved having a famous cousin. Krista, unfortunately, was in a women's prison, and the last time Megan heard from her, there was no parole in sight. And Beverly left the family for foster care the year after Bunny drowned. She went to live with a family better equipped to take care of her in the years following her trauma. Bunny had been Beverly's best friend and they'd been together in that little rowboat when the storm rose up suddenly and Bunny was lost. Her foster family became her family of choice, though she did stay in touch with her mother, Jo. And Megan got Christmas cards with little notes. But the idea of Beverly going to the lake? After what had happened there? It was at best a very slim possibility.

Since it wasn't likely any of them would come, Megan decided to reach out to Aunt Jo and Grandma Berkey. Aunt Jo would never go to the lake without an invitation from Louise and no one knew why or how Louise had that kind of power over her sister. They hadn't been close since Bunny died. And Grandma Berkey was in a nursing home—someone would have to fetch her. With a little guilt and a sigh of resignation Megan thought that Charley would do that if she wanted it badly enough. Or John would. At the moment Meg had some very persuasive powers.

The only one she didn't send a note to was her mother. She hadn't even told Louise what they were doing. She'd deal with that later. But she did put stamps on her notes and took them out to the mailbox for the postman to pick up.

She told John what she'd done. "But I don't think I'll tell Charley," she said.

"I can take a leave this summer," John said. "I want us to be together."

"Come on the weekends," she said. "Let me stay with Charley during the week. Go to work. Your patients need you, you need them and you need to live a normal life." Then she rubbed her cheek against his. "I might not be around forever, my darling. And I want you to carry on. In fact, the only thing I will ever ask of you is that you carry on."

She put on some classical, cell-fortifying symphony music, reclined on the sofa in the den, took deep meditative breaths and pictured Lake Waseka as she remembered it, when it was at its best. She began to see them all as children, before the last year, six little blondes with bodies like brown sugar, freckled from the sun. Dirty, with calluses on their bare feet from not wearing shoes all summer, flushed and happy, gamy and healthy and strong. Giggling late into the muggy summer nights. Summer after summer. Everything that had nagged or bothered all year long disappeared as it was left behind. It was an escape from the real world. Grandma and the judge covered the expenses, from gas to groceries, so the material burdens were fewer and Lou and Jo were almost equals. This was significant because Aunt Jo worried about money all the time and it made her fretful. At the lake she was carefree. Happy. And there was almost nothing prettier than Aunt Jo when she was happy.

Their mothers became best friends again; there was laughter and what Grandma used to call shenanigans. They were fun. Young men passing in speedboats noticed them. Both Lou and Jo were attractive women. Lou was statuesque and bold and brazen while Jo was small and lovely and buxom and fragile. They were opposites who complemented each other. Lou often groused that Jo was the pretty one but it wasn't exactly true. Lou could be pretty, too, when she was in a good mood, laughed and smiled. It was only the frown of envy and anger that made her plain.

At night they'd play cards or Scrabble and sometimes turn the radio up and dance—line dances and disco and boogie-woogie. All the little girls would dance, too. It was like having a party with your best friends every day of the summer. Then Lou and Jo would sleep together in Grandma's big bed just like having a pajama party and whisper and laugh late into the night. There were eight bodies and five beds; when their husbands showed up on weekends they'd pile the kids on top of each other or make them take to the screened-in porch, but that big king-size bed of Grandma's served them very well when it was just the two of them and the six kids.

Jo giggled more than Lou but Lou gave more advice than Jo. Whatever it was about their mysterious and complex relationship, it worked every summer. Lou would be her hardy self—capable and energetic and take-charge. And Aunt Jo would regress a little when around Lou, becoming her sweet, slightly incompetent self, but she would do whatever Lou suggested, which seemed to please them both tremendously. If you needed snuggling, like if you'd been stung by a bee, Aunt Jo was the one to go to. But if you wanted to try swimming across the lake, it was Lou who would coach and follow in the boat. Lou would teach the girls to dive; Jo would play dress-up with them. Between the two of them, no matter what problems they had all winter at home, every summer at the lake was a huge, raving, laughing, shining success. Before everything went so horribly wrong.

As Meg relaxed, she began to remember the time she fell apart. She lost her mind when she was fifteen. She'd been packing for the lake.

Carl, Meg's father, stayed in the city to work and came to the lake on weekends. It was okay to ask him to bring something from home now and then, but he hated to be asked by everyone, all the time, week after week. He had a wife and three daughters, after all, and sometimes their requests for things that had to be searched out of closets and drawers frustrated him, made him cranky and not very helpful. So they tried to pack everything they needed for the summer. Meg tried hardest of all.

She could hear Charley and Mother fighting downstairs in the kitchen. As usual. Their voices would rise to screaming now and then; every year older Charley got, the more she swore at Mother. Mother swore, too, then denied she ever used a bad word. Whenever Megan heard them fight she renewed her own vow never to put herself through that useless exercise. Did Charley really think she was going to win against Mother? Did anyone ever win an argument with Louise?

It also meant no one was helping Bunny pack. Being the baby, Bunny tended to lack focus, expecting a big sister or her doting mother to step in and finish whatever she was doing. Bunny was spoiled. She was the only one Louise never yelled at. So, when someone gave her a chore, she didn't take it seriously. She might pack a couple of things and then get sidetracked, dressing a doll or reading a book. Megan went down the hall to help her.

Bunny's room was gone. Oh, the room was there, but the bed, dresser, toy chest, bookcase and Mary-had-a-little-lamb lamps were gone. Instead, Mother's sewing machine was set up there. Also an ironing board, a trestle table covered with fabric and patterns, a sewing chest, a model-form and rocking chair. Megan felt disoriented. This was all wrong. She put a hand to her temple, feeling dizzy.

She walked around the upstairs hallway, stupidly looking for the missing room. All four bedrooms were accounted for—her parents', hers, Charley's and... But Bunny had no room.

"You'd better watch who you're talking to, young lady," Mother was shouting.

"Yeah? So what are you going to do about it? Send me away, maybe? Wouldn't that be *awful*?" Charley shouted back.

"Maybe if you'd mind your manners, you'd find life here could be pleasant. Not to mention plentiful!"

Meg walked into the kitchen. Charley had changed. Megan stared at her, dazed. Who was this? Her hair was long, straight and stringy, a band tied around her head. She was so skinny, like a toothpick. Her clothes were terrible—torn and patched jeans, some kind of symbol sewn onto her little butt, and you could see her bra right through the gauzy shirt that only accentuated how flat her chest was. Her bare feet were filthy and her cheeks sunken. And the rage on her face was astonishing. Megan had seen Charley mad before, but nothing like this.

Louise had also changed. She was heavier, her hair very gray, and her face was deeply lined. Her skin was especially crepey around her eyes and under her chin. She looked like she'd been awake for a year. Her down-turned mouth was grim...but then it was usually grim when she wasn't having her way.

"Where's Bunny?" Meg asked.

They stopped fighting and turned to look at her.

"Where's her room? Her stuff?"

They gaped at her. A look of absolute horror crossed Louise's face.

"What's going on?" Megan asked. "Where's Bunny? You know, *Mary Verna*?"

"That's not funny, Meg," Louise said.

"Funny?"

"About Bunny," Charley said.

"Where is she?" Megan demanded, tears gathering on her face, her voice shaky. She was confused and frightened.

"She's dead and you know it!" Charley snapped.

Louise didn't say anything. They stood in the kitchen in heavy silence, looking at each other. Then Megan noticed the kitchen was just a little different and everyone, including herself, was wearing clothes she hadn't seen before. Meg grabbed her stomach like she was going to be sick and made a loud, moaning noise. "Dead? No! Where's Bunny really? Where?"

"Oh, Jesus Christ," Charley swore, whirling around and presenting her back in disgust. But Louise got a strange look in her eyes and walked very slowly toward Megan as though she might bolt like a frightened fawn if anyone made any quick moves.

Megan's ears were ringing so that it sounded like her mother was talking into a tin can when she said, "Charlene, please call Dr. Sloan." Then Megan started screaming and running through the house, calling out to Bunny. She began tearing things apart, breaking things, ripping things off the walls, out of closets, pulling whole bureau drawers out and letting them fall upside down on the floor, looking for evidence of Bunny somewhere, finding none.

The police and ambulance came, someone gave her a shot, the world became very slow and quiet. The only sound was whimpering. Her own whimpering.

Megan had begun packing to go to the lake on May 8, 1989, and woke up a year later on May 12, 1990, without remembering a single thing. It was as though a slice was taken out of her brain. She spent two weeks in the hospital being treated for what the family doctor and the hospital psychiatrist decided to call a nervous breakdown. Later, when Megan became an RN, she recognized it as a psychotic break due to the psychological trauma of the past year. Bunny drowned, Charley was sent away to have and give up her baby, the family had become completely estranged. The family that had spent every summer, holiday and most Sunday afternoons together was gone.

Charley and Louise stopped fighting that summer. At least out loud. Instead, the summer was spent keeping Megan calm and remembering things to her. They all took turns—Louise and Carl and Charley. Sometimes Grandma Berkey and the judge came to visit, but the judge mainly grumbled that there weren't any screws loose on his side of the family, so he could only guess where all this psychiatry bullshit was coming from.

At the end of that summer, Charley took her leave. "Once I get a little settled in the dorm, I'll call you. I promise," she told Meg.

"Oh, Charley, can't you go to college around here?" Meg wept. "I can't live here without you! Can't you go to the university and live at home?"

"It'll be better here without me—no more fighting, yelling, swearing, threatening..."

"But what if you get hurt or something? Or what if I need you? And you're all the way in California?"

"If you need me, I'll come if I can. I think my being here... I think it's made you sick and made you forget."

"No! That can't be the reason! Oh, Charley, I just lost Bunny! I can't lose you, too. Please don't go!"

"I have to, Meg. I hate her and she hates me." She took a deep breath and squeezed Meg's hands. "I'll never forgive her. Them," she said, for it was the judge who came to Louise's aid when she said she wanted to send Charley away to have her baby. Carl was not convinced Charley should have to go but he didn't argue with Louise and the judge. "And as soon as I can, I'm going to start looking for my baby. Here," she said, handing Megan a cigar box filled with letters.

"What's this?"

"It's every letter you wrote me while I was in Florida. It will help you remember. You wrote me almost every day, Meggie. I think you kept me alive."

"But I can't keep you home!"

Her lips formed the word, but Megan didn't hear the sound. "No."

Charley didn't cry. Not when they talked about their dead sister, her lost baby or leaving home. Megan never asked but had always wondered if she knew it was a trait she seemed to share with Louise.

When Charley was away that first year, Meg spent a lot of time rereading her letters to her sister. The chronology of a year she couldn't remember. Some of the letters were smeary with tearstains that Meg assumed must have been her own. It was hard to imagine Charley crying, even in private, she was so strong. Meg had written about the quiet of the house, about how their father seemed to grieve in deep silence and withdraw further and further inside himself, no match for Louise's insistent and relentless anger. Louise had always been the more talkative of the two, but Carl no longer even responded with his usual grunts and humphs. She had written about missing Bunny but also missing her cousins—the only one she ever saw was Hope and it was as though Hope didn't know her anymore.

"I'm pretty sure no one has ever been this lonely," she wrote in one of her letters to Charley. And in the margin Charley had scribbled, "Except me!"

Charley called from Lake Waseka every day with good news and then better news. She went into the biggest real estate office in the nearest big town, Brainerd, and asked if they could help her find a competent decorator and a crew to empty the lake house of old furniture and trash. The decorator, Melissa Stewart, recognized Charley from television and they shared instant rapport.

While the junk was removed, Charley and Melissa discussed the interior design. She wasn't going to completely redecorate the place; she wanted it spruced up, painted, furnished and restored. They talked colors, appliances, mattresses and rugs. Melissa said she could text Charley pictures and make purchases on her approval.

Charley went again to Brainerd and bought new appliances, even though the electrician hadn't checked the wiring yet. They had to be purchased, anyway, didn't they? And luck was on her side. The very next day the electrician spent six hours checking the house. He wanted to make a few repairs, put in a new fuse box, replace some switches and outlets, and they'd be good to go.

Megan was so excited at the reported progress she started pulling out dishes and glasses she could spare to be taken to the lake. The kitchen counter was full of the stuff. She'd barely begun when she got tired. Bone tired. Excruciatingly tired. She wanted to lie down and thought for a second about just lying on the kitchen floor. No one had adequately prepared her for the power of the fatigue. *Cancer is a pain in the ass*, she thought.

She'd only rested for a few minutes when the sound of her doorbell brought her back to reality. All the way back—it was her mother. That, with the fatigue, turned her cranky.

When Louise made an unannounced visit in the middle of the day, it could only mean one thing. Drama. But, in a way, Meg had been expecting this. She thought Louise might get wind of the reunion she was planning even though it was destined to fail.

"Mother. Funny enough, I was just thinking about you."

Louise flapped the small envelope addressed to Grandma Berkey. The invitation Megan had sent, inviting her to come to the lake. "Have you lost your mind? Or does it give you such great pleasure to hurt me like this?"

"Come in, Mother. Please. Let me get you something to drink. Another of what you've recently had?"

Louise made a wincing gesture. "It's my bridge day. We had wine with lunch. Otherwise, as you know, I rarely drink."

"Oh, really? Is that so?" Meg said sarcastically. "So? What's the problem?" she asked, leaving her mother to stand in the doorway as she made her way slowly back to the den. She needed to sit down. She was weak. And bald. And thin as a noodle. You'd think the sight of her wasting body would intimidate Louise, make her think about someone besides herself.

"Do you have any idea how much trouble Grandma is when someone puts an idea like—"

"Sit down, Mother," Megan said softly. "The doctor said it's very bad for my cells when you stand over me, talking down at me. It's upsetting."

"Oh," Louise said, taking a seat. And instantly she picked up where she left off. "You can't imagine how difficult and obstinate and tiresome Grandma is when she's got some idea—"

"Sure I can," Megan said. "I've heard her rant for years. What's new?"

"What's new is that now she wants to go to the lake!" Louise barked.

"Well, I invited her. Why don't you bring her?" Meg asked this as though she had forgotten that Louise had not gone to the lake in almost twenty-seven years.

Louise's lips thinned and she leaned stiffly back in the chair. Megan could tell she was grinding her teeth. "Just what are you trying to prove?" she asked very sternly.

Megan took a deep breath. Then she sighed. "Nothing, Mother. I just want to go back to the lake. I loved the lake…"

"The lake that tore our family apart? The lake that swallowed up your baby sister? The lake that—"

"The last place any of us loved each other?" Megan asked, voice escalating to match Louise's.

They were silent for a long moment. "This is ridiculous," Louise said, rising as if to leave Meg's house. Or, more likely, rising so that Meg could call her back and apologize.

"No, this actually makes sense. I'll tell you what's ridiculous—that five years ago when John and I wanted to go to a lake up north for a vacation, we rented a house on a different lake so that your feelings wouldn't be hurt...when in fact we have a wonderful lake house in the family! And what's even more ridiculous is that no one ever questioned the sanity of that. That's what's crazy."

"Well, Megan, I can see I'll have no success in discussing this issue with you. I was trying to spare you, but you're going to do what you're going to do."

Spare herself, *she meant.* Meg knew Louise had never tried to spare anyone anything in her life. Louise dished it out but she didn't take it well.

"I have nothing further to say."

Hah! A trap! Louise never ran out of arguments! "Fine. Good," Meg said.

"If you're going to go, you're going to go."

"I just hope I live long enough to go," Megan said.

"You've been trying to hurt me with your impending death for four long years now, Meggie. And I don't think I have any fight left in me," Louise said.

"Mother, darling, you don't have to fight. You just like to. I *have* to."

"Oh, God, you never quit. You've become so mean-spirited."

"And cranky. And foulmouthed, too. This cancer shit's a bummer. But don't worry, Mother. I'll probably quit before you do."

"I'm leaving. I can't take any more."

"Drive carefully, will you? That wine you had at bridge smells a lot like bourbon."

Louise lifted her chin stoically. She headed for the door.

"Unreal," Megan muttered as she wearily rose to follow Louise to the door. "You act like you're afraid we're going to finally find that goddamn body buried under the porch."

Louise was brought up short with a gasp. Her skin took on an ashen pallor and she actually swooned slightly, leaning against the door. Then she slowly collected herself and left.

Chapter Three

Charley was able to accomplish a great deal in just a few days and was pretty confident that the decorator, Melissa, could finish what needed to be done in a few short weeks. Melissa could supervise the refurbishing of the wood floors, send in a chimney sweep, schedule the interior and exterior painting, stock the kitchen with small appliances, plates, glasses, pans and cutlery and buy new mattresses and porch furniture. She promised to text pictures before making purchases and Charley promised to make sure she was paid within a week of any purchases no matter how large or small.

And then the house would be like new. Oh, they would still need odds and ends—linens, comforters, rugs large and small. Melissa hoped to haunt some of the thrift shops and antique dealers to see if any side tables, a dining table and chairs and such could be added to make the place special, and Charley approved of that idea. The existing wood furniture, dressers, end tables, etc., looked like they'd be okay after some cleaning and polishing but Melissa thought she could do better with a little effort and not much money.

Just seeing the place after it had been cleared of trash and cleaned made Charley feel good about being there. It was a functional and cozy house—wide-open from living room to kitchen. She'd arrange a sofa, love seat and two large chairs in front of the fireplace, something rarely used during summer visits. A large area rug would have to be bought to cover the wood floors. The wood kitchen table that could seat six—and with extra leaves opened up to seat ten—sat behind where the sofa would be placed. Beyond that was a breakfast bar and work counter fronting the spacious kitchen. There was also an island with a vegetable sink.

Really, the kitchen needed to be gutted and remodeled with new cabinets, sink, countertop and updated work island, but for now the existing cabinets would be fine. More extensive work could be done later, when the house wasn't in use.

Melissa promised to have the cabinets cleaned, wiped down with lemon oil and in good repair for now and do the same with the bathroom cabinets and countertops.

"Are you sure you can get everything done, Melissa? I promised my sister we'd be here by June."

"Four weeks isn't even mid-May," Melissa said. "I work with some remarkable subcontractors."

"The porch furniture, Melissa. Make it nice. When the weather is good, which is most of the time, the best place to be is on the porch. The one thing Meg said she wanted was to sit on the porch on one of those sunny summer mornings and look at the fishermen out on the lake."

"It'll be resort quality," she said. Melissa pursed her lips for control and her eyes got a little wet. "You're such a good sister."

"She would do this and more for me," Charley said. "Four chaise lounges, a couple of chairs with ottomans—wicker, maybe, I don't know. A couple of simple side tables. It'll all be moved to the boathouse for winter. And pick a good quality screen material—we don't want the bugs in but we want to see out."

"Absolutely."

"I hope you can do this," Charley said.

"It will be my priority. I don't have any other big jobs right now and I have help. Let me clarify—okay to text you as often as necessary as long as it's during business hours?"

"Certainly. And thank you."

"And I'll take a look at the boathouse, if you like. You said it once served as a guest room?"

"Go ahead," Charley said. "I doubt we'll have need of it. If we have more than five people at one time, I'll faint. In fact, I think it will be me and Meg, her husband on weekends, maybe a visit from my two guys, my son and his father. Otherwise... I'm not betting on anyone."

"But you want the house ready in case?"

"I want it like it used to be," Charley said.

"Are you leaving now?" Melissa asked.

"In an hour or so. I'm just going to look around a little."

"You must have had such a wonderful childhood here," Melissa said.

"Mostly," Charley said.

The summers *were* mostly wonderful, even that last one, right up to the end. That summer, when Charley was sixteen, would turn seventeen in late July and was headed for her senior year in high school, she fell in love. She was tall, lithe, pretty, smart and brazen and he was twenty-two. She'd had boyfriends before, hadn't missed a winter formal, prom or homecoming dance yet, but she'd never been in love before. Not like this. And with all the summer romances and flings she and Hope and even Krista and Meg had had, for Charley this one was special and a little forbidden. Hot and heavy. His name was Mack and he was so handsome her knees buckled when she looked at him. He was a graduate of the University of Minnesota and headed for Harvard Law School. So, she fudged a little bit and said she was eighteen and had just finished her freshman year at Berkeley and was home visiting her family for the summer. She threatened Hope, Krista and Meg with dire consequences if they sold her out.

It was Mack's first summer working at the lodge. His father was a rich attorney in Minneapolis and wouldn't even consider letting Mack lay around all summer waiting to go to school back East. He liked to talk about work being a virtue. Mack figured the best way to work and play was a job at the lodge.

The girls used to sneak across the lake to the lodge on hot summer nights when some of the waiters and waitresses had parties after they got off work. Charley would've braved the wrath of Louise every night, but the workforce didn't play every night. The lodge employed a lot of local kids but about a dozen were from out of town and for them there were a couple of small dormitories—cabins with bunk beds and chests. They didn't dare party on the lodge premises; they'd get canned. They went around the bend to a cove that was just right, just private enough, for a lot of messing around. They'd have a fire, and most of them drank a few beers. Someone usually managed to pilfer some snacks. They'd sit around and tell jokes, stories and probably lies. There was a lot of sneaking off behind the trees or bushes; there was a lot of making out in plain sight.

Charley picked out Mack right off the bat that summer. He told her about himself, his important dad, his plans to be a kick-ass prosecutor and put away all the bad guys. She told him of her plans to be a broadcast newscaster. She let him get to first base, to second base; she went to second base on him and then she found herself in over her head...

"Come on, Charley. I'm too old for these games. We gotta either do it or move on."

"What games? This isn't a game! I'm not exactly ready. I'm not on the pill or anything."

"Why not?" he asked. "Man, you're the first college girl I've ever met not on the pill!"

"I didn't have a reason to be on the pill!"

"You didn't have a boyfriend...ever?"

"I've had plenty of boyfriends, but never one who threatened to break up with me if I didn't get birth control!"

"Seriously?" He laughed. Then he grabbed her and kissed her and said, "That's sweet. But I'm too old for this. We have to get on with it."

"I told you, I'm not ready..."

"Then let's get ready," he said, snuggling her to the ground and going after her mouth with his. "I have protection. I have a condom. Let's just take our time, how about that?"

"I don't know..." she said. But the truth was, she was getting turned on and she had begun to have fantasies. She thought about moving out to Boston while he attended Harvard, working while he went to school. She never thought about the fact that she was probably smart enough to get into Harvard herself. She'd killed the SAT; her grades were excellent, always had been. But instead she thought about being his forever girl, then his supportive wife. They'd both be very successful, be a power couple, maybe even have children someday. They'd live in a big rural house, commute to the city, go home to each other every night—a lifelong love affair. They'd have lots of friends, join a club, have parties, go to dances at the club, take trips together.

While she was busy thinking about how ideal their life would be, he was sliding off her shorts and pressing himself against her. He was whispering, *Baby, baby, baby.* He had his fingers on her, in her, and she was about ready to explode. She tried to ignore the fact that it was a little uncomfortable. He was a little clumsy. Or maybe she was; she was the one without experience, after all. So she snaked her hand down between their bodies to touch him as intimately as he was touching her.

She felt herself because he was pressing right into her.

"Mack," she said softly. "Where's the condom?"

"Ugh," he said. "Crap. Just kiss me a second while I get under control..."

So she did. And while she was kissing him, he was pushing deeper and groaning. He was pushing inside her.

"Mack!" she said, panicked.

He pumped his hips a couple of times. He moaned. "Crap," he said again. "Oh, man. I shouldn't have had so much beer. It's okay."

"What's okay?" she asked.

"Nothing really happened," he said. "It'll be fine. But you shoulda told me you were a virgin."

He pulled out and tucked himself away. He helped her pull her shorts up. He kissed her deeply.

"Yeah, I think I did! And something happened, all right," she said. "And it happened without a condom!"

"Sorry," he said. "Don't worry. No one ever gets caught the first time. It'll be fine."

She sat up and slugged him in the arm. "'I have protection,'" she mimicked. "'I have a condom!'" she said. "You idiot!"

He flopped over onto the grass, his hand on his forehead. "Don't bitch, Charley, okay? I got a little hot. Your fault, you turned me on so much. But I'm telling you—it'll be okay. Trust me."

"Fat chance I'll ever trust you again!" She got to her feet and walked through the bushes to the lake.

"Come on," he cried. "Come on!"

"Up yours!"

"Charley," he called, following her. "Hey, come on!"

But she walked right into the lake and began to swim.

Charley swam across the lake in the moonlight, unable to cry after the first half mile. Waseka was a large lake and from the party site to the Berkey cabin was about a mile. The girls were fish, all of them, but swimming at night while under the influence and emotionally upset was a very dangerous thing to do. Charley knew it but really didn't care at that moment if she died.

She should have at least made him say he loved her first. He couldn't get a piece of her fast enough. And then he berated her for being a virgin? She would have to rethink growing old with him.

"You went all the way, didn't you?" Hope whispered that night.

"Shh, don't let the little girls hear you," Charley answered. "They're big mouths. I don't know."

"What do you mean you don't know? How can you not know?"

"It…it happened so fast. It hurt. I wasn't that sure…"

"Did he…did he *rape* you?"

"Shh. No, I said okay. But I shouldn't have and he didn't use anything…or pull out…or…"

"Oh, *Charley!*"

Charley was upset by what happened and she needed time to think things through. She hung close to home, where she got a clear reminder of why she had been avoiding the place. Her mother was irritable and preoccupied; Aunt Jo was more spacey than usual. There was another couple who

Uncle Roy had brought and they stayed on, upsetting the balance of things for a while. It was some Russian guy and his much younger girlfriend and things were tense for some reason. Charley didn't understand why but they created drama. Then, before Charley could get a grip on her own issues, the Russian guy took off, abandoning his girlfriend, and Lou took the young woman to the bus station in Brainerd, and after that Lou and Jo did nothing but bicker. Lou was in a foul temper that rose every ten minutes; you didn't dare spill or talk back or leave a mess—she was constantly on a tear. And Jo was withering, clearly very upset, probably with Lou. When asked what was wrong, the malady was described as "family trouble."

"Well, no shit," Charley muttered under her breath. Though no one knew exactly what had set the sisters at odds that summer, it was definitely made worse by the strange couple. Years later Charley realized that up to that point, that summer, her mother always seemed to be capable and decisive. Aunt Jo had always been sweet, supportive and attentive. They bickered as sisters will but rarely, and making up quickly. That summer they both fell apart. They became unaccountably useless as caretakers.

Charley described her own withdrawn behavior, which was barely noticed by her mother and aunt, as cramps. Not that anyone cared.

After about a week of thinking things through, she went back to the party spot across the lake. She asked several waiters where Mack was. "Gone."

"That fast?"

"Didn't hang around to talk it over." One of the girls she knew said, "You should've told him you were only sixteen, Charley. Turns out you scared the shit out of him. He hit the trail."

"Who said I was sixteen?" she asked.

"Your cousin Hope."

The worst thing, even though Charley had made up most of the biography she'd given Mack, was it never once occurred to her that he might make up some of his. She heard he was not twenty-two but nineteen. He was not a graduate or even a college student and law school was not in his future. At least not anytime soon. His daddy was not a rich lawyer but a humble farmer and he didn't have any way of escaping his fate if he had sex with the underage granddaughter of a superior court judge.

"You should've told Mack ol' Grandpa was a judge," said one of the waiters Charley had known for two summers. "You shoulda seen his face. I didn't know a person could get that color!"

"I didn't know anyone knew that!" Charley said.

"Hope told me. Hope told anyone who would listen about her rich, powerful grandpa."

Well, that's just great! Charley thought.

Gone. Gone. Gone.

Charley's heart didn't break because Mack had run off and left her lonely, nor was she in a panic about him getting in trouble because she wasn't going to accuse him of anything. Nor did she hurt because he was a liar who had used her. The lesson that hit her in the chest with the weight of a hundred-pound boulder was that she'd *fallen for it.* That was something that would stay with her forever—she could take almost anything but looking stupid. That was the worst pain she could imagine.

When it was just the six cousins and their mothers, no daddies or grandparents or unwelcome guests present, the four oldest girls slept in sleeping bags on the screened porch, their mothers slept in the big bedroom together—when they were speaking, that is—and the little girls, Bunny and Bev, got to sleep in the upstairs loft, which had two bedrooms. Of course they wanted to be outside on the porch with the big girls, but they were exiled as "babies." So, Charley tucked into her sleeping bag night after night, sometimes weeping soft, silent tears as she wondered how she could have been so easily duped by such a well-known male trick. She rarely fell asleep before dawn. She had dark circles under her eyes. She wasn't hungry. But only Hope noticed. Only Hope tried to console her. And as far as Charley was concerned, Hope had caused the trouble by bragging about the judge.

Even though Charley and Hope were best friends, they were nothing alike. They were as different as Jo and Lou. Charley wanted to be Barbara Walters or at least Jane Pauley, and Hope wanted a nice, rich husband. "Rich as Grandpa Berkey and ten times as handsome," she would say. So, to help Charley with her tears Hope would say, "Ohhh, don't cry, Charlene, you'll find another guy—a better one!"

It was only a couple of weeks after Charley lost her virginity that Bunny drowned. And suddenly the summer was over. The summers at the lake to come never would.

The lake house transformed under the fierce and yet gentle hand of Melissa Stewart. Charley often thought if she'd had an assistant like Melissa during her talk show days, her life would have been almost carefree. During the month of April Charley returned to the house on the lake three times and every time she saw such growth and improvement she was completely impressed.

"I've paid some of the best designers available in a big city and never saw results like this," Charley said. "You've done amazing things, under budget, sourcing everything in small towns."

"Maybe that's the trick—small towns," Melissa said. "I've lived here all my life. I know everyone. When I put the word out that I need a new dinette set that will seat ten, I get calls. When I email subs I've worked with that I'm considering a kitchen cabinet redo, I hear from cabinetmakers to renovators to antique dealers who are artists at restoration. Not just antique restoration but I know a guy who can make 1950s cabinetry look like it was built yesterday. You're going to be ready in plenty of time."

With the help of Melissa at Lake Waseka and John able to spend extra time looking after Megan, Charley thought it was time she go back to Palo Alto to spend time with Michael and Eric. Playing it safe, she called Michael and asked him if he felt like seeing her. "Of course," he said.

"Can we do this without fighting?" she asked.

"I could have my lips sutured shut," he said. "But then you might let something slip out and I'd have to defend myself."

"Oh, I'm not going to let anything slip out," she said. "I want to enjoy my family for a few days."

"And I want you," he said.

Because it had been so long since she'd seen them, both Michael and Eric went out of their way to clear their schedules as best they could to spend time with her. They had a lovely day in Carmel, went into the city for a great dinner at the wharf and Eric actually spent a night at the house rather than on campus with his friends. They watched a couple of movies, played Scrabble, sat out on the deck at night to enjoy the spring in the Bay Area.

One thing she did not do—she did not visit with old colleagues from the station or the network. There were still friends among them and several who kept in touch by email, but she admitted, only to herself, that it had hurt to be unceremoniously dumped by her station. There had even been talk of a farewell event, but she made excuses—she wasn't planning to stay in the area for the immediate future. To a couple she had said, "My sister needs me. She's been ill." Michael, who knew her better than anyone, said, "You had twelve years of extraordinary success on that dying of beasts, the daytime talk show. That counts for a lot. Maybe you could take the high road. Attend a special luncheon or something. Thank the suits for all their support."

"I could," she said. "Except that would make me want to shoot myself."

Seriously? she thought. Thank the people who fired her? Maybe someday. Right now she couldn't do it.

Michael's plans to spend six months in England studying Britain's electoral system would begin in September. He stuck to his word and didn't badger her about going along but he threw out some bait, just the same. Eric had expressed an interest in a year of study at Cambridge. Michael thought he could get a little help in facilitating that.

"Not see either one of you?" Charley asked, stricken.

"Don't be silly," Michael said. "Even if you never warm to the idea of joining me there, won't you visit? Provided Meg can do without you for a while?"

"But both of you?"

Michael chuckled and lifted her chin. "I know it gives you a sense of security to think we're both waiting for you here in Palo Alto but it isn't like that anymore. Eric has things to do, people to see, a life to live. We get together for dinner every couple of weeks and that's it. I guarantee you, if he gets to go to Cambridge, he won't be hanging out with his dad! And if he stays here while I'm away, you're not going to get much of his time, either. He's grown, Charley. He's busy building a life."

"All these changes," she said. "All at once…"

"I'll make sure to visit you this summer at the lake," Michael said. "I'll make sure Eric comes. When did you last take Eric to Minnesota?"

"I think he was six. He hated it. After that I went alone. My obligation visits."

"He's more mature now," Michael said. "In most ways."

Nights in Michael's arms brought back such memories it only left her confused, wondering what was wrong with her. She couldn't imagine a woman on the planet who wouldn't rush to hold him in some marital knot. He was so perfect. They'd been together so long, and yet when he touched her, she still came alive with desire. Better yet, she had only to whisper to him and he was ready for her. Familiarity was such a blissful aphrodisiac—practiced love meant they had a beautiful routine together. He knew where to touch, she knew how to move, he knew what to say, she knew what sounds turned him on. When he rolled her onto her back and pushed her shoulders into the mattress, she lifted her knees and spread them for him. That always made him chuckle a little. "In a hurry, honey?" he would ask. "No, take your time," she would always say. And he would. He would tease and tempt and make her beg him to hurry, to finish. Michael would always make sure she had two orgasms and he would take one. He could work her body as though he'd programmed it.

But she could do the same to him. She knew exactly where to touch, kiss and caress to drive him mad. Making him a little crazy was not only her favorite thing. It was his. "Why do you do that to me?" he would ask. "Because you want me to," she would say.

About nineteen years ago, when they'd been together about three years, after one of their wonderful lovemaking sessions while he was still above her, she touched his cheek. "Michael, I'm pregnant."

He had merely lifted his eyebrows. No gasp, no grimace. "How'd that happen?"

"I think I might've missed pills or something."

"What do you want to do?" he asked.

"Do?" she asked.

"Do," he repeated. "We're good together. Please say you want to have it."

Her heart soared, but she kept a poker face. "I want to, but it will be difficult. Inconvenient. I have a job. A good job."

"You'd have to take some family leave, at least a couple of months, but my schedule is pretty flexible. I'd be involved. I swear."

"Right," she said. "I'm holding you to that, Michael. We have to do this together or not at all."

"I agree."

And they had.

It was the end of April when Charley returned from California to find Megan looking quite well, for all she was up against. There was now a thin, fuzzy cap of hair covering her bald head. It wasn't much, but it was there. She looked as though she'd gained a couple of pounds and her color was improved.

"How was your visit?" Meg asked.

"Perfect," Charley said. "I think the advantage of seeing Michael so rarely is that he takes time. I don't remember him ever having so much time to spend with me. Of course, I was a bit short on free time myself."

"I hope you're not grieving the show unnecessarily, Charley. This is a temporary setback. A small break in the action, that's all."

Charley began idly looking through a stack of magazines. There was a reason Meg had so many subscriptions when the rest of the world seemed to be getting their news and articles online—she had to rest a lot and couldn't sit at the computer for long periods of time. Just like the magazines, TV talk shows were an endangered species. "That would be encouraging, but I'm afraid it's not true. Talk shows like mine have been on the decline for a while now."

"But maybe your next step will not be a televised talk show."

"What do you suppose it will be?" Charley asked, for that was the real dilemma. The network hadn't offered her a position. She feared that at forty-four she was considered too old for television. There were other positions, of course—at the executive level, behind the camera, in the field. But she'd loved her show.

"Hey, look at this," Charley said, holding up a purple envelope. "A letter from Hope! It's opened. You didn't mention... What did she have to say?"

"Same old Hope," Megan said with a shrug.

"Can I have a look?" Charley asked.

"I guess you might as well," Meg said.

"But if it's private..."

"It's not," Meg said. "Really, go ahead."

Charley opened it and read.

My darling Megan,

How wonderful that you're opening up the lake house for summer! We'll be there! I'll have to get back to you on the exact dates. We usually spend a couple of months at the Cape but of course we'll cut that short this year if there's a chance to get together with the family. I won't know whether Franklin will come for the duration until closer to the date—he's so overwhelmed with his company. I know he'll do his best! And Bobbi and

Trude will be thrilled. They'll have such a good time. Does the lodge still have a stable and horses to use? And is Grandma Berkey going to be able to come? I'll dash off a note when we have a few more details about our summer.

Love, Hope

Charley fanned herself with the note card. "Oh, Meg, what have you done?"

Meg shrugged again. "I didn't think you'd mind."

"How many of them did you invite?" Charley asked.

Megan briefly bit her bottom lip. "All of them."

"*All* of them?" And Megan nodded. "Oh, God," Charley said.

"Don't worry, they'll never come. Hope surprises me…but I bet anything she'll change her mind. The lodge is no longer like a country club the ladies can go to for bridge. It's just a hotel now. I don't mean 'just.' It sounds like a nice hotel. But I don't think the guest services are available to the lake people, just the guests."

Charley raised an eyebrow. "And you know this how?"

"I looked into it," Megan said.

Charley eased down into a chair. Megan reclined on the sofa. The den was a small, cozy room. It contained only a sofa, one chair, a side table and coffee table, a bookcase and a small flat-screen TV in a niche in the bookcase. Charley looked at Megan, huddled in a knit wrap. She was perpetually chilly, having so little meat on her bones. Eyeing her now, thin and nearly bald, her cheekbones so prominent and her constitution weak, it was hard to remember what a force of nature she could be.

"I forget how stubborn you can be," Charley said. "Have you heard from anyone else?"

"Everyone, I think."

"Care to expound on that?" Charley pushed.

"Well, it shouldn't surprise you, Hope was the first. Beverly called. She said she was very doubtful—she's pretty sure she's not in a good place with that yet. But she'll keep it in mind. Aunt Jo said it sounded to her like just the thing this family needed—time to get beyond all the trouble and angst and move on. Of course, she also said she wouldn't feel right about going unless Louise asked her. And I don't see that happening."

"And Mother?" Charley asked.

"Oh, she's furious. But there's not much she can do. I guess she could arrest us and post a guard." Megan laughed rather brightly. "I wouldn't put it past her, to tell the truth. But she's mostly angry that I invited Grandma Berkey and now she expects to be carted down to the lake and Mother's pitching a holy fit about it."

"You didn't…"

"Of course I did," Megan said. "I wouldn't leave Grandma out. The house belongs to her."

"Oh, brother," Charley said. "Well, I think you take after her. Did any of the others ask how you were feeling?"

"Oh, yes, they're actually very lovely people, our family."

Charley just shook her head. Hope hadn't asked. Typical of Hope. She didn't think about other people much. "You know the best part about your recovery? You're not going to get away with this shit anymore!"

"Lighten up, Charley. It'll be fun. Even if it's just the two of us."

"I have a feeling it'll only be fun if it's just the two of us," she said.

Chapter Four

When Hope Hempstead Griffin received the little note from Megan, something came alive in her that had been dormant for years. How long had the note been there? She hadn't collected the mail in days! It was four in the afternoon when she opened the front door of her palatial home, stepped over the custom-hooked doormat that read Hope and FR Griffin and walked down her curved brick driveway in her terry-cloth robe and furry slippers. She pulled an armload of bills and catalogs out of the box and waddled back up the drive at a slow pace, leafing through the mail. Once every month or so she got a letter from her mother, sometimes a small package addressed to the girls, all of which she threw away unopened, but other than that there were only rare items personally addressed to her.

She dropped all the other stuff on the kitchen table and tore open the note. "The lake," she whispered in a reverent breath. She read the few lines over and over. She held the note in her right hand and clutched her robe together over her pendulous breasts with her left hand. She absently ran a hand through her messy hair as though she were suddenly concerned with her appearance. Her lips began to move in nervous, meaningless, silent chatter. With a sweep of her hand she cleared a month's worth of newspapers, magazines, catalogs and junk mail into the trash can. She put the note, alone and prominently displayed, in the middle of the table. She went to a cupboard in search of a coffee cup, but she found the cupboard empty. She rummaged through mounds of dirty dishes in the dishwasher and then the sink until she found one that wasn't too nasty and slowly washed it out, her lips moving the whole time.

The coffeepot was permanently stained but she rinsed it out and loaded it with filter, grounds and water. While the coffee began to brew she went into the downstairs powder room and fussed a little with her hair. It was perfectly hopeless. Ha, ha, she thought. Hopeless Hope. Well, it would have to do for now. She hadn't had a proper coiffure in months. She hadn't washed her hair in days. Or showered, for that matter. "Coffee. Shower. Dress. Hair. Clean kitchen. Manicure. Take out trash. Run dishwasher. Unload. Reload. Vacuum. Sheets. Clothes…clothes…summer clothes…" Her lips moved over these words but the only sound was an occasional squeak.

When her coffee was brewed she sat down at the table with her address book. She flipped through the pages, and when her eyes lit on a name she mentally approved of, she reached for the phone and dialed. She hadn't talked to her friend Maxine in so long. They had served on so many fundraising committees together and had carpooled, belonged to the same country club. It would be so nice to tell someone like Maxine her news.

"Maxine? Max? Hi, it's Hope! How are you?"

"Hope? I'm fine. But how are *you*?"

"Oh, great. How about Bob and the boys? Good?"

"Excellent. Tennis, track and baseball are just about in full swing so you know what I'm going through. And the girls?"

Hope's laughter was melodious. "Oh, they're ridiculously

busy. Lessons, meets, games, drama club, cheerleading. Everything you can squeeze into a day! Having teenagers is so busy!"

"Busy doesn't even touch it. What are you up to these days?"

"Frantic. Simply frantic as always. No rest for the weary. And making summer plans already, too."

"Really? What are you doing this summer?"

"Well, we had planned another summer at the Cape, but I think there's going to be a change of venue this year. It seems my family... You've heard me speak of my family? Back in Minnesota? Charley Berkey? From *Chatting with Charley*, Channel 10? Well, it seems the family has decided to summer at the lake house on precious little Lake Waseka. It's the most charming place in the world. I grew up having all my summers there—riding, tennis, boating, everything you can imagine!"

"Won't that be nice for you! I'm so glad you're making plans for yourself!"

"Oh, the girls are thrilled. They haven't seen Grandma Berkey in ages! And she raised me, after all. She's eighty-eight now, and still kicking up a fuss. Ever since my grandfather the judge passed, she's become more cantankerous every year. I do love the old darling. Filthy rich, you know. In fact, I'm quite sure this reunion has to do with her estate. She probably wants to discuss her bequests. It was actually her family who had the money to begin with..."

"So the girls are going with you, then?"

"Of course! I don't know if Franklin will be able to go or not. He's been in London all month and I haven't even run this by him yet. He does love the Cape but I'm sure once he knows..."

"*Frank?* What about...what about Pam?"

Hope laughed indulgently. "Pam? Maxie, darling, sometimes you have such a passion for indiscretion! Franklin might take liberties with my feelings...successful men are used to giving orders and having their way, often taking their wives completely for granted. But I doubt even Franklin would be so crude as to bring Pam along on our family vacation!"

There was silence on Maxine's end. Hope began to fidget.

"Pam is temporary, Maxine. If it hasn't worn itself out yet, it will soon. In any case, I'm going ahead with our plans for the lake. It was the highlight of my youth and I'm sure the entire family will be there."

It wasn't that Hope had read an awful lot into a little card. It was how she lived—building castles in the air. She had a whole imaginary life. On some level she knew what was real and what was fantasy, but as it happened, she preferred her fantasy life. Her hands began to tremble slightly.

"Hope, forgive me, but I don't think Frank regards Pam as temporary," Maxine said.

Hope laughed again, but her laugh was hollow this time. "But of course she is! Just the other night Franklin said something that sounded awfully like he was just this close to coming home. Of course, I don't intend to make it that easy for him. He'll have to make a few changes, that's for sure! I'm not going to allow him to just stomp all over my feelings for the rest of my—"

"Hope! He divorced you! Years ago! He's remarried! They have a *child*!"

Hope's voice was weak and pathetic. "We have children, too."

"Yes, two adorable teenage girls who really deserve to have a mother who is living in this world! Hope, darling, I know this has been hard on you, but you really must consider talking to someone about this. A professional. A therapist. You need help!"

"Maxine." Hope sighed, remembering now why it had been so long since they'd spoken. "Sometimes you're so... so...*bold*. I'm fine. I'm perfectly fine. It's not that I need a therapist to tell me that my husband has divorced me. Believe me, I'm more than aware of the fact. It greets me daily. The problem is very simple. I married for life. The vows I took are permanent."

"Oh, really? And how's that working out for you?"

"I won't keep you! You have carpooling and meetings and probably some fabulous function at the club. Say hello to Bob and your handsome sons. I'll call you again when we're all home from the lake and settled in. Until then—"

"Really, Hope..."

"Goodbye, Maxine. Have a lovely summer!"

She hung up the phone and shook her head sadly. Why were all her friends so willing to give up? So quickly? So easily? Well, not her! She had things to do!

She gathered up discarded shoes, slippers and clothing on her way up the stairs to her bedroom. She shook dust balls off those items that had been on the floor for a long time and made a mental note to mop the foyer and kitchen floors. Soon she stood under a steaming shower and mentally ticked off all the things she had to do right away. What a scandal she'd become, letting things go as she had.

Hope's husband had left her six years ago. Her daughters were then eight and ten. He told her he wasn't happy. He hadn't been for a long time. He didn't like their life. He'd felt unfulfilled and suffocated by her. The arguing, for one thing, as if that was her fault. It was Franklin, in her opinion, who constantly avoided intimacy and who also seemed to avoid home in general. She had been very clear about her needs and more than specific about how he needed to change to meet them. But Franklin could be a thoroughly selfish man.

She had painstakingly built the perfect home and family for him and he was perpetually unappreciative! In addition to keeping a flawlessly ordered and spotless home—thanks to a little domestic help—she volunteered at the school, at the church, and was almost exhausted from her country club and Junior League activities. She made sure they had season tickets to the symphony; she hosted a fabulous summer barbecue and a Christmas party for the corporate officers of Franklin's company every year. If it were not for her judiciously chosen charity work they would not have been present at every glittering, star-studded event in Philadelphia! All this so that Franklin would look good to his colleagues, to his rich family. And did he care? Hah! When she thought about how she impeccably choreographed their every family trip, right down to what each of them would wear every day and where they would eat every meal, she couldn't imagine that he'd last very long living alone in an apartment! It was ludicrous.

And of course he hadn't. Lasted long in an apartment, that is. He was soon living in a rather spacious town house with a woman named Pam. Younger than Hope, naturally. And from a simple miner's family! It was all part and parcel of the old midlife crisis. Franklin had been all of thirty-eight when his crisis struck, but then he'd always been precocious. And this Pam was a CPA. Married before, of course. So they had that much in common. They could sit up late at night and talk about number crunching and ex-spouses.

Ex. Ex. Ex. Ex.

Franklin divorced Hope after a one-year separation. He gave her the six-thousand-square-foot house, the car, and worked out a time-share agreement with her for the house on the Cape. She could use it for the last two weeks in July.

Big deal. He continued to pay her living expenses and had given her half the stock he received when he left the investment firm. He paid the taxes, utilities, phone, gas, cable TV and even for bottled water. But he refused to continue her country-club membership, pay her credit card accounts, or for a housekeeper, beauty shop, florist or spa. He paid alimony and child support and told her to figure out how to budget for the first time in her life. He said what he had given her was generous. *Given!* As though she hadn't worked her ass off for fourteen years to create the most perfect, flawless home and family for the vice president of finance of a major investment firm!

A year after the divorce he had married Pam, who Bobbi and Trude said was nice. But she convinced herself that nothing had changed. She wouldn't take the family portraits off the walls, wouldn't pull up the personalized welcome mat and kept sending out Christmas cards signed, "The Griffins— Franklin, Hope, Bobbi and Trude." She wrote an annual newsletter that chronicled every family member's achievements for the year, including Franklin's. She kept going to her volunteer posts and kept talking as though she and Franklin were still living together, embarrassing the girls and everyone around them. She wouldn't stop going to the club even though she was no longer a member until one of the managers had to ask her to stop coming unless she came as the guest of a member. She was mortified to realize no one ever invited her. But it didn't change her thinking.

Nothing would change her thinking, not even the gradual disappearance of all her friends. Her behavior definitely further deteriorated when her daughters went to live with their father. They told her she was crazy. That's when she let herself and the house go into the tank. She'd gone through all the money from the stock in short order, stunned to realize after it was gone that it had been a few hundred thousand dollars. She stopped going out. She kept running into people like Maxine, who were interested only in confronting her with her divorce. She only cleaned and dressed when the girls were coming home for a weekend, but even then she didn't do a very good job. Then they started begging to be allowed to skip their weekends with Hope. They claimed the house was a mess. Well, it was hell without help. Hope's best housekeeping efforts had a rather smeary, lackluster effect that she'd gotten used to. She'd bust her butt if Franklin would even get out of the car when he picked up or delivered the kids, but since he didn't care, she didn't care. She had her groceries delivered. She had gained something in the vicinity of eighty pounds. Thirteen pounds a year. Roughly one pound one ounce per month since Franklin left her.

She spent her days and nights on the couch, watching TV and cutting pictures out of catalogs. Earlier on she spent most of her money paying for the useless things she'd bought from the shopping channel; Franklin had bailed her out of credit card disasters twice but on the third time around he refused and her card was canceled so she was reduced to catalog snipping until her monthly check was due. Then she ordered COD. She frequently overordered and had to send packages back.

But all that was going to change now. She was going home. Home to her rich family. Grandma Berkey had piles and piles of money and was older than dirt. She probably wouldn't last much longer… Hope would finally get her inheritance… Maybe she would move in with Grandma Berkey and start over… Oh, God, she needed to lose some weight! She needed to get her house in shape! She would have to get in touch with the girls and let them know what they were doing this summer.

Somehow, in the fever of all this, she pushed aside the fact that Megan had cancer. Hope's mother, Josephine, had chronicled all she knew about Megan's illness and treatments in her regular letters to Hope, but Hope almost never read them. If she did open a letter, she merely scanned it in search of something of importance to *her*. It had not for one second occurred to Hope that Megan might be spending her last months at Lake Waseka.

Hope dressed in the only clothes that would fit her and began the most thorough job of housecleaning she had done in at least five years. She heaved out so much trash—from papers to cans to dead houseplants—she completely filled the Dumpster at the far end of the alley. She scrubbed, scoured, dusted, washed, wiped, shined, vacuumed and waxed. She laundered and ironed. She phoned in a grocery list that was largely fresh greens and cleaning supplies. She called carpet cleaners and window washers. She wrote checks for those services she couldn't cover immediately and made appointments to have her hair and nails done. And her legs waxed.

Hope's house had twelve rooms and even though she had been the only one living there full-time for five years, it took days to snap it into even tolerable shape. She was never going to be a very good housekeeper. She drank a lot of coffee, didn't eat any sweets and only slept for a few hours each night on the sofa in the den. Then she called Franklin.

"Is this the Franklin Griffin residence?" she asked the woman who answered the phone. She pretended not to know Pam's voice even after all this time.

"Just a moment, Hope. I'll get him."

It annoyed her very much that Pam would take that kind of liberty with her. She grimaced and tapped her freshly manicured finger on the streaked kitchen counter.

"Hello, Hope," Frank said. "How are you?"

"I'm fine, Franklin. And yourself?"

"Well, thank you." He waited. She didn't speak. "What can I do for you, Hope?"

"Nice to talk to you, too, Franklin."

"All right, then—"

"Wait! Wait a minute," she begged. "I'm making some summer plans and I have to discuss the girls' schedules with you, among other things."

"Shoot," he invited.

"Well, my family is opening up the lake house for the summer. We haven't been back since the judge died," she explained, which she knew was not the truth at all. Her brow wrinkled. She'd taken him to the lake the summer they got married...1996? It had only been seven years since the family had stopped going there but the years had been very hard on the house. Was that when Franklin first began to doubt that she came from a very rich, prominent family? Was that why he *really* left her? "It's been completely refurbished," she informed him quickly, hoping first that Megan would at least buy some new appliances, and second that her daughters would lie to their father about its condition. "I'd like to take the girls there for six weeks or so this summer. From about the tenth of June to maybe the end of July."

"No can do, Hope. We're going to be in New York and the Cape until the middle of July. The girls are expecting you to join them at the Cape and bring them home by the first of August. As usual."

"Franklin, this is my *family*!" She stopped herself just short of demanding that he be there with them. Despite what she said to others, she knew Franklin was not inclined to spend any time with his *old* family.

"Maybe we can work out some compromise, but the girls

are going to have a say in this. They don't have to go with you at all if they don't want to."

"Franklin, why do you persist in trying to turn my own daughters against me? Isn't it enough that you've taken them away from me? My own children?"

He sighed into the phone. "We've been over this, Hope. They love you very much but they hate this game you play, pretending we're still married. Not to mention all the other airs you put on."

"I don't do that," she insisted, her voice beginning to tremble. "Believe me, Franklin, I'm well aware that you're not married to me anymore." She wouldn't go so far as to admit that she was not married to him, however. That was too much. She *loved* Franklin! "All I want to do is take my children home to see my family. We haven't seen each other in years."

"All right. I'll talk to the girls about it. Maybe something can be worked out. It won't be for six weeks, though. That's too long. But maybe a little longer than—"

"And, Franklin? I'm going to need a little extra money. To buy some clothes for myself and the girls and to—"

"The girls have clothes," he said irritably.

"The *right* kind of clothes. I know how to buy my daughters' clothes. I'm not taking them back to Minnesota dressed like a couple of punk rockers. I have to get a few simple, inexpensive things for myself and I'm going to need some travel money. Also, I've just put some work into the house… It was quite falling down around me. I'd happily pay for all this if I had any money, but unfortunately on my limited income…"

"Hope, I give you two thousand dollars a month and pay all your bills, including gas for your car. You have only to buy food and clothes. You have a college degree. Have you ever thought of going to work?"

"Can't we call it a loan, then? You could simply *advance* me a few months of that allowance you give me..." She could *not* call it alimony. No matter how hard she tried.

"And add it to what you already owe me? No, I'm afraid not. Sooner or later you're going to have to be accountable."

"At least May and June, then! At least send those checks early! For God's sake, Franklin, would you like to see me beg? Am I not quite humiliated enough for you?"

"Overdrawn again, Hope?"

She was silent for a moment. "Does this young girl you're living with know what a cruel bastard you can be?"

"Do you mean Pam? My *wife*? Who is only eleven months younger than you?"

"Please, Franklin," she whimpered, but it was more a plea for him to stop throwing that truth in her face than a plea for money.

"I'll send May's check now," he relented. "And I'll talk with the girls and call you next week to let you know what time they're willing to compromise from their summer plans. And...if you decide to drive to Minnesota, you can use the gas card as usual, but I'm unable to fund plane tickets."

"*Drive?* You expect me to *drive?*"

"Actually, Bobbi would probably be thrilled to do the driving. I don't know if your nerves can take it, but she's coming along with experience."

"Ohhh, Franklin..."

"Is that it? Money and vacation plans?"

"Yes," she said, suddenly very tired.

"I'll be in touch, then. And, Hope? I want to remind you that the insurance coverage you have will pay for counseling...if you're interested."

She stiffened. She had told him many times before that she would indeed consider counseling—marriage counseling. She was about to remind him of that when she remembered she needed that check right away—to cover the carpet cleaning, window washing and beauty shop expenses. Where did her money go? She couldn't eat that much every month. And there were only those few little COD catalog purchases... "Thank you, Franklin," she said as sweetly as she could. "Please convince the girls to extend their vacation time with me. Please. It's very important to me...and I ask for so little."

"I'll speak to them," he said.

She was so tired. All that cleaning and primping. All that stress and worry. She would have to rest now and wait. It was going to be all right. Once she saw Grandma Berkey again everything would be fine.

She didn't think about Megan's four-year battle with cancer. Her oblivion was so complete that if someone asked her, right now, how the family fared health-wise, she would say, "Very well, thank you!"

In 1989, the year the Berlin Wall came down and the Game Boy was introduced, right before Hope was due to become a junior in high school, she took her last realistic look at her family. Her cousin Bunny was dead. Her parents had had a very troubled marriage and her father, Roy, had run off, couldn't be found and didn't send money. Her mother was sick—depressed and emotionally unavailable. Her mother had no job, no husband and no money. Her sister Krista couldn't stand to be at home anymore and was running with a bad crowd, skipping school and getting into serious trouble. Twice the police brought her home in the middle of the night. Her youngest sister, Beverly, had been Bunny's best friend and was broken by her loss. She was in even worse shape than Jo. Her cousin Charley had been exiled to Florida to have and give up her illegitimate baby. Charley's last letter to Hope said, simply, "I'm going to run away the second I get back to Saint Paul so don't expect any help from me...unless you want to come with me."

"Mama," Hope entreated. "You have to ask Grandma and the judge for help!"

"The judge can't help us," Jo said.

Hope later learned that the judge had offered help with the condition that Jo agreed to divorce Roy and live by Berkey standards. Jo refused.

The family was in utter chaos after Bunny's death. And that was when Hope started looking for a better life.

As a little girl Hope had spent hours looking through the photo albums at pictures of her mother and Aunt Lou dressed for their formal dances at the club and pictures of their incredible coming-out parties and unbelievable weddings. Aunt Lou had twelve bridesmaids—like Grandma Berkey before her—and so did Hope's mom. There were trips to Europe and carriage rides through the streets and ice-skating at the winter carnival. What the hell had happened to them all? How could this be? Falling apart was one thing but this whole family was ready to be shot and buried—they were that humiliating.

Grandpa Berkey was still on the bench and she went to him. "Please," she begged. "I'll do anything you want, act any way you please, just let me live with you and go to a decent high school and maybe get into college somewhere. Please, I'm begging you. I want to have the kind of life you planned for your daughters."

Charmed, her grandparents took her in. They dressed her, showed her off, sent her to a private school. And she did as she had promised. She followed their every wish from crossing her legs at the ankle to getting home before ten every night. She went with them to the club for dinner every weekend, danced with all the old codgers, learned to play bridge and wore long, lacy dresses when torn jeans, bra tops and exposed garter belts were all the rage.

She had a coming-out party, got her college degree and met a man from a rich family. When she got married in Saint Paul, a simple but elegant affair held at Central Presbyterian Cathedral with dinner at the country club, she introduced Franklin's wealthy family to Grandma Berkey and the judge as the people who'd raised her. She had whispered to the Griffins that her biological mother was emotionally unwell and Hope hadn't lived with her since she was small. Jo didn't argue with this story. Hope's father, they said, was deceased. No one else from the family came to the wedding. No one seemed to think this odd. Nor did they ask any questions.

Chapter Five

B y the middle of May both the house on Lake Waseka and Megan were looking much better. Even several visits from Louise couldn't bring Megan's spirits down as she anticipated the summer, and Louise definitely tried to put the kibosh on their plans. Louise steadfastly insisted she would not join them. If they wanted Grandma Berkey at the lake, they'd have to find someone other than Louise to deliver her.

There was very little left to do in the house and Charley went ahead of Meg to see it done. John had agreed to help Meg pack, make sure she had her medication and drive her and her luggage north to the lake. He wanted to be there on weekends whenever possible. There were just the finishing touches, things that Melissa had offered to take care of but Charley wanted to do herself. In fact, Melissa had come close to begging, but Charley insisted. Charley's hands-on involvement in fixing up the place had been pretty limited and she looked forward to adding the accessories she'd shopped for in the city. She had fluffy towels, crisp sheets, thick rugs, soaps and creams, place mats and napkins, comforters and down pillows. She bought a set of eight wineglasses and as many tumblers and cocktail glasses.

After putting her new purchases in the house, Charley lit off for the nearest large grocery to stock up, looking forward with great longing to the summer days when the farmers would begin to put their fresh vegetables out on roadside stands.

She settled in, smoothing sheets over the mattress in the master bedroom, shaking out and putting down fluffy rugs in bathrooms, in front of the door and kitchen sink, beside the beds. The new down pillows almost hugged her back when she squeezed them. Everything was in place before the sun lowered in the sky and she took a glass of wine onto the porch, sat in one of the chaises with her feet up and began to do what Megan had been doing—remembering the summers that were filled with laughter and fun.

It wasn't hard when she focused. When it was just them— the girls—it was carefree and filled with pleasure. It wasn't harmonious every second, of course. Six little girls could squabble and bicker, especially when the rain forced them inside, but their conflicts were short-lived. They just enjoyed the heaven that escape to the lake provided. They loved to spy on their mothers late at night. Getting caught was almost as much fun as the spying, which never turned up much besides gossip about their marriages. They had swimming races and diving contests. Since they spent so much time in the lake they hardly ever took baths. In fact, they washed their hair in the lake. Aunt Jo would give them a bottle of shampoo to take to the lake every few days. They had an old outdoor shower at the boathouse but they used it sparingly because the water was freezing.

Her cell phone rang and she held her breath when she saw it was Michael. She prayed they wouldn't fight. "Hi," she said.

"I was just thinking about you. I just got here this afternoon. The place is all put together and I'm by myself."

"Where's Meg?" he asked.

"John's bringing her in a few days. I wanted to come ahead, make sure it was clean and comfortable and stocked with healthy food."

"John's okay with her spending the whole summer at the lake?" he asked.

"He's planning to come on the weekends. But how are you?"

"Ready for the semester to end," he said. "Listen, I hope you'll take this as good news. Eric was able to get a slot in an exchange program at Cambridge. He's coming with me in September."

"Oh, Michael," she said. "Is he happy about that?"

"He's ecstatic. Of course, all he can talk about is the fact that he won't be staying with me. He's planning on staying in a student flat. But we'll be in the same city. And I'll be able to check on him."

I wonder where I'll be, Charley thought. "Both of you gone? I don't know if I can stand it."

"Charley, *you're* gone," he reminded her. "You can come with us, you know."

"You know that depends on a lot of things, mostly Meg."

"And how is our Meg?" he asked.

"She's looking so much better. And she's stronger. I'm filled with hope. But she's thin and still needs two naps a day, so…"

"I'll bring Eric in the summer," Michael said. "In fact, I can't wait."

At least he didn't say he'd *send* Eric. "I wish you could see it right now," she said. "School isn't out yet so the lake is still quiet. You can hear a fish jump now and then. Someone will whistle for a dog or maybe shout the dog's name. No speedboats but the occasional putter of a motor on a bass boat out in the big lake. It's so peaceful. Restful. Good for thinking."

"I'm sorry Meg's illness was what took you away, but after the shitty way your year started out, this might be just what you need. Has Louise reared her ugly head?"

Charley laughed. "Oh, yes. She tried saying she wouldn't allow us to come here, but when Meg said she'd have to call the police and arrest us, she tried other tactics. She won't be joining us. We're not at all sad about that. But guess who says she's coming? Hope. She says so, anyway."

"And Beverly?"

"She says she's not sure if she's ready for that much reality."

"It might be just the two of you all summer," Michael said.

"I'm perfectly all right with that idea," Charley said. "Being here alone I tried to remember all the good things that happened when we were children. That's what Meg's been doing. It turns out it's not that hard to do. I'm remembering so much."

"Too much?" he asked. Because of course Michael knew about that summer romance that went awry, leaving her an unwed mother.

"Actually, I'm remembering that last summer more kindly now. Do you know what never occurred to me at the time? In fact, it didn't occur to me until very recently. My summer love who ran for his life when he found out my grandfather was a judge—he might've been afraid of a statutory rape charge. I was sixteen. He was nineteen. We both lied about our ages. And he said he was from the city, but I heard from one of the other waiters that he wasn't—he was a local kid. If I'd been near here when I found out I was pregnant I could've tracked him down, but I wasn't, and then they sent me away. When I made contact with Andrea seven years ago, all I could tell her about her father was that he was nineteen and he'd said he was Mack but that wasn't his real name."

"You could ask around now," Michael said.

"You think he could still be around after twenty-seven years?" she said. "Maybe after I'm here a little while." But what she didn't want to say, what she couldn't quite say, was how she still found it so embarrassing. She was made to feel humiliated by the way she was sent away. Thinking about facing the locals to say there was a man out there who should know he has a child who was now twenty-seven, married, with children of her own, was intimidating. Yes, the sophisticated talk show host might be able to spit out something like that in the big city, but out here in the small farm towns, facing old-fashioned Methodists who went to church every Sunday was different. Feeling like a fool had always been her weak spot.

But she vowed she would try. After she got used to the idea.

The next day Charley put her iPod in the speaker bay she'd brought along and, to the comforting strings of Vivaldi, she folded freshly laundered towels and put them in the linen closet. She hung two fluffy yellow towels in the bathroom. It had been such a relief to sleep amid smells of lemon oil and pine needles rather than the motel's economy disinfectant that bore a ghastly resemblance to cheap talc.

She went to make a pot of coffee. Just as she turned on the machine she caught sight of something out of the corner of her eye. She was drawn to the kitchen window for a closer look. There was a young girl sitting across the lawn in one of the freshly painted chairs that Melissa had put out in the yard. She had a small suitcase on each side of the chair. For a second Charley almost felt like she was looking at a memory; the girl's hair was stringy, her jeans ratty, her T-shirt ragged and grayish, her jacket a cheap, dated corduroy. With a closer look, she realized it was not a girl, but a woman. A small, familiar woman.

"Krista," she whispered. "What the hell?"

When they were little girls, aged one through six, they looked like towheaded clones, but as they grew older they each took on more individual characteristics. Charley was tall, her face angular, her hair a dark auburn, while Megan was only five-three and when she'd had hair their mother had called it dishwater blond. She hadn't seen Krista in a long time, a couple of years since she'd visited her in prison. In fact, Charley had only visited her a handful of times the whole twenty-three years. But from the distance of one hundred yards she looked the same as she had the last time she'd seen her, her brows thick and straight, her hair that nondescript and shapeless brown, her mouth harshly set. She was Megan's height and probably didn't weigh a whole hundred and fifteen pounds.

Charley wondered, not for the first time, what kind of baggage prison would leave Krista with. She could have visited her more often. But she hadn't. The whole experience of visiting Chowchilla had been so horrid.

It was odd the way she sat out there, watching the house. What was she doing here? Meg had sent her a note telling her the lake house would be open from June through August but it wasn't yet June. And Krista was supposed to be in prison, for God's sake. Last Charley had heard, she wasn't even eligible for parole.

It was sunny but chilly outside. Charley shivered and found her heaviest sweater. She turned on the oven to begin to warm up the place, then on the spur of the moment opened a can of biscuits, tucked them into a pan, covered them with butter, sugar and cinnamon and popped them in the oven. But the cold air, smell of coffee and hot cinnamon biscuits and sounds of music hadn't drawn Krista to the porch.

Well, Charley decided, *she's having trouble with this. So I'll have to bring her in and get her story, find out what she expects of me. I've done that for a living for years.*

Charley tucked a woven lap blanket under her arm, poured two steaming cups of coffee and went out into the yard. Krista watched her cautiously as she approached but she didn't move. She neither rose to greet her cousin, nor did she bolt.

Charley knelt before her, placing both coffees on the ground. She unfurled the blanket and wrapped it like a shawl around Krista's shoulders. Then she placed a warm mug in Krista's hands. "Krista, why are you sitting out here? Did you escape?" she asked.

Krista shrugged.

"Really?" Charley said with a sarcastic laugh.

Krista's lips moved into a smirk. "Once I got here, I realized you might not be happy to see me. I was giving you a chance to send me away."

"Why would I do that?"

"Because I'm a convicted murderer, maybe?" Krista replied with sarcasm of her own.

Charley put on her impatient interviewer face. "I know you didn't murder anyone, Krista. How'd you get out?"

"A miracle. Some big-shot lady lawyer got me out. I stopped believing something like that was possible a long time ago."

"That's a relief. I'm glad I don't have to harbor a fugitive." Krista made a face and Charley smiled. "Wanna come in? Or you wanna sit out here by yourself?"

"So you're okay with this, then? Me being here?"

"I'm not afraid of you, Krista. I think in all fairness I should be asking you if you're okay with *me* being here. We haven't even talked in a couple of years. And I wasn't able to do anything to help you. Aside from some letters, I was hardly any support to you while you were in prison…and I knew you didn't deserve to be there."

"Oh, I don't even think about that, Charley," Krista said slowly, getting to her feet. "I mean, first of all, I did deserve to be there—just maybe not for the reasons they said. And second, I wasn't much help to you, either, as I recall. I don't think you had it that much easier than me."

Charley's head slowly tilted to one side as she listened to Krista. This woman had just come out of twenty-three years of hard time while Charley had been considered a minor celebrity making lots of money. Yet she had sympathetic words for Charley. It was almost unheard of that anyone would express such a kindness to her, especially a member of her family. That her success had come at great labor and sacrifice was irrelevant to most people. She was unaccustomed to genuine concern for her feelings.

She bent to pick up one of the two small suitcases. "How'd you like a nice hot soak in our new bathtub?"

"That would be so cool," Krista answered. "You just have no idea how cool."

Charley gave two taps on the bathroom door before entering. The bubbles were high, nearly covering Krista's head. Charley picked up the empty coffee cup and replaced it with a new one. "This is Amaretto Crème," she said. "With a little dollop of whipping cream on top for good measure."

"I don't drink."

"It's just the flavor—no booze. Krista, I have to say something quick before I lose my nerve. And I don't think there's any way to preserve your dignity when I say it."

"Go ahead, babe. I don't have hardly any dignity."

"I peeked in your suitcase. The stuff you brought with

you…your clothes. The underwear and jeans? It's no good. You have to let me replace it all for you. With new stuff."

"You don't have to do that."

"Yes, I do. Orphans in third-world countries have better underwear than you. I've spent more on lunch…many times… than it would cost to buy a few new outfits for you to wear this summer. And you'll need a bathing suit."

"Gee, we were all girls at the last place I lived, so when we went to the beach, we just skinny-dipped," Krista said, laughing harshly.

"Maybe some nightclothes. You obviously don't need nightclothes or robes or slippers in prison."

"Shower thongs, Charley. Not slippers."

"Well, you need slippers and beach thongs. Flip-flops."

"Charley," Krista said.

"And we'll get you a decent haircut in Brainerd, if you like."

"This is so much how I pictured you, Charley. A perfectionist. Throwing money at everything."

"Please, I don't mean to hurt your pride, Krista. I just want to help. I want you to be comfortable and feel safe. Don't deny me the pleasure of—"

"Oh, don't worry, I won't deny you your pleasures. I don't do things to hurt myself anymore," Krista said, raising her arm high above her head and watching the soap suds run slowly down. "Spend as much on me as you want, Charley." She laughed. "I didn't have time to stop at Victoria's Secret on my way out of Chowchilla. And my beautician was all tied up."

"Who cut your hair in prison?" Charley asked.

"Whoever could be trusted with scissors. It was usually a guard. But we did have a little beauty shop there, if you use the term loosely." She sank down in the tub, letting the water and bubbles cover her head. She rose up again. "Way loosely."

"Well, for right now you can wear some of my stuff."

This made Krista laugh. "Really, Charley, I can get by for the time being. All right?"

Charley left the bathroom and came back directly with some underwear and and a pair of soft white socks. She dangled them toward Krista, then put them down on the closed toilet lid and left.

"Charley?" Krista called. "When do you expect the phone to be hooked up?"

"Couple of days. Why?"

"I haven't called my mom yet. I never really believed I was going to get out so I didn't tell anyone what was happening. I just came straight here."

"I have a cell...you can call her whenever you want..."

"Maybe in the morning, then. And, Charley?" The sound of the drain gulping bathwater accompanied Krista's yelling. "I have to check in with my parole officer in Grand Rapids... it was the best I could do... Do you suppose...?"

"I'll take you there myself. I'll be your sponsor here."

"I don't think I need a sponsor. But, Charley? Oh! Oh, Charley! Oh, my God!"

Charley rushed to the bathroom. There stood Krista, her skin pink from the hot water, wearing Charley's cotton underwear and matching undershirt. Bright soft whites. Krista was running her hands up and down her sides, over her little rump, around her hips, over her little breasts. "Oh, Charley, these are the most wonderful things I have ever had on my body!" she said with reverence. "I will never take them off!"

"Yeah, well, I think that's what happened to the last ones."

They had to share a bed, Charley told her, because they had only the one mattress so far with two more being delivered. And there was only the one heating pad to keep them warm. Fortunately, there were plenty of quilts and comfort-ers and pillows. "Just like our mothers used to do," she said. Charley took the flavored coffee and hot cinnamon biscuits to the bedroom on a tray and they nibbled and sipped while they talked.

"Tell me what prison was like," Charley said.

"Oh, not now," Krista said, sinking back against the down pillows. "Just let me smell and feel these things. Charley, your life is so rich, do you know that?"

She picked up her coffee cup, warming her hands with it, and smiled. She did know. She worked hard for it—she ap-preciated every moment of it.

"Do you smell all these smells? The lotion and pine and linen and soap...soap that isn't lye, I mean. The dirt and the lake and the...the...furniture polish?" she asked.

"Yes. And varnish," Charley said. "I had the hardwood floors sanded and varnished."

"There's paint and wallpaper paste and lemon oil." She closed her eyes and twitched her nose in the air. "There's va-nilla somewhere, some sweet-smelling cleaning fluid. The smell of brand-new muslin and ages-old cotton...what a great combination."

"Can you smell the wicker? Does wicker have a smell?" Charley wanted to know.

"Sure it does—it smells like a basket or a straw hat. And you know what else? There are a thousand different blos-soms around the lake. In fact, this is the best the lake is ever going to smell," Krista said. "When everything is just com-ing in bloom. Except maybe the way it'll smell in fall, when the leaves change and drop off, when the fireplaces are all going, when the pies and turkeys are—" She stopped talking for a moment to sip from her steaming mug and think about smells. Later, when they had run out of things to talk about, she might tell Charley how prison smelled. Maybe. But she'd really rather forget.

"I never think about smells that much," Charley confessed quietly. "In fact, the only time I was ever made tragically aware of odor was once, after Megan went through a big chemo treatment and she kept saying, 'I smell like chemicals, don't I?' Her skin had a tinny odor to it. It was very strange."

They were both quiet for a moment. "How is she?" Krista finally asked.

"Well, she's better now than she was a couple of months ago. She's gained a couple of pounds, she's growing hair and her color isn't pasty. Did she or your mom write you about this latest treatment?"

"She just wrote me what she was going to have done. She said the results have been very good. She said she was optimistic."

"She had lung, liver and pancreatic metastasis, not to mention some lymphatic involvement. When she was in remission they got her as strong as possible and she donated her own bone marrow for the surgery. Just in case. Once she recovered from the harvest, when the cancer was evident again, they literally wiped her out with chemotherapy. Killed everything that moved, so to speak. Then gave her a cell transplant with her own healthy cells. There isn't anything more to do now. Except wait."

"Wait? For how long?"

Charley let out a small, rueful laugh. "From now on, that's how long."

"Well? How does she feel?"

"She's pretty weak, but she claims she's feeling stronger every day. She's emaciated. The doctor has her drinking protein supplements to try to put a little weight on. And she was bald, of course." Charley shrugged. "She takes at least one nap every day but other than that she seems to be doing okay. That doesn't mean anything, of course."

"Why doesn't it?"

Charley took a moment to answer. "She's lying about the odds, Krista."

"Huh?"

"Not lying, that's not what I mean. They have had good results with this bone marrow transplant after chemo treatment...but unfortunately not on patients whose cancer is as advanced as Meg's. That's what this is all about, I think. This opening up the lake house, writing everyone to tell them to come back here one more time. I think she wants to come here to die."

"Maybe not," Krista said hopefully.

"Yeah, maybe not," Charley said. But there wasn't much hope in her voice.

To see dawn sparkle across the lake water...this was something Krista feared she would never see again. She'd hardly slept since she'd been out of prison, but was not in the least tired. It would have been impossible to sleep through any sight that underscored her own freedom—like the rising of the sun on Lake Waseka. She sat cross-legged at the end of the dock in the purplish predawn, wearing Charley's underwear and socks and her own old, ratty corduroy jacket.

She heard the new dock creak behind her and she looked over her shoulder to see Charley coming toward her. Charley wore her warm, furry robe, toasty slippers, and carried two steaming cups of coffee.

"I didn't mean to wake you," Krista said. "I was trying to be quiet."

"You didn't wake me. I get up before sunrise every day. I'm trained."

Krista accepted the coffee gratefully. "That's how you became so famous. Famous Charley—that's what we call you."

"*We?*" she asked.

"Me, Meg, my mom…"

"Aunt Jo calls me that?" Charley asked, aghast.

"Not really…it's how I've referred to you a couple of times, and when my mom wrote to me, if she mentioned you, she'd put it in quotes. She didn't mean it disrespectfully. She's very proud of you." Krista sipped. "She'd write, 'I caught "Famous Charley's" show today. She had on Sylvester Stallone. Who knew what a good sense of humor he has.' Stuff like that."

"Hmm."

"You did all this, then? Fixing up the house and stuff?"

"Uh-huh. With the help of a local decorator."

"For Meg?"

"I'd buy the lake for her if I could. I only have one sister left, you know."

Krista reached out and patted Charley's knee. "And I have two—and haven't heard a word from one of them in years. *Years.* I get a holiday card every year from Bev. I think Ma makes her do that. I always heard from Meggie, though. Isn't she the best one of all of us?"

Charley stared down into her coffee cup. Meg was going to be here in a few days. She hadn't done all this just to spend the summer crying because her sister was probably dying. But yes, she thought. Megan was the best one of them all.

"How does it feel to you to be back here?" Krista asked her.

"Surprisingly positive. Or maybe it hasn't really hit me yet. If it had, surely I'd be banging my head or tearing out my hair. This place…the last summer here… I think it must have been the pivotal point."

"Bunny…"

"Actually, I wasn't thinking of Bunny," she said. "I was thinking of Andrea."

"Andrea?"

"Andrea, the baby I was forced to give away. I found her... Rather, she found me, about seven years ago. She's a mother herself now. She's incredible, Krista. So beautiful, so smart. She has two darling little girls of her own. I was only seventeen when she was born. I did a kind of crazy thing."

Krista began to laugh. "Sorry—I don't think you even qualify..."

"No, I mean, just lately. I called Andrea, told her where I was spending the summer and why. I couldn't really invite her to the lake for the summer, tempting as that would be. The little girls—I think it might be too much for Meg. But I did suggest to Andrea that she try to come this way if possible. I told her I'd pay for their lodging in a nice place nearby. She could see her extended biological family. Some of them, anyway. And if she's still interested, she could do a little detective work on her biological father."

"Detective work? You don't know where he is?"

"I don't even know *who* he is. I mean, who he really is. I thought he was a twenty-two-year-old Harvard law student when I fell for him, but when some of the other lodge waiters told him I was the underage granddaughter of a superior court judge, he ran for his life. It turned out he was a nineteen-year-old local boy who hadn't gone to college at all. He said his name was Mack and that's all I ever knew. What are the odds Mack is his real name?" She laughed bitterly. "We were whisked away before I even realized I could be pregnant. Before I could even go back to the lodge and ask what his full name really was, although I didn't want him by then. He really took me for a ride."

"But...did you want to go on that ride?"

"Oh, yes," Charley said. "Or no. I wanted to kiss and hug and cuddle and feel love and passion and fantasize about how much better I was going to make my life than our mothers made theirs. And the reality is that if I had not had that awful summer, I wouldn't have had the volatile power and focus to do what I did. All that anger. It's what I used to get everything I ever got."

"I guess if Meg is the best one of us all, then you're the most successful one of us all." Krista drank her coffee and looked off in the direction of the first pink streaks of dawn. "And I'm the baddest one of us all. But who cares? Who could care when you look at something like that? God, Charley, have you ever seen anything more beautiful?"

Charley felt the tangy presence of her own sentimental tears—sheer joy at seeing Krista's reaction to dawn outside the walls of a prison. This was something she hadn't even considered, that she'd have this kind of reunion. Both with her cousin and with her own consciousness. She could not have appreciated the sunrise half so well without Krista to exclaim on its unique beauty. "Ahhh," was all she could say, for certainly she had seen dawns more beautiful than this. There was one on the China Sea that had moved her to tears, another from a mountaintop in the Greek isles. Perhaps the most beautiful of all—over the crown of her newborn baby boy's head, born at dawn eighteen years ago.

"I'm so glad you're here, Krista."

"No one's more glad of that than me! So, who actually owns this place now?"

Charley shrugged, thinking. "I suppose Grandma Berkey does. It obviously hasn't been sold. Which raises some interesting questions, now that you mention it."

"I should know who actually owns the place," Krista said, paying little attention to the prospect of interesting questions.

"I know Meg invited everyone to visit this summer, which is nice, but I need a place to stay and I have to have the permission of the owner. You know?"

"You have my permission," Charley said dismissively.

"No, you don't understand," Krista said. "I really have to know who to ask. I have an obsessive need to do things the right way." She touched Charley's arm, drawing her attention. "There are rules. Understand?"

"Sure," she finally answered. "We'll take care of that." Then, remembering something, she said, "Krista, I looked in the other suitcase, too. Last night. I wasn't really snooping. I was looking for your clothes and then for what else you might need."

"You were snooping," Krista said.

"Where'd you get the typewriter?"

"My mom sent it. I asked her for it—she found it at a thrift shop. She said she wished it was a laptop, but she couldn't really afford it. But she wanted me to have something for writing."

"Can I buy you the laptop?"

"I really don't need it."

"I want to. Because you're doing the one thing no one could do. You're writing about it. Trying to get it down. I saw the pages. God, I'm so relieved. I'm so glad it's you and not me."

"It's hard. I'd like to do it right. I mean, correct. I mean, true. Shit, I don't know what I mean."

"Where are you getting the stuff? The information?"

"Well, I'd ask a question here and there of my mom or Meg. I could get Meg to go undercover to Grandma Berkey. I think she even enjoyed it. Plus, I remember things. Meg doesn't, Beverly won't talk about it, you and Hope were pretty scarce with other things on your minds."

"They know about the book, your mom and Meg? The story? Whatever it is?"

"No. I told them it's for my therapy. So I could get 'well.' And get out. I lied."

"That's okay. You do what you have to do. Writing it down is important to everyone, even the ones who don't know it. And you're on the right track, I can feel it."

"You read it?" Krista asked.

"The first sentence. It's a very good first sentence."

They had a moment of silent communication as they both thought about that first sentence.

My grandfather kicked my grandmother in the stomach when she was pregnant with her first child, so it's a wonder any of us are here at all.

Chapter Six

Krista had adored her father but she knew at an early age he was trouble. Roy was ten years younger than his brother, Carl. He was about twelve times more handsome, too. And he could charm the socks off a centipede. He was funny and handsome, could sing beautifully, tell jokes all night, and just the sight of him dancing with Jo was enough to clear the dance floor—people backed away to watch.

While Hope was trying to fantasize another kind of life and Megan couldn't remember a thing for a whole year, Krista was the observer. She noticed everything and seemed unable to close her eyes to her family's problems. She had a couple of prominent memories. One was from when she was four or five and the family was getting ready for Christmas Eve with her grandparents and cousins. "Did you wash the dresses like I told you?" Roy asked Jo.

"I don't see why..." Jo said.

"So they don't look like we bought 'em for the Christmas inspection!" he shot back. "So the judge and your tight-assed sister don't say anything about it! And if your sister asks where your ring is, you say you left it by the sink. You got that?"

"Don't get all worked up, Roy," Jo pleaded. "That's usually your excuse to drink."

"How the hell am I supposed to get through six hours of listening to the old bastard without a couple of drinks under my belt?" he asked. Jo began to weep. "Oh, come on, baby, come on. I forget it's hard for you, too. I'll fix you a little something to take the edge off."

Krista remembered the tension before and after every holiday or weekend gathering at Grandma and the judge's house. Her other prominent memory was of the secret meetings in her parents' kitchen. This was something her cousins wouldn't remember even if they'd been paying attention because Carl and Louise came to Jo and Roy's house without the kids, after Krista and her sisters were in bed. They'd talk quietly in the kitchen. Krista had spied and eavesdropped a few times. She'd hear her father say things like, *I had to get rid of that car because it was a lemon, falling apart on us all the time. I got screwed.* But she knew the truth was the car had been repossessed. Or she'd hear her father say, *If you can't loan me the money, I'll have to sell some stock and I'm trying to hang on to it for the girls' education.* There was no stock.

Carl Hempstead had owned an electronics firm that was prosperous and a couple of times Roy worked for him. It had not gone well and there had been more of those kitchen meetings. Louise would always say, "Family is the most important thing. We will forever and always put family first and we'll never speak of this again." What they were never speaking of remained a mystery but Krista had some guesses. She suspected that every time Roy was down on his luck and needed the help of his older brother to dig out of a debt or pay off a loan, there was a kitchen meeting.

Krista had fashioned some of these memories into short stories for a class she'd taken in prison. The writing teacher had praised her work and asked her if she'd ever considered putting it all down on paper, from her earliest memory on. "You have talent," the teacher said. "Plus, it's an amazing way to clear the cobwebs—writing about it. The truth about it."

"People in my position are very flexible about the truth," Krista said. Her position was one of convicted felon, serving two and four. Two counts of murder, four of armed robbery. Now that was a story in itself.

Krista had had lots of therapy in prison. Most inmates didn't really take to it but Krista was fascinated and she liked drawing some conclusions about the turns her life had taken. She had some individual and group counseling. It had been suggested that if she wanted to figure out where her problems had come from, she might take a closer look at her family.

That seemed pretty obvious to Krista. In fact, she suspected she knew where it all started. She thought she might be somewhat biased since the judge wouldn't help her when she was in deep shit, but she suspected he was the root of all their problems. In fact, she'd be disappointed if she learned he wasn't. But she wanted to gather as much information, the secret kind of information, the kind no one was supposed to talk about, to write it down. She wasn't sure she'd ever publish something that personal that touched so many lives, but the first step was writing it. And writing it accurately. She started by asking Jo a lot of questions.

"When your dad and I needed a loan or a little help, Lou and Carl would come over to the house after you kids were in bed to talk about the terms. We'd set up a payment schedule and a small amount of interest, but Lou and Carl never expected to get repaid. So as a backup, as collateral, I'd promise to forfeit a part of the inheritance I'd share with Lou. Maybe my half of the silver or my half of a piece of art, of which there was a lot. Like my half of the Matisse."

Yeah, Krista thought. *That's what I'm talking about.*

She was careful to space her questions carefully so as not to draw too much attention to the fact seeking she was doing. And she had a nice, steady communication with Megan right up to the last couple of years when to talk about anything other than Megan's health was selfish and even cruel.

Her mother visited the prison a few times, but it was costly for Jo and she didn't make a lot of money. She got by and seemed pretty content, but Krista was well aware there were no extras for her mother and for her to spend the money to travel to California to visit her was an extravagance. But those were the times Jo would tell her things about the family. In her letters, Krista could tell Jo was uncomfortable putting it to paper and their phone conversations had to be kept short because there were always people waiting. But when Jo visited, they could talk for a few hours.

"Your grandmother started saying bizarre things after the judge passed away. Things I never heard her say while he was alive. Like the fact that she brought the money to the marriage. He'd have had everyone, including his family, believe that his wealth came from his great success as a lawyer and a judge. But Grandma said that was bull. She said he was a threadbare young attorney and she was the only child of a successful Chicago businessman. Her father literally picked the judge out for her, threw them a big wedding—a huge wedding. There was a fantastic dowry and it was her parents who gave them that enormous house on Grand Avenue. No young lawyer could afford that kind of house unless he had family money and the judge was the only child of a widow who lived from hand to mouth. Grandma said the judge was bought and paid for. And she was angry about it."

"What kind of business did your grandfather run in Chicago?" Krista asked.

"He was a mortician!" Jo said. "A very successful mortician! And, after they got married and were living in Saint Paul, Grandma said the judge got mean. He had a temper, she said. He slapped her around and threw things. Back in those days, one never talked about domestic abuse, never. But Grandma was too smart for the judge. She called her father. And her father had what she called *connections*. Grandma said a couple of men visited the judge and explained, very carefully, that her parents were worried about her and didn't want to think for one second that she wasn't being well cared for. After listening to her talk like this for a couple of years, I got the idea my grandfather, Grandma's daddy, was connected to the mob in Chicago. But your aunt Lou thought Grandma was senile. That's when Grandma said, 'Senile, eh? You're lucky to have been born. The judge hit me, knocked me down and kicked me in the stomach when I was pregnant with you!' We'd never seen the judge raise a hand to our mother. Though there was no mistaking he had a temper."

And he had a mean streak a mile long, Krista knew from experience. He was known as a hanging judge. And when she had appealed to him for help, he refused. Not that she blamed him. Krista had been both defiant and incorrigible.

But that was then. Twenty-five to life had filed down all the jagged edges.

Charley called Meg to let her know that Krista was with her at the lake house. After a tearful conversation, Krista handed the phone back to Charley.

"Would you like to call your mom now?" Charley asked while they ate a light breakfast of fruit and toast.

"The first person I have to check in with is that parole officer," Krista said.

"Will you have to see him or her right away?"

"It's a woman. And I won't know until I call," Krista said.

"Well, if she wants to see you, I'll take you. But I have an idea. I can drive you into the city and you can see your mother. Today. How does that sound to you?"

"I like that idea," she said.

"Can I leave you with her for a couple of hours while I run a few errands?" Charley asked.

"She'll be at work," Krista said. "We'll have to ask her if it's all right if I hang around. She's not expecting me."

"Call her," Charley said. "Do you have any money?"

"Seventy-five dollars," Krista said. "The parole officer will help me with some paperwork to apply for some interim assistance while I look for work."

Charley opened up her purse and gave Krista another fifty. "Take your mom to lunch so you can talk, if she can escape the shop for an hour."

"Charley..."

"Don't even think about it, Krista. I've been lucky. If I can help you make this transition, it'll be good for my spirit."

"As long as your spirit doesn't go broke," she said.

They headed for the city, chatting the whole way. They recalled how it had been such a long drive when they were children but now there were good freeways that cut the time by at least a third. They turned the oldies on the radio and sang along. They laughed about the games they played in the back of the station wagon, their mothers in the front seat. It was a wonder no one got hurt! Games like *Who can we suffocate the fastest?* And pushing on the stomach of whatever girl had to pee. And laughing until someone *did* pee!

They pulled up in front of a respectable-looking little flower shop in an older section of Oakdale. "Want me to come in with you?" Charley asked.

Krista looked up and down the street. There were a couple of fast-food restaurants, an Italian place, a park. "No, I'll be fine. This is good. I should see her first before I do anything else. What are you going to do? If you don't mind me asking..."

"I'm going to see my mother," Charley said. "We need to figure out who owns the lake house. And we need to be sure your mom feels okay about coming if that's where you're going to be. If you decide to stay here with your mom, that's not a problem, you know. Everyone would understand."

"Everyone? As in you and Megan?"

"Or anyone else," Charley said.

"Listen—for twenty-three years Megan has been my faithful best friend, correspondent, spy and sister of the heart. I don't know how much time she has left. I want to be there."

That made Charley tear up. "Thank you," she whispered.

"Don't thank me," Krista said. "I haven't earned the right. But I really want to be with her and both of you seem to want me to be at the lake. You have no idea how much I appreciate that."

"I love you, Krista," Charley said. "I'm so glad we have this second chance."

Charley dropped Krista in the small park across the street from the flower shop and drove to her mother's house. She'd seen Louise several times while she was staying with Meg but she hadn't been back to the house she grew up in for years. Not since Eric was six years old. She always stayed with Meg.

Just walking up to the door, her gut churned. She thought, *My God, I'm forty-four years old and still afraid of my mother! I don't want to be alone with her!*

Funny, Charley thought, *I've been less nervous facing neo-Nazis on my talk show than I am dropping in on my mother.* And as far as that went, she wasn't merely dropping in—she had called ahead after leaving Krista at the flower shop. "Mother, it's Charley," she had said.

"Oh?" Louise replied.

"I'm going to be in Saint Paul this morning. I wonder if I might stop by?"

"Well, I suppose so. If you feel you have the *time*."

"I'm pretty busy actually, but I'll squeeze you in," Charley said. Automatic sass. Instantly she knew she'd been had again. Louise's tongue was like pistol fire at her feet. Dance, dance, dance. Louise would bait her and Charley always took the bait.

Louise had been old for over twenty years. In fact, when Charley's father passed away Louise was forty-one and she'd already been old. Not wrinkled, tired or through too many hard times; it wasn't that. She was already complaining about how hard the floors were on her knees and hips but she was neither arthritic nor crippled. Her hair was gray and she didn't color it. It must be hard to find a beautician who could still create that twenty-or thirty-year-old weekly hairdo... Charley thought it was called "the wedge." Lou wore no makeup, not even lipstick, as she had when she was young. Her brows were shapeless and she wouldn't pluck them. Her clothes were expensive but dowdy and she didn't update them. But more than anything it was the sourness on her face. It could scare children. She could be so fierce and mean looking it could make you wince and step back. It put thirty years on her.

Before that terrible summer she used to laugh. She was smart and funny, happy and attractive. She gave up so long ago.

The very first time Charley had taken Eric to meet his grandmother he was six years old. He was bright, funny, handsome and daring. But when he saw Louise, he had gasped. Right out loud. And the most complimentary thing Louise had said of him during their entire visit was, "Small for his age, isn't he? And a bit of an attitude. I know where he gets that."

Charley had a few pictures of her family members taken at her grandparents' home at the time of her father's funeral—when Louise was three years younger than Charley was now. Louise had looked at least sixty.

Cut her some slack, her conscience had said at the time. *She's been through hell with her kids and her husband just died.* Louise couldn't be blamed for what happened to Bunny, Charley said to herself, but the rest of us she drove away with her anger, her lack of empathy. Even Daddy. Louise behaved as though everything that had gone wrong happened only to her.

She knocked on her mother's front door before she let herself think too much about her father. Her father, who was so inherently good, so loving and generous, yet in all their familial crises he never found a way to be the least bit useful.

Louise had lived in the same spacious split-level since Charley was about twelve. The house was in an upscale neighborhood. It sat at the end of a cul-de-sac on a half-acre lot with lush trees and shrubs. Charley could hear the sound of the lawn trimmer outside and the vacuum cleaner inside. A housekeeping service van was parked at the curb.

Charley was already angry. She was pursing her lips against rage. Her mother had a gardener and maid, but Aunt Jo could only afford a small apartment? They were both single women, had once been so close. You'd think Louise would want to take care of her sister. How could they allow this arrangement to continue?

"Charley, I didn't expect you to get here so quickly."

"I dropped Krista at Aunt Jo's flower shop and came right over." She shrugged.

"Jo's flower shop?" Louise asked. "She has a flower shop now?"

Louise knew better but Charley responded, anyway. "I believe she has worked in the same flower shop for years, Mother," she managed to say without snarling. "Don't you see her?"

"I see her every week," Louise said. "As you know."

Ah, so this had not changed since the last time Charley was home. Jo and Louise accompanied Grandma Berkey to church every Sunday. Jo took a bus to the nursing home and Louise drove herself there. They put Grandma in the front seat of the car, Jo got in the back seat and they went to the big Presbyterian church downtown. They sat on either side of Grandma and barely spoke to each other. They took Grandma to lunch, each paid for her own plus half of Grandma's and talked mostly to Grandma. They took Grandma back to the nursing home; Jo left there by bus and Louise drove herself home. Charley wondered if Louise had ever offered her sister a ride. Jo never asked for one. The settings had changed over the years but the bottom line was the same: they were often together, at least once a week, and in twenty-seven years had not had any real conversations.

Charley took a breath. "Actually, I'm here to talk to you about Aunt Jo."

"Would you like to talk in the doorway? Or would you like to come inside?"

"Why do you have to be so damn sarcastic, Mother? I'd like to come in! I'd like you to say you're glad I stopped by! I'd like you to offer me a cup of coffee or tea or maybe a good belt of something stronger! My God, you're no more welcoming than you were the last time I came to this house some twelve years ago!"

"Maybe I don't show my feelings so much anymore because I'm a little tired of being hurt, Charley. As you said, it's been twelve years since you came to my house. By all means, come in." And with that Louise turned and strode into the house, leaving Charley to follow.

How the hell does she do that? Charley asked herself. Though Louise had not phoned or written one time to say she was missed or asked her to come for a visit, it was somehow Charley's fault. It was all about Louise. *This is the last time*, Charley vowed. *The very last time. She is an unredeemable narcissist.*

She started to follow her mother, but the giant clog of jumbled furnishings slowed her pace like quicksand and she stopped to take it in. Well, this had changed. The house was a turmoil of contrasting florals and patterns and textures and styles—it swam before her. Charley looked at the walls, the pillows, the paintings, the bric-a-brac; this was how her mother spent her time—filling every inch of space. It actually seemed to move, it was so busy. Charley stopped in the foyer, the jam-packed living room on her right, cluttered dining room on her left. She slowly turned. It wasn't so much the disarray; it was the amount! She began to feel claustrophobic. Had Louise become a hoarder?

She thought she recognized a painting. Then a familiar candelabra. And then with a gasp she realized that Louise had stuffed every last possession from Grandma Berkey's Grand Avenue manse into her house. How the devil did these maids for hire dust it all?

"The coffee is in here, Charley," her mother called from the kitchen.

There were two buffets and Grandma Berkey's breakfront, filled with silver, crystal, china and collectibles. The walls were literally covered with paintings, gilt mirrors, sconces, clocks. The antique furniture and accoutrements alone were worth tens of thousands of dollars. Charley remembered her grandparents' home and all its plenty. She'd wondered just how the Berkey wealth had been disposed. Since Aunt Jo couldn't seem to afford a car anymore, it was possible all of Grandma's valuables had been moved right into Louise's possession.

Well, that could be dealt with another time. Grandma wasn't dead yet.

She pushed through the swinging door and tried not to react to the junk-shop atmosphere of the kitchen. But again, Louise had surrounded herself with tons of useless, though perhaps valuable, possessions. She had refused to part with a single thing. It would have to be inventoried by someone smarter than Charley. It struck her that she might be the only surviving daughter when Louise died and she'd actually be stuck with this mountain of expensive junk. She shivered at the thought.

"It isn't cold in here, Charley. In fact, I've been baking," Louise said, putting a cup of coffee on the kitchen table. No baked goods appeared.

Charley pulled out a chair, picked up the cup and took a sip and sat down at the table, cup in both hands. "Mother, sit down, please. Let's talk."

Louise had a turn to her lips that said resistance, but she sat.

"Krista came directly to the lake house from jail. It's very important to her to do things right after all she's been through. She wants permission to stay at the lake house for a while. She wants to ask someone and have someone tell her it's okay. So—who is the owner now, Mother? Would that be you?"

"Hmm. That's more than you and your sister thought to do."

"Yes, correct, we—or really Megan—*assumed*. Or would that be *presumed*? But that's beside the point. Call us rude, I don't care. But I think it's important to honor Krista's request to have official permission."

"If I didn't give her permission, would it cause the rest of you to leave and stay out of that house?"

"Not a chance."

"Then tell Krista she has her permission. I don't expect any of you cares how it makes me feel."

Charley decided to let it go. "Are you the official owner?"

"I'm the official trustee to Grandma Berkey's trust and executor of her estate. I disposed of her other real estate, pay her bills and taxes, control her income—which goes directly to the nursing home. I take care of all her needs. I alone."

"Aunt Jo doesn't help with any of that?"

"Hah. She's barely capable of taking care of herself."

"I see. Okay. Just out of curiosity—if you're the trustee and you hate the lake house so much, why haven't you sold it?"

"Grandma objected. I'm merely honoring her wishes. She always hoped we'd open it up again one day but I have no use for that place." Then Louise looked away in obvious discomfort, making Charley wonder just who wouldn't sell that property.

"I know it's none of my business but does Aunt Jo get anything? When Grandma dies?"

Louise looked back sharply. "Grandma has a will. For the time being her worldly goods and accounts and social security and pension are being used to pay for her care. When she dies her will goes into effect. She made her decisions about that a long time ago."

She knows, Charley thought. *But she won't tell.*

"There isn't much, Charley," Louise said. "A lot of widows my age go on vacations and cruises and have their nails and hair done but I stay home and make sure Grandma is cared for. It's more than a full-time job. That's all I've done for almost twenty years."

Charley decided to call her bluff, just for vicious fun. She leaned back in her chair. "I have some time on my hands, Mother. Why don't I take care of Grandma's needs for a month or two while you do some traveling? You could sell off what's in that breakfront and cruise around the world a couple of times."

"When my daughter has cancer and could be dying?" Louise countered.

"Megan is planning on staying at the lake," Charley reminded her.

"Surely not for the rest of her life!"

"Very possibly," Charley said. But then Louise had been told more than once. She just hated to deal with it.

"I just can't believe that!"

"Well, you'd better. Which brings me to another matter. Aunt Jo. She won't go to the lake unless you invite her. She's adamant. I want you to call her and tell her that you have no problem with her going to the lake."

"I don't even know her phone number," Louise said churlishly, crossing her arms over her chest and looking away.

"I'll be glad to give you the number. Now, Mother, I think Aunt Jo is being very sensitive to your feelings on the matter, but not only does she deserve a chance to be with Megan, both Hope and Krista will be at the lake this summer and those are her daughters."

"Hope?"

"Yes, and her daughters, though I don't think Frank is coming. Hope wrote to Meg something about business in Europe. He's a big shot, you know."

"Hmph. What else would Hope deign to have?"

"You don't like Hope?"

"She's a snotty social climber. I don't have much use for that."

Charley was again given pause. She was confused. "When did you last see Hope?" she asked Louise.

"Does it matter?"

"Well... Yeah, it matters. If you haven't seen Hope for over twenty-five years and still have this impression of her... I mean, you don't know anything about her. Anymore at least."

"I'm sure she hasn't changed," Louise said decidedly.

"She probably hasn't," Charley muttered, noting her mother's expression of satisfaction. "Not that you'd know anything about it. Now, back to Aunt Jo. Please, tell her you don't mind if she goes to the lake. It's her family, too."

"But I do mind," Louise said. The expression on her face looked as though she might cry, but her eyes didn't so much as cloud. "I mind everyone going. I mind my daughter, who is sick, going to that god-awful place. Doesn't anyone care what it will do to me if two of my daughters die there?"

What it will do to me? Doesn't anyone care about me? Do to me, to me, me, me...

Charley took a sip of her coffee to keep her mouth from sagging open forever. Then she put her cup down on the table and looked at her mother, shaking her head. "The rest of us were thinking of someone else, Mother." She took a deep breath. "Will you please do this for Megan? She's too sick to argue with you about it."

"I saw her just a week ago. She seemed quite feisty to me."

"A note," Charley said, ignoring her. "Just jot out a little note to Aunt Jo. I'm going over there to pick up Krista. I'll pass it to her. Just say, 'Jo, you're welcome to go to the lake anytime you like. Lou.' That should do the trick. And believe me—we'd all appreciate it very much. You'll just never know." *And hurry,* Charley thought. *If I don't get out of here quick, I might have to kill you.*

But Louise didn't move. She sat there staring at Charley.

Charley heard the ticking of at least three clocks. It seemed to last forever.

Finally, Louise rose from the table, went to the cupboard from which she withdrew a blank recipe card from a box and a pen. She scrawled the requested note and angrily thrust it at Charley. "Do you have everything you need?" she asked meanly.

Charley took it slowly. Then she stood. They were both tall women; they looked eye to eye at about five foot ten. "Mother, you should see someone. You don't have to be this miserable."

Louise forced a smile that looked positively psychopathic. "Who says I'm miserable? I have a good Christian life. I have the Lord at least, which is more than I can say for some people in my family. You have your permissions, Charley, you don't have to stay here with your mother a minute longer than necessary. But there's one thing you should know—I'll be damned to hell before I'll go to that house again."

A little spittle caught on Louise's lower lip when she spat the last sentence and Charley was reminded of some of her mother's insane rages when they were small. Most of them were at her, of course. Charley slowly turned, picked up her purse and left the house. When she closed the front door behind her, she whispered, "Thank you, God. I owe you one."

Louise never asked how she was, how Krista had fared after twenty-three years in prison, how her grandchildren were. She never asked about Charley's job, though she probably knew her show had been canceled. No, there was nothing about anyone else. Louise thought only of herself. How lonely she must be.

Charley looked at the note.

Josephine—Go to the lake house if you must, though it will probably kill me! Louise

In spite of herself she began to laugh.

"Hi, Ma."

Josephine heard it clearly but she was afraid to look up from the flora she was arranging in a basket. She was afraid it might not be real. She slowly turned, lifting her eyes hopefully but fearfully. Her head began shake in wonder and tears came immediately to her eyes. "Oh, baby, oh, Krista, oh, baby," she cried. She walked shakily toward Krista, her hands reaching out for her daughter's face.

Krista stood still, smiling, giving her mother some time to reach her and touch her. Jo's hands were roughly textured, marked by hard work and long cold winters.

Jo pressed Krista's face between the flat palms of her open hands. "Krista," she said breathily. "Oh, my God, my baby, my darling, my Krista!"

"I got out a little early," she said.

Jo let her hands flow down Krista's shoulders, arms, back, waist. "You're so little. Have you always been so little?"

"I'm right about your size."

"Well, height, maybe," Jo said, a laugh almost breaking through her tears. Jo was softly, roundly padded. A little stooped from being on her feet all day for years and years. "My baby. Home," she whispered, kneading her upper arms. "You're small—but you're strong. Feel your muscles."

"I'm very strong, Ma. Runs in the family, huh?" By now Krista could not hold back her own tears, fogging up her vision and tingling her nose. She resented the intrusion of tears. She wanted a clear vision of her mother. It had been a couple of years since she'd seen her. Jo had written faithfully at least every week, sending fifty dollars every month without fail, but she had rarely visited.

Jo's skin was soft and wrinkled but she was still beautiful. She'd worked hard over the years; anyone who thought the floral industry was a bucket of posies didn't know anything. Her light brown hair was threaded with gray and was thinner and wispier than it had been. But her smile, her smile was so sweet, even with tears catching in the wrinkles under her eyes. Krista took her into her arms and gave her a hearty hug. "Ohhh, Mom," she said, holding her close.

"Didn't they feed you? Are you okay? You're pale. You're too thin."

"I'm fine, Ma." Krista looked around the little flower shop; there didn't seem to be anyone around. "Can you sneak away for lunch?"

With precision timing, a woman stood in the doorway leading to the back of the shop. She was much younger than Jo, maybe thirty-five, and stocky. She looked at Krista suspiciously. She probably knew, Krista assumed.

"Sure I can, honey. I'm the manager. I don't know that I could possibly eat, but we can go for a walk at least. I don't like to take too much time away—"

"Go on and go, Jo," the woman said. "I'll handle the shop."

"Oh, Margie, I didn't see you there. Margie, this is my daughter Krista. Krista, this is Margie Ripley. She helps out part-time." She looked back at Krista. "I haven't seen Krista in a long time, Margie. She's been...she's been..."

"In the Army," Krista said, reaching around her mother and extending her hand toward the younger woman. "I just got out of the Army. This week, in fact. How do you do?" Margie was very slow to take Krista's hand. Krista bobbed. She did everything but salute.

"Go on then, Josephine. Take a little bit of time with your daughter. You betcha."

"Thanks, Margie. I won't be gone too long." Jo eased herself past Margie and into the back room to get her purse. Krista could hear the sound of a woman's voice, that nasal Midwestern twang, asking where she was going, but she couldn't hear her mother's reply.

Jo tucked her arm through Krista's as they left the shop. "You want something to eat, honey? There's a grill down the street a ways. A sandwich place over there. Or, if you don't mind a crowd, there's that pizzeria…"

"I mind the crowd, Ma. I want to talk to you more than anything. Find out how you are. If you're coming to the lake. You know. We don't need a big crowd on our first visit. How about that little park over there? That's where I sat while I was getting my nerve up to come into the flower shop."

"You needed courage to come to see *me*? You don't mean that, Krista. Not really."

"Not because of you, Ma. Because of me. I'm such a disappointment. It must be hard to be my mother, huh?" she asked, only half-facetiously. "Someone who's been in the Army for twenty-three years." Then she laughed with the painful truth of it.

"I'm proud of you, if you want to know. You worked hard in there—counseling, your GED, even some classes with college credits. How did you get here?"

"Charley brought me and dropped me off. She has some errands and will be back in a couple of hours. If it's not a good idea for me to hang around the shop, I'll just get a soda and come back later."

"Will you stay with me? I only have the one bedroom but I'll take the couch. It's small but nice and it's only a block from the bus."

"Where's your car?" Krista asked.

"I got rid of it years ago."

"I thought you'd be getting another one," Krista said.

"I wasn't using it too much. I took the bus most of the time to economize. After a while I thought, I don't need that car at all, not really. It wasn't just the gas but every time I turned around it needed some mechanical fix. I like not having a car, to tell the truth. But do you want to stay with me?"

"I want to spend as much time with you as possible, but I'm going to try to stay at the lake with Megan and Charley. If I don't find work nearby I might have to come to the city, but Megan...you know about Megan. I want to spend time with her, too. For right now, I'll be at the lake," Krista said. She steered her mother toward the little park just down the street. There were a couple of benches, a sandbox and some swings and a slide. "Maybe for the whole summer, depending. Charley is going to pick me up here, right where she left me off, and we're going to swing by Megan's house so I can say hello. You can come with us, too, if you want. Today, if you want to."

They sat down on the bench, still clutching each other's hands. Jo didn't say anything.

"I'm going to get a job as soon as I can, Ma. I don't want you to feel obligated, but if you want we can get a place together. It's up to you, okay?"

"I'd love that. Maybe after you're all settled," Jo said quietly. "You should get your life settled. You shouldn't have to worry about me."

Krista laughed and pulled Jo into a hug. "I'm not worried about you, Ma. I want to be with you if we can work it out! You shouldn't worry about having a place for me. I should worry about having a place for you!"

Jo turned her watering eyes and gazed at her daughter's

face. She patted her cheek. "You're such a good girl, Krista. How do I deserve such a good girl as you?"

Krista laughed again. "Only a mother could say that to a kid who just wrapped up a twenty-five-year sentence. You haven't lost your sense of humor. So, how about it? Want to go tell what's-her-name... Margie...that you're taking a little time off?"

"I wish I could, honey. I wish I could, that's for sure..."

"Sure you can! I'll take care of you now. I don't know exactly how, but we'll figure it out."

"Krista, honey, I know it doesn't look like very much of a job, but it's a good job. The owner has been really good to me—I have a decent paycheck and benefits and she's flexible with my schedule. I wouldn't take off without notice—I'm the manager. Margie just couldn't handle it. She thinks she could but... It wouldn't be fair of me—even if it's because you're home now. And me being sixty-five and without very many skills—good jobs don't come along every day. You might think you're going to get yourself a big fancy job that pays for both of us, but, Krista, honey, it just isn't that simple anymore. We're gonna have to take this a little slower, honey."

"I know, I know," Krista agreed, though reluctantly. "But, Ma, you have to come to the lake right away...please? Charley has it all fixed up—it's more beautiful than it's ever been before."

"It is at that," Charley said from behind them. They both jumped in surprise and turned to look at her over the back of the park bench. "I didn't mean to sneak up on you. I parked over there," she said, jutting a thumb over her shoulder. "Hi, Aunt Jo. It's been a while."

"Charley, look at you! Pretty as on TV!" Tears sprouting anew, Jo jumped to her feet and reached for Charley over the bench. They embraced, nearly crushing Krista in the process. "It's so long since we've been together," she wept. "So, so long..."

"Well, this doesn't even resemble the welcome my mother gave me." Charley chuckled.

"Oh, don't you pay any attention to her," Jo said, wiping at her tears. "She can't help herself. That's just her."

"I agree with you on one count, but I do believe she *could* help herself. Which reminds me—I have something for you." Charley pulled away so she could reach into her purse. She pulled out the recipe card. "I hope this makes you laugh."

Josephine looked at the scrawled note from her sister. A small huff escaped her, but she was not as overcome as Charley had been. "It will be hard to pass up an invitation like that," she said. She passed the note to Krista. Krista did not laugh at all.

"Good, I hoped you'd say that," Charley said. "There was a little travel agent's shop not far from Mother's. I ducked in and picked up some round-trip bus passes for you. I don't know what your schedule is like, but you should have these passes..." She flipped through the small envelopes as though counting dollar bills. "Three for you, three for Krista... Now you can get back and forth to see each other whenever it's convenient. Aunt Jo, I know how you feel about Mother giving her okay for you to visit the lake house, and I know this note isn't quite what you had in mind, but you're just going to have to swallow your pride. Hope and the girls are coming in July."

Josephine didn't even look surprised. She just stared at the tickets. "I know, I know. Thank you, Charley. It's a little more complicated than pride, but that will have to do for now." She looked up at her tall, slender niece. She smiled appreciatively. Charley was elegant looking even in shorts and a T-shirt. "You've thought of everything, haven't you, sweetheart?"

"Not everything. Have you had lunch? I'm starving!"

"Mom says she couldn't eat and—"

"And I can't take too much time," Jo said. "There are a lot of orders today for some reason. If I don't finish up, I'll be staying late."

Krista frowned. She didn't like the way her mother fidgeted over that job. It didn't look like the kind of flower shop that had too many orders. And that Margie… Well, Krista hadn't been around civilians in a long time. But if Margie worked for Jo, shouldn't she be more accommodating?

"Charley? Want to get us a couple of sandwiches from that sub shop and just eat them here? If my mom only has a little time, I don't want to waste it ordering food in a restaurant."

"Good idea," Charley said, lighting off for the sub shop immediately.

Krista pulled her mom back down on the bench. "Isn't it amazing how I can ask a TV star to run an errand, go get me food, and she goes?" Krista laughed. "Ma, no one's going to fire you for taking an hour or two with a daughter you haven't seen in years. Come on, relax. I can only stay a little while, anyway."

"Oh, Margie will probably try," Jo said. "She's ornery. But the owner is not, so I'm going to spend what little time I have with you."

"When are your days off? When can you come to the lake?"

"That Charley," Jo said solemnly. "She's just thought of everything, hasn't she?"

"I don't know, Ma. You tell me. Can you come to the lake pretty soon? Maybe before Hope and the girls come? So I can have you to myself?"

"I'll try, honey. I'll talk to Margie today and find out when she's free to help out. She's a good worker—I just worry about her scaring off the customers. Maybe I can take a couple of days here and there..."

"What about your vacation?" Krista asked.

Jo merely laughed. "Krista, honey, we never even talked about it."

Chapter Seven

As Charley drove toward Megan's house so Krista could see her, she yakked excitedly. After all her hard work, things were coming together pretty much the way she had hoped. Even though items that had been ordered would continue to arrive for the next couple of weeks, the house was basically ready enough to take on summer visitors, once a couple more mattresses arrived. They could get Megan settled when John brought her in a few days. Hope and the girls were due in a month and Aunt Jo and Krista had their bus passes so they could see each other. "And as long as my mother keeps her word and promises not to come—" She laughed suddenly.

Krista was quiet.

"Oh, I'm sorry, Krista—you must have hated to leave your mother so soon," Charley said.

"What do you suppose she's hiding?" Krista asked.

"Hiding? What makes you think she's hiding something?"

"She was so fidgety. So nervous about little things—taking time off, her job, going to the lake…"

"Krista, she's probably worried and nervous about everything! Not the least of which is what she's going to do if she pisses off my mother! You know, you haven't seen Louise in a very, very long time, but she's changed. She's so bitter, so angry. It's understandable that losing a child would take a serious toll, but nursing that anger for this long? I can't imagine the effect on Jo. Jo always depended on my mother. Go easy—Jo wasn't expecting you and she's got a lot to juggle. Louise, having you home, seeing Hope and darling little Brattie and Turdie..."

"That would be Bobbi and Trude." Krista laughed.

"Oh, heavens, my mistake! You know, when Eric was ten years old I had a business trip to Philly and I took him along so he could meet his cousins. I had already scared the shit out of him with Louise, then we went to Philadelphia, where Hope was struggling with these two subhuman creatures... Wait till you meet them, Krista. At fourteen and sixteen, spoiled and rich, they've got to be a treat. Just what Hope puts in the Christmas letter about them is enough to—"

"I don't suppose you saved any?" Krista asked.

"Hope doesn't send you her world-famous Christmas letter? The one that lists their latest vacations, brand names and important people they've socialized with during the year? I swear to God, she includes everything but Frank's annual income."

"She wrote me once," Krista said. "When she was addressing her wedding invitations it occurred to her that if she was going to keep me a secret, she'd better tell me not to put the prison's return address on the envelope if I ever wrote to her." Krista cleared her throat. "That turned out not to be a problem."

"Does she know you're out of prison?"

"Well... *I* didn't tell her."

Charley chuckled and it had a decidedly evil sound. "This should surpass interesting," she finally said.

★ ★ ★

After a brief reunion between Krista and Megan, Megan could not sustain the wait to get to the lake. She begged and pleaded until John brought her two days later, provided the new mattresses had arrived. They had. John and Megan both raved about how perfect the cabin looked, how homey and welcoming, making Charley proud.

John stayed only one night, then left to get back to the city to work. "I think he really left because he wasn't able to stand three women talking and laughing nonstop," Megan said. "That's okay. He'll be less in the way once we've had a chance to catch up."

"Did you get unpacked?" Charley asked. "I can help if you haven't."

"Everything except these three boxes—I told John to leave them alone. I shouldn't be the only one here who gets her own room this summer," Megan said. "I can double up, too."

For the time being Krista was keeping her belongings in the master suite but taking the third bedroom for sleeping, keeping the drawers and closet free for Hope. When Hope and the girls arrived, Krista was okay sharing the big bed with Charley.

"Maybe. We'll see. Depends on how you feel," Charley said. "I just don't want you to have any trouble sleeping, that's all. And you should have a room of your own that John can share on weekends."

"I've been sleeping like the dead lately," Megan said. Then she winked at Krista, whose mouth hung open.

"It takes a little getting used to," Charley told Krista.

"I have a surprise you're going to love," Megan said. "In one of these boxes...let's see..." She read the contents as described in black, heavy marker on the outside of the boxes.

Dishes, pans, linens, clothes, shoes… "Ah! Here!" She began to tear open the box.

"Shoes?" Krista questioned. "I'd heard you women on the outside were very big on shoes, but…"

"Not this time," Megan said. "We don't need many shoes at the lake. This was just a ruse in case Mother stopped by."

Charley turned her attention to them now—the idea of getting something over on her mother held instant appeal.

"I stole these," she said, lifting several large photo albums out of the box to expose a cache of loose pictures in the bottom of the box. There were also a couple of large padded envelopes full of old snapshots. "When Grandma went to the nursing home and Mother was getting ready to have an estate sale and get rid of the Grand Avenue mansion, I went over to Grandma's in the dark of night, with a flashlight and my key to the back door, and poked around in an old box of photos. John came with me. That was before I got sick. We had a blast."

"Why didn't you just ask for them?" Krista wanted to know.

"Well, I asked for and got a couple of the big albums…the formal ones… Remember how we used to pore over them when we were little? Our mommies' proms, parties, coming-outs, weddings? And the years and years of formal sittings after we started being born? I'm surprised they held together for all the little hands pulling at them. So, she said I could have these, but to tell the truth, I didn't trust Mother with the rest of the pictures. She's so damn angry about the past, I figured she'd either hide or destroy them. Like all the lake pictures, there are hundreds of them, and we're all ages. There are a lot of faces in here I don't know. We'll have to sort through them, identify them, maybe make some new albums."

"Look at this," Krista was saying, leafing through piles of loose pictures. "Our mothers in puberty…out on the dock…"

"Oh, my God, the Berkey-Hempstead cousins in braces!" Charley said, howling with laughter.

"Oh, Jesus, is this what I think it is? This was taken moments after Beverly was born, in Grandma Berkey's bed, here at the lake!"

"Let's see. Oh, boy, you're right, look at them grin! Mother and Jo, like they planned it. Mother said Jo had miscalculated, as usual. You know," Charley said, putting the photo down and looking upward as if for an answer of some kind, "for years that event was told as a funny story, but after the summer of '89, it became another example of Josephine's incompetence."

"Of course my mother says she could have made it to the hospital, but Louise was bossy as usual and insisted they stay at the lake."

They looked at each other and laughed. Then they dug around to find another picture to tell another story.

"I knew they'd come in handy," Megan said softly, watching Charley and Krista plow through them, laugh, groan, gasp, light up in recognition. Meg pulled out the largest of the albums, leather bound and gold embossed. She sat on the sofa with it on her lap. Small as she was, she resembled a child reading an oversize book.

On every holiday from the time Josephine and Louise were born, they were dressed up and seated for a formal picture. The photographer would come out to the house. Christmas, Easter, Thanksgiving—in the study by the fireplace, in the living room on the satin sofa, in the rose garden behind the house. There was also a wedding book for each daughter and then, as would naturally follow, formal pictures of the extended family. Louise and Carl, Charley, Megan and Bunny. Josephine and Roy, Hope, Krista and Beverly. Presiding over them, year after year, the judge and Grandma.

The portraits, all eight-by-ten color behind vinyl sheets, pulled them out of their lives and put them into this fairyland that could be viewed forever. You couldn't tell, when looking at the portraits, that Roy was frequently drunk and out of work. Nor could you see that it was Lou, in the other family group, who was given to violent rages against her mostly silent husband, more often verbal than physical but in many ways more destructive.

Charley remembered. She was quite young when she heard, *You think you can treat me like that and get away with it? You'll see when I'm not here anymore and it won't just be me, but me and the babies. I'll take them with me. Check in the basement when you come home next time and see if we're not all hanging there, dead!*

Her mother, mouth twisted in rage, railed at her silent and stoic father. She might've been young but she was old enough to have carried that screaming threat straight into adulthood. There were a few times when, as a budding teen, she came home to an empty house and for a split second wondered if her mother and sisters were dead in the basement.

But no. No. That had not happened, only threatened.

Megan flipped the page of the album to Christmas 1985. They were coordinated in black and red velvet; the men wore dark suits and red ties, the little girls wore red jumpers and black Mary Janes; the women wore black velvet and pearls. In '86, they wore ensembles of red and white. In '87, they were decked in black and silver with touches of red and green here and there, on the men's ties, in bows in the little girls' hair. In '88, it was red and green—the Roy Hempsteads in red and the Carl Hempsteads in green. The judge and Grandma reigned over them in black formal attire.

Their last Christmas together as a whole family.

Whatever it was that had held them together, whether it was the controlling hand of the judge or the denial of the dysfunction and brutality, whether it was the need to give an external impression, whatever it was, you had to give it some credit because they sure looked damn good. They didn't look like screamers or drinkers or bed wetters or nightmare victims or insomniacs or nervous wrecks. It sure didn't look like pending amnesia or attempted suicide or homicide.

"Did everyone know our homelife was crazy?" Charley asked Krista.

"*Your* homelife?" she asked with a laugh. "Did your father have to get blitzed to go to the judge and Grandma's?"

"My dad didn't drink much, that I recall," Charley said.

"See, that's what would be worth untangling," Krista said. "We remember everything differently. We came from different families. We weren't the same at all. Just because our mothers wanted us to think we were a set didn't make it so."

Megan began to remember what things were like when they were children. She could see it almost as if she was back in her mother's kitchen and she was approximately thirteen years old. But she was seeing it with a new perspective.

She was pouring two glasses of Kool-Aid, probably for herself and Krista, watching and listening to her mother and aunt discuss the meal, their husbands, kids, parents, their conversation speckled with laughter. Hope and Charley were upstairs in Charley's bedroom listening to music and reading magazines and talking about boys. Bev and Bunny were in the rec room down in the basement playing Barbies. There was the distant sound of some sporting event on the television; Carl and Roy occasionally erupted in cheers or groans of misery.

"Don't slice the eggs yet, they'll get dry," Lou commanded.

"I could devil them up?" Jo asked. She would always ask how Lou would have her do things.

"I think we'll do the eggs last. Here, let's make the patties and relishes."

"You betcha."

"Do those pretty radishes like you do," Lou said.

"You betcha. Should we put the girls at the picnic table?"

"Let's keep 'em in. It's a little cold yet. We'll put them downstairs."

"Want to warm the buns in the oven again?"

"Oh, yeah, I loved that before, didn't you? Toast them a little."

"Aw, shit! He coulda had that! Jo! Bring me and Carl a beer!" Roy shouted from the living room.

"Don't bother taking one to Carl," Lou said. "He doesn't need another one."

"Roy doesn't *need* one, either, but you think anyone could tell him that?" Jo said with heavy sarcasm.

"How many is that he's had so far?"

"A hundred or so," she said. Then she popped the cap off a cold beer, took a swig and passed it to Lou. "I'd rather have one than count his. Share?" she said with a grin.

Lou laughed. "Why not? They're both a little easier to take when we've had our beer."

"After Roy's had his, there isn't anything to take, if you know what I mean."

"Carl doesn't need as much as Roy, if you know what I mean."

Meg remembered there was always lots of laughter. Helpless laughter. Secret laughter. *We. Our. Them. Us.*

There were many weekend days like that, most of them spent at Lou and Carl's because Roy and Jo were always moving from one little low-rent house to another. When there wasn't a command performance with the judge and Grandma, Lou and Jo brought the husbands and kids together so *they* could be together.

Even though Roy was Carl's younger brother and the

brothers had married sisters, they weren't naturally drawn to-gether as friends and companions. Roy was ten years younger than Carl and they hadn't spent much of their childhood to-gether. But Lou and Jo were only a year apart and had been inseparable almost from the day they were born.

Suddenly Megan understood what had happened to the family. It wasn't the deaths and abandonments and all the dysfunction that had torn them apart—it was only one thing. The rift between Jo and Lou.

Louise was too harsh and temperamental, but Jo always softened her outbursts. Jo was too passive and needy, but Lou propped her up and gave her strength. Lou was tall, Jo was short; Jo was frilly, Lou was sturdy. What Louise could not do, Jo could do with her eyes closed and vice versa.

No matter how hard she tried, Megan couldn't remember the fall of '89 at all. The shade went down in '89 when Lou and Jo were attractive, energetic women in their thirties and the curtain came up over a year later to find them both dev-astated by losses that stronger women could not have borne alone. The weight of it on Louise made her coarser and more rigid, but the losses turned Jo into herself and made her more helpless. Stretching her memory for all it was worth, Megan could not remember her aunt Jo being so weak before the women parted angrily. Louise had always been bossy and controlling but upon losing her softer sister there was no re-lief from her temper.

Megan had closed her eyes so she could see the vision growing in her mind, but when she opened them the album was gone and a blanket had been drawn over her. The sun was low; Charley and Krista were keeping their voices de-liberately soft as they fussed over some food in the kitchen. Charley was telling Krista how to chop the vegetables while Krista was asking questions about the bread and soup and salad being prepared. Megan realized she may have created a dream or scene around the back-noise of their conversation, which sounded, in muted tones, like Lou and Jo. As she sat up on the sofa, the women in the kitchen turned her way.

"Well, good morning," Charley said. "How about some tea?"

"How long did I sleep?"

"Gee, I think it's been two hours. Did we wake you? I decided it wouldn't be a very good idea to put off dinner when—"

"No, but I had this dream. This wonderful dream. About our mothers, working together in the kitchen, just like the two of you are doing now, just like our mothers did a million times, for so many years. For a second there I had a glimpse of what went wrong. The one single thing that, if you could change it, would make it all right again."

There was a moment of complete quiet. "You do that, too?" Charley finally asked.

"I do that all the time! Do you?"

"It's like an obsession with me—this pulling out the thread of the bad thing, removing it, and now everything is all right. Krista?" Charley asked.

"Oh, please," Krista said, chopping. "With my life, you have to throw out the whole fucking loom."

"The thing is, even your problems didn't start until after Bunny drowned," Megan said, grabbing the blanket and wrapping it around her shoulders. "In my dream, though, it wasn't about Bunny at all. Or even about Daddy or Uncle Roy or the judge or anyone else. It was only about Lou and Jo and how, since they were born, they were totally inseparable. And then *rrripppppp*, they're torn apart. And everything changes. And collapses."

"Oh, honey, it's not as though there weren't plenty of problems—" Charley said.

"I know! There were a million problems—why wouldn't there be? With that domineering old man in everyone's business all the time, passive-aggressive Carl playing the White Sheep and devil-may-care Roy playing the Black Sheep. And six kids in six years? Jesus, life was complicated to say the least! But as long as Lou and Jo stuck together, everyone made it. Charley, if Mother and Aunt Jo had been speaking at the time you were pregnant, Aunt Jo wouldn't have let Mother send you away. She never approved of that and she said so. And if they'd been speaking, Aunt Jo and the kids would have been living with us—Jo would not have been alone, sinking deeper and deeper into depression. And Hope would not have moved in with the judge and Grandma, and Krista would not have run off with Rick French—"

"May he *not* rest in peace," Krista put in.

"I've always wondered, what did that feel like? Did it feel like, 'Oh, no, what have I done?' or did it feel like, 'Die, you son of a bitch, die'?" Charley asked.

"I zoned out. Almost completely. Like I had no choice. It was sort of automatic, like jumping out of the way of an oncoming train."

"Hey. What about it? You think I could be right?" Megan asked.

Charley and Krista seemed to consider Megan more than the question. She looked like a waif, her frail body wrapped in a blanket, her crown of thin peach fuzz spiked, her eyes huge against her emaciated face.

"And if you're right?" Charley finally asked.

"Well," Megan began, then stopped. "Well..." she tried again, but paused. "I suppose we could try to get them back together?"

"No!" Charley and Krista said in unison.

★ ★ ★

Charley was reflective after the pictures came out. She'd been at odds with her mother for at least thirty years. They started squabbling when she was about thirteen, which was textbook—pubescent girls and their mothers were famous for it. But then there was the baby and their bickering escalated into warfare. Nothing could make Charley so insane as to have someone say, *You're just too much alike!*

But there was a time they'd been so close. Louise might've had a quick temper but Charley had loved her so much, admired her, thought her beautiful. Louise had been tall, athletic, strong, encouraging. It was Louise who taught her to swim, Louise who drove her to ice-skating lessons and sat on the bleachers and watched her moves. Louise had somehow gotten her through high school chemistry and algebra II. And Louise helped coach the cheerleading squad.

Charley remembered wanting to be like her mother—she was decisive, got things done, took charge. If not for Louise, two women and six kids could never have gotten to the lake every summer.

There were those times Charley curled up on the couch next to her mother to watch *Cagney and Lacey* and *Magnum, P.I.* and *The Love Boat.* If she closed her eyes she could still feel the softness of her mother's turquoise velour robe. And while Louise divided her cuddle time with the other girls, Charley felt like her favorite. If she wanted to give Bunny a little extra time, she apologized to Charley. "I'm sorry, honey. Let Bunny sit by me for *One Day at a Time.* And after the younger girls go to bed, we'll turn on *Magnum.*"

Charley would cuddle Meg or share a bowl of popcorn with her.

There were lots of those times until Charley hit thirteen and still quite a few after that. She was the firstborn of the lot, had the most confidence and the most responsibility. And she had loved her mother. She thought of her as a best friend. Louise was fearless and so strong and reliable. If Charley got sick it was Louise who knelt behind her in the bathroom and held her hair back. Louise made those midnight runs to the emergency room. Louise sat up until Charley was safely home. True, if she was late there was hell to pay, but now that she was a mother she understood—Louise couldn't sleep until all her chicks were tucked in.

When Charley got pregnant she let Louise down. Her brilliant daughter had been trapped and Louise was furious. That was to be expected. But any compassion or understanding had been leached out of her by Bunny's death.

And when Charley needed her mother the most, Louise sent her away.

Charley had had the thought a time or two of exploring the possibility that she and her mother could make peace, but the thoughts never lasted long. Louise was stubborn and bitter, still very angry. Charley had called her toxic.

Louise was also alone. For the last twenty-some years Charley talked to her every few months unless Louise called her, which was so rare it was laughable. It was usually to report something like Grandma Berkey broke her hip or some distant relative Charley couldn't even remember had died. In fact, Louise hadn't placed a call to Charley in the past seven years, but Charley dutifully called her every couple of months, sent her Mother's Day, birthday and Christmas gifts. Louise sent a sausage and cheese gift basket at Christmas and an annual birthday card with twenty dollars in it. And when Charley did talk to her, who did her mother mention? Only Grandma or Megan. Charley had no idea who her mother's friends were, though she'd played bridge with the same group of women for years. She didn't date, though she'd been widowed for twenty-five years. At least, Charley didn't think she did—who would date her? Megan and John had checked on her regularly, had her for dinner sometimes, up until the cancer.

Louise would die without them making peace. Charley had accepted that.

The first of June was ripening the flora and more activity could be seen at the lodge across the lake. The sun was coming up earlier; there were always fishermen out on the lake by the time the sun came up. There was one cold rain shower, cold enough that Charley put a couple of logs in the fireplace because Megan shivered. The three women sat on the same couch, sharing a blanket, listening to the crackle of the flames.

"I'm going to have to get a job of some kind," Krista said. "If I can come up with a list of places to apply, will you give me a lift, Charley?" Krista asked.

"Of course," she said. "Do you know what to look for?"

Krista shook her head. "Manual labor, I think. Washing dishes, cleaning hotel rooms, that sort of thing."

"I'll write you a letter of recommendation," Charley said. "You must be nervous."

"No," Krista said. "I'm completely terrified."

"I can imagine," Charley said. "But do your best and do so knowing we'll keep you afloat until you find the right thing."

"There is no right thing. I hope to find anything. And I hope I don't have to take you up on much of that," she said. "I mean, I'm already wearing your underwear, for God's sake."

"You're wearing Charley's underwear?" Megan asked.

"Mine wasn't up to her standards," Krista said. "It kind of looked like twenty-five to life. Charley's is exactly what you'd expect—pristine, perfect, bright white, flawless."

Megan giggled.

"Before we get around to jobs and all that, before my mom

or anyone else shows up for a visit, I wonder if we could do something. If it's not upsetting to you, Meg. I want to know if our memories of a couple of things match." She chewed her lip. "That morning, for starters. When we lost Bunny. I remember you brought Beverly in, Charley. You were the strongest swimmer. I know you remember."

"Vividly. Meg?" Charley asked.

"That's all I want," Megan said. "You know, I've got nothing! Do you have any idea how awful it was having people shield me from the truth? Cleaning it up all the time?"

"I don't want you upset. Your health…"

"My health needs some honesty. God above! Tell it, Charley. Tell it like it really happened, not the way you told me before, when I was a little crazy."

"You weren't crazy," Charley said. "You were in shock!"

"Let's have it," Megan said.

A couple of weeks or so after Charley lost her virginity, she was awakened by a horrible, high-pitched scream. Then came many screams. Then yelling and hollering and door-slamming. "Beverly! Baby! Come on, baby! Beverly!"

Aunt Jo was in the water up to her knees in her nightgown, calling to Beverly, who clung to the overturned rowboat about a hundred feet from shore. Charley and the other girls all ran to the water's edge. Louise was sprinting back and forth from the house to the shore, yelling, "Where's Bunny? Where is Bunny?" She was looking inside, outside, in the boathouse, loft, shed, under the dock, everywhere. Their neighbor, Oliver, came over to see what was happening, but all the action was really onshore. In the early dawn, all they could see out there in the lake was a very still, overturned boat, surrounded by fog and the unmistakable bobbing of Beverly's head.

Charley didn't even think. She was the strongest swimmer.

She ran into the water, dived and swam. It had stormed the night before and the water was like ice. She reached Beverly quickly. She was alone, silent, holding on to the side of the boat with one small, blue hand. Her eyes were fixed and dilated, her lips were purple edged, her teeth were chattering.

"Where…is… Bunny?" Charley asked breathlessly.

Beverly couldn't respond.

"Beverly, can you swim back with me?" Charley asked. "Will you put your arms around my neck?" she begged. But Beverly wouldn't let go of the boat. Charley could see that Beverly's condition was poor—she was in shock and probably had hypothermia. She didn't want to waste a lot of time trying to convince her to swim.

"Oliver!" Charley called. He was already approaching them in his little fishing boat.

They had a little trouble getting Beverly into Oliver's boat, but once she was wrapped in a blanket, they tied a rope to the overturned rowboat and towed it in, too. There was no sign of Bunny anywhere.

Apparently the two littlest girls had grown adept at sneaking out. So adept that no one noticed, not their mothers, sisters or cousins. How many times they'd pulled their prank was unclear because Beverly was hardly talking at all. To anyone. All she said was, "We like to rock to sleep on the lake." She was catatonic and had to be hospitalized.

The police, sheriff and fish-and-game people were all called, but it took days to recover Bunny's body. They all stood at water's edge again as divers brought in Bunny's swollen, discolored, nibbled remains from the cold water. The baby of the family—Mary Verna—sweet Bunny was only twelve years old. Near as anyone could discern, Bunny had slipped from the boat during that nighttime storm but Beverly was somehow able to hang on. When the storm cleared as the sun rose, the boat was right in front of the house…close enough to have called for help or dog-paddle in.

Louise never cried. Charley thought about that often—she never cried. She had horrible black rings under her eyes, her lips were cracked and her face was gray, but she was dry of tears. When Aunt Jo embraced her to comfort her, Louise kept her arms locked at her sides and turned her face away. Aunt Jo kind of leaned back to look at Lou's face, questioning this avoidance of affection. Then Charley heard Louise's very quiet but vicious voice. "Somebody had to pay for what happened here this summer, and we damn sure know it wasn't going to be *you*. It's never *you*."

Over twenty years later those words and the icy tone with which they were delivered could still make Charley shiver. She never understood what they meant.

Bunny was buried and the family was rocked to its core. The unraveling began immediately. Uncle Roy had already abandoned them and he never returned, leaving his family adrift and unsupported. Aunt Jo sank into a deep depression. Beverly slipped into some kind of psychosis and had been taken to a hospital. Krista started skipping school, shoplifting and hanging out with hoodlums. Hope left her miserable mother and hoodlum sister and moved in with Grandma Berkey and the judge. Louise was filled with rage. Megan withdrew from everyone and seemed to hum quietly to herself all the time. All the time. Like she was off her rocker, too.

Charley couldn't do anything to help her family. She was struggling as much as the rest of them and she needed her mother, but Louise was not emotionally available. Charley waited as long as she could, hoping to find Louise alone, receptive and of stable frame of mind.

"Mom?" Charley said one day in October. She had looked for the right moment and even now it didn't seem right but she couldn't wait any longer. "Mom, can I talk to you for a minute?"

Louise looked at Charley over the top of her sewing machine. She had immediately cleared out Bunny's room and set up her sewing there. She sewed from morning to night—clothes, curtains, place mats, slipcovers, pillowcases, aprons. Things no one wanted or needed.

"Mom, I have a problem. A really big one," Charley said, then hung her head and looked at her feet.

Some instinct must have propelled Louise out of her chair. She came around the machine and stood in front of Charley.

Charley took a deep breath and lifted her head. She looked into her mother's eyes and said it. "Mom, I'm pregnant."

For a moment the storm simply gathered in Louise's gray eyes and then, like a shot, her hand came from nowhere and slapped Charley across the face. The sting temporarily blinded her.

"How *could* you," Louise shouted. "How could you do this to *me!*"

"Is that how you remember it?" Charley asked Krista very softly, a catch in her voice.

"Pretty much," she said. "I didn't hear what our mothers said to each other. For a long time I thought my mother must have loved Bunny more than her own kids. She seemed oblivious to us—we were hitting the skids. Especially me. I think I get it now."

"What's there to get?"

"Something else happened here that summer. Something Louise blamed my mom for. She couldn't have possibly blamed my mom for Bunny's death. No one was at fault there—it was a terrible accident."

"Can you ask your mom?"

"Eventually," Krista said. "I have a lot to atone for before I'm going to be trusted with secrets. You okay, Meg?" she asked.

Meg wiped her eyes. "I'm happy," she said.

"How can that possibly make you happy?" Charley asked. "It's a horror story!"

"It's the real story," Meg said. "Not the tidied-up version."

"It is that," Charley said. "And that's when Mother really changed. Louise was never easy. In fact, she was damn difficult at times. She always had an ugly temper."

"But not around Aunt Jo," Megan reminded her.

"That's why summers were so great," Charley said in a somewhat reverent breath. "Aside from some occasional bickering, there was no craziness. I used to like my mother."

"I loved Aunt Lou," Krista said. "She was strong and brave."

"And funny," Charley said. "So funny she'd have us all wetting our pants."

"And decisive," Meg said. "No matter what came up, she knew what she wanted to do. She never hesitated."

"It's like all the good parts of Louise were sucked right out of her," Charley said. Then more quietly: "I used to depend on my mother. I used to love her. But when I needed her most she turned on me."

Chapter Eight

A couple of days later Krista decided she couldn't put it off another minute—she needed a job. The enormity of this challenge threatened to paralyze her, so she thought she'd better get right to it. She didn't drive and she had no vehicle; she would have to find work close by or impose on Charley. Plus, her job skills were worse than minimal; they were felonious. She could see only one option at the outset—the lodge.

As she approached, she was impressed by the condition of the place. It had been renovated and expanded. It didn't appear to have gone a year without fresh paint; the grounds were lush and immaculate. The big central lodge rivaled any major citified hotel—she knew this from pictures in magazines. She looked through the brochure she found in the huge lobby—there were banquet rooms, a large dining room, cocktail lounge and gift shop. There were over a hundred rooms. The facilities included tennis courts, riding stables, outboard docks, boat ramps, a bait and tackle shop. There were also cabins—a long string of them along the shoreline. The cabins had their own kitchens and patios and were reserved long in advance of the peak summer season.

When Krista was a kid, the lodge had been a summer place only, but one glance at the brochure showed it was now a year-round destination. There were no major hills for ski slopes nearby but the lodge boasted ice fishing, cross-country skiing, snowshoeing, snowmobile rentals and year-round trail riding.

She wore her nicest new shorts and tennis shoes to the lodge and, thanks to anal Charley, she now had a fashionably cropped haircut. Makeup was beyond her but a little lip gloss, at Charley's and Megan's insistence, was not out of the question.

She approached the front desk. "I wonder if you're hiring?" she said to the desk clerk, her voice quaking.

The young woman might as well have said no. Instead, she looked at Krista as if she'd peed on her shoe, as if she already knew Krista's entire history, but she reached under the desk for an application. The encounter was so negative Krista almost left. But she knew it might be the only game in town. "May I borrow a pen, please?" she asked, anxious to get the whole thing over with.

She looked around the lobby for an out of the way place to sit to fill out the form. There was a small, round table in the corner by the front window. From there she could take her time with the application and also watch as vacationers pulled up to the lodge. In fact, she watched three families arrive while she considered how to fill in the blanks. She was going to tell the truth, of course. She was too damn stubborn not to, but she wasn't sure how to go about it. It was all so unacceptable. Who would hire her, knowing her story?

"Excuse me?" a voice said, pulling her out of her thoughts.

She looked up to find a man in his forties leaning both hands on the table, looking down at her. When she acknowledged him, he smiled and stuck out a hand. "My name is Jake

McAllister, I'm the manager here. One of my jobs is hiring and right now I'm looking for kitchen and housekeeping staff. Any chance you're interested in either of those positions? Or maybe another position I can help you with?"

"Ah," Krista began tremulously. "Ah, yeah... I mean, yes. Maybe. I don't, ah, have a lot of work experience actually."

"They're entry-level jobs. Why don't you fill out the application as completely as you can and bring it to my office? Just tell Elizabeth over there when you're ready. She'll bring you around the desk." He indicated the rude girl with his chin. "And you're...?"

"Krista Hemp... Um, Hempstead."

"It's a pleasure, Ms. Hempstead."

He wasn't going to be this nice, she realized, once he found out she was an ex-con. She might as well enjoy it now. "Krista is fine," she said.

"Good, Krista. Call me Jake, if you're comfortable with that. I'll see you in a few minutes."

"Do you have a lot of openings... Jake?" She wanted to know what the possibilities were. Before he clammed up, anyway.

"I'm always looking for good people, Krista. This place once relied almost solely on college kids, but since I've been here we've been trying to balance the staff a little better. I hope we can find something for you. We'll see."

He turned and walked away. Her eyes followed him. He stopped and talked to a young bellman in the lobby for a few moments. Both laughed before parting ways. He gave some smiling instruction to the concierge, who also appeared to like him, then he told Elizabeth that Krista would need an escort to his office. That caused Elizabeth to direct her rude stare at Krista.

Krista smiled at her and waved with her pen. Elizabeth

looked down at something on her desk. *What is up her butt?* Krista wondered.

Well, no need to worry—it would be a short relationship. *Chowchilla Federal Women's Penitentiary,* she wrote, *1993–2016.* That should do it.

Krista felt a strange compression at the back of her throat; it was an alien sensation and caused her to frown in bewilderment for a moment. She thought about crumpling up the application and walking out; she thought about her mother's old slacks and smock, worn shoes and the twenty-dollar bill she had slipped into her hand as they parted company; she thought about Charley buying her decent underwear and clothes; she thought about wealthy Hope neglecting their mother. Then she realized what she was feeling in her throat was the threat of tears—something banished twenty-three years ago and not heard from until now. Today. Because she had to face the outside world with her shame.

Well, shit, she thought. *I sure paid for it. And then some. And right now I need a job. So I can buy my own goddamn underwear and give my mother a twenty now and then. There is only one way through this and that's straight through.*

She took a moment to write on the application some of the things she had learned to do in prison. She'd done some piecework sewing, some cooking—though surely not the kind needed here—lots of kitchen cleaning and of course her reading and writing. She had actual college credits now. Someplace here, probably the cleaning, there had to be a job for her.

Jake McAllister's office was barely large enough for a desk and a couple of chairs, which put Krista pretty close to him. Her knees would have bumped up against his if it had been a table instead of a desk. She could watch him closely while he read over her application. She didn't want to miss the look of shock wash over him when he saw it—twenty-three years in the pen. He'd think she must be one badass to do that much time. Then he'd want to know what a person has to do to get sent up for that long.

While she watched him, she noticed that his hair was probably as much silver as blond, thinning in front. But there was still a sort of boyishness about him. Maybe the way his hair kind of flopped over his forehead, even though it was sparse at the crown. Or the slightly pocked complexion, a legacy of teenage acne. Then, of course, there were the blue-blue eyes—something you had to get used to all over again if you hadn't lived in Minnesota for a while.

"Looks like most of your experience would put you in Housekeeping, Krista, but I think that would only be a big headache for you. You don't need the stress—cleaning rooms for guests. Our guests regularly lose things, go over the top and insist the maid took it, then they find it in their own suitcase… Frankly, it's a pain in the ass. For you, it could cause you some anxious moments, getting it resolved."

"Huh?" she asked, dumbfounded.

"Do you think you'd have any problem as a server, if we provided good training?"

"As a…waitress?"

"The dining room would be an obvious place to start. Lucky for you I have all the bussers and dishwashers I can stand…so this is a bad week for starting at the bottom. And there isn't anybody here I'm looking to promote right now, beginning of the summer, you know. Lots of high school kids need work. So, if you could work mornings at first—breakfast and lunch—that would be great. We're busy but not overwhelmed at that time of day. I'm not understaffed there at the moment, which would give you plenty of time to learn without the pressure of being too rushed. What do you think? Think you could handle that?"

"I, ah, sure I could. But—" She left it hanging. She didn't have any buts.

"You didn't fill in the space about expected salary," he pointed out, turning the application back toward her.

"Because…" She left that hanging out there, too.

"Well, we used to start the servers below minimum wage and let them make up the difference in tips, but I've finally put that to an uneasy death. How about nine dollars an hour? We'll give you one uniform and you can deduct the cost of a second from your paycheck if you like. You're allowed to add a fifteen percent gratuity to the check if you serve a party of six or more. We pay your busman—kind of generous on our part, I think—and you'll have to split your tips with your trainer the first week. A good waitress tips the busman, if she's smart and wants good service." He smiled at her. He had a very kind smile. "Give you some incentive to draw good tips."

She nodded vigorously. She couldn't speak. He was just giving her a job? Without worrying that she'd freak out and kill them all? Or rob them blind? Or kidnap the children?

"You'll need uniforms, shoes, your food service license— you can get everything at this address in Brainerd. Do you have someone who can take you there?"

She nodded. "My, uh, cousin. I'm staying with my cousin. She'll take me."

"Good. We have a few forms for federal and state withholding. We have a benefit package—not great, but good enough. I'd like to improve that, too, but one thing at a time. Now," he said, putting down her application and folding his hands on top of it. "Is there anyone I'm supposed to call? To verify your employment?"

"No," she said, finding her voice at last. "She'll call you. Patricia Driver, parole office, Grand Rapids."

"Okay," he said, smiling again. "Tell her to ask for me and

not to talk to anyone else." He reached into his shirt pocket and pulled out a business card.

"Listen," she said, scooting forward on her chair. "I really don't know how to thank you for this. I really need a job and I—"

"I need good people, Krista. The staff here is friendly. Hardworking. You're going to like it. Let me know if I can be of any further assistance." He stood, stretched out his hand.

"Hey, did my cousin call you and offer to pay you to hire me?"

His look was one of such shock she abandoned the notion. "Well, really, thank you. I mean, thank you for giving me a chance. Thank you so much. You have no idea—"

"I base a lot of my decisions on first impressions and character assessments. And I like to give people the benefit of the doubt. You should try it sometime."

She tilted her head. "Yeah. Maybe I will."

"Personnel records are supposed to be confidential, Krista. I keep them in my office. I don't have a secretary—just the desk clerks and payroll administrator. I lock my door when I leave at night. But..." He thought about what to say.

"I won't be naive about it," she said, helping him.

"I guess that's what I meant. Can you get your license and uniform taken care of right away? Start on Friday and work the weekend?"

"You bet."

He laughed at her. "Around here we say, *You betcha.*"

"You betcha, then."

He leaned down and whispered to her. "The guests are almost all Midwestern tightwads. Friendly as hell but the tips suck."

"I'll be okay." She laughed. She wanted to jump up and

down. To throw her arms around him and kiss him. To shout to the heavens that her life was now officially beginning.

After completing the rest of the required paperwork, having a tour of the dining room and kitchen, meeting a few of the staff and learning how to punch in and out, Krista began the long walk back to the house. It was late afternoon, nearly four. A nice time of day. She hadn't let Charley drive her over, though of course she had offered. Surely Charley had not called this nice Mr. McAllister and begged him to give her a job, then act all surprised if Krista mentioned her? No, Mr. McAllister's surprise was genuine. And he had this thing about giving people a chance, that was easy to see. Everyone liked him there, too; people couldn't fake that all the time. Except Elizabeth, the sourpuss, who didn't like anyone. People made faces when her name came up, though no one said anything.

Krista wouldn't ask about her. She wasn't going to ask any questions! She just wanted to work; she wanted to pitch in for groceries, give her mother some money, buy her own underwear, live a real life.

Halfway home she passed an empty lot with a boat ramp and dock. Not an uncommon sight. Many people bought a lot, erected the dock and plowed a ramp, but were years away or maybe never intended to build a house. They might bring a trailer up here or camp for a couple of weeks each summer and leave the land as it was.

She walked down the sloping lot toward the lake. There was a nice swing hanging from a broad-boughed elm. *People must not steal much around here*, she thought. She sat on the swing, took off her shoes and leaned back, guiding the swing to and fro with her toes on the grass. Staring out at the beautiful, still lake.

There was that feeling again. In her throat. And along with

the feeling came thoughts of work, her mother, Meg's cancer, seeing Charley's son, maybe even seeing Charley's long-lost daughter, then work again and the idea of buying her mother a cell phone. And then she let it go. Let it all flood out of her in great gulps and sobs. Loud cries, unlike anything she'd done in years. You didn't dare show this kind of weakness in prison. "Oh, God, oh, God, thank you, God, thank you, God, thank you, God," she cried. And then she drew up her knees, embraced them with her arms and laid her head down for a good, healthy, cleansing cry. Everything was going to be all right. Finally. Finally. Finally. It flooded out of her in relief such as she had never known.

Krista let herself cry for a good half hour until it left her eyes feeling swollen and her cheeks chapped. She never let herself obsess about the past, but today it all came back. Megan and Charley knew her story, of course, and they didn't expect her to go over it again. But she asked herself, *What would I do if Mr. McAllister asked me?* She'd tell him, she decided at once. Because not only had he earned the right, taking a chance on her as he had, but if he wanted to, he could look it up. No convicted criminal's story was private.

She'd written about it in the autobiographical story she'd been working on. That, in fact, was a relatively short and simple account. Krista started getting into trouble early, at about the time everyone bailed out and left her, at the age of fourteen, to hold things together. It was an impossible job. Her cousin drowned, her dad fled, her little sister was put first in a hospital and then in foster care; her mother fell into a dark and relentless depression, and her older sister, Hope, had somehow convinced their grandparents to remove her from the discomforts of her dysfunctional family and take her in. Hope had been like that all her life—able to detach herself from reality while she concentrated on her fantasy life. Krista often tried to imagine how that worked. *Let's see—Mom can't get off the couch, Dad's gone, Bev's in the booby hatch, Krista's in jail... Do you think we could have squab at my graduation party, Grandma?*

Krista was fourteen when she was the only one left but her mother. And her mother was not up to speed, as they say.

"And how about you, Krista?" the judge had asked after Hope went to him. "Are you of a mind to come and live with us, follow our rules and meet our expectations?"

Krista wouldn't leave Jo. The judge was willing to give his daughter a little money on which to survive and there was some government check of some kind because there was no income to support them, but unless Jo agreed to let the judge work a divorce from her wayward, missing spouse, she was on her own. Krista didn't quite understand why Jo wouldn't do that but there was a young, inexperienced part of her that felt a certain relief that Jo didn't completely give up on Roy. It made no sense, but he was her father. How could Krista leave her, too? And live in that rigid mausoleum on Grand Avenue with Aunt Lou dropping in regularly to count the silver and look down her nose at Hope and Krista? And be in by nine p.m. and wear frilly crap to church every Sunday? So, in her first step on the road to rebellion to her grandfather, she said, "Hell, no. I'd rather eat shit and die."

Krista did it her way. She hung out with bad kids, got in trouble for everything from shoplifting to possession of marijuana, dropped out of school—to the relief of her teachers— and verbally abused her mother, who she loved. After about three years of that Krista ran away at the age of seventeen with an older guy named Rick French and they lived day to day and town to town all the way to California.

There was no question in Krista's mind she deserved to go to prison for the bad things she'd done. She and Rick stole, did drugs and sometimes sold them; she prostituted herself for money and kept downright evil company. But she never owned a gun and was opposed to doing bodily harm to anyone. One could argue that selling drugs was doing bodily harm but they only sold to addicts and never tried to coax any pure-blooded youngster into trying drugs. They were too hard up for money to give away drugs!

When she realized Rick had used a gun to rob a gas station she panicked and tried to leave him. He responded by finding her and beating her senseless in the bedroom of a house while there was a party going on. A bunch of people were right outside the door and could hear his fists crunching into her face and body. They heard her screaming, heard her begging. When she found out Rick had actually shot a man, who later died, in another robbery, just the fact that she showed fear and remorse caused him to beat her again.

A few months later they stopped at an all-night gas-and-convenience store for beer and cigarettes. Rick must have made a spontaneous decision to rob the place. The store was empty but for Rick and Krista and she was looking at magazines. She heard Rick's voice. "I'll have all the money in the till, Bud."

There was silence for a second. "Now!" Rick said. Then he called out to her. "Got that beer, babe?"

Next, Krista heard a loud shout and the sounds of a struggle. She ran around the aisle and saw that Rick and an overweight, middle-aged clerk were struggling over the counter. The gun, which had been knocked out of Rick's hand, lay at Krista's feet. The clerk had a grip on Rick's leather jacket. Rick was straining to break free as Krista bent to pick up the gun. Rick tore himself loose; Krista trained the gun on the clerk. And froze.

"Shoot him, baby. Then we'll go."

She stood stricken. Paralyzed.

"If you don't shoot the son of a bitch, I'll shoot you. Let's do it, Krista."

Shoot him? It was bad enough all she had done. Looking back on it, she realized she could have gotten away from him when she first knew how dangerous he was, but at the time she didn't understand that. She was afraid of him, afraid he'd find her and kill her. At that time, chemically impaired and battered and all of seventeen, she saw no way out. One thing she did know for absolute sure, and even time and sobriety and knowledge would never change the fact, was that at the time of that holdup she had no way out. If she didn't follow his orders he was going to kill her.

Rick made an exasperated grunt and moved toward her. She pointed the gun at Rick and fired. The force blew Rick backward, crashing through a floor display of paperbacks, onto the floor. Her vision cleared and she saw him lying there in a rapidly growing dark red puddle. Not moving at all. Her first clear, logical thought was that the bad part of her life was finally over. It felt so good.

"Call the police," she told the clerk. Then she waited for them to come and get her. Believing, all the while, that her mom or grandpa or Aunt Lou or someone would help her explain this huge misunderstanding and she would gladly go home and live a quiet and law-abiding life.

The facts slowly became self-evident. Grandpa Berkey had no influence in California and his hard line against criminals prevented him from paying for a defense attorney, it would seem. Krista got a not-very-talented public defender. The abuse Krista suffered at the hands of Rick was inadmissible and she was an accomplice/accessory in all the crimes he had committed, all of which she helped the police determine. Including the armed robbery while she sat in the car with no knowledge he even owned a gun. Her criminal history since the age of fourteen was all admissible, of course. It gave her the appearance of something a bit more dangerous than a misunderstood teenager. She became the Bonnie of Bonnie and Clyde. They kicked her ass and took her name. She got two life sentences plus the armed robbery convictions.

Her grandfather the judge wrote her a very long, very moralistic letter in his shaky old hand and advised her that she had no grounds for appeal in his opinion. He had obviously followed the case but wouldn't help. He died shortly thereafter. Grandma and Aunt Lou never wrote. Krista heard from her mother when she finally got medical help and rose out of her depression. Jo was devastated by what had happened to her children.

Krista wished uselessly and restlessly for some kind of reprieve, but never really believed it possible. She did finally get some ritzy female lawyer from a big-deal law firm to handle her case pro bono, but it was something she saw as the futile crust of bread, a little charity work for a rich broad, the Gospel Mission of law. Every lifer had a lawyer. Who knew if they could do anything? Krista never contacted her or asked about her progress.

There sat Krista for almost twenty-three years, not even eligible for parole when Charles Manson was. So imagine her surprise when her hoity-toity lady lawyer appeared one day to tell her that she had petitioned the California Supreme Court and they agreed to hear Krista's case, which could finally include the battery in her defense. Rather than scheduling a costly trial, Krista's sentence was miraculously reduced, and she was suddenly eligible for parole. The board approved her release and relocation to Lake Waseka, Minnesota. In May 2016.

★ ★ ★

Jake McAllister put in much longer hours than necessary, so it wasn't uncommon for him to walk the grounds of the lodge, or even take a walk along the lake for a breath of fresh air and to stretch his legs. He heard someone crying and calling out to God and he ducked behind a tree. It was by complete coincidence that he'd come upon her. He crossed his arms over his chest and leaned up against a tree where Krista couldn't see him. He had a lump in his throat as he listened to this emotional outpouring.

He went quickly and quietly back to the lodge, feeling pretty good about his day.

Krista suspected it was getting close to dinnertime when she finally left that rope swing, her eyes dry and feeling lighter, freer. She couldn't wait to tell Charley and Meg she had a job. She couldn't wait to call Patricia Driver and give her Jake McAllister's number. Then her mother…she'd call her mother.

She could hear Meg and Charley talking in the kitchen when she walked across the porch. Meg was sitting on the stool at the breakfast bar while Charley was across from her, tearing up clean lettuce for a salad.

"Hey," Krista said. "You're not going to believe this. I got a job!"

"At the lodge?" Charley asked, eyes wide.

"It's the only place I went. I told the manager I'd take anything but he's going to give me a chance to waitress."

"Oh, my God, I thought it was going to be a challenge," Meg said. "Guess you've got that handled! First place you looked!"

"That was easy," Charley said. "But you look a little… Are you disappointed? Was it terrible?"

"It was very good," Krista said. "I told the truth, and he

gave me a job. And then on my way home it just… It hit me. The road to a waitress job has been a long one. I'm wrung out."

"Too tired to celebrate?" Charley asked. "Because I'm prepared." She opened the refrigerator and pulled out a chilled bottle of sparkling cider. She pushed aside her salad makings and put out three glasses. "Selfishly, I'm glad it's still just the three of us. We'll drink it out of champagne glasses. But I'm warning you both—I'm not sticking to this diet. After we've toasted the new start, I'm hitting the wine."

"You do what you gotta do," Krista said. She sat at the counter next to Meg, tired to the bone.

"Gimme a second," Charley said, excusing herself from the kitchen. She returned a moment later with a white box tied with a red bow. She put it on the counter and poured their cider.

"Now what have you done?" Krista asked.

"I thought it would take a while for you to get a job but I was determined to be ready. I'm glad I didn't wait. It was killing me just waiting this long. Krista, here's to you. You're the bravest person I know and I'm proud of you."

"Here, here," Meg said. "Me, too."

"I didn't expect a party," Krista said. "That's really optimistic of you. Presents and everything. I hope it's more underwear."

"It's not underwear," Charley said, pushing the box toward her.

Krista lifted the lid, parted the tissue paper and looked at a rectangular metal folder. She'd seen these before. Some inmates had these or similar tablets, though they weren't allowed to hook up to the internet. Even knowing what it was she asked, "What is it?"

"It's called a Surface," Charley said. "For your writing. And your research."

"I've seen these," she said softly, lifting it out of the box.

"It's all charged," Charley said. "You give yourself a password and then write your brains out and no one can read it but you."

Krista slowly lifted the top to look at a flat, black screen and the keyboard below. Charley reached across the breakfast bar and pressed a button on top and it came to life.

"I can't believe you'd do this for me," Krista said.

"I did it for all of us."

Chapter Nine

It was almost humorous, the amount of pride Krista felt putting on her waitress uniform. It was a simple pair of khaki shorts and a dark green knit shirt, but it was a costume that put her in the world of the working class. She didn't get an extra set; every penny counted. She laundered it every evening and even though it was polyester and needed no ironing, she touched it up with a hot steam iron. Her creases were sharp and her seams flat. She was up at four thirty a.m. to get to work by five thirty. And she had warm smiles for even the earliest of customers.

Of course, one of the first people in for breakfast every day was Jake McAllister. She would never complain about her hours after taking note of his. He was there at least twelve hours a day, sometimes more. "But this isn't exactly my work schedule, Krista," he said in good humor. "I live at the lodge, it's that simple. I was brought in from a resort back East in the Catskills to help the owner get this place in shape. Seemed it needed a little freshening up. My specialty is sprucing up or shutting down a resort. It requires some moving."

"Your family must hate it," she observed.

"I'm divorced—my son's in the Army, my daughter is in

college. Since I don't get to see that much of them, I might as well enjoy my work."

Krista settled into a routine, relieved by how quickly she was adjusting to being out of prison. There were no nightmares or panic attacks. She wanted to boast about opening a bank account; she wanted to flash her shiny new credit card. She wanted to sing about how great it felt to write her mom a check, to empty the change out of her pockets every afternoon and watch it fill up the mason jar on her dresser—and be safe there. Untouched. In prison, not even your toothbrush was safe. Her small change and minimum wage salary was nothing compared to the money Charley must have, but to Krista it was a personal fortune. She might as well be a brain surgeon, she felt so important.

One week of work and the job came easy to her. Her training was brief and simple and she was on her own in no time. The staff, as Jake had promised, were friendly and accessible. They seemed not to know she was an ex-con. She said she'd just returned to Minnesota to spend the summer with cousins after living in California for twenty-three years; she liked it here and thought she might stay on since her mother wasn't far away. When asked what she'd done in California, she answered, "Nothing as interesting as this," as if to imply her life was dull beyond imagination. Then she deftly turned the subject back to them. People were universally predictable; when offered a chance to talk about themselves, they invariably took it.

Jo rode the bus to Brainerd and came to the lake house for one day and one night and it was the greatest treat Krista could remember having. Jo brought homemade cinnamon rolls and carried one little overnight bag that must have been thirty years old. The four of them talked over coffee, remembering past summers at the lake. When it was time for lunch Jo took up her place in the kitchen beside Charley. "Tell me what to do," she said, and Krista had a clear memory of Aunt Lou telling Jo exactly what she wanted done in the kitchen and Jo following instructions. "I've been so lazy, living alone all these years. I'm bad about grabbing something fast and easy on the way home from work."

"It's all for me," Meg said. "Charley's never going to make me believe she was so fussy about her diet before. I visited her, remember."

"I've always been fussy," Charley insisted. "How do you think I keep this youthful figure?"

"By being the one member of this family with a metabolism that can whip through chili dogs and cheesecake!" Meg said. "Anyone but Charley would gain fifty pounds in a year."

"Lord knows I can't get by with that," Jo said.

"I was always on the run a lot," Charley said.

Krista was in heaven. She couldn't believe how natural it was, the four of them, talking and laughing and then being quiet together, as though no time had passed. When Meg rested in the afternoon, Krista and Jo went for a walk and ended up on the fringes of the lodge. Jo didn't want to go in, didn't want to invade that space. "It's where you work, Krista. Keep it to yourself for a while. I can tell you're happy there."

"I'm happy *here*," she said. "Just to be able to walk around the lake, to earn a little money, to be with friends."

"After all that's passed, you're not bitter," Jo said.

"I am bitter," Krista said. "There's a dark place deep inside me where the bitterness lives. I just won't let it come out of that cave I keep it in. I'm afraid it would keep me from smelling the lake, feeling Charley's fancy linens, eating the food she makes to try to keep Meg alive."

Jo touched her daughter's cheek. "Don't let it eat a hole in you," she said.

"I won't. I'm too stubborn for that."

Jo laughed softly. "I never thought I'd be grateful for your stubbornness."

Krista showed Jo her new sleek, small and efficient computer and told her she'd been writing, journaling, trying to put all the pieces together. "I want to know what became of us all," she admitted.

"Well, when you do, be sure to let me know, will you?" Jo said with a laugh.

Of course Krista didn't do any writing while her mother was visiting, but there was a moment that stuck with her, that she planned to look at more closely later, when her mind was clear. It was bedtime. Krista had a double bed in her room and Charley was in the master bedroom Jo and Lou had shared for so many years while the kids were little. Charley said Krista and Jo should take it—share that big king-size bed. It was completely refurnished, of course; the mattress was new. But Jo said, "No. I think I'll just take the couch."

"Oh, Ma, it brings back memories, doesn't it?" Krista said.

"It's okay," Jo said, not exactly answering. "You take your bed as usual. I'm used to sleeping alone."

"I know," Krista said. "The boathouse! Charley had it cleaned, prettied up and furnished with two double beds. We can hear the water lapping underneath."

Jo shuddered slightly; it was unmistakable. But she smiled and said, "Oh, sweetheart, I'd just pee all night. I have an idea! Let's bundle up our pillows and blankets and sleep on the porch!"

Krista hesitated, wondering what had just happened. Then she said, "Sure. I have to get up really early."

"That's perfect," Jo said. "I've got the early bus home and I'm going straight to work. But I hope to be back next week!"

She put the incident from her mind because she couldn't

help grieving the fact that it would be at least a week until she saw her mother again. For the first time since she started working at the lodge, she had a hard time getting excited about going to work. She tried to slap on that happy smile for the carefree summer people but it was harder than usual. Just the idea that her mother wouldn't be at the cabin when she got home put her in a quiet mood. She thought maybe if she wrote about it in the afternoon it might put things into perspective. She didn't want to waste the happiness of that time they had together by dreading their parting. She began to concentrate on remembering all the details.

She was on her way around the lake when she saw Jake walking toward her, three ducks following him. The sight made her laugh.

"There's that smile," he said. He pulled a couple of pellets out of his pocket and tossed them to the ducks. "Was it my imagination or were you a little down in the dumps today?"

She bristled slightly, though she wasn't sure why she should. It had been obvious, after all. "Keeping a close eye on me in case I snap, turn dangerous or something?"

"I keep a close eye on everyone, Krista," he said. He handed her a fistful of pellets for the ducks. "I have an employee whose husband is disabled and he's been known to have some hard nights. I have a man who got hurt on the job a few weeks ago and I think he's back at work a little too soon. He might've been worried that taking time off made him look lazy. And I have a valet who actually is lazy—but he's young and it's time he learned you have to work for a living. One of the women who works here has not one but two special-needs kids at home. I can tell a lot about how they're doing from her moods."

"Well, don't I feel stupid," she said.

He laughed. "I didn't mean to make you feel stupid—I meant to make you feel less suspicious."

"My mother visited for a day and a night. She had to leave this morning—she has a full-time job back in Saint Paul. I haven't seen very much of my mother over the years. I was a little bummed. I hated to say goodbye again."

"I can imagine. Will you have another visit soon?"

"In a week," she said with a shrug. "It's not so long, I guess. It just feels... It's been so many years of not being near the people who are important to me."

"I can imagine. You're doing a very good job for us, Krista. If you find you need a day or two extra to visit family, I'm sure it can be arranged. Don't suffer in silence."

Suspicion reared its ugly head again. "Are you this accommodating with everyone?"

"No," he laughed. "Some I'm very tough on, some I grow impatient with, some would get on the nerves of a saint and some I don't trust very much. But when I have a hard worker who seems sincere and has earned a break I can make an extra effort. I don't know the gory details but I'm sure what you've been through was no picnic."

"Huh," she said. "I'll tell you what you want to know..."

"I didn't ask," he said. He handed her some more duck pellets. She accepted them, tossed them to the ducks. "You're entitled to some privacy, for God's sake."

"I just meant it's all public record, if your curiosity gets the best of you. By the way, I am grateful you haven't shared that with anyone...that I know of."

"I haven't."

"If you know so much about everyone, what's up with Elizabeth?" When he didn't reply right away, she said, "That was unfair. You won't talk about another employee..."

"That one I would," he said. "I'm trying to figure out what

to say. Someday I'll figure her out. She's smart and very efficient. Why isn't she nice to people? Who's she mad at?" He shook his head.

"Assuming you've talked to her, she needs counseling," Krista said.

"Of course I've talked to her, but I can't mandate counseling. Let me walk you a little way. Here," he said, handing her some more duck pellets. She laughed and tossed them behind her. Three ducks waddled toward them. "Chaperones," he said.

"What are you doing out here?"

"Just taking a break. I get a little sluggish about this time of day, especially after lunch. You walk to work every day?"

"I do. It's great. My cousin would be happy to drive me but I'd rather walk. I'm staying with two cousins at the old family lake house we stayed at as kids. They're sisters. One of them is sick. She's been fighting cancer. She just came through a powerful round of chemo and no one knows what's next— recovery or...you know...the end. Even she doesn't know. It's been a rough battle and she says she's done with treatment, no matter what. She's the one who insisted we open up the house and spend the summer here. That's the main reason I'm here. To spend time with her. We were always close."

"Jesus, Krista!" he said sympathetically. "You come off a tour like you had only to face a possible loss like that?"

"It would be okay not to mention that, too," she said. "I just told you because you gave me duck pellets."

"Of course not," he said. "I hope you get lucky on this one, Krista. I hope your cousin stays well."

"Thanks—me, too. She's pretty amazing. Her attitude. I think she's made peace with the thing, you know?"

"I saw that in my father. Same disease, same fight, same attitude, eventually. When he came to the end of his patience, he let us know he'd had enough and that was that."

"And your father…?"

"Unfortunately, he passed," Jake said. "But he seemed serene. He enjoyed his last months and we were all with him."

"Are there a lot of you?" she asked.

"A sister and a brother. I'm the youngest." He laughed then. "How many are there in your family?"

She gave him a brief rundown of the sisters and cousins. "And obviously I've been out of touch. Not everyone will be overjoyed to see me if they come this way."

"They haven't been in contact?"

"A couple have," she said. "The two cousins I'm staying with now and my mother, of course. But really, some are pretty embarrassed…"

"Don't we all have those dark shadows in our past?"

"I don't know too many people who have shadows like mine," she said. "But tell me more about you. It's probably so much nicer."

He told her about being a farm kid, filling her with envy. He talked about hayrides, harvest parties when they buried corn and potatoes in hot coals for a cookout, regularly rescuing stranded motorists in winter by taking the tractor to the road to pull them out of the snow. To him it was austere and rugged—a tough way to grow up. To her it sounded like freedom. They walked and talked for about fifteen minutes and then he said it was time he got back. And she told him she was almost home.

Over the years Krista had nurtured many a fantasy, but living at the lake house of her childhood had never been one of them. Perhaps because she could not even have imagined a life of such lovely tranquility. Of course, this lake house, renovated by Charley, was ten times the place of her childhood. On the days Krista worked, she was back home by two thirty. Quite often Jake would accompany her about halfway.

"Aren't you afraid people will talk about you always walking with one of the waitresses?" she asked him.

"Nope," he said. "Not worried at all. If you'd rather be alone…"

"It's okay," she said. Truthfully, she looked forward to it every day, so grateful he didn't ask her personal questions.

After work Krista could stretch out on a lounge on the porch with Charley and Meg, or fish off the dock, float on a raft or nap in the hammock. She was frequently admonished by Charley for walking around outside in her beloved Jockey underwear. On days she didn't have to work, she took the bus to Oakdale and treated her mother to a long lunch. Then she'd slip her mother a twenty-dollar bill. Sometimes she wondered if she had died and gone to heaven.

Meg's husband, John, came every weekend, and on the Fourth of July Jo also came for the holiday weekend and they had the most wonderful time, barbecuing, having a picnic outside in the sweltering heat. There were fireworks over the lake, set off by the lodge, and the lake was busy with boaters and swimmers. She even had a brief fantasy of inviting Jake to join them but she knew she wouldn't have the nerve. And even though she worked every weekend it was such a treat to come home to a full house, including her mother.

She restricted herself from thinking too often or for too long about her years in prison, about the people she knew there. It had the shock and ache of an amputation, but she longed so fiercely to have never been there at all she practiced this conscious denial. *I can suffer about that later,* she would tell herself. *For right now I want to enjoy this respite, live in the moment, be with my cousins and best friends.*

Of course, she knew Hope would be coming with her daughters, though no one seemed to know exactly when. Their very presence would force the issue of her twenty-three-year imprisonment. She tried to mentally prepare herself for her sister. It was a matter of scraping away a thick, sticky layer of anger and resentment. *Maybe,* she told herself, *if Hope can manage not to hate me for what I've done to get myself locked up, maybe I can manage to not hate her for abandoning me.* But forgiving Hope for ignoring their mother would be harder.

Krista had been at the lake over a month. Meg seemed to be doing pretty well. Early July was hot and humid and life seemed generally peaceful. Pleasurable. Then the moment she'd dreaded arrived. Krista walked home from the lodge, the smell of grilled cheese and Caesar salad dressing clinging to her clothes. Lost in her thoughts she was surprised to find a silver Mercedes parked in the drive behind the house. She stopped and studied the vehicle. Pennsylvania plates. She approached it cautiously and put a hand on the hood—it was hot. She hadn't been here long. She could hear the high-strung and excitable voice of her older sister emanating from the house, but she couldn't make out what she was saying. Whatever, she was saying it fast. The nervous edge to Hope's voice carried and it had not changed in all these years. *Please be nice,* Krista begged herself. *Remember the summer is not really for her, or for you, but for Megan. It's Megan's summer.*

It was that last thought that propelled her up the porch steps—the thought that this could be Meg's last summer. She so wished they could become old women together.

Krista was actually smiling as she walked in the house. She stopped immediately, of course. All she had to do was look at them, the three of them.

Hope sat on the sofa alone while Charley and Meg sat in two adjacent wicker chairs; they each had tall sweaty glasses of tea on the large square table that separated them. And directly opposite Hope, across from the glass-and-wicker table, sitting on a single chair, were her daughters, Bobbi and Trude. Alias, Brattie and Turdie. They were almost identical blondes, though Krista knew that two years separated them in age. Both had long, thick, straight hair, multilayered makeup, especially so around their eyes—they wore mauve shadows, liner, heavy mascara. Their wet-look lipstick, identical to their mother's in color and style, was lined with a darker lip pencil around the edges.

Krista sauntered into the room, but stopped dead in her tracks, shocked in spite of herself. She just hadn't been prepared for it all. First of all, Hope was a good fifty pounds overweight, but Krista had never seen a woman more plucked, pruned, primped and polished. Her fingernails and toenails were shiny with perfect enamel, her brows penciled with a sensual slant, her clothing obviously tailored and expensive. Her hair was permed and frosted and fluffed into a fancy short style that accented her bright and shiny gold earrings. Though she wore shorts and sandals, the shorts were cuffed above the knee and she also wore a blazer and plenty of jewelry, including a large diamond ring and thick sparkling tennis bracelet.

Krista turned to the girls. Now what were their ages again? Thirteen and fifteen? Fourteen and sixteen? Whatever, too young for this, yet they, too, were manicured and pedicured, their nails matching their glossy outlined lips. Krista had been away a long time, but she hadn't been deprived of TV during this time. These two were more overdone than twenty-one-year-old beauty contestants. And their pouty mouths showed their frank displeasure at being there. No one can snub like a beautiful teenage girl! With their crystalline blue eyes they resembled the alien children from the *Village of the Damned*. The younger one, who sat on the arm of the chair, was thinner than the older. Much thinner. In fact, her collarbones, elbows and knees seemed to jut out. They, too, were dressed to kill in their overlong shorts, jackets and accenting silk scarves.

"Well, Bobbi and Trude, I presume?" Krista asked politely.

Hope turned her head toward Krista. The girls simply gave her an abbreviated and suspicious nod.

"You guys missed the turn to the yacht club," Krista said. She plucked an apple out of the bowl that sat on the counter. She took a big, noisy bite. No one responded to her remark. "Hey," she said, her mouth full of apple. "I'm completely unarmed!" A small huff of laughter escaped Meg but Charley appeared to be bracing herself for more. Krista met her eyes ever so briefly and took note that Charley might be waiting too eagerly. Krista bent at the waist for a closer look at their feet, both pairs crossed at the ankles. "Are the bottoms of your shoes clean?"

They both tucked their feet back with speed. The older girl took the hand of the younger, giving comfort.

"You have us at a disadvantage, Krista," Hope said. "I didn't know you'd be here."

Krista took another noisy bite and chewed. "You didn't?" she asked with her mouth full. "Then I bet you just about shit when you found out."

"Kris—"

"Don't talk to me in that superior tone of yours or I might lose my temper and deck you. Believe it or not, no one else ever treats me like that." She turned toward the girls again and leveled them with her hard expression.

Boy, do I have a mean streak, Krista thought.

"Bobbi and Trude," Hope said. "This is your aunt Krista, my younger sister. We haven't been in touch for many, many years…which would explain why I haven't exactly mentioned her."

"Oh, I don't think *that* would explain it, Hope," Krista said. "Have you told your daughters that I exist at all?"

"Krista, please. Don't be confrontational."

"I've been away," she said, directing her gaze at the princesses. "Charm school. Forty years and two life terms… Really, we can't blame your mother for being uncomfortable. I wasn't supposed to be here. I was supposed to die in prison. But it was all a misunderstanding and the California Supreme Court apologized for the inconvenience and gave me parole." She grinned. "And here I am."

"You're just trying to scare them," Hope said. "Girls, your aunt Krista isn't really a dangerous—"

"Where's Frank?" Krista asked.

"Dad…" one of the girls began.

"Frank couldn't get away from work, Krista. He has a lot of responsibility. He's depended upon by too many people to take a vacation right now."

"That's too bad. I was looking forward to meeting him."

As Krista spoke the younger, thinner girl leaned down to whisper to her sister, her hair forming a canopy over both of their faces. Then she rose and the older girl spoke. "Mom, may we please be excused. You and your sister can catch up on old times and we'll put some of our stuff away. Please?"

"Sure," Charley said, before Hope could interfere. "You can have the whole loft to yourselves. Change into bathing suits if you like—there's still plenty of sun today."

Neither of them said *thank you* or *excuse me*, but fled quietly toward the back stairs, picking up a couple of bags each as they went.

"Well, dang, they damn near talked me to death!" Krista pronounced, biting into her apple again.

"You haven't changed at all, have you?" Hope asked with

hostility. "You once enjoyed shocking the grown-ups and now it's the children you want to shock with your crude behavior."

"Kiss my ass, Hope."

"Charley," Hope entreated. "How do you imagine we can make this situation work? I certainly can't subject my children to—"

"Charley isn't in charge, Hope," Krista said. "You and I have one or two things to sort out. Maybe when we do that and you get off your high fucking horse, we'll make this work by being equals, a thought that must make you wanna puke. Hmm?"

"Charley? Meg?" Hope pleaded.

Megan shrugged her thin shoulders. "I don't think this has anything to do with us. Does it, Charley?"

"I don't have any issues," Charley said. "Except that I'm not interested in spending the next couple of weeks listening to you two snipe at each other."

"Oh, God, I should have known you'd side with her," Hope said, resting her forehead in her hand. Weariness seemed to wash over her. "I would never have come if I'd known this was what was waiting for me! I can't put the girls through this!"

"Through what?" Meg asked. "Your reunion with your sister, who they didn't know existed?"

Hope lifted her head. "She's outrageous. Indiscreet and confrontational and inappropriate...and she's been in *prison*, for God's sake. Yet she's somehow implying that I've made some grave familial error!"

Krista scrunched up her face. *"Familial error?"*

"I came back here with the best of intentions—hoping upon hope that a reunion of our family could put everything right at last and allow Grandma Berkey to die in peace. I wanted her to see the girls once more. I wanted to satisfy our obligations, pay my respects, perhaps thank her for making me feel loved and cherished when I was a young woman without family. I'm ready to put a final stamp on our family business and tidy up any legal complications. But I did not come back here to haggle with Krista over whether or not we're equal!"

Megan, Charley and Krista all looked at each other in total confusion.

"Legal complications? Hope," Charley said patiently. "What the hell are you talking about?"

"The will!" Hope nearly shouted. Her eyes were glassy, her cheeks rosy and her impatience a palpable thing. "I came back to settle my inheritance. And that's all!"

Silence enveloped them, a silence heavy with confusion. Megan, Charley and Krista made eye contact, asking the non-verbal question over and over: *Will? What will?* But however Hope had concocted this in her mind—that this was a last call for the purpose of seeing a will—might remain forever unanswered. She'd been doing this for years, as a teenager and young woman, living a delusional life in which she was a fairy princess and not related to common folk.

Remembering that, Charley laughed. Meg joined in. Before long Krista was holding her sides in hysterics.

"As soon as they're asleep tonight, I'm outta here," Trude told her sister in a hushed voice. She sat on one of the two double beds in the loft and whispered to her older sister. "You can take me or I'll go alone. Either way, I'm gone. They're all nuts, Mom at the head of the pack."

"We could give it a day or two," Bobbi suggested. "We could see how it shakes out. Check out the place. Get a tan."

"I can't," Trude insisted. "Dad said if she was acting crazy, we didn't have to stay. She's been crazy all the way here—making us promise to keep it a secret that she and Dad are divorced, making us promise to act like we have a perfect life or she doesn't know what she'll do, throwing away our jeans, making us have manicures and facials and… Shit! And this place is crazy as she is! She's got a sister who's like right outta jail! Jesus! I'm like… I'm all… She won't take us to the airport so let's take the car and go to the airport, park it, fly home, and Dad can handle her. She's fuckin' loony tunes, okay?"

"You let it get you too upset," Bobbi said. Bobbi was also upset, but being the older sister and sixteen, she was able to maintain an appearance of calm. She could be the leader for her sister, take care of her in as much as Trude would allow it. Their therapist said they should work on accepting their mother as she was—and if she was crazy, accept her crazy. Without taking on her burdens.

Trude had been taking on her mother's burdens and recriminations for a long time. That was one of the many reasons she couldn't eat. She'd hoped if she could be more perfect, her mother would be less crazy. Although she could see the intellectual absurdity of such reasoning, even at her young age, emotionally she was still locked in that behavior pattern. Plus, she felt guilty about refusing to live with her. And Hope was no help. She played on that guilt and anxiety and just got crazier as the years went by.

"*I* let it get me too upset?" Trude argued. "Look, one of them is just out of prison, one of them looks like she just escaped a concentration camp and then there's our mother, Hopeless. That Charley might be the only sane one in the group and I'm not real sure about her yet." Tears came to Trude's large blue eyes. "I feel like a fucking Barbie doll that she dressed up all the way from Philly to here. I feel stupid and nervous and like I might barf. Please, Bob. Take me home. Please."

Bobbi put her arms around her little sister, so frail in her embrace. She was anorexic, another reality Hope wouldn't address. "Leave everything packed for now," she said. "Let's go for a little walk outside, check out the lake, have some dinner, then we'll do what we have to do. When have I ever let you down, huh?"

Bobbi and Trude sat at the end of the dock, sandals lined up perfectly straight behind them, and dangled their feet in the water. It was five thirty but the sun was a long time from going down. The clinking of dinner plates being placed around the table could be heard from the house; the smells of cooking wafted pleasantly on the breeze.

"It might not be so bad," Bobbi said.

The creak and groan of the dock boards behind them told of a visitor and they turned to see Krista. "Hey," she said, moving barefoot down the dock. She wore only some shorts and a Jockey T-shirt through which the pink of her nipples were visible. Both girls' eyes grew wide at the sight. "Ah, I wanted to talk to you guys for a second, if it's okay."

They looked at each other, then back at her. Bobbi nodded.

Krista plunked down on the dock behind them, cross-legged. "Ah… I don't know anything about talking to kids, okay? So don't be surprised if I say all the wrong things. Your mom and me—well, we never did get along all that well. You two—it looks like you two are actually pretty close. Me and your mom, we just never were. Your mom and Charley were best friends when they were little, but about the time Charley was…well, sometime in high school, they started wanting different things. And going different ways.

"What I'm trying to say is—your mom had it all wrong about coming to the lake this summer. Megan wanted to open up the lake house one more time. She's been fighting cancer for years, that's why she's so bald and skinny. From the chemotherapy. We haven't been here together in twenty-seven years. The year Charley and Megan's little sister Bunny drowned, that was the last time any of us were here. Our mothers pretty much demanded that no one come to the lake again, which was not a real honest and up-front way to deal with the grief, but…we come from a family that isn't real honest. I wish that weren't true…

"So, back to your mom. She seems to have some idea about a will, an inheritance, something like that. We don't know anything about that. We're all here because Megan wanted to spend the summer here. She just doesn't have much fight left in her. She might get better or she might not. We're here for her. And maybe a little bit for each other. To give each other a little moral support, something our family also hasn't been known for. It's hard, you know? Being estranged like this all these years, feeling like we have no family, feeling alone…

"But it's nice to have one more chance, to get people together, to see what kind of family survived all the sadness. Me and your mom, shoot, we don't understand each other. Never have. I always overreacted to everything, usually by doing something that got me into trouble, like getting drunk or getting in a fight. Your mom? Her way of dealing with crisis was to pretend it wasn't there and invent some completely fictional scenario around herself. I remember once when our little sister, Beverly, was taken to the hospital and your mom—"

"There's *another* sister?" Trude interrupted in a voice that was near panic. It was also the most she had said to anyone besides Bobbi in an entire afternoon. Three whole words.

Krista didn't answer immediately. Instead, she contemplated these girls. She was inclined to dislike them. They were frilly, they were Hope's and they were anything but friendly.

"You know what?" Krista said. "It's good you're here. Meg

brought a million pictures, plus the albums of our families when we were growing up. I doubt your mom was able to give you a detailed biography of the family—she was always on another planet." Trude's gaze dropped to her lap as if in embarrassment. "Hey, that's not the worst place to be! Look where I was!" When Trude's gaze came up it was hostile. This wasn't going to be easy, Krista realized. These girls might be as fucked-up as Hope.

Krista got to her feet. "We've got a million pictures. You want to know more about your mother's family, there are plenty of people around to answer your questions truthfully. Also, your grandmother would love to see you."

"We heard she's in a nursing home now," Bobbi said.

"No, she lives in Saint Paul. Your great-grandma Berkey is in a nursing home. She's eighty-eight but still pretty feisty, considering."

The girls looked at each other, confused.

"I'm talking about my mother," Krista said. "Your mother's mother, Josephine. Josephine Berkey Hempstead? That grandma?"

Bobbi was slow to reply but finally her voice came. Softly. "We…we don't know too much about her. We only know about Grandma Berkey. The rich one."

A punch in the gut could not have hurt Krista as much. But why should she be surprised? Hope pretended she had no sisters, since one was homicidal and the other had been suicidal. And Hope had long pretended she had no mother since Jo didn't meet her expectations.

Well, it was going to be hard not to kill Hope, after all.

During dinner, Krista lost all hope that the summer would be restoring for Meg. It was horrid. Hope prattled on about every expensive trip she'd ever taken with her husband, her country club, her charities, their house on the Cape, her big house in Philly. By itself that kind of grandiose talk could drive a person insane but in addition to that the skinny girl didn't eat and the heavier one hardly ever made eye contact with anyone. Charley and Meg made a few attempts to draw the girls out a little but it was futile—Hope cut them off and did their talking for them. By the time dinner was over Bobbi and Trude had not uttered a word and simply fled to their loft.

Krista took most of her belongings to Charley's room, giving her room to Hope. There was no possible way she could share space with her sister.

When the lake house was finally darkened for sleep that night, the sounds came out. There was something about the heating/cooling system that connected all the rooms and brought out every sound. Charley and Krista both remembered that from their childhood. They slept together in the big king-size bed; they looked at each other several times, but never spoke. Hope, alone in Krista's bedroom on the main floor, was still chattering and humming and laughing to herself. It was so eerie; it was like background music for a movie about a psychiatric hospital. Then came the heartbreaking over-noise of soft crying coming from the loft.

After about an hour of this noise, Megan came into the master bedroom carrying her pillow and dragging her quilt, like a small child fleeing to her parents' bed. Without a word Charley moved over and held the blanket back for her to climb in. And there were the three of them, cuddled against the lunacy of the night. Just before they began to drift off to sleep, Krista made the only whispery comment. "And we're the sanest ones we've got? Jesus Christ."

Chapter Ten

The pounding on the door came at 4:17 in the morning, just a few minutes before Krista was supposed to be getting up for work. It jolted the three women awake like the shock of ice water in the face. Charley was the first to get to the door and ask who was there, even though all she had was one flimsy hook-lock on the screen to keep the bad guys out. "Sheriff Tom Doherty. Is this the Berkey-Hempstead residence?"

"Yes," Charley answered. "Who are you looking for?"

"Well, anyone who might know the Griffin girls—Bobbi and Trude Griffin? There's been an accident. A pretty bad one."

With that Charley swung open the door to find it really was the sheriff and he'd been telling the awful truth.

Charley got just the briefest information about what had happened. Bobbi and Trude had taken Hope's Mercedes and headed for the Twin Cities. To what purpose was as yet unclear. Out for a spin? Hoping to get in a little party time while their mother slept? Running away? If it was Charley, she'd have been running from that crazy mother. Hell, it *had* been Charley and she *had* run away. Sort of. She chose the college as far as she could get from Louise and had to be forced to return for holidays.

Bobbi and Trude hadn't gotten far. They were just south of Brainerd, entering I-10 South, when a drunk driver traveling in the wrong direction on the interstate hit them head-on. They'd probably be dead if not for seat belts, airbags and the fact Hope's six-year-old Mercedes was built like a brick shithouse. Even so, Bobbi, the driver, had a possible head injury, possible internal injuries and had been flown by medical helicopter to the county trauma hospital in Saint Paul. Trude, banged up pretty good but not as seriously, had been taken to Brainerd's sixty-bed Saint Catherine's. The sheriff said that probably the worst of it for Trude was her hysteria over her sister, who had been taken to a different hospital. She'd had to be sedated.

As the women absorbed the news, Hope was useless. Either she was listening and completely unresponsive or she wasn't listening at all. *They really should have named her Hopeless*, Charley thought.

"They need to be together," Krista said immediately. "Anyone can see how they depend on each other, how they seem to be all they really have. Their father is too busy for them and their mother is crackers."

"I could pick Trude up at the hospital, if they'll release her, and take her with us to Saint Paul," Charley said, thinking out loud.

"I'm no doctor," the sheriff said, "but it's my guess she's not leaving the hospital right now unless it's AMA."

"AMA?" Krista asked.

"Against medical advice," Meg said. "But we can get a doctor to have her transferred to Saint Paul. Hope and Frank are rich—it shouldn't be a problem even if the insurance won't cover it."

Charley flew into action, taking charge in the way she knew best. Networking and giving orders and asking favors. She told Meg to call John. He was on staff at the trauma hospital where Bobbi had been taken. John would do anything for Megan; he'd lasso the moon for her. One call from Meg to John started the ball rolling before anyone even left the lake house to head to Saint Paul. John would make it to the hospital right behind the emergency helicopter. Then he would phone Saint Catherine's and instruct them to transport his other patient, Trude Griffin. In the interim, Charley called Frank. She tried to get Hope to do it but she could barely come up with the phone number. Hope was trembling, panicked, twittering and asking a million questions, very few of which seemed to have anything to do with the accident.

"It's too soon to even get the emergency room to grade the injuries," Charley told Frank. "But my brother-in-law is a doctor and has gone to the hospital to look after them and I'll be taking Hope there shortly. All I know is that Bobbi was driving, and she was unconscious when she was airlifted. Trude is banged up but not hurt badly, they say, but is hysterical about her sister's injuries, so my brother-in-law is having her transported to the same hospital. John is a pediatrician with lots of pull in the ER and hell of a great guy besides. His name is Dr. John Crane and he's expecting to hear from you." She rattled off the phone number.

"What the hell were they doing out driving in the middle of the night?" Frank asked.

"No one knows. You don't suppose... Could they have been running away?"

"Oh, Jesus." He sighed heavily. "I shouldn't have made them go. I was so optimistic."

"Optimistic about what?" Charley asked. They hadn't seemed particularly happy to be there, but *forced*?

"It's complicated. I'm coming out immediately. Tell the girls to stay calm. I'll explain when I get there. How's Hope?"

Now it was Charley's turn to sigh deeply. "Not good, Frank. She doesn't seem to have much aptitude for crisis."

He laughed into the phone but Charley could tell it was not from humor. "I'll be there as quickly as I can. Meanwhile, see if you can keep her away from the girls. I imagine their stress and anxiety is enough without their mother's…well… just keep her away from the girls for now."

"If I can," Charley said. She noticed that through all the bad news and planning and networking, Hope walked around in circles, twisting her hands and muttering. She let Charley, Meg, Krista and the sheriff make phone calls and decisions. Eventually Hope was told to get dressed if she wanted to go with Charley to the hospital. It turned out she was pretty good at taking instruction. Charley wondered if she was on something—some kind of tranquilizers or something—she was so out of it.

Charley had a fleeting thought—Louise was always complaining that Josephine was completely incompetent. Compared to Hope, Jo looked like she could run Ford Motor Company. But having to put up with bullshit behavior like this? If that's what Louise had to deal with with Jo, it could certainly be fodder for a feud.

There was only the one car now—Charley's. Krista and Meg would stay at the lake together while Charley did what only a saint would do—put Hope in the car to take her to the city. And almost immediately she yelled at her to shut up.

"Now look, I don't really care how crazy you are, Hope. You are not going to mutter and whine all the way to Saint Paul. If you do, I'll pull over and shove you out and leave you by the road."

"I wasn't talking. I was just asking myself a few questions

so I can plan, like will Frank be called and will he come and will he tell them we're married and do they have clothes for the hospital and are they appropriate and—"

"Hope! Shut up!" Her foot tapped the brake as a warning. Only Hope. *Her daughter is unconscious and she's worried whether her clothes for the hospital are the right clothes?* Hope quieted. What was this business about Frank telling them they were married? Hope was not silent, but at least she only mumbled absently, like the hum of new tires on coarse asphalt. Good enough.

"Charley?" Hope asked quietly. Meekly. "Do you think they're alive?"

Charley frowned. It was so strange to have her ask a question like that without any emotion. "They're very much alive, Hope. John Crane is a wonderful doctor and he's gone to the emergency room to see what he can do to help. Frank is on his way. For now you should pray. Very quietly so I can drive."

"I failed them," she whispered. "I should have planned better. I thought I had everything worked out but I should have planned better."

Charley just shook her head. She was dreadfully sorry about the accident but she was grateful there would be an opportunity to put Hope back in Frank's hands. He would have to take them all home. He would surely understand this wasn't good for Megan.

The sun had risen by the time Charley pulled into the hospital parking lot. She had to wake Hope and pull her along by the hand. It had to be drugs. How else could a mother sleep on the way to the hospital? Once inside the emergency room, Charley found a quiet corner and placed Hope, childlike, on a chair and told her to rest while she found the doctor. Hope did as she was told, curling into herself and closing her eyes. Charley backed away from her suspiciously. When she turned, she ran into John. Literally.

"Oh, God, John! You scared me to death!"

He put his arms around her and hugged her. "Charley, how I hate that this has happened but so glad you were there to take care of things."

She hugged him back. "You're so sane. How did someone in our family have such a perfectly normal relationship?"

He laughed. "Nothing about my relationship with Meg has been normal for years. How are you?"

"I was doing real well until I was reunited with my cousin Hope." She jutted her chin over her shoulder toward the sleeping woman. "This was all Megan's idea, you know. Opening up the lake house, having the family get together."

He got a sentimental smile. "Why not? She never liked the status quo. How'd she hold up through this crisis?"

"Like a rock. She's doing okay, I think. Krista will take good care of her while I'm away. Meg maintains a great sense of humor if you have a strong stomach."

"Yeah, the death jokes."

She shrugged. She couldn't talk about that now. "Tell me about the girls."

"Bobbi Griffin, sixteen, the driver, has a concussion and they want to observe her for a while, but she looks to be okay. Doesn't appear to have any spinal cord damage but the orthopedic surgeon is looking at her now. She's had an MRI. She's had some abdominal pain but it was a negative CT. She's been worried about her sister, but all in all they're two very lucky little girls. The little one has gone to have her knee wrapped and that's all. Lucky." He looked past Charley. "They haven't asked for their mother."

"Thank God. Their mother is a nutball."

"Do you want to see Bobbi?" John asked.

"Oh, yes, I need to. Surrogate Mom, I guess. Their dad is on his way."

Seeing Bobbi lying there, all that heavy makeup washed off, her blond hair smoothed away from her face, she looked so young, so innocent. Harmless and sweet. It was a reflex that drew Charley's hand to Bobbi's brow, touching her. The girl's eyes fluttered open and Charley smiled reassuringly. "How do you feel?" she asked in a tender, maternal whisper.

"I'm okay," the girl croaked. "Is Trude okay?"

"She'll be right back—she's just having her knee wrapped." She struggled to sit up. "I should go with her…"

"No, no," Charley said, gently pushing her back down. "You can't get up for a while. You hit your head. You're lucky to be alive."

Her eyes filled with tears. "You don't understand, Aunt Charley. My sister can't handle anything without me. She's not very strong…"

Aunt Charley? That stopped her for a second. She wasn't this girl's aunt. And the girl wasn't even friendly enough to have chosen the term out of affection. Hope again? Delusional? Or just a liar?

One thing at a time. "Bobbi, I called your dad. He's coming immediately. First flight he can get."

All the stress seemed to flow out of the girl's body and she lay down with a *flomp*. "Oh, God," she whimpered. "Thank you! Thank God. When will he be here?"

"Well, it'll take a few hours. Your, ah, mother is in the waiting area."

"Oh, please, I can't deal with her right now. Please? Tell her I'm too sick or something. Is Pam coming?"

"Pam?"

"My step… My dad's wife. Pam."

"Wife?" Charley asked in a soft breath. "Your dad said the situation was complicated, but I don't think he adequately prepared me. What's going on?"

Her eyes bubbled with tears. "Can I have some water, please?" she asked.

"Sure. Let me ask." Charley went outside the drawn curtain, hailed a nurse and fixed Bobbi up with a little glass of water. She fluffed her pillow. Then she smoothed her cool brow again. The girl slowly got a grip so she could attempt an explanation.

"We don't know what's wrong with my mom. She won't get counseling. My dad divorced her five years ago. He hasn't lived with her in six. He's remarried and I have a little brother and we live with Dad and Pam…but my mom still pretends to be married to him."

"Oh, for the love of God! What about those Christmas letters?"

"Those letters are so embarrassing. Up to two years ago she drove all the way across town to our school to volunteer and she'd carry on, talking like we all live together. They had to finally ask her to stop volunteering because she was disruptive. She'd talk about vacations we were never going to take. They almost had to arrest her to get her to stop going to the country club where she and my dad used to be members. She had to get checked out by the shrink or we weren't even going to have to go there for weekend visits, and the shrink says she knows what's real and what isn't, but it doesn't seem like it. She acts so crazy."

"Oh, Bobbi…"

"Do you know what it was like driving out here with her? We just can't do that anymore. Trude can't take it—she's too fragile. She's anorexic, anyone can see that. I think my mother's craziness made her that way. It gets worse every time we're with my mother. On the way out here Trude could hardly eat anything. When our mother was throwing out our jeans and stuff, buying us this fancy summer wardrobe that we hated and getting us done over, I thought Trude was going to just lose it. Mom had all these rules we had to follow so none of her sisters would know about Dad or Pam or little Matt…"

"Sisters?" Charley asked.

"You and Aunt Meg. We didn't even know about Krista. And now I hear there's another one!"

"Oh, honey, I had no idea. I mean, I could see she was pretty strange, but this is just sounding worse all the time."

"I can take it. I don't let her get to me. But Trude just can't handle it anymore. I don't care what Dad and the counselor say, Trude needs to not see our mother."

Charley was devastated by this story. She leaned down and pulled Bobbi into an embrace and held her. "Oh, you poor baby," she crooned, rocking her. She didn't even bother to tell her the truth, that Hope was her cousin. It only took seconds before Bobbi was crying softly. So much for her being able to take it. "Were you running away? Is that what you were doing?"

"Oh, God, I'm sorry! I hope I didn't hurt anyone. I never even saw—"

"It wasn't your fault, Bobbi. It was a drunk driver. And don't say you're sorry for running away. It sounds like you had to!"

"We were just going to go home. We have a credit card for emergencies. We had to, that's all."

"Of course you had to!"

"You mean…you understand?"

"Absolutely. And I'll talk to your father about this when he gets here. I don't care how busy he is…he has to keep you safe from this lunacy."

"Charley?" John said from behind her. "I'm sorry to bother you, but could I see you for a moment? She'll be right back, Bobbi. Okay?"

Charley and Bobbi both nodded and wiped at their eyes. Then she followed John.

"Sorry to pull you away, but this is important." John held her elbow and escorted her toward the waiting area. He stopped in the doorway and let Charley see for herself.

Hope was perched on the edge of her chair, tilted toward the man next to her, talking in an animated fashion. But the man was sound asleep. He was snoring, and with each out-breath, his dentures moved. He looked to be about ninety and, by his clothing, might be homeless. This had no impact at all on Hope, however. She talked in earnest; she waved her hands for emphasis. Her voice was soft but high-pitched and people were staring at her. Charley crept closer to hear. Just as Hope didn't seem to realize the man was sleeping, she was oblivious to the fact that other people were listening.

"We've actually had the house on the Cape since Trude was about three years old, but sometimes we don't see it for a year. I'd like to spend June and July, but Franklin is just too busy. And if he has business in London or Paris while the girls are on summer hiatus, I like going along, take the opportunity to shop, see a few plays. It's good for the girls, don't you think? But no, we'd never rent out the house on the Cape! Not any more than we'd rent out our own home while we're abroad! I couldn't bear to have strangers in my house! This summer we aren't going to the Cape at all, of course, because we're having our summer at the lake house, just like I did when I was a girl. I don't know when to expect Franklin. He's been quite tied up. That's the price—he's a senior partner—men in power, you know, have a nasty habit of forgetting they have a family sometimes. But don't even get me started on that! Fortunately, I have many friends who share that lot in life, women married to powerful, wealthy men. I meet most of them at the club. Some I've become close to through my charity work in the city..."

Charley was mesmerized by this speech Hope was giving to a passed-out bum. She gaped and couldn't seem to look away. After a while she felt someone tugging on her elbow and she allowed John to pull her away. Charley, unlike Hope, was speechless.

"I've called for a psych consult, Charley. She doesn't seem to be causing any real problems at the moment. We'll keep an eye on her to make sure she doesn't wander off."

"John, what the hell is all that?"

"Not my bag actually, but she's definitely out of reality. Could she be bipolar?"

"Hell if I know. John, she sounded just like that at dinner last night! It's all fabricated, Bobbi tells me. All that business about her vacations with her husband and children? Her houses? Her clubs and charities? According to Bobbi none of it is true. She hasn't been married to their father for years!"

John raised an eyebrow and tilted his head slightly. "I've heard of people not adjusting to the divorce, but that's a little extreme."

"She's been a little like that all her life. One of her sisters attempted suicide and another was locked up in juvenile detention and Hope wondered if lavender would be too spring-like a color for the winter formal." She shook her head. "I had my own problems. I never had the time to think of her as crazy. We all had our own problems. In fact, at the time, her behavior was the least crazy."

"Not anymore," he said.

"I've got to stay with Bobbi," Charley said. "I need to talk to her. Can we get her out of emergency soon?"

"As soon as the orthopod clears her. We'll see if we can

find a semiprivate room for the girls. But, Charley, don't wear the kid out."

Slightly distracted, Charley ran a hand through her hair. "She thinks I'm her aunt! I've got to try to explain our family to her."

"Jesus, on top of a head injury?" John said. "If she didn't see stars before…"

"Oh, that's right. You've met my family."

By noon Frank Griffin had arrived and the girls were together in a semiprivate room. And Franklin was a complete surprise. He was a youthful and fit forty-five. Though his hair was thin up top, he wore a six-inch ponytail. He was tanned and healthy looking as if he spent a great deal of time outside. After he assured himself that his daughters were all right, he impetuously embraced Charley and squeezed her until she squeaked. When he let go of her he had grateful tears in his eyes.

Hope had prepared Charley for a distracted, insensitive business executive. A picture of a starched white shirt, double chins, abrupt and dismissive behavior came to mind. A man without time for his family—hadn't she said so? Not true of this Franklin, who preferred to be called Frank. He was sweet, relaxed, casual and attractive. And he wasn't a business executive.

"Oh, I was. A CPA and vice president of finance for a small but very successful investment firm. I left that job years ago for a quieter, more manageable life as a shop owner. That's how I met my wife, Pam, also an escaped executive who was tired of the rat race and wanted to have a baby. We're dropouts. We sell bikes, and also have a large add-on to the store where we sell imported tea, herbs, vitamins and natural supplements."

"You're kidding!"

"We're cyclists. Long-distance riders. I left the job before I left the marriage and I think that's what did it to Hope, put her over the edge. She's been like this for years now. Somewhere along the way I must have hurt her very deeply..."

"Hope has been like this since she was a teenager," Charley said. "If she didn't like the way things were, she invented something she liked better. And right now I suppose she's making up a life for a psychiatrist. She's been escorted to the psych ward."

"Oh, man," he said, shaking his head.

After a long afternoon in the hospital, Charley and Frank retired to a restaurant for a badly needed bottle of wine and food. They had permission from Bobbi and Trude—two tired and relieved little girls in possession of their father's cell phone number if they needed him.

"What makes you think it was *your* doing?" Charley asked.

He shook his head sadly. "She barely resembles the sweet young woman I married. She was so filled with good intentions. She tried so hard to please my mother, to get her approval. It was impossible but Hope never seemed to understand it had nothing to do with her. My mother was an old snob. No one in the family ever took her seriously. There are only two or three people on the East Coast she truly admired." He shook his head and laughed. "Hope was so determined. She was going to do everything the Griffin way! She would make us the toast of Philadelphia. I broke her heart when I told her nothing could make me more miserable."

"Oh, Frank..."

"I finally couldn't take any more of it. My God, her lists alone were enough to drive me mad. If I'd wanted to marry my mother, I could have chosen from a parade of Philly girls already picked out for me. When we divorced, no matter how many times I told her it was because that uppity lifestyle just made me unhappy, Hope never believed me. She always thought I left her because she just hadn't done it well enough. There was just no—"

"Frank, it wasn't you," Charley said.

"It was mostly pretense with my mother, too, God rest her. My sisters and I, we were usually amused by Mother's efforts to be...well... We were amused when we weren't pissed off. Our family has some money from a good furniture business that my father and uncle built plus some clever investments. If you bought land a few generations ago, urban growth being what it is, there was money to be made. But Hope could never quite get that straight, that my mother was just a wannabe rich matron who was born to a farmer. She told people her ancestors came over on the *Mayflower*. It was rubbish."

"But, Frank, this has been going on with Hope for years, since she was about fifteen. She moved in with our grandparents about then and pretended they were her parents because they were rich and socially prominent."

Charley put her hand on Frank's arm. "Your girls haven't met their grandmother, Hope's mother. They've only met their great-grandmother. Their grandmother, Josephine, lives a very simple, low-key existence and manages a flower shop. She's one of the kindest, loveliest people I know. And I'm not Hope's sister, I'm her cousin. Her sister Krista was just released from prison. Hope had some notion she was coming home to get an inheritance... There's no inheritance. I could go on but you'd need a chart."

Frank stared at Charley in disbelief.

"We've got some catching up to do," Charley said. "I hope you're going to be around for a couple of days. For the girls' sake, you should hear the reality of our family. They deserve a shot at a normal, healthy life and part of that depends on them understanding their roots. Denial doesn't make sense anymore."

"Spoken like a true talk show host."

"*Canceled* talk show host. Right now I'm just on the mop and bucket detail..."

"Which means?"

"Cleanup crew. Looks like we've got three or four generations to tidy up before summer's over. And I just can't imagine how that's going to be done while keeping Meg's health as the priority." She took a deep breath. "I'm tempted to shut the whole thing down right where it is. Krista and I can take care of Meg. But Hope needs more help than we can give."

"You can count on me," he said, pouring the last of the wine into Charley's glass. "She's the mother of my children. I have responsibility there."

She smiled at him as she covered his hand with hers. "I'm sorry we never got to know each other, Frank. You're a good guy."

Chapter Eleven

After what was, under the circumstances, a perfectly lovely visit with Frank, Charley drove only as far as Megan's house in the city. She had a key and warned John that she'd be staying there for the night. She'd checked in with Meg and Krista several times throughout the day, reassuring them that the girls and Hope were all fine, which they weren't really. But they were in no imminent medical crisis and Charley decided to give the full story in person. In case all of it upset her sister. It was possible Meg could feel some responsibility, having set up this summer reunion as she had.

In fact, Charley couldn't remember Megan ever being emotionally upset. She had always been strong and serene and philosophical. Why she would have cancer was such a mystery. Why anyone would have that awful scourge was perplexing but Meg had done all the things Charley had convinced herself were necessary to avoid the beast—she laughed often, she loved thoroughly, she didn't hold grudges, she exercised and ate healthy foods and she'd never been particularly vulnerable to illness. She was small of stature but hardy. The only blight on an almost perfect marriage with John was their inability to conceive. Even with the help of doctors and piles of money.

And yet here they were. The already crazy family was imploding and Meg was probably dying. Charley was asking herself, what would be the greatest gift she could give her sister now. The answer was out of her reach.

She had breakfast in the hospital cafeteria with Frank. He had spent the night in the chair in his daughters' room. They didn't really need him there but he didn't want them to wake in a panic and wonder if they were safe. They had another fantastic visit but this time Frank wanted to know more about Charley and her personal life.

"Michael," she told him. "We've been together for twenty-two years, have a son, Eric, but we haven't married. Michael wants to marry now. My life is so crazy right now—don't you think I'd love to just turn my back on all of it and escape into matrimonial bliss with the love of my life?"

"No," Frank said with a smile. "I don't think that for one second. Trying to sort a few things out, are you?"

She rested her forehead in a hand and groaned.

"I've been there, Charley," Frank said. "I left my wife, though she was clearly vulnerable. I had to rescue my daughters from their mother and it wasn't easy. I made so many mistakes, and yet I did the only things I could do. I'm still doing all I can and I'm not sure it will ever be enough. Just do yourself one favor—tell the truth about how you feel and what you're going through."

Trite, she thought. *Oversimplified. We're dealing with mental illness, cancer, family dysfunction. Plus, I'm fired and unemployable. And I'm in some kind of weird romantic power struggle with the man I love. How I feel is* fucked.

But she loved Frank and his ponytail and his dropout lifestyle. And she was starting to love those high-maintenance girls. They were young. With the right kind of guidance, they could be okay.

She called Meg and told her she was staying in the city until the girls were discharged and on their way home with their father. Then she drove to the flower shop that Jo managed and found her behind the counter. Thankfully there were no customers in the store. Jo smiled when she saw Charley enter.

"Is your helper here?" Charley asked.

"Not yet. She doesn't come in until eleven."

"Good. I have a very complicated story to tell you. It's family business."

Jo's smile faded. "This doesn't sound like it's going to be good news. Is Meg okay?"

"She's hanging in there. This is more about your family. Hope and the girls came to the lake."

"They did?" she asked, wide-eyed. "They actually came?"

"It didn't last long," Charley said. "It didn't go well."

Charley carefully went through the details, mapping out as best she could all the disjointed family relationships Hope had concocted. It was one of the most difficult things she'd ever done. Jo was calm and listened raptly, even asking a few questions, but it was Charley who felt a tear spill over as she explained Trude and Bobbi didn't even know who their grandmother was. "All this time Hope has given me billing as her sister, apparently you've become a distant relative and Grandma Berkey is the woman who raised her. I was so furious I thought I'd strangle her. But it isn't just her fantasy life. It turns out she's legitimately delusional. With John's help, she's in the temporary care of the psych ward, where she's being evaluated. She's going to need someone to see after her, legally if nothing else, and I'm afraid it's not going to be me."

"Of course not," Jo said. "I suppose that should be my responsibility. But first, I have to see the girls. Let me call Margie and see if she can come early. Are you going back to the lake now?"

"Not just yet. I'll be glad to take you to the hospital."

"Do you mind if we stop by my apartment?" she asked. "I'd like to put on my nicest summer pants and top."

"Of course we can," Charley said.

It was nearly noon by the time they arrived at the hospital. Frank stood up from the end of Trude's bed as they entered the room.

"Frank, this is Josephine Hempstead, Hope's mother. I'm sure you met at least once…"

"Yes," he said, sticking out a hand. "But—"

"I know," Jo said. "You were told Hope was raised by her grandparents. That wasn't entirely true. She did live with them for a couple of years in high school and they sent her to college. I wasn't there for Hope in the ways she wanted or needed. I regret that I let her just have her way about that. Maybe all this confusion is really my fault. I thought it might hurt more than help if I demanded you and everyone present know the truth. She wanted a more proper and more financially able family to present to your family and my parents were only too happy to conspire in that. I was a great disappointment to them in those ways."

"I'm afraid the girls think you're an aunt," he said.

"And I'm here to explain if I can," Jo said. She looked at the girls. "My darlings, you are so beautiful, so perfect."

"Excuse me, Mrs. Hempstead, but I was told you and Hope were estranged, that you hadn't been in touch in years," Frank said.

"I wrote and called every month," Jo said. "I sent little gifts for the girls. Nothing flashy, but… But let me see if I can start from the beginning and explain what is real and what isn't. Hope has always exaggerated and fantasized, but when she was fifteen, when our family was at the lowest, when one of the cousins died suddenly, the youngest one, when Hope's father abandoned us and the girls and I were left poor and emotionally crippled, that's when Hope seemed to decide she wasn't just going to wish to be someone else, she was going to become someone else. She moved in with my parents, where they were happy to do everything they would do for a daughter—buy her beautiful dresses, give her a debutante's ball, pay for a prestigious college, an expensive and showy wedding—all the things Hope seemed to crave and need. I admit, I was angry. I felt rejected and had two other daughters who needed me. But I promise you, I never knew she was beginning to believe it. And now maybe I can see...she needed me most of all."

Charley listened in wonder and admiration as Jo explained in vivid detail each small fantasy Hope concocted and how everyone in the family called them her "castles in the air." How no one took her seriously.

Jo explained the whole family tree—Jo and Louise marrying brothers, having a daughter each year until there were six, summers at the lake where they were protected from the real world for three months. How it hurt her so much when Hope rejected her, how she longed to be with her granddaughters. "I didn't realize for years that we were all in such a bad place. There'd been a family tragedy, you see, leaving every single one of us so badly unable to cope. Hope's irritating refusal to face reality honestly seemed like the least of our troubles. In fact, I thought she'd somehow escaped the craziness that seemed to oppress the rest of us. I had no idea..."

"*She's* crazy," Bobbi boldly put in.

Jo nodded solemnly. "I'm told by your cousin Charley— Hope is ill. I'm going to visit her today, but I'm not optimistic that she'll snap out of it. She's going to need help. I admit, I don't know what to do. I'll ask Megan's husband, Dr. Crane. He's always so willing to help. But I promise I'll do what I can." Then she smiled so sweetly. "I've lost so much time with you," she said. "Hope always sent me pictures. But if I asked to visit she said you were going to Europe! So many trips to Europe."

"We went once," Trude said. "We went to France with Dad and Pam. To see the Tour de France. Dad and Pam are big cyclists."

"I sell bikes. We make custom bikes," Frank said.

"But... I thought you were with an investment firm," Jo said.

"I left that firm years ago," he said.

"Oh, my God, it's going to take a lifetime to untangle everything!" Jo just shook her head. "I'm so sorry."

Bobbi laughed and said, "Why even bother!"

"It comes in handy later," Frank said. "When you're trying to decide exactly who you want to be. Reject some of this, keep some of that, laugh at some, cringe at others... I'm the last person to poke fun. My family had some pretty wacky characters. I heard my father talk about a family feud a few generations ago, back when there were wakes in people's houses. Two sides of the family hated each other so meanly and fought so bitterly they put the casket on wheels and rolled it between rooms—the Hatfields in the parlor and the McCoys in the dining room."

Bobbi giggled. "You're making it up!"

"There are a million stories like that," Charley said. "Some families are doomed to keep repeating their problems. The Hatfields and McCoys can't even remember what started their feud."

"I heard it was a pig," Frank said. "One of them stole a pig from the other one and ate it before they'd get caught."

"I'm totally going to barf," Trude said.

"I thought it was a marriage situation," Charley said. "A

Hatfield son ran off with a McCoy daughter who was engaged to someone else."

"That came later," Jo said. "After the feud got started. They intermarried a lot—it was probably just a matter of forbidden fruit being so desirable. At least that's always been my excuse." She stood up. "I should never have left you all alone just because Hope was being herself. I should have come to Pennsylvania to see you, get to know you. One of my many mistakes. But I'm going to get about the business of trying to get things right. First thing on my list, I'll see what I can do about Hope." She went to Bobbi's bed first. "I don't want you to worry about your mother—I'll keep you informed but you don't have to take on this burden."

Jo opened her arms and Bobbi gave her a hug. "Thank you. Please let us know. We love her but—"

"I understand completely," Jo said. "I'll get phone numbers from your dad and I promise to stay in touch."

She opened her arms to Trude, and while the younger girl hesitated, she finally let herself be hugged. "Don't be too mad at our mom," she said.

"I'm not going to be mad at her," Jo said. "Not now. Now I think it's time we make up and get well. Right?"

Trude nodded. "We never got any gifts…"

"I know, darling," Jo said. She kissed Trude's forehead. "We have lots of time in front of us."

Charley had been very reluctant to leave Jo at the hospital, even though Jo insisted she could navigate the bus system. "Believe me, I can manage," Jo assured her. "I've done so many times."

"You don't even carry a phone," Charley said.

"I'm going to take care of that, too," Jo said. "To tell the truth, I never felt the need before. I have a perfectly good phone in my condo and at the shop and survived many years without a cell phone. Remember, life used to be like that. If we went shopping we made our calls when we got home. What a concept!"

"But, Jo, no car and no phone? What if the bus doesn't come? Or what if there's some bad character on the bus?"

"You're spoiled, Charley. The bus is probably safer than a parking garage. But now that my daughter is at the lake, I'm rethinking the car also. Suddenly I have a lot of running around to do. And a lot of people to call. For today, I'll be perfectly fine. Go back to the lake, see if you can explain all this to the girls while I dig a little deeper."

"I don't want you taking the bus after dark…"

"Go! I'm as capable of taking the bus or a train as you are! I don't know how long I'll be in trying to see Hope and talk to a doctor."

"I can see Jo home," Frank chimed in. "I'll even tell John she's loose on the mean streets of Saint Paul—I'm sure he'd be happy to provide car service, as well."

"Everyone is being ridiculous," Jo groused. Then she turned and went to the elevator, trusting everyone she was leaving behind to go about their business.

Her first mission was extremely frustrating. Hope was in a locked ward, listed as a patient in observation. She was an adult, a single adult making her own decisions unless a psychiatrist said otherwise. And she wasn't to have visitors for forty-eight hours while she was being evaluated.

She went back in search of Frank and eventually John. Charley was thankfully gone. To her relief she found that Frank was more than willing to help in any way he could but he didn't think it would be beneficial to Hope or the girls for him to step in as a legal guardian. But he did offer to help Jo in that capacity if necessary. John was friendly with a couple of the psych doctors and could find out when she'd be able to visit and what she could do to help. Then John drove her home.

But Jo didn't stay there. John had barely pulled away when she was off again, on the bus. This line she was quite familiar with—she rode to the stop nearest her sister's house. She rang the bell and rapped on the door. It was a long moment before there was a shadow over the peephole and the lock slid.

Louise towered over her. The expression on her face was equal parts surprise and displeasure. "What are you doing here?" Louise asked.

"I've come to ask for your help."

The corners of Lou's lips turned up. "Well, isn't that a surprise."

"We're losing our children, Lou," Jo said. "And our grandchildren. It's time to put this bitterness behind us and pull it together."

"And how do you suppose we're going to do that?"

"I imagine it will take hours if not days of negotiation but I believe we can do it. We have to for the sake of our family."

"I see. You're willing to negotiate? And what do you have to offer in the bargain?"

"The truth," Jo said, standing as tall as she could. "We'll work some things out or I'll tell."

Louise flinched. "No one would believe you!"

"I'll risk it," Jo said. "But what I'd rather do is talk. Louise, I'm sorry for what I did, and though you haven't said so, I know you have your own regrets. Let's end this. We've already lost so much, not the least of which—each other."

Louise seemed to think about that for a long, difficult moment. Then she backed up and held the door open for Jo to enter.

★ ★ ★

Krista was not surprised to see her boss waiting near the lot with the swing. He walked her most of the way around the lake every day. Sometimes he held her hand for a few seconds. He smiled when he saw her coming. She smiled back, knowing it was a little crooked.

"Want to talk about it?"

She laughed a little. "You really don't have time."

"Long story?"

"About three generations. Listen, why do you hold my hand? Are you coming on to me or something?"

"I know you've been locked up for twenty-three years but you said you had television. Don't you get it? I like you. I like your determination. Your boldness."

"Boldness," she said with a laugh. "I'm hard, that's what I am. Didn't your mama tell you not to get mixed up with hoods?"

"You're no hood," he said. "Are you having some kind of PTSD about jail or something? Anything wrong with work?"

"The work is great," she said. "My family is a wreck, that's all. And I'm sure I'm part of the problem. A large part of the problem. Can you imagine what it must be like to have your sister or your auntie be an ex-con? And you know me—I don't soft-pedal it. They get squeamish and I have to shove it right in their faces."

"Really on a roll, aren't you," he said with a laugh. "What happened?"

"You really want to hear this? My sister came with her daughters and was acting so crazy that her girls borrowed her car in the middle of the night, got in an accident and everyone's in the hospital. They're okay but it turns out Hope isn't just an uppity bitch—they put her in the psych ward because she's delusional. Maybe bipolar or something. And man, I was so hard on her. She's crazy and in need of help and what did I do? I came down on her."

"But they're okay now?" he asked.

"They're going to be fine. Except Hope. Hope's going to need help and who knows if she can get better."

"I'm sorry, Krista. You must have so many adjustments to make. And families, by their very nature, get messy regularly. I can relate. My own family has had similar ups and downs. We had some messes to clean up…"

"What kind of— Oh, I'm sorry. That's none of my business…"

"I brought it up, you didn't. No one went to jail or anything, but not for lack of trying. I got into trouble when I was a kid—I didn't want to be a poor farm kid. I wanted to be a rich city kid, one whose way was paved with money. So I tried to hang with the rich guys, tried pretending to be one, then took it out on my family when dishonesty didn't work out for me. I drank too much, drove too fast, partied with the best of them, and once I finally made my way to college, I got tossed out for not only failing but getting into trouble."

"What kind of trouble—I'd love to know."

He took her hand and they walked a bit. "Well, let's see— on a drunken dare, I streaked through a Gophers' football game. A couple of friends of mine and I put a skunk in the dean's office. And there were multiple instances of disorderly conduct. It just took me a longer than average length of time to figure out the world didn't owe me anything. Meanwhile, my parents were furious and confused, my sister was ashamed of me—she didn't invite me to her wedding. I married the first girl who would have me, had a couple of kids I couldn't support, stumbled from job to job and messed up every one until my wife did the smart thing and divorced me. That's the condensed version."

She stopped walking for a minute and looked up at him. She was fascinated. He was such a stellar boss, such a supportive and understanding man; it was hard to picture him that stupid. That irresponsible. She smiled at him. "Kid stuff," she said.

He laughed.

"What turned you around?"

"Well, busted, a broke failure in all the ways I thought I knew better, I just went home to the farm. And of course I didn't make that easy on anyone. There was an adolescent piece of me that tried to make it all their fault, but they're old-school country people and didn't take the bait. Instead, they put me to work. Little by little, year by year, I guess I built myself up morally, got an education. My wife remarried and took the kids out of state and I wanted to be close to them so I got the only job I could find in Arizona—at a resort. And that began the resort trade for me. Many disappointments and failures led to me finally landing on my feet, after being bounced on my head many times."

"How old are you, Jake?"

"Me? Forty-six."

"Where will you go from here? Another resort?"

"I might have one or two more in me," he said. "But I kind of like it here. I bought a lot on this lake. Someday I'll put a house on it. This is where I'm from—I grew up around here. My mom and dad are gone now but my sister and brother are here and my kids are pretty much raised."

"What happened to the farm?"

"My sister's husband farms. Sometimes I help, like around planting and the harvest, but they bought me out. I always thought it was a poor farm, that we were poor. We weren't poor but my folks didn't indulge—you never know when a bad year is going to just about wipe you out so you don't go buying your kids fancy things when you need a new combine."

"What's that?"

He laughed and dropped an arm around her shoulders. "A harvester. Would you like to see the farm sometime?"

"I would," she said somewhat excitedly. "But... Well, I don't have a lot of extra time. There's my cousins at the house, my mom coming on days off or sometimes I go to Saint Paul on my day off. And...you know... But I'd like to."

"One afternoon when your house is kind of stable and your cousins can part with your company, after you get off work, we'll drive over. I'll introduce you to the combine." He gave her shoulders a squeeze. "Feeling any better about your family issues?"

"I am, now that you mention it. But I'm not sure why."

"You talked about it, for one thing. You're not alone, you know. I'm really glad you decided to give Lake Waseka a chance."

"Listen, have you dated a lot since your divorce? I mean, are you collecting women or something? Because I'm pretty awkward when it comes to this boy-girl stuff and I don't want to be stupid."

"Nothing will make you stupid, Krista, but that's a fair question. I've been single fifteen years and I've had a few girlfriends. I was with one for a couple of years and I guess everyone thought we'd end up married but we didn't. I was transferred and we talked about her coming with me, but it ended up we spent too much time thinking about it. I guess it wasn't quite right or it would've worked out. Right?"

"Did *she* work for you?" Krista asked.

"She's a high school teacher. Listen, there's no policy forbidding employees from dating each other. But there is a stern policy against sexual harassment, so if you ever get the feeling your job is at stake because I like you, all you have to do is say something. I understand. It has to be mutual, right? I don't want to make you uncomfortable."

"Oh, now that's a first for me," she said.

"Huh?"

"You don't watch prison movies for fun, do you?"

He seemed unable to help himself. He laughed at her. "No."

"Not even *Orange Is the New Black*?"

"What's that?"

She put her hands on her hips. "What do you watch on TV?"

"Um…news. Golf tournaments. I don't watch a lot of TV. Do I make you nervous?"

"No," she said. "I've just never had anyone like me before."

"That's not true," he said. "You're really popular in the restaurant. You work hard, smile a lot, make everyone laugh. And they don't even know what I know. Do you think someday you'll introduce me to your family? Your cousins?"

"I don't know," she said. "First, the farm."

"It's a deal. I have to get back to work soon."

"Which lot is yours?"

"The one with the swing," he said, urging her along.

She actually gasped. "I love that spot! Did you put up the swing?"

"I did. I'm working on some house plans—just rough sketches. I'm going to turn the house so I'm not looking at the lodge from inside the house. I'll be able to see it from the yard but I want a pure view of the lake."

"What about winter?" she asked.

"Same view in winter," he said.

She giggled. "You know what I mean."

"You've been away—winter here is brutal but beautiful. You shouldn't live in a place like this unless you have things like plowing worked out. It's important to stockpile food and firewood in case of power failures. As long as you plan, winter on the lake can be good."

"How long are you planning to work at the lodge?" she asked.

He shrugged and put his hands in his pockets. "The company that sent me says the owners are pretty happy with the place right now. So, a while. Maybe a year, maybe a little less. I'm pretty sure they'll want me to take it through another winter. Last year was the first winter we offered winter sports and it did pretty well. What usually happens if I can turn a place around, they hire their own manager and I move on to the next challenge."

"It sounds…maybe fun," she said. "And you're good at it, aren't you?"

"Mostly," he said. "Sometimes I have to shut 'em down. I hate that. People out of work, a good property closed, sometimes bankrupted owners who really hoped for the best… I do my best. I love a place like this. A few changes, a little face-lift and we're doing great."

"That's so cool," she said. "Go back to work. I've got to get home and get the update on today's dysfunction. I'll see you tomorrow." She trotted off. "Remember, you promised I could see the farm."

"I'll remember," he said, watching her go.

She jogged the rest of the way back to the lake house. Meg was on the porch with a book in her lap.

"Did you have a decent day?" she asked.

"I had a great day," Krista said.

Chapter Twelve

When Jo entered her sister's house, she took a deep breath. The clutter was choking. "I don't know how you can live like this," she muttered.

"It's better than an empty apartment and no car. We'll go in the kitchen," Louise said. "I'll make tea. You can state your business."

"Tea. Good idea," Jo said. "Hope and my granddaughters are in the hospital. It's a long story, one that I didn't know before today." She sat down at the kitchen table, pushing a few things out of the way to make a place for her tea when it was ready. "It seems that when Hope left my house to move in with Mother and the judge, that was approximately her last touch with reality. I thought she was just a liar. Embarrassed by the family she came from. How could I blame her?"

"Our family was nothing to be embarrassed about," Lou said defensively.

"Yours wasn't, maybe. But the homelife we had with Roy was rocky and unstable on the best days. And when we got back from the lake that summer it went completely to hell. Roy had wandered off and this time it was different. He never came home. I knew too much had happened and he wasn't off on some bender that he'd call a business trip when he came home. My children were falling apart and he was gone for good. Poor little Beverly was in the hospital, almost catatonic, barely holding it together. I had nowhere to turn and collapsed."

"You were never strong," Louise pointed out.

"Not in the ways you were."

"The judge offered to help you," Louise said. She delivered a cup of tea to the table.

"There were conditions," Jo said. "When I couldn't tell him where Roy was, he hit the roof. All this tragedy and loss in our family and my husband hadn't been home or at his office in Rapid City? Hadn't been in touch? The judge said I should pack up my house and come to live with him and Mother and he would find Roy and secure a divorce for me and I could start over. A single mother living with her children and her parents."

Louise put milk and sugar on the table and sat down. "I don't know why you would hesitate. That bum never did do anyone any good."

"You know exactly why I hesitated," Jo said. "I couldn't have the judge looking for Roy and finding out he was connected to other missing persons. So I just said he was the father of my children…"

"You loved him!" Louise said. It shot out of her like an accusation.

"Oh, Lou, I hadn't loved Roy for a long time by then. He was an irresponsible drunk. I'll be the first to admit that when I met him it was like magic." She stirred milk and sugar into her tea. "For a while, everything was like a dream come true. I thought it would last forever."

Judge Berkey and his family weren't exactly high society in Saint Paul, but they were damn close to it. Mrs. Berkey brought family money to their marriage and the judge was very influential. They belonged to a prestigious country club in Maplewood where the judge golfed, Mrs. Berkey played bridge and there were regular social and charity events. Louise and Jo grew up in that club; it was where they had their debutante balls. They were both popular in high school, where they were cheerleaders and homecoming queen candidates. Louise was introduced to Carl Hempstead at the club right after her college graduation and a wedding was in the works within a few months. Carl was a young businessman, already successful at the age of thirty-four, ten years older than Louise, and that made her feel extremely sophisticated. They were planning a wedding and simultaneously building a large house in Maplewood.

Josephine was finishing her last year of college during the wedding planning and was to be the maid of honor, of course. She almost didn't graduate because of the swirl of social events surrounding Louise's wedding, but she squeaked through, got her degree in communications just before the wedding, a degree she didn't expect to put to much use.

Just days before the wedding Roy called Carl to say he was going to make the event, after all. Carl said he hadn't even talked to his brother in a year but had called him to tell him he was getting married. They were ten years apart in age and after their parents died Roy, while still a boy, had moved in with an aunt and uncle. Roy had been in the Army but was discharged and couldn't wait to meet the new bride.

"You'll have to move groomsmen around a little and make him your best man," Louise instructed. "He's your brother!"

"I don't know," Carl had said, scratching his chin. "We're not close. He's young and not exactly what I'd call serious..."

That was possibly the first time Louise had called Carl an old fogy.

Then Roy sauntered into the groom's dinner party at the club and took everyone's breath away. Louise was the first to nearly swoon when she saw him—tall and lithe with fierce blue eyes, and the light brown hair that flopped over his forehead was streaked by sunshine. He had the devil's dimples in his cheeks, straight and strong white teeth and was dressed in a new, tailored Yves Saint Laurent suit. He kissed Louise's hand and she said, "I can't wait to introduce you to my sister."

It was like a fairy tale. The best man and maid of honor got more attention for their dancing at the wedding than the bride and groom...

"But I didn't care," Louise remembered, sipping her tea. "I never dreamed anything so perfect could happen at my wedding. The groom's long-lost brother shows up, looking like Robert Redford but better."

"Carl was a very good-looking man," Jo said.

"He was, and he looked even better standing next to Roy. That Roy, he sure knew how to play to the crowd..."

"How long was it before we realized he had no job, Carl bought him the suit and the haircut, that he wasn't just very social, he always had an angle. He flirted with all the old ladies, paid Mother a ton of compliments, schmoozed the judge..." Jo sighed. "I should never have been taken in by him. I shouldn't have married him."

"Hah! Only a woman with no nerve endings would have turned him away. He was like a sex machine!"

"No, he looked like he should be a sex machine. The truth was after several drinks all his equipment shriveled and died."

"He got three on you," Louise reminded her. "Three in four years."

"The price was so high," Jo said. "The joblessness, the arguing, the shame. Every time he let us down, every time we had to ask Carl for a loan or a job or a gift, I wanted to die. Then he'd go on the wagon, shape up a little bit, get a job, help with the girls. It never lasted long but it seemed to be exactly the right amount of time for me to trick myself into thinking things would be okay. I knew we'd never have much but I didn't care as long as we could stay one step ahead of the poorhouse."

"Remember when we used to drive by the county home and the judge would say, 'There's the poorhouse. That's where you end up when you can't pay your bills. Take a good look.' And we were terrified of ending up there," Louise said.

"Looked pretty decent to me," Jo said.

"Well, it wasn't actually a poorhouse, how about that?" Louise said. "It was a county-funded nursing home."

"I think we were doomed," Jo said. "I think on the day Roy turned up, we were doomed. There was always all this tension between us. You had the well-off husband and I had the loser, but the handsome loser. How'd he always know the latest dances? All the most hilarious jokes?"

"He hung out in a lot of bars," Louise said.

"He went to a lot of parties," Jo said. "No wonder we had issues, you and me. My situation, my husband, it would drag down anyone."

"And then Carl got quieter and quieter. He got old. At thirty-four he was a handsome and sophisticated young businessman and at almost fifty he was gray, balding, thick around the middle, tired…"

"I loved Carl. He was good to his brother. Better than he should've been. He did that for you and me, I think," Jo said. "So we wouldn't end up like Carl and Roy—estranged and strangers. I'm so sorry—it was my fault. I should've divorced Roy and gone on welfare. The outcome would've been better. I should have seen it—you and me—we were destined to end up like this. We were doomed."

"Except at the lake," Louise said.

Jo picked up her teacup. "We're going to need something a little stronger..."

By the time all of their daughters were in school, Lou and Jo had each been married over a dozen years. They needed a break from their city lives, from their husbands, from their parents. Life for Jo was always a struggle and Lou's existence had become dull and monotonous. But in the summer they could leave it all behind.

Jo recalled that one of her best summers was when Beverly, her youngest, was eight and Roy had a good job. He worked construction and it was hard work but the pay was good. He was exhausted and dirty, but he only drank on the weekends. Carl drove them both to the lake on Friday nights and when he arrived Roy needed a beer, a shower and a back rub, in that order. Nothing brought Jo so much pride as seeing her handsome Roy come in wearing those tight jeans and dirty work shirt, his eyes tired, his hands roughened by calluses. He'd held down this job for months and even Carl was more animated and talkative. It was such a great summer, Jo and Lou even talked about whether it was possible to just stay at the lake year-round.

It didn't last. The school year started and they were back in the city. Carl became quiet and distracted by the heavy burden of his company; Roy was laid off a few times and unemployment not only made him irritable and Jo cautious, but the judge and Grandma always had opinions about how the sisters conducted their marriages.

In the spring of '89, Roy got a job in sales in Rapid City. He wanted Jo to move to Rapid City with the girls and she really didn't want to, but she still nurtured hopes that her husband could break through his personal cloud of perpetual failures.

"Oh, God, you can't be serious," Louise said. "When has Roy ever kept a job for more than six months! You'll no sooner get there than you'll be headed back here! Or somewhere else!"

"Maybe if we start fresh, somewhere new, somewhere he's not carrying the load of his past reputation, maybe it will make a difference," Jo said.

"You'll have no one!"

"Roy complains that I value my relationship with you more than my relationship with him," Jo said.

"He doesn't complain of that when he needs money!"

"Don't throw that in my face," Jo said. "It's cruel."

"Think about the winters, Jo," Lou pleaded. "If you think they're tough here, wait till you try South Dakota!"

Jo played the middle ground. She told Roy she refused to move anywhere until he'd been in that job long enough for it to be a secure position. She told Lou she hoped to move to Rapid City for Roy as soon as he could offer her some reassurance he had a solid, long-term job.

"That'll be the day," Lou said.

"Nice," Jo said. "Can't you at least say you hope my marriage can recover and last?"

"I'd love to," Lou said. "If I thought there was a chance in hell."

Roy was only able to get back to Saint Paul for a couple of weekends in more than three months, but he looked great. Or maybe Jo was looking through the lens of a woman missing at least the illusion of a happy marriage to a handsome, sexy man. She may have lost the glow of true love but she never forgot the fairy-tale quality of meeting him and falling for him. It had seemed that her dream man appeared out of no-where and shook her to her core.

"I think maybe Roy has really changed," Jo told her sister.

"How many times have you believed that?" Lou said sourly.

"We should have something to eat," Louise said.

Jo looked at her watch. It was getting late. The summer sun was low. She knew she had to pay attention to the time and think about catching that last bus. In this part of town they stopped running at ten. "I didn't mean to stay so long. I know it's going to take more than one conversation. I can come back tomorrow, after I've been to the hospital. I'm sure after tomorrow the girls will be gone—home with their father. Hope's going to be another story."

"But she'll be okay?"

"I don't know," Jo said. "I'm not even sure what's wrong with her, other than the fact she's been lying to herself for so many years she believes her fantasies. Charley said Hope was telling herself some nonsense about coming home to hear about Mother's will."

"Will?" Louise said. "What about her will?"

"Apparently she thinks there's a fortune to be left to her."

Louise laughed. "By the time it gets down to her, she'll get enough to be able to take herself out to a nice dinner."

"I had no idea she was suffering from a serious mental ill-ness…"

"It's not your fault. I'll scramble us some eggs, make some toast." Lou pulled out a frying pan, a couple of plates, a dozen eggs and a loaf of bread. And a bottle of Jack Daniel's. "Since we're getting to the serious stuff. Say whatever you like about me, I don't think I'm ready to talk about that summer with-out a little of this."

"I was the one to say we'd need something stronger," Jo reminded her. "May I have an ice cube, please?"

"Would you like a glass with that?"

"No, no. I have a perfectly good teacup."

Louise cracked eggs into the pan, her back to Jo. "Do you still think about it?"

"When I can't stop myself," Jo said. "You were so angry with me before anything went wrong. We barely spoke on the way to the lake."

"I couldn't believe you'd leave me. Us. Move away? I knew it was a stupid idea."

"See, you always do that," Jo said. "I'm well aware of all my shortcomings. Calling me stupid isn't going to help us now."

"I didn't call you stupid!" Louise said, sliding bread in the toaster. "I said it was a stupid idea and I stand by that. Roy had let you down and disappointed you for over fifteen years—I couldn't believe he was actually going to come through for the first time, do right by you and the girls. I couldn't believe you'd be happy."

"I knew I wouldn't be happy," she said, pouring a small amount over an ice cube in her teacup. "I thought I'd probably cry every day, but I was going to give it one more go, make the ultimate sacrifice, move away and devote myself to my marriage and my family. And then, when it didn't work, I was going to be finished. I was going to admit I'd done everything I could and leave him for good. But I just couldn't do that until I knew I'd tried everything. One more ice cube, please. No, two more."

"You never said that," Lou said, handing her the ice cubes from the freezer. "You never said that," she repeated.

"No, I didn't. Because it would have put a fire under you. You know how you are—when you want your way, you're just so fucking relentless!"

"And you're just so fucking stubborn!"

Jo took a tiny sip. "I'm still stubborn. I think things through for a long time. Sometimes too long. But you make up your mind in a second and that's that."

"Well, be grateful I could make a quick decision when you needed it most or who knows what would have happened."

They went to the lake the day after school was out as usual. Roy said he'd come in two weeks, stay a few days. Jo hadn't seen him in a long time, six weeks or so. They talked when they could and he sounded happy. Excited and motivated. He hadn't been slurring. He'd even sent her some money! "Baby, this is it! This is what I've been looking for! I'm leading in sales for our team—time-shares everywhere."

"I thought it was investment properties," she said.

"It is," he said. "Some people want to use the properties for vacation for a few years and then sell them and upgrade—it's complicated. It's a point system for those but we have some investment properties for sale. Big sales bring big commissions."

"People want to vacation in Rapid City?" she asked.

He laughed. "Some do but our properties are worldwide. I can sell you a time-share in Maui from here. I can get you a summerhouse in Morocco! It's real estate, just not the usual thing. We don't sell them to live in so much as to invest in— buy and sell. This is the company headquarters but there are lots of offices. I've even looked into some transfers later, after I've proven myself. Maybe Florida. Maybe Hawaii. How do you think the girls would like to live in Hawaii?"

Jo was almost afraid Roy might pull it off, turn into a responsible man, though doubt and fear clouded her vision. She dreaded the idea of moving away. But to Lou she remained positive and optimistic. Lou was all too ready to condemn Roy and Jo wasn't going to give her any fuel.

Lou and Jo were at each other. The strain it put on their relationship to dance around the idea of being separated by so many miles was tearing them apart. Nothing had ever kept them apart for very long—a week or two at most. They talked every day even if they didn't see each other. Two or three times a day sometimes. The anticipation of Roy coming to the lake had them both a bundle of nerves.

He was making the long drive from Rapid City—over eight hours. By the time he arrived it was after eight. Jo wore her prettiest sundress and fixed her hair. When he pulled up to the house she flew across the porch, down the steps and across the yard and into his arms. He kissed her wildly and for a moment she was transported back in time and became that young girl who saw her prince appear in a formal ballroom.

But only for a moment. Roy was not alone.

A second car had followed him onto the property and a couple was getting out.

"Roy?"

"Oh, babe, this is Ivan and Corky," he said, turning her toward the couple.

The man, who was about forty, was striking with his dark hair and eyes and a thin mustache. He smiled and she thought his teeth were so white they gleamed. He gave a small bow. "How do you do," he said with a slightly foreign accent. "Roy has been talking about you for weeks. He's so proud of you."

Me? she thought. Roy had said a lot of flattering things to her but never that he was proud.

"This is my companion. She's called Corky."

Corky was beautiful but very young—early twenties. Her blond hair was silky, her boobs full and perky, her lips red, and she smacked her gum. "Nice to meetcha," she said.

"Ivan is one of our biggest clients, Jo. I invited him to stay at the lake for a couple of weeks."

"You what?" she asked.

"I invited him to use the lake house for a couple of weeks. He was saying he really needed to escape the business of money and finance and get away, get back to nature, relax. He didn't want to be in a resort or hotel. I suggested the lake. I told him I was going for a few days and that you and Lou would make him feel welcome."

"Oh, Roy, I don't—"

"Ivan, come and meet my beautiful sister-in-law, Lou Hempstead." He pulled Ivan to the porch where Lou stood, curious, waiting to find out what was going on. "Lou, this is a business associate of mine, Ivan."

"Indeed a great pleasure, miss," he said, taking her hand.

Jo had dressed up for Roy but Lou was wearing shorts and a halter top; her feet were bare, her hair pulled into a pony-tail. Carl couldn't make it for the weekend so she didn't fuss about her appearance, but with her long legs, she made those shorts look fantastic. She wore no makeup but her cheeks were rosy from the sun, and on her face her expression was thoroughly nonplussed.

"But how long have you been here? Already tan as a beach beauty!" Ivan looked around. "I envy you this little hidden paradise! It's perfect! You are so kind to have us. It's my intention that you never even know I'm around unless I'm doing something to help you."

"Mr....?"

"Just Ivan, my dear girl. You'd never remember the last name. I've brought some provisions to add to your kitchen. I'll get them in a moment. Will you show me around your little paradise?"

"I...suppose..." Lou said.

Lou was clearly gobsmacked. This was unprecedented. They never had guests at the lake. That Roy would do this without even asking must have stunned Lou to the depth of her being. Jo leaned into Roy and whispered, "What are you thinking? They can't stay here!"

"Why not? There's tons of room. We can give him the boathouse. He's an important client, Jo, and this is exactly what he said he was looking for. You wait, you're going to love him! The women all love him!"

"We haven't even seen each other in weeks!"

He nuzzled her neck. "Believe me, we're going to spend plenty of time together. Where are the girls?" He wandered away from her, yelling, "Girls!"

They came flying from all corners of the house—two from up in the loft, two from down by the dock, two from the second bedroom, all of them running to throw themselves on their daddy or uncle. Within moments the house was teeming with people—Lou and Ivan had completed their short tour and now were laughing in the kitchen, working together to pull out snacks and drinks. Ivan made his "companion" a drink and she settled at the table with it. Jo noticed she was quiet but smiling all the time. She was so well put together, her long, red nails and matching toes, glossy lips. She didn't say a word for the longest time until she pulled a pack of cigarettes out of her small purse. "Mind if I smoke?"

"I saw an ashtray beside the lawn chair on the grass, Corky," Ivan said. Then he leaned over and whispered something to Lou and she *giggled.*

Lou and Jo sat with their teacups holding a splash of Jack Daniel's on ice and tried to remember how this suave and handsome stranger with the young, blonde appendage had insinuated himself into their sacred summer retreat. It started with drinks and snacks that lasted until after the children had gone to bed. Ivan had them laughing at his exploits, told them crazy stories of all his travels and the odd people he'd met along the way.

"He was an expert flirt," Lou said. "He always found an excuse to whisper in my ear or touch my knee, and when I got a little nervous he whispered, 'Don't worry, I'm not going to put you in an awkward situation.' I asked about Corky, who seemed to only come in the house to freshen her drink and then was gone again. And he said something like he was clever with money but he seemed to make mistakes with women. He said they weren't a couple. He said, 'You'll see.' Then he asked if there was a bed somewhere in the house she might use. He was bound for the boathouse. Clever—he let me know right off they weren't sleeping together. And that he wanted a private place of his own..."

"I should go," Jo said. "I have a long bus home. I'll come back tomorrow. We'll find some way to negotiate a truce. I hope."

"You started this," Lou said. "You brought it up. I think I was the one who wanted him to stay."

"I think so, too," Jo said, looking into her teacup. She took a sip.

"It was the dumbest thing I've ever done, to take that lying bastard seriously."

"I've had a lot of experience in that if you'd like some pointers," Jo said.

"I was having fun. I hadn't had fun in so long. He made me laugh until I couldn't sit up and then he'd ask me all these questions about myself, my education, my life, about motherhood. He'd wanted children, he said, but he'd never met anyone he thought could be his companion for a lifetime. He could see how my husband was so lucky. And he wasn't just fun in the evenings with his charming stories—the first morning they were there I got up to find him in the kitchen getting breakfast together. 'What do the children like?' he asked. And in the afternoon I'd see him sitting alone on the dock and find him reading some sophisticated book in a foreign language. He couldn't stay away from the Wall Street news. He had that damn phone—that cell phone the size of a brick. He needed to be in touch with his investment adviser and broker. And he said, 'My dear,' in that fancy accent. 'My dear, I'm afraid I may have to leave suddenly. There's a hotel in Cabo I've been watching…a great investment opportunity…'" She shook her head. "He'd leave from time to time, alone, come back with something—steaks, liquor, wine, fresh vegetables, sweets…"

"My Jesus, wasn't he slick," Jo said. "What was that accent? British but with a little Russian affect?"

"Who the hell knows? It was all fake."

"He knew what he was doing, that's for sure."

"Magnetic," Lou said. "If you ever tell anyone this I will find a way to punish you forever. I'm more embarrassed by being suckered by him than what I really did to him."

Jo was shaking her head. "You shouldn't be. He was a professional. A con man. A gambler. How long was it before he started talking to you about property?"

"It wasn't too long, a little while," Lou said. "I was pretty worried when Roy left, but there didn't seem to be any reason—Ivan was a perfect gentleman. Aside from being charming and helpful and wildly sexy, he didn't make any demands at all. I think he'd been there a week." She laughed suddenly.

"I haven't heard you laugh in years," Jo said.

"I can't believe we're doing this," Lou said. "I don't want to talk about this. I want to shut it down. Bury it."

"We tried that," Jo said. "Listen, neither of us is happy. Before that summer, despite all our issues and problems, we counted on each other and we were happy. Not giggling fools,

maybe. But we managed. We've got to get back to our families. My daughters need me and yours need you, too. Megan
is not well, Lou. You don't want her to slip away without
mending things, without letting her know how much you
love her. And Charley..."

"Charley hates me," Lou said. "I failed her."

"You were a grieving mother when Charley needed you
and you just didn't have the energy to focus on her accidental
pregnancy. You should have. I should have. We did the best
we could. But she's found her daughter and has a relationship
with her and her children. Charley is a grandmother! And
there's Eric, your grandson. We have to pull it together. We
should've pulled it together years ago."

"I thought you hated me," Lou said.

"Well... I did," Jo admitted. "But I also loved you. And
I was so hurt that you turned your back on me. So I turned
away, too." She smiled a lopsided smile. "Sisters. Best friends
and enemies."

The first week Ivan was at the lake he stirred curiosity
about his experience and travels and wealth so they asked
him many questions. He explained that he'd started small and
sold property at a profit, doubled his investments and sold at a
greater profit, doubling again and again. It was pretty simple
math. And he bought in places almost guaranteed to bring
an excellent return.

After a week Ivan started asking Louise about her and Carl's
investment strategy. He offered to put her in touch with some
successful financial advisers. Had she considered investing
in property? Vacation and recreational property. He'd done
business with the company Roy was working for since long
before Roy had been hired. Roy was a new kid, Ivan said,
but he liked him and thought he'd go far. The resale value

on his condos, hotels, apartments and houses was amazing. He didn't buy hotels alone—he was part of many limited partnerships. They were safe investments, he said. He always chose resort communities—Hawaii, the Bahamas, Mexico. Romantic getaways.

"I'd be willing to meet you in any of those places to tour the properties. Your children are nearly grown. Maybe you should start dabbling in these opportunities."

"Meet me?" She laughed. "I'm sure Carl would like that idea!"

"Bring your sister along and we'll have Roy meet us. It's very doable."

She started having fantasies of escaping to some sunny, sandy island without her husband and children. She knew that would never happen but Lou was thirty-nine and it had been a long time since a man paid attention to her. And this wasn't just any man—he was sexy, handsome, rich, educated, sophisticated.

She didn't ask herself why a man with these exclusive properties all over the world would want to spend a couple of weeks at a stranger's lake house. It was a nice lake house. But it was a family house! Full of children.

Then there was Corky. She was stingy with her words and only said things like, "Perfect day for a tan," or "Such a cute sundress." And she drank a *lot*. She was passed out early every night and very slow to rise every morning.

"Where'd you find her?" Lou asked Ivan.

"Poor thing was left stranded by a fellow I know so I've been looking after her for a while. I know her family. I've partnered with them on investments a time or two. I'm going to ship her home to her brother once I hear he's back in the country."

"Why would you look after her if she isn't your girlfriend?" Lou asked.

"Because I'm a very decent guy," he said with that beautiful smile.

"You should ship her to treatment," Lou said.

"Has a bit of a problem with that, I'm afraid," he said kindly.

That was the thing about Ivan; he never slipped. He never contradicted himself or acted in a rude or capricious manner.

Lou was smitten.

She might have fantasies about lovers and islands and getaways but she was not out of reality. She knew better. Carl managed their money and he kept his fist tightly around it. He did well with it, too—Lou and Carl lived comfortably.

But when Carl called to say he couldn't come for the weekend again, Lou almost broke out the champagne. She was being thoroughly seduced and enjoying every second of it.

"It was that second week," Lou said. "It was only the second week! And I realized later, that was when I gave him so much information. 'What's a house go for in your part of Minnesota, darling?' he asked me. And I told him what we paid for ours and what it was worth and he said, 'But that's splendid! What about a cabin like this?' And I gave him my best guess. He asked about Carl's company and if he was happy because that was the most important thing, that a man be fulfilled! And I told him I had no idea. Carl never seemed particularly happy to me. He seemed worn down by work. And Ivan said that was a tragedy. For me as well as Carl."

By the time they got to this last chapter, they were propped up in Lou's king-size bed, pillows behind them, more Jack Daniel's in their dainty little teacups.

"It was all so lovely," Lou was saying. "Like visiting a posh vacation spot. Every day he would pull some treat out of that Lincoln. Filets for dinner, Bloody Marys in the morning, wine coolers in the afternoon."

"He made the most delicious and rich stuffed mushrooms—a chef in France showed him how," Jo said.

"I haven't been able to eat a stuffed mushroom since," Lou said.

"He gave us bracelets he bought in Mexico."

"A wrap from Spain…"

"By the third week we were putty in his hands…"

Corky, always a bit tipsy, had opened up—Ivan was a friend of her brother and father. Ivan was her protector, almost like a guardian, and when she was dumped by a man, left with only a suitcase, not a dime, heart in tatters and her family out of the country, no help in sight, Ivan took charge. He said, *Don't worry, darling. I'll look after you until your brother is back. It's no bother.*

"Really, no bother at all," Jo said.

And where were the children during this party atmosphere? They were about—checking in, looking for food, wanting someone to watch them in the lake, asking to take out the rowboat. Jo and Lou were experienced mothers and, even with the distraction of Ivan, they checked on the kids, counted heads, kept track. The girls were safe at the lake, as long as they had boundaries and lifeguards, though every one of them swam like a fish. Carl called to check on Lou and the kids but as long as there was such a houseful, he said he had plenty to occupy him in the city—his company was demanding of his time. Not unusual for Carl the past few years. He seemed not to take note that it was so exceptional to have guests at the lake and strangers at that. He promised to be down the next weekend.

One weekend too late.

Chapter Thirteen

L ouise, the most practical and least romantic of the two Berkey sisters, was experiencing a change in perspec- tive. Ivan's allure was quickly capturing her. She con- fided in Jo that the idea of being with him was unbearably tempting and she wasn't sure how long she could fight it. It had been so long! Carl was not the most romantic of hus- bands. Maybe she could find a way to take a brief trip. Carl never denied her anything, and if she said she had a desperate desire to take a break in midwinter and do a little shopping in Miami, he might just go along with it to keep the peace.

"Don't lose your mind," Jo said. "I know you're having a struggle right now and it seems perfectly logical in your mind, but it wouldn't be worth risking your marriage, your family."

She was simply so turned on she wasn't sure she could stop herself. Ivan had stolen a few nuzzles here and there, his lips briefly on her neck, a brief touch now and then. And what was the danger? Wasn't he just the most wonderful gentle- man? Look how he cared for Corky, who was a mess.

"I thought they were staying for a couple of weeks," Jo said to Lou one day. "They've been here almost three weeks!"

"So? Are they in the way? Are they intruding? Not really.

Besides, Ivan brings food and flowers and gifts constantly. We've never been so pampered."

Jo watched her sister, so unsentimental, so immune to emotional displays, being stung and becoming a featherhead. She realized this was how she'd looked to Lou all these years that she couldn't be sensible where Roy was concerned. She was constantly falling for his charm, believing his lies and, worst of all, lying to herself.

"The way Ivan and Corky drink, you want to get mixed up with that? After seeing what I've gone through with Roy's out-of-control drinking?"

"Well, clearly Ivan can handle it even if Corky can't," Lou said. "It hasn't stopped him getting rich, has it?"

"What if he's not really rich?" Jo asked. "Maybe he's just a braggart. Big talker like Roy!"

Lou leaned close and whispered, "I peeked at his checkbook. *Tons* of money. He said if I want to meet him somewhere, he'll pay for everything."

Jo wanted to ask if they'd had sex yet but she knew it was unlikely—they were almost never alone together. But it was coming, she knew. Desperate and fearing she might lose her sister, she watched vigilantly. For the first time she noticed the way Ivan and Corky looked at each other. Once in a while they exchanged very brief, meaningful glances or a few whispered words. He would tell Jo and Lou he was running to town to look around and then on his way to his car he'd whisper a few words to Corky. One early evening when the kids had dispersed, the little ones to the loft and the oldest to the beach parties with the lodge waiters and waitresses across the lake, Ivan said he was going off to take a shower before a nightcap by the outdoor fire. Lou decided it was a good time for her to dash into the shower in the master bedroom. That left Jo in the house and Corky in her lawn chair outdoors beside the ashtray.

Jo sat at the breakfast bar, paging through a magazine, watching. She was surprised she hadn't noticed anything odd before. Corky waited just a couple of minutes and then crossed the yard to the boathouse. She'd followed Ivan to the boathouse before. She was something of a pest; she wasn't enjoying the lake house as much as Ivan was and would rather have been at some resort.

Jo crept down to the boathouse and went underneath, where the boat and some supplies were kept. The finished room was on the second floor, up a flight of outdoor stairs. When you stayed up there you could hear the water lapping against the dock all through the night. And when you were hiding where the boat sat, you could hear the voices of anyone inside.

She didn't hear voices. She heard a soft thumping. Squinting into the darkness, straining to hear, she thought there was heavy breathing. She frowned. Then came the moans. A couple of hard grunts. And the inevitable giggle. She heard Ivan's voice: "Jesus, you're crazy. We don't want to throw this whole thing for a fuck."

"You like me crazy," Corky said. "Oh, baby, how long do we have to stay here?"

"A few more days, I think. I've almost got her. She's ready to be plucked."

"Do that to her and she'll cash in her entire inheritance," Corky said. "Oh, Ivan, I want you back."

"A couple more days is good for a couple hundred thousand. Now get out of here before someone notices. Go get drunk and stay out of sight so I can work my magic."

"Ohhh," she groaned. "I just got here! You can make up

something. Tell them what a complainer I am! Tell them you had to calm me down!"

"You have the 'I've just had sex' look all over your face," he said. "If things are quiet later, come back after everyone's asleep. I feel like something real dirty."

"I can do that," she said with a laugh.

Ivan, Jo noticed, had no accent. The sick feelings that spiraled through her were manic. She crept out of the boathouse in time to see Corky disappearing into the house. Jo then walked up the boathouse stairs to the bedroom loft and opened the door.

Ivan turned while still fastening his belt, grinning at her. "Well, my little chicken, you could have caught me just stepping out of the shower." He laughed lightly, unconcerned.

"Did Corky catch you just getting out of the shower?" she asked.

"No, thank goodness, but it was close. At least I had my pants on."

"But they didn't stay on for too long," she said. "Wouldn't want to blow the whole deal on a fuck."

He frowned. "I'm afraid you have me at a disadvantage…"

"Just tell me one thing," she said. "Was Roy in on it?"

"Darling, what *are* you getting at here? What crazy talk is this?"

"Drop the accent and tell me the truth. Was Roy in on it? Setting up my sister and trying to con her out of investment money?"

He stood tall and unsmiling in front of her. "I'm sure I don't know what you're talking about."

"I'm sure you do," Jo said. "He had to have known. The bastard, parking you here to take complete advantage of us. Of his family! I want you out of here. Tonight. Get your shit together and clear out!"

He stepped toward her. "I don't know what has you all worked up but let's calm down and just talk it through."

"I want you *out!*"

"Why? Because of Corky?" Finally, the accent was gone. He took another step toward her and gone was the princely fellow. "Roy found Corky. I usually work alone but she's a little addictive and Roy likes to share his good fortune. Roy said you'd probably be fine with this idea but I could tell in ten minutes that wouldn't happen. You're too wrapped up in old Roy and your sister has you jumping through hoops. Tell me something—did Roy ever suggest to you a little doubling up? Maybe adding another person to your entertainment? Because you and Corky...there's a thought I could get into."

In spite of everything that was happening—her husband setting up her sister, this bastard conning them, catching him just seconds before it all fell apart—she blushed at the thought of a three-way! Perceptive, that made him laugh. Charming Ivan's warm and inviting eyes turned sinister. Suddenly she was frightened.

"Did Roy tell you that my father is a judge? I bet you have a record twenty miles long. When I tell the judge you were set up to rob us, he won't sleep until he finds you and locks you up."

"I don't think so, sweetheart." He reached for her, grabbed and pulled her hard against him. He laughed as she pushed against him, fought against him, cried out for him to let her go. Her mind raced, what could he do to her? Beat her? Rape her? Drown her and say she fell?

"Stop it! Let me go! Don't you dare touch me! Stop! Help!" she shrieked.

He turned her around, a hand plastered over her mouth, and fell on top of her on the bed. His hand suffocating her and his long body pressing her down, she couldn't get out a sound.

"Always a little awkward when you get found out," he said, evil laughter in his voice. "Doesn't happen often, but there's always a risk. It's the risk that makes it fun." She bit his little finger and he howled in pain. "You bloody viper!" He drew back his hand and slapped her across the face so hard she wondered if he'd broken her jaw. He began choking her.

Then there was a loud *thunk* and he fell on her.

She pushed and struggled to get out from under his limp, heavy weight, her vision slightly blurred from the blow and her fight. She blinked several times to clear her vision. Louise was standing at the end of the bed holding an oar.

"Oh, God," Jo said.

Lou's face was angry and Jo realized she was angry with her.

"What did you do?" Louise spat out.

"What did *I* do? I found him out, that's what I did! While you were in the shower I saw Corky follow him up here and I spied! He had no accent, Lou! It was all a con and Roy had to have been in on it. He was trying to con you out of money!"

"You don't know what you heard," Lou said.

"I know *exactly* what I heard, and I confronted him, told him to get out tonight! I told him the judge would track him down and lock him up and he attacked me! I wouldn't lie to you!"

"You told me I was foolish!" Lou hurled.

"Turns out we both were! I foolishly believed Roy and we both fell for Ivan's bullshit story." She rolled him over. "Maybe we should tie him up…"

"Don't be ridiculous, he can't hurt both of us. Call the police or something."

"Um… Lou?"

"What?"

"He couldn't be… Come here. Help me find his pulse…"

The oar dropped and the two of them searched his neck, wrist, pressed ears against his chest, listening for a heartbeat.

"I can't tell," Jo said. "My own heart is beating so hard…"

"I think he's dead. Can you feel his breath?"

Jo leaned her cheek up to his nose. "I can't feel his breath but he smells like a distillery. Call the police. Or an ambulance. Or something…"

"What if they don't believe us?" Lou said.

"He was attacking me. You saved my life. Look at my face—he hit me!"

Lou squinted at her. "You only have a little pink slap mark."

"Oh, God. We'll leave him. Put that oar back on the wall. Corky will find him. It can be her problem."

"Was he really planning to rob me?"

Jo bit her lip and nodded. "He told Corky to go get drunk and stay out of sight so he could work his magic."

"I can't believe it," Lou said. Then she let out a bitter laugh. "I guess it wasn't possible someone actually wanted me." And then there were tears running down her cheeks.

"Don't be stupid—that's not what this is about! The only reason it was you is because he knows I don't have anything! Roy would've told him that. Damn Roy—he'd sell his mother." She looked around. "Lou, we're sitting here with a dead man."

"I killed him," Lou said. "I'm probably going to rot in jail. We spent three weeks with him—no one will believe he suddenly attacked you and I saved your life by hitting him from behind."

"Maybe we can get rid of him. We can throw him in the lake and everyone will think he fell."

"So our kids can swim around his dead body?"

"Oh, my God, what are we going to do?" Jo started to panic.

"Can we get him to his car?" Lou asked.

"Down the stairs? We'll probably all be dead after that. Why?"

"Corky's getting drunk and staying out of sight in her room. The girls are either across the lake or in the loft. If we can get him in his car maybe we can drive over to Winslett Lake and drive him right in—there's that drop-off. And it's five minutes away. There's never anyone around there."

"Oh, I don't know," Jo said. "What if we get caught?"

"Is it worse than murder?"

"I don't know. We have to decide right now. Before Corky comes looking for us or something. We either call the police and take our chances or bury him and tell Corky he left her here."

"What about his stuff?"

Lou looked around. There was one small suitcase. Corky had bags but it seemed as though Ivan kept going to the trunk of that Lincoln when he wanted something. Anything. Food, gifts, treats, clothing. "He's probably all packed so he can make a fast getaway."

Jo shuddered. "He said it was awkward when he got found out." She swallowed. "He didn't know the half."

"Go see if there's anyone outside. Hurry up."

"You sure about this?"

"I can't change anything," Lou said. "He was going to rob me and rape my sister but I don't have any evidence of that."

Jo took a breath. "I think we have to do this."

"I think he moved!"

They both stood stone-still for a long moment, watching him.

"He didn't move," Jo said. She poked him. "I think he's getting cold."

"Okay. Okay."

Jo scampered down the stairs and looked around. The light was on in the loft, where the younger girls were probably watching a movie. The older girls had gone across the lake in the boat to that cove where the secret teenage parties happened—and they knew they had to be home by eleven or else. The light shone from the room Corky was using—staying out of sight and getting drunk like a good girl.

Jo ran back into the boathouse loft. "No one around. Did he move?"

"Not at all. Oh, my God, what have I done?"

"Try not to think about it," Jo said.

Lou reached into Ivan's pants pocket and got his keys. She moved his car closer to the boathouse along the path used for the boat launch. They wrestled him down the stairs with great difficulty but then managed to get him into the front seat of the car.

Jo began to fasten the seat belt.

"Are you kidding me?" Lou asked.

"You don't want him bobbing around, do you?"

"I guess not. Follow me. I might have to drive around or circle the lake or something if I see people."

"Okay. And then when they catch us we can ask to share a cell."

"Oh, God, let's get this over with!" Lou said.

Jo snatched the keys. "I'll do it." She pushed Lou out of the way and got in the driver's seat. She pulled out of the property and onto the road slowly, casting furtive glances over at Ivan. To a passerby he might look like a passenger, maybe a sleeping passenger. If a police officer pulled her over, she would say he was drunk. He certainly smelled it. But in all their years at Lake Waseka when had they ever been pulled over or even seen a car pulled over by police?

Jo drove so slowly she was crawling. Lou was close behind her and Jo tried to pick up speed, but it was so hard. Her hands were shaking. When she got to Winslett Lake she drove along the dirt road that circled the lake. There was not so much as a light anywhere—no fires, nothing in the few cabin windows, no headlights. She stopped the car, cut her lights and just stared at the lake. There were No Swimming signs. It was very deep about six feet from shore. She knew she was going to have to go in with the car but she dare not leave any sign that she'd been there. She couldn't afford to lose a shoe; she didn't have a purse.

She was frozen. Lou, sitting in her car on the road, killed her lights. Just to be sure, she poked the body one more time. Nothing.

She put all the windows down, opened her door and held it open with one foot. Then she gunned the engine, popped the car into gear and shot into the lake. There was hardly a splash as the big Lincoln floated right in. As an afterthought, she unclasped Ivan's seat belt—if they did find him, he couldn't be strapped in to the passenger side of the car. She rolled out of the car and made her way slowly toward shore while the Lincoln floated on top of the water.

She stared at it for only a few seconds, then she got in Lou's car.

"It's not sinking," Lou said.

"That's all right. If someone sees it they'll think he had an accident. If they find him they'll think he drowned in whiskey. Let's just leave, please."

"But what if it doesn't sink?" Lou asked.

"There's nothing we can do! Want me to swim out there and jump on it?"

Lou didn't answer. She sat there, staring.

"Lou, I swear he was smiling," Jo said.

Lou gasped. "Look! What's that? Is that his body?"

"Is there a current?" Jo asked. "There's no current to pull him away!"

"I bet he *was* smiling, the bastard."

"Just hurry and go!" Jo said. "I'd rather not know!"

Lou drove slowly down the road away from Winslett Lake.

Jo showered and they both got into the big bed they shared when their husbands weren't around. They barely talked, though neither of them slept. They were terrified and shocked by what had happened and there were just little whispers between them. *We're going to hell. No, we're going to jail on our way to hell. There's no coming back from this. He was a bad person. But should he have died? I didn't mean to kill him, just stop him! We meant to sink him, though. It was self-defense. We're going to hell. I'm so afraid.*

They were awake at dawn because they'd never been to sleep. Corky, as usual, was very slow to rise. Of course she had a miserable headache. She didn't say anything to the women and finally Jo urged the children to the lake so Lou could handle Corky.

"Where's Ivan?" she finally asked.

"Guess," Lou said. "We found you out. Did Roy tell you our father is a superior court judge? He has tons of influence and resources. I bet there is no investment property, is there? No company, either? I told Ivan he could have a head start— I'm going to call my father."

"He wouldn't leave me!"

"Wouldn't he?" Louise asked. "It must be difficult to seduce rich women with your girlfriend tagging along. He said to put you on a bus—you'd know where to find him." Corky looked panicked. "Oh, dear, you're not sure where he is, are you? Maybe you should call that mobile phone..."

Without another word, the young woman turned and left the kitchen. She was back in less than five minutes with two suitcases. They were mighty big suitcases for such a little girl but Lou didn't offer to help.

The drive to the bus station was silent and far too long. When Lou got back to the lake house after the best piece of acting she'd ever done, Jo was waiting for her. "What did she say?"

"Not a word. Not even thanks for the ride."

"God, what if she talks to someone?"

Lou shook her head. "You think she's going to report him missing?"

"What about Roy?" Jo asked.

Lou's lips twisted. "I knew he took advantage of us. I knew he tried to lie his way out of messes. But throwing me to that wolf? His own brother's wife? His own wife's sister? How low can a man go? The real question is—did you know?"

"You can't be serious!"

"But I am! Did you know Roy was sending a con man in to strip me of whatever I had? No matter how much Roy does, no matter how bad he is, you not only forgive him, you defend him."

"Lou, I wouldn't hurt you."

"Well, you certainly could," Lou said. "You've got something on me now, something big. You could get back all that stuff from our inheritance you signed away. While I rot in jail."

Jo looked at her sister with horrible disappointment and anger. "I'd rather starve," Jo finally said.

Six days later Bunny drowned. Lou was so cold, so angry. She believed she was being punished. "We'll leave and never come back," she pronounced.

The sisters talked till four in the morning, sitting in Lou's big king-size bed not even acknowledging that this was how they'd been that night. It was that night that everything changed. At some point they both dozed off, then woke before eight because it was in both their natures.

"I hope you got what you wanted," Louise said. "I have a miserable headache and that summer is all in my head again like it was yesterday."

"Well, I never got over it, did you?"

"No, of course not. But I managed to not think about it most of the time. After the first couple of years."

"I want you to know I'm going to talk to Krista about it."

"Oh, damn, I knew it—you have to make a confession!"

"Sort of. Krista went to prison for killing a man. She had to do it. He was coming at her. But they didn't really believe her. She paid the debt for herself and for everyone else. I will ask myself until I die if we just lost our minds that night."

"Do whatever you want, Josephine," Louise said. "I'm too tired to argue."

"Krista will keep it in confidence," Jo said. She started making up the bed out of habit. "God knows I can't tell Hope. And Beverly just doesn't deserve that burden—she's been so happy the last dozen years or so. You should consider telling Charley—see if you can have a conversation with her about why things were the way they were at the time she needed you. Really, think about it. I just wanted you to know what I'm going to do. I don't want you to be confused—it's not to punish you. I think you did what you had to do. I think your decision in the one second you had to think about it was the right one. I know you did it to protect me, and believe me, I was in danger."

"There's something you never made clear," Lou said. "Roy. You wouldn't divorce him. You said he ran off. Did you never hear from him again?"

"Oh, I heard from him. Not very long after. I imagine

Corky found him. I was so furious I could barely speak and it's a wonder he understood my blabbering. I raged at him for putting Ivan on us, to use me and con you. And in our family home. I told him I would never forgive him. He said he was sorry. And asked me to tell the girls he said goodbye."

"Why in God's name didn't you divorce him?"

"I did," she said, straightening up. "I wasn't going to let Daddy hunt him down and find out what kind of business he was caught up in. Besides, I wanted to do it myself. It took a while, but I finally pulled the money together."

"Do you know where he is?"

She shook her head. "I had to place ads to try to locate him before my divorce could be made final but there was never a response. He would be sixty-seven now if he's alive. With his high-risk behavior, what are the odds?" Jo looked around, plucking the nightgown that she'd borrowed. "Thanks for the loan of a gown. Louise...look at all this stuff. Have you turned into some kind of hoarder?"

"You think I enjoy this? I've been saving it."

"What the hell for?"

"I don't know," she said. "For us. For our retirement. For something urgent or otherwise unaffordable."

"Us?" Jo asked. "What us? We've been in a feud for almost thirty years!"

"Yes," Louise said. "But if something happened to you, who was going to take care of you? One kid chose herself a new family. One moved to Philly to be a princess who never even called home. One was in prison. There was only me."

Jo put a hand on her hip. "Louise, if you were planning to take care of me in my declining years, why the *fuck* wouldn't you talk to me at church?"

"I find that language very offensive," Lou said. "And I

don't know why. I did my best. Everyone seemed mad at me when I had done my best."

Jo looked at her and just shook her head wearily. "You giant pain in the ass."

Four days after the sinking of the Lincoln, Lou spotted a small piece in the weekly *Winslett News*. A man had been found wandering the back roads of Winslett disoriented, injured and soaking wet, though he was a few miles from the lake. He was admitted to the hospital with a head injury and amnesia. He couldn't tell anyone his name. Then he wandered away from the hospital without being released. Anyone knowing the identity of the man was asked to call the local police. They printed a picture.

It was Ivan.

Chapter Fourteen

After several cups of coffee and a long, sobering shower, Jo headed for the hospital. She visited with the girls briefly; they were going to be discharged later in the day and hoped to go home. Frank was unsure if he should go so soon. Leaving the girls to shower and dress, she went with Frank to the hospital cafeteria.

"I'm sorry about the misunderstanding, Jo," he said. "You should have had more time with the girls."

"It wasn't a misunderstanding, Frank," she said. "Hope left me behind when she was a teenager. She knew what she was doing. She didn't want me to be their grandmother."

"It was wrong," he said.

"I'm not sure she could help herself," Jo said.

"I have an appointment with the psychiatrist at one o'clock," he said.

"She's not your responsibility anymore, Frank."

"She's still the mother of my girls. I think at this point they'd like to walk away and forget about her but that wouldn't be good for anyone. Not Hope, not them. Why don't you sit in with me?"

"I'll do that, though I don't know how I'll help. I'll try, Frank. I'll see what I can do."

"Hope has assets," he said. "And she has medical benefits— I saw to that. Not because I want to take care of her but because having anything happen to her without resources would just be a burden on the girls. They're so young. They're not spoiled." He laughed abruptly. "I thought Hope must be very spoiled, the way she talked. I was determined to prevent Trude and Bobbi from being like that if I could."

"She wasn't spoiled," Jo said. "She was deprived. At least, I felt she was. Her childhood didn't resemble mine—my parents were well-to-do. But the man I married couldn't hold a job to save his life. We struggled constantly. Hope always longed for things other girls her age had, things her richer cousins had. Things she thought I had had. But I fell for an irresponsible man. In the end he was my doom. The doom of everyone."

"I'm sure you did the best you could," Frank said.

"I thought so at the time," she said. "Looking back, I could have done so much better. All I did was blame people. I'll do what I can to help Hope through whatever it is she's going through but the important thing to me now is the chance to get to know my granddaughters. My youngest daughter, Beverly, has two children—a boy and a girl. We're not exactly close but we have a nice relationship. Trude and Bobbi have cousins. I'd just like to get to know them, Frank."

"I'll be happy to work on that with you but you're going to have to remember, the girls live in Pennsylvania."

"I'll find a way. And I promise not to crowd them," she said.

"I'm not sure if I know anything about you and your family," he said. "I'm not sure what's fabricated and what's real. Can you imagine my shock to learn you had a daughter just released from prison?"

Jo laughed slightly. "I'm starting to see the merits of an imaginary life. I'll be happy to tell you anything, Frank. It's not really as horrible as it seems on the surface, but it is complicated."

He looked at his watch. "We have a couple of hours before the doctor will see me."

She laughed again. "That should get us started."

There was not only enough time for Jo to tell Frank whatever he wanted to know about their family but also time for her to learn about his transition from VP of finance to bike shop owner. There were times during their conversation when he had to pause to read and send a text. "Excuse me," he said a few times. "One of the girls, wanting to know where I am and what I'm doing."

"Should you go to them?" Jo asked.

"No, they're fine. I'm right in the same building and they're safe."

Jo also learned some very disturbing things about the state of Hope's marriage. The most upsetting was to hear that for the past six years she would not admit to anyone that they had separated and divorced. "My son is now three years old. You'd think by now she'd recognize my marriage to Pam."

"Oh, she is in desperate need of help," Jo said.

"I think you're going to find she doesn't want help," he said.

"That's the most serious symptom of all," she said.

When the time came for the appointment with the doctor, Jo and Frank went to an office on the fourth floor. Frank introduced Jo to the doctor, but they didn't even sit down.

"I'm afraid I'm not able to give you any information on Mrs. Griffin's condition. We're very sensitive to issues of confidentiality and Mrs. Griffin hasn't given permission for either one of you to be informed of her condition or to make

medical decisions on her behalf. In fact, the only visitors she
has approved so far are her daughters."

"Wait a minute," Jo said. She put a hand on Frank's fore-
arm. "Doctor, will you give us a second?"

"Sure. I'll be right here."

Jo stepped into the hallway with Frank and spoke softly.
He nodded. Jo gave his hand a fond pat. Then she went back
into the doctor's office alone.

"Can you please give my daughter a message?" Jo asked.

"I'd be happy to."

"Please tell Hope that I'm available to help her but there
will be conditions. Therapy, for one thing. Maybe therapy and
medication if that's what you recommend. But her ex-husband
and her daughters are no longer taking her calls. You can tell
her the car they were in was a total loss but fortunately her
daughters survived without serious injury. So, I guess Hope
is on her own unless she wants help from her mother. But I'm
not willing to do that unless I have permission to speak with
her medical providers. If I'm going to help her and perhaps
take care of her, I'll need to know her medical condition.
How long do you imagine you'll keep her?" Jo finally asked.

"I don't know," the doctor said.

"Let me write down my number in case she doesn't have
it." She pulled one of the doctor's business cards from its
holder on the desk and scribbled her name and number on
the back. "I really must get one of those cell phones." She
took a second card for her purse. Then she put out her hand.
"Thank you, Doctor."

"I hope all goes well, Mrs. Hempstead."

Frank was waiting for her in the hallway. "I don't know
about this," he said. "I don't want her homeless, crazy and
wandering the streets."

"I don't, either. I'll check on her—I have my own sources.

Say, Frank, there's something you can do for me. I must have one of those cell phones. I've made it this long without one but now I find I have to cave in. Something affordable. Can you tell me what to buy? I really don't have time to do a lot of research."

"I can do better than that. When Trude and Bobbi are ready to go, we'll take you to buy one. There are no finer experts than two teenage girls. And it will help you stay in touch with them. They mainly communicate via text."

"Oh, I'm dangerously behind," she said.

"You'll be amazed at how fast you catch on," he said, dropping an arm around her shoulders.

A few days later Josephine found her life had changed in a hundred ways. Probably the most shocking was the iPhone. She called Charley, who passed her phone to Krista so they could talk. She called Louise, who answered in shock, amazed that Jo had come so far. She called Hope's doctor, who said that Hope, unsurprisingly, would like to see her. She called Frank.

She didn't have to call her granddaughters. They were with her when she picked out the phone, which Frank insisted on buying for her. Then they all went out to an early dinner and giggled helplessly as Jo learned to text, get email and use Google and other fundamentals of cell phone life.

She had an appointment with Dr. Sam Benoit, the psychiatrist. They shook hands and then Jo took her seat in front of his desk. She clutched her purse on her lap in front of her and he smiled reassuringly. "So, all these years without a cell phone and now you've become just another slave like the rest of us."

She smiled back. "That part didn't take any time at all. My

granddaughters taught me to text. After not really knowing them we're making up for lost time."

"Do you mind if I ask, how did that happen? No contact with your granddaughters?"

"I was always in contact with Hope, but we weren't at all close. She left my house and moved in with her grandparents when she was fifteen because they were well-to-do and could give her the lifestyle she wanted. Frankly, I grew tired of her judgment and disapproval and didn't try very hard to gain her acceptance. When her children came along she told me, not very politely, that she would send pictures and give them my letters but her husband was a very important man and she didn't want her daughters embarrassed by some of our family issues—predominantly her sister serving a prison sentence for murder. It was self-defense. It was tragic. But twenty-three years have passed and Krista's home now. Home and I must say emotionally much more stable than poor Hope. But back to your question—it wasn't true that Frank forbade us to have a relationship." She laughed uncomfortably. "Frank said he asked about me from time to time. He never even knew about Krista's prison sentence. I guess that was what Hope intended."

"People cover up things they find embarrassing," he said. "I suppose we all do."

"Is that all that's wrong with Hope?"

"Not exactly. Hope seems to suffer from a delusional disorder. She knows the difference between fantasy and reality but that's not likely to impact her interpretation of her life. Not now, anyway. Hope prefers her version of reality even though she knows it's mostly fabricated. She's in denial and has many creative excuses. I've prescribed a mild antidepressant and she should have therapy. I recommend an inpatient facility for thirty days followed by outpatient therapy. I'd like you to be prepared for something—this has gone on for so long I don't expect it will be easy to resolve. And in fact, it might never completely resolve. But she's functional. She's not a danger to herself or others."

"Is there something off in her brain?" Jo asked. "Is this a mental illness?"

"It's borderline. It is identified in the *DSM*—the *Diagnostic and Statistical Manual of Mental Disorders* published by the American Psychiatric Association. It falls into the same category as other disorders that are borderline, like narcissism, jealousy, that sort of thing. It's not curable but people who seek change through therapy have good results. That's the rule of thumb in most things—you can't change people but people can change. They have to want to."

"Hope doesn't want to, does she?"

"Not at the moment, I'm afraid. But that isn't necessarily permanent. Let's see how it goes."

"What am I going to do with her?" Jo asked. "I don't have a place for her."

"She might choose to go back to Pennsylvania. Doesn't she have a home there?"

"But no family support. They're done with this craziness."

"That might change her perspective," the doctor said. "There are other options, too, depending on Hope's acceptance—like transitionary housing. A halfway house. But let's not get ahead of ourselves. We have a long way to go."

Jo shook her head wearily. "I wish I understood why..."

"There could be a dozen reasons," he said. "Sometimes people fictionalize their lives for attention. Sometimes they're looking for excuses. Some think a good story will explain them better than the truth will. Some suffer from low self-esteem and think their fictional story makes them more interesting than they really are, while others were abused and an imaginary life helps them escape the reality of abuse. Then there are those who think if they tell the story long enough it will become true just as those who have told their story for so long it blends with the truth so thoroughly they begin to believe it. Whatever the cause, when it's protracted it becomes compulsive. It's a habit hard to break."

"How do you explain her meltdown?"

"Keeping up with the stories and dodging the consequences is very stressful—many sufferers change friends and even families often. And we all know them—some are more intense than others. There are some more popular than others. There were so many men claiming to be Navy SEALs that there's a website dedicated to exposing the frauds. The editor in chief of a major city newspaper spent his entire career claiming to be a decorated retired colonel who served in the war—he was exposed as never having served in the military."

"And people who lie to con you?" she asked. "To trick you into giving them money or something?"

"Not in the same category, I'm afraid," the doctor said. "That's a whole different thing. Criminal, deliberate, felonious...not represented in the *DSM*. No, people who make up false but entirely plausible stories and know they're not true but can't seem to stop doing it—that's a disorder we're familiar with. It pops up all the time."

Jo was intrigued. "It's so wrong to deceive people like that..."

"That's the irony," he said. "Most people aren't fooled. The taller the tales, the more doubt associated with them. There seems to be an interesting inverse correlation—true heroes seldom brag. People with solid marriages feel secure and don't seem to need to constantly remind the world how happy they are. Wealthy people seldom publicize their net worth. This isn't always true, of course—some people just have to toot their own horn. But it's often true that grand tales of heroism or wealth or romance are usually in play to cover up some sense of a deficiency. And of course delusional disorders like all disorders come in all sizes. I'd venture to say almost all Christmas letters are a little delusional."

"My daughter was sending Christmas letters signed Hope, Franklin, Bobbi and Trude for years after their divorce. She wouldn't accept it."

"She must have been so lonely," the doctor said.

"Do you think she'll get well?"

"I think she is well," he said. "The question is, will she stop fictionalizing her life? Let's see what comes with some therapy."

Jo went to see her daughter after her conversation with the doctor. Hope didn't look good to her, but she imagined that was to be expected. She was drawn and looked sleepy; her hair wasn't fixed and she wore scrubs. Someone had given her scrubs. Jo would find a way to get her clothes.

She embraced her. "Oh, Hope," was all she could say.

"I've made a mess, haven't I?" she said.

"Nothing that can't be worked through," Jo said.

"I think Franklin has left me for good," she said.

Jo pulled back, holding Hope's upper arms. "I believe he did that about six years ago. He has a wife and son."

"But once he thought it over…?"

Jo was shaking her head. She didn't have to say anything. Hope just sighed.

"Let's get you back on your feet," Jo said. "You're young. There are lots of possibilities for you, but only if you get help."

"I think it's too late," she said. "I have no one. Not even my children."

"Well, you have me, but only if you follow the doctor's recommendations. If you don't, I'm afraid you're on your own."

"Oh, I doubt he'll be much help," she said. "He wants me to go to a hospital. A hospital for crazy people."

"That's not correct," Jo said. "It's a rehab facility for people recovering from depression and other mental and emotional disorders. The doors are not locked."

"I bet they have rubber rooms…"

Jo laughed and smoothed Hope's hair. Then she clutched her hands. "It's all up to you, Hope. You still have family, but only if you're honest and truthful. You might be able to repair your relationship with your daughters in time, but they aren't going to help you pretend—they've been clear, they're done with that. I'll be there for you but only if you get help. So what are you going to do?"

"I'll do what you want," she said. "But I'm so sad. Do you think I'll ever stop being so sad?"

"What are you so sad about, darling?"

"I mapped out the perfect life. Absolutely perfect. And it didn't work."

Jo was flabbergasted. "That's because it was pretend."

"It was still perfect," she said.

Jo sighed. "I don't know if a month is going to be enough."

Jo couldn't help but feel she had failed her children, even though there wasn't much more she could have done. Hindsight is so excellent—now it was clear that had she contacted Frank Griffin years ago, things might have been better. She had met him at the wedding, of course, but it was like meeting him for the first time now. She liked the bike shop owner so much more than the VP of finance. The old Frank, in the company of his rich, stuffy parents, was so uptight. He had looked thoroughly bored and unhappy. What a shock to learn he was! But this Frank, comfortable in his own skin, was so charming and kind, so thoughtful and concerned.

She thought of Krista back then. She could not have stopped her from acting out no matter what she tried. Likely in the face of her family disintegrating around her she gravitated toward teenagers who she could attach herself to, feel acceptance—and they were a bad lot.

Her thoughts turned to Beverly. Beverly had come a long way—she was the content mother of two. But getting there had been such a struggle and no one could have made it easier for her. Beverly was the one who had been with Bunny when she drowned, Beverly felt guilty and responsible for twelve-year-old Bunny's death; sneaking out on the lake in the rowboat had been her scheme. She spent years in therapy.

Not many months after Bunny's death Beverly's counselor reported that her depression was not responding to medication and she was concerned by her suicidal thoughts. The counselor recommended a foster home where she might have a better chance of getting her life back. It was a farm in southern Minnesota and there were usually six teenagers at a time. They thought Beverly could benefit from a few months there—there were farm chores, animals, even riding horses. The couple who operated the farm were both social workers and could provide counseling as well as close supervision. Just a few months, the counselor said.

Beverly never lived at home again. She bonded with the Swensons, Joy and Glenn, and she blossomed through high school, even helping with other teenagers in residence. But Beverly was the only one who stayed on as the closest thing to a family member they had.

Fortunately, Jo and Beverly did stay in close touch and saw each other regularly. If Joy and Glenn came into the city, they brought Beverly to see her mother and there were days Jo could drive or take the bus to the farm to spend a day with them. That first year was so hard, being separated from her youngest child. But as Beverly grew stronger and happier, Jo realized it had been a godsend. A gift.

Beverly was forty now and it had really been no surprise— she was thoroughly a country girl. Her children, a boy and a girl, Alex and Becca, were twelve and fourteen. She had married a man who came from a big family farm near Red Wing and the kids had lots of 4-H blue ribbons for everything from canning to raising a calf. Though Beverly had never stayed a night with Jo, Jo had spent a few nights at Beverly's farmhouse. She loved Beverly's big, quiet husband, Tom. If Jo was visiting Beverly and her family, Glenn and Joy often made it a point to visit, as well. And it was no surprise to Jo when Beverly and Tom became foster parents.

Jo called her youngest daughter. "Beverly, it's Mom," she said. "You'll never believe what I'm calling you from—my very own iPhone. I'm even doing email."

"Get outta town!" Beverly said. "Tom," she yelled. "My mom has a cell phone and email!"

"Did hell freeze over?" he yelled back.

Jo laughed happily. "I have some things to tell you—I'll try to give you the condensed version." She explained about Hope and the girls and especially about Frank. She told her Megan was hanging in there but she certainly wasn't robust looking. Charley was managing all the details, Krista was working at the lodge and seemed happier than Jo would have thought possible and Jo and Lou were speaking again. "Not everything is resolved between us but I'm very hopeful."

"How in heaven's name did you manage that?"

"I think we can give credit to Hope, in a backward kind of way. I swallowed my pride and went to Louise. I told her our girls need us and we can't fail them a second time. Megan is sick, Hope is in the hospital, Krista is trying to get on her feet—we need to stop being angry and start supporting each other. We talked about everything. We talked all through the night. I think there's more talking to do, but unless I missed all the signals, Lou is ready to make amends, too."

Beverly's voice was very quiet. "I haven't seen her in twenty-seven years. I'm sure she still hates me."

"I don't think she ever hated you, Beverly. For a while she was angry with the world, and who wouldn't be. But it's been a lifetime. Surely we can all move on in a lifetime. You haven't seen very many of our family."

"Will Hope be okay?" she asked.

"I think so. But it's up to her. Krista has a good chance—she's a new person and she's amazing. Meg... I don't know what to expect. I've seen her a few times and she says she feels well but the disease and the treatment have taken their toll."

"And you, Mom? Are you okay?"

"I'm better than I've been in a long time, Beverly. I felt like I was in a holding pattern all this time and now I'm finally doing something. I'm making some plans, taking care of my girls, back in touch with my sister, spending time with my nieces, texting my granddaughters. I must start texting with Alex and Becca. Will you give them my number and ask them to try me? Tell them their grandma is rocking it—that's what Bobbi and Trude say. They taught me. I'm messing up all the acronyms, of course—they love that and LOL like mad."

Beverly laughed.

"I'll talk to Louise, Beverly. I'll make sure she's made peace with that night Bunny drowned. If she hasn't, I won't lie to you. All right?"

"All right. Does Krista have a phone?"

"Not yet. Charley shares hers but I'm thinking of gifting her one."

"Will you ask her to call me? It's been so long."

"Of course. And if you decide you'd like to show her the farm, she's really figuring out the bus."

"Mom? Will you please tell Aunt Lou I'm sorry?" she said.

Beverly hadn't said anything like that in many years and it broke Jo's heart. She didn't want her reliving the pain of it. "If you'd like me to, sure. But, Beverly, she knows it was an accident. Kids just doing what kids do—no malice and no wickedness, just a very sad accident. You have children—you know how hard we try to keep them from taking chances and we know they do, anyway. That night, that freak storm, it was just the wrong place at the wrong time..."

"That night it was Bunny who wanted to go, not me. But it was me other nights. It was my idea first, a year before. It was as much fun to sneak around, spy on our big sisters, creep out of the house and take out the boat after dark as anything we did at the lake. We used to spy on you and Aunt Lou. Listen to what you said."

"You did?" Jo said.

"Sure. We were never very sure what you were talking about, though. Usually complaints about Daddy and Uncle Carl."

That night, she thought. *That night she hid in the boathouse to listen in on Ivan and Corky the boat was there so the girls hadn't gone out.*

All this time that Beverly had felt the accident was her fault, Jo and Lou had felt the same way—that they'd been preoccupied with Ivan and Corky, that they hadn't been paying enough attention, letting the kids run wild. Not only were Bunny and Beverly sneaking out in the boat, Charley got pregnant!

"You'd been doing that for a year?" Jo asked.

"Yes. The big girls got to go to the parties with the other kids across the lake but we always had to stay in, play with

Barbies. It was as much fun to get the best of the big girls as anything. You're right, it's what kids do. Krista did it. Krista and Meg, I remember. When Charley and Hope wouldn't take them to the beach parties, they snuck out and spied on them."

"But if they took the boat to the parties…"

"You could walk there, remember? It wasn't close but you could walk there. Or you could untie the boat next door— that old guy's boat. Charley even swam home once, all the way across the lake, at night, no lifeguard…"

"Dear God," Jo said. "So much going on we didn't know about."

"You had six teenage girls," Beverly said. "We're foster parents and our kids are not always the best kids. I've learned to be vigilant, but a lot of that comes from the knowledge of what me and my sisters and cousins managed to get away with."

"Well, it served a purpose, then," Jo said, suddenly tired.

"Weren't we once the perfect family?" Beverly asked.

Jo couldn't speak? *Perfect?* They were never perfect! Horribly flawed and dysfunctional was the truth of it!

"At least that's how I remember it," Beverly said. "We had the best time. We were so close. Until Bunny died."

Jo talked to her daughter awhile longer. When they hung up Jo called Louise. "I'd like to have you come to my apartment tonight. I'd like to make you dinner. I'll buy us a very good bottle of wine. There are so many things we've forgotten to talk about. Good things."

Chapter Fifteen

The end of July at Lake Waseka was hot and steamy and there seemed to be more than the usual number of mosquitoes. It was just the three of them again— Charley, Meg and Krista. John came on the weekends and stayed as long as possible, sometimes leaving at three a.m. Monday morning so he could get to the hospital for early rounds and often taking Friday off to maximize his time with Meg. He gave Jo a ride to the lake once; she took the bus back to the city but came on her own another time, spending a night. When John or Jo visited, there was an air of quiet celebration, a big dinner, a lot of chatter and laughter.

Jo tried sharing memories with them, particularly the ones the girls were too young to remember, like the night Beverly was born right there in the lake house and how Lou took charge and helped her through the birth. She talked about Lou teaching the girls the latest dances and confessed there were a few times when Lou and Jo went skinny-dipping under a full moon after the girls went to sleep—until that one chilly summer night when Oliver, their next door neighbor, took a lawn chair down to his dock and plopped down there to enjoy a cigar while they nearly froze to death waiting for him to leave. It was a very big cigar and they shivered for hours afterward.

"You've been talking about my mother a lot lately," Charley said. "I'm starting to think you miss her."

"I suppose I did," she said. "We've had dinner a couple of times. We're trying to patch things up."

"Is Mother trying?" Charley asked.

"If you want the truth, Louise has been the lonely one. I had my work at the flower shop, the neighbors in my condo complex, the customers in the shop and all the other people who work in that little business district. I have a nice relationship with Beverly, and while she doesn't come to stay with me, I've spent time with her family at her farm. We've spent several holidays together. I've been busy all the time. Lou never worked and had only those women she saw for cards sometimes. I don't know how she lived like that."

"That's what stubbornness gets you," Charley said.

"If she decides to be less stubborn you just might try letting her off the hook. Or you could find you are just like her."

Krista shuddered at the thought.

What was she going to do when the summer was over? Where would she go? Maybe there was a small place for rent in the area and she could just keep her job at the lodge. Her job and her boss had become so important to her.

Krista had no normal role models or experiences in romance, in developing relationships. She didn't know how; it was that simple. She was mixed up with all the wrong kinds of people before she went to prison and more scary people when she was inside. Her only experience with dating was what little television she'd seen in prison or discussions with her therapist about how to have healthy adult relationships.

She couldn't believe how quickly her life had changed. She had only been back in the real world for a short time and she had a family to support her and she was being walked home by a sweet, handsome man almost every day. He had even kissed her. At first he had given her a peck on the cheek, then a brief kiss, then, most recently, they'd stood with their arms wrapped around each other and shared a deep and consuming kiss that rattled her bones. It took her breath away and terrified her. She'd felt suddenly weak and giddy; she was simmering inside with a heat that begged to be doused in satisfaction. She cautiously opened her eyes and found him smiling.

"That was nice," he said.

"Is there steam pouring out of my ears?"

"You look perfectly normal," he said with a laugh. "But I want to kiss you again."

She let her eyes drift closed. "Okay," she said, leaving her lips slightly parted.

He obliged. After that it became routine for them to walk together and then stop at the place where the swing hung from its sturdy branch, where they'd share several hot and exciting kisses. Jake had a way of holding her so tightly and yet she felt cradled rather than confined. She wished for him to hold her all the time. "What if someone sees us?" she whispered against his lips.

"I'd have to admit I have a big crush on the new waitress."

"I think you should know something—I'm scared. I've never been with a man who was nice to me. I don't know what I'm doing. This will probably end very badly."

"Why?" he said. "Is something wrong?"

"I don't know. How would I even know?"

"Krista, you're smart and intuitive. I watch you at work. You relate to people easily and you seem to instinctively know which ones to avoid. If anything about our being together like this doesn't feel right to you, you have to say so. I want both of us to enjoy ourselves."

"And you're enjoying yourself?"

"Oh, yeah. You're fun and you feel good. You're also smart. And pretty."

"I'm not pretty!"

"Yes, you are. The head valet, Dennis, has the hots for you."

"Dennis is seventy-five! By the way, why is he still working at seventy-five?"

"He gets the job done and he wants to work. I have an idea. We should have a proper date. What would you like to do?"

"I don't know," she said. "I guess we could go out in a boat."

"That's not a date," he said. "There aren't a lot of great restaurants around here and we don't want to have dinner at the lodge. We could drive over to Brainerd. Want to do that?"

"What happened to your marriage?" she asked abruptly.

"I'd be happy to tell you every detail but it is a long story. Basically we were unhappy together and my wife said she thought we'd both be happier if we weren't married. She also pointed out that arguing wasn't good for the kids. And she was pretty sure she outgrew me. We saw a counselor— twice. It was awful for a while. But then my wife remarried and wanted someone to take a turn with the kids sometimes so she could have a break, take a vacation now and then, and that's when things got much more agreeable. We're much better at being divorced than we were at being married."

"Would you do it again? Get married?" she asked.

"I don't know," he said. "Maybe. But to be completely honest, I don't want to rush into anything. And neither should you. You who claim to have no real experience with dating, with men."

"No, I have only bad experiences," she corrected.

"Well, look, I'd like this to be a good experience. Not

just for you—I'd like it to be a good experience for me, too. You're not the only one who hasn't been with anybody for a long time."

"What about sex?" she asked. "I suppose that has to be part of the experience, too."

"That wouldn't hurt, but it's not a bargaining chip. I think sex should happen between two people who like each other. And respect each other. That's the next level. You're not ready for that."

"How do you know?"

He raised his eyebrows. "You're worried about being seen kissing! You're not nearly comfortable that we're right for each other!" He kissed her forehead. "Sex will happen when we're comfortable with each other."

"Well, I can't wait for that."

He grinned at her. "For us to be comfortable with each other?" he asked. "Or for the sex?"

"All of it, really," she said.

"I love that you're so honest. You're not afraid to say what you think."

"I do feel afraid, though," she said. "I know I'll make so many mistakes living in this world—I just don't want to hurt anyone with my mistakes."

"You are a good, honest person, Krista. Follow your instincts and you'll be okay. So, how do you feel about dinner at a restaurant with me?"

"Will there be sex?"

He laughed. "No pressure, eh? No. No sex on our first date. We want to be very good friends first. We've done a lot of talking but there's more to be said. We both have baggage. I know you think you're the only one with baggage because of your stunning prison record..."

"You gotta admit..."

"I've had my own issues, just not as dramatic. I'm sure they'll show themselves before long and you'll have to decide if I'm worth putting up with. My wife said I was a selfish bastard who never thought of anyone but himself."

"You've obviously changed since you were married. I appreciate that you're afraid if you move too fast you'll traumatize me," she said. Then she smiled her impish smile. "I like you enough to call you my friend. Okay. I'll go on a date with you. I don't have a dress, by the way."

"We'll go somewhere not too fancy the first time. It's summer. Lots of campers take a night to go out to dinner. But don't you think I should meet your cousins before I come to pick you up?"

"Oh, you're going to pick me up?"

"Did you think I was going to make you meet me somewhere?" He put an arm around her shoulders and then resumed walking toward her house. "I'll go with you now if you like. I won't stay. I'll just say hello, then get back to work."

"You won't be missed?"

"I'm not on the clock. Elizabeth is covering for me."

"Oh, Elizabeth," she said. "You better check when you get back. Be sure she hasn't offended most of the guests."

"I know," he said. "I think she's getting better. Little by little…"

"Not very much. Every time she sees me I get the feeling I slept with her husband or something and just can't remember it."

He laughed. "Elizabeth has a husband? See—miracles do happen!"

They talked and laughed the rest of the way. Jake had his arm around her shoulders most of the way; she loved leaning against him. She liked him so much she couldn't wait to see what being very good friends felt like. It must be heaven to feel that sure of someone.

They walked down the drive and found her cousins sitting on the chaises inside the screened porch. Both of them reclined and both were reading in the balmy heat of the afternoon.

"Hi," Krista said. "Charley. Meg. I want you to meet my friend and boss, Jake. We're actually going to go on a date one of these days. Out to dinner. So we thought you should meet."

Charley sat up and then stood, her book left behind. She walked slowly to the screen door and opened it, taking a couple of steps down. She just looked at him for a long moment.

"Charley?" he said.

"Mack?" she said.

"Wow," he said. Then he laughed uncomfortably. "Charley! It's been a long time." He ran a hand around the back of his sweaty neck. "I'm not even sure when that was…"

"Ah, 1989," she said. Her voice was ominous.

"That's right," he said. "I was maybe nineteen."

"You said you were twenty-two," she said.

Again the uncomfortable laugh. "I was a young idiot. I apologize. I've completely given up trying to be cool. It's good to see you. I got older while you were doing something else with your time."

"Mack," she said. "Krista said her boss was Jake. That name didn't ring any bells."

"Everyone called me Mack back then. I'm officially Jacob McAllister but I go by Jake. Are you okay?"

"How long have you worked at the lodge? Not all these years?"

"No," he said. "I've moved around a lot the past twenty-five years or so. I work for a corporation in the business of renovating or closing aging resorts. I've been here a year but grew up around here so it was good to get home."

"You're from here?"

"Hey," Krista said, interrupting them. "How do you two know each other?"

Charley shifted her attention to Krista. "There's no way to do this delicately. Jake and I should talk privately. Right away. Before you have your date. Would that be all right?"

"You know each other?" she asked, knowing the answer already.

"We knew each other that summer. Twenty-seven years ago. Then we all left. And I didn't know where he was. I didn't remember his last name or maybe I never even knew it. We left the lake for good. We were young."

"Oh, God," Krista said.

"What's going on here?" he asked, clearly uncomfortable.

"Let's walk down by the lake, Jake," Charley said.

"It's great to see you, Charley," he said. "Although this is a little awkward."

"So you do remember," she said.

He stopped walking and looked at her. "You lied about your age, too."

"What happened?" she asked. "A few days after we were together I looked for you. I asked your friends about you. You weren't a law student and you weren't twenty-two."

"I was nineteen," he said. "I was a kid and I thought getting a job at the lodge instead of spending my summer pitching hay bales was my big chance. Hanging with the cool guys." His color darkened. "The rich, sophisticated girls. Getting lucky."

"And you bit off more than you could chew," she said.

"Look, Charley, I'm really sorry about the age thing. It was wrong of me. Really wrong. But we were both—"

"I got pregnant," she said, interrupting him.

His face went pale. "No," he said. He shook his head. But she was nodding. "How the hell...?"

"How well do you remember that night?" she asked him. "You were prepared, you said. Then you said you must've had too much beer..."

He hung his head. "Oh, God," he said quietly. "Oh, God. What did you do?"

"I had her. I gave her up for adoption."

"Oh, Charley, my God..."

"And then later I found her. Or I should say she found me. She grew up fine. She's happy. Married. She has two little kids, very young kids. She wanted to know about you and I didn't have anything to tell her."

"You didn't try to find me?"

"You ran!" she said. Then she looked over her shoulder and saw that Krista was just standing there, watching. Waiting. "Look, here's how it went. I went back to the lodge to find you a few days later and the other guys said you found out I was under eighteen and that my grandfather was a judge and you ran for your life. Quit your job and took off. I didn't know I was pregnant—I just knew the guy I gave it up to dumped me and ran. I didn't realize I was pregnant for another month or two. We were back in Saint Paul. And all I knew about you was your name—Mack. And that you'd lied about everything else."

"Didn't you ask someone to find me? Didn't you ask a few more questions? Because I was here. Just a few miles from—"

"Not long after I went looking for you there was an accident. My little sister drowned. They had to drag the lake to find her body. We packed up and left. This is the first time we've been back since then."

His mouth hung open as he tried to absorb everything. His

eyes squinted while he tried to remember. "A kid drowned," he said softly. "I remember thinking I was glad I wasn't working at the lodge when that happened. It was big news around here."

"You should've seen the people," she said. "They were lined up along the shore everywhere, watching. Waiting to see something gruesome."

"Oh, Jesus, I don't even know what to say..."

"Maybe nothing. Right now."

"I don't know where to begin to make amends..."

"Let's not talk about amends—there's plenty of blame to go around. We were kids. It was my misjudgment as well as yours. The only one you should probably make amends to is Andrea... That's her name, Andrea. She's beautiful and smart. And I'm not sorry she was born, hard as it was at the time. She was lucky—she had great adoptive parents. Did you marry? Have children?"

He looked shell-shocked but answered. "I'm divorced. I have a son and a daughter. My son is in the Army and my daughter in college. Charley, I can't imagine what it must have been like for you. Sixteen and pregnant." He groaned and shook his head. "I think at the end of the day you're lucky you couldn't find me. I don't know what I could've done to make the situation better. I wasn't known for wisdom back then. And you? Married?"

She shook her head and her eyes clouded with tears. "In a long-term committed relationship. We have a son. I know this is a lot to absorb..."

"Oh, Jesus... Krista," he said, turning. She was gone. "I have to talk to Krista..."

"Jake, let me," Charley said. "You should just let me. I'm not in shock."

He grabbed her upper arms suddenly. "Charley, I never

would have deliberately hurt you. If I'd known, I'd have done anything to help, to step up, but… I'm so sorry you went through all that with no one. I hope your family was supportive."

"Easy there, big boy," she said, shucking off his hands. "It was a tough time but in the end we have a daughter who is lovely and well adjusted, no thanks to us. I wanted to keep her but it's probably better that I didn't. She understands. We were young and stupid."

He ran a hand through his hair. "God. I want to meet her, of course. Will she want to meet me? Does she hate me for abandoning you? I should talk to Krista…"

She put her hand on his arm. "I think you should try to untangle your brain, Jake. Krista will be fine. You can talk to her later. You have a phone on you?"

"Yeah," he said, pulling it out of his pocket.

She held out her hand. "Unlock it and I'll add my number to your directory. You can call when you're calmed down, and if you want to talk to Krista I'll tell her. Okay?"

"You're pretty calm," he said. "You don't seem angry."

"I've had a long time to think about things," she said, keying in her number. "I've already answered all those hard questions—like why I had to give her up. You're pretty blameless. Except for that tiny inconsequential detail that you lied about your age and then ran like the chicken you are." She delivered that last with a sympathetic smile.

"I'm so sorry," he said.

She laughed lightly. "I thought I was in love with you, you know."

"You were too good for me. I liked you a lot. I figured I was doomed. I couldn't figure out how I was going to tell you I wasn't a college kid but just a poor, dumb farm kid. A nineteen-year-old farm kid with no college degree."

"It was a long time ago. You better not be lying to my cousin, though. If you do that I'll come after you. She just doesn't deserve any more bad breaks."

"I told you, that was then. I'm not that guy anymore."

"Go home, Jake. Clear your head."

He turned and started to walk away. Then he turned back. "Charley, thank you. Thank you for having our daughter."

"Where is she?" Charley asked Meg.

"I heard bathwater. Was that him?"

"How could it happen like that, huh? How could the father of my baby turn up dating my cousin? My cousin who has never had a boyfriend in her life?"

"Well, there was that one she shot," Meg said, making a face.

"That wasn't a boyfriend, that was a kidnapper."

She knocked on the bathroom door. "Are you in the tub?" she asked. "Can I come in?"

"What for?" Krista called back.

Charley opened the door. Krista was covered in bubbles. "I told Jake I would talk to you."

"You don't have to. I don't think I need the details. I get it. He's the guy who knocked you up."

"That's right," Charley said.

"Your heart was broken, I remember that. You were a mess. You suffered magnificently."

"I think you should listen to me," Charley said. "My heart was broken regularly and dramatically for at least a few years and your friend Jake wasn't the only culprit. You missed a whole fundamental part of adolescence because you were running wild with creeps and miscreants. Tragic broken hearts, one right after another, is the hallmark of being a teenage girl. I was also in a deep and bloody battle with my mother and Jake was the only thing I could fantasize into a way out of my predicament. But even though I had a crush on him and ended up pregnant, he wasn't what I really wanted. I thought I wanted who he was pretending to be, but that wouldn't have worked. And I ended up a pregnant teenager sent away to Florida to have and give away my baby."

"Is that what I'm supposed to understand?" Krista asked.

"Who are you angry with?" Charley asked.

"Myself!" Krista said. And then she slid under the water. She rose a moment later and wiped the bubbles from her face.

Charley sat on the closed toilet lid. "I had twenty boyfriends in high school. Most of them lasted a few days but there were a couple that lasted weeks. It didn't matter if I broke up with them or they with me—I was always crushed. I do think Jake was one of the cutest ones."

"Why'd you have so many boyfriends? Because you were pretty and popular?"

"You don't remember right—I was kind of a late bloomer. I was better looking in my twenties. I really came into my own when I got a talk show. Nothing makes a woman beautiful like self-esteem and confidence. But back to your Jake…"

"He's not mine! And definitely not now!" She dunked again.

"Oh, settle down. So, Jake lied to get his job at the lodge. He said he was older than he was, said he was a law student with an important father. We hooked up and of course, being the brilliant teenager I was, I wasn't on the pill. Can you imagine me asking Louise for birth control pills? I'd rather ask Godzilla. And the genius Jake said he had a condom but he didn't get it out fast enough. Hmm," she paused, thinking. "The whole thing was bumbling and clumsy. I wonder if it was his first time? Well, I'm not asking him. So—there you have it. We'd been flirting and making out about three weeks, tops. And it changed a lot of lives. But we're not long-lost lovers, Krista. We're both pretty embarrassed by how stupid we were. I was as stupid as he was, all right? Let's have that straight, should we?"

"You must have loved him," Krista said.

"I loved love! I wasn't going to come even close to figuring out what it took to really love someone for at least another five years. Krista, teenagers have no sense. Poor judgment is more normal than good judgment. In fact, those who traveled through those years without major fuckups were lucky."

"I'm living proof of that," she said.

"I don't know that you have to be nervous about Jake because of our history any more than you would be distrustful of me. But there is a favor I'm going to ask."

"I'd do anything for you, Charley. You gave me my first good underwear."

"Andrea wants to know who her father is and I'm going to tell her. She will want to meet him. Know him."

"So?"

"That might happen around here. She was undecided about coming to the lake for a quick visit but when I tell her... It may change her plans."

"What about him?" she asked. "Does he want to meet her?"

"Oh, yes, though he was pretty blindsided by the news. And he's scared she'll hate him, but she's not that kind of person. He, ah, thanked me for having her."

Krista went underwater again.

She finally came up and sputtered soap out of her mouth. "Stop that!" Charley said.

Krista wiped the soap off her face with a washcloth. "Is this dating in the free world?"

"It can get a lot rockier than this. Jake seems to have turned out all right."

Krista shrugged. "How will we know for sure?"

"We watch and learn. He was very nice. He actually got a little teary. I wonder what it's like to find out you have an adult daughter and grandchildren." Charley smiled. "I'm an accomplished investigative reporter. Want me to research him?"

"No," Krista said, standing up in the tub and reaching for a towel. "If he can take me at face value, I can do the same."

"But you don't have to," Charley said. "You have very good reasons to be cautious."

Krista toweled off. "I missed a lot of social skills in prison but I learned a few things the rest of you didn't. I can hot-wire a car, slip a wallet out of a breast pocket and I can read the hell out of people." Then she grinned.

Chapter Sixteen

August was upon them and Charley was growing restless.

"You probably need to get back to work," Meg said. "I can't imagine you lying around some lake house all summer long. Go back home. Krista and I will be fine. I'm doing well, John comes on the weekends and Jo is a frequent visitor. You're bored."

"I'm not bored. This is lovely."

Meg laughed at her. "You're so bored you're boring me. Go home. Find a great job!"

Work would help if she could bear to be away from Meg, but there was no work for her to go back to. She really thought Michael would have come by now. She knew it would be easy enough for him to get away during the summer session. He was preparing for Cambridge. And he was holding a hard line. They'd talked but they hadn't made much progress. And she'd only been home to see him once since April. They'd never spent so long apart. No job, no Michael? There were times she felt that at forty-four her life was over.

"It's Michael, isn't it?" Meg said. "You've been dancing around the subject all summer."

"We talk all the time," Charley said. And they quarreled a lot. Enough so that Charley always went down to the dock to talk to him.

"Right," Meg said. "Unless I missed something, you're no closer to resolving your standoff. Charley, what are you afraid of?"

"Look who's talking," Charley said. "After all your health problems and all the uncertainty, you moved away from your husband to spend a summer at the lake with your crazy family."

"That was a good idea. For John as well as me," Meg said. "I'm not the only one who needs a break from cancer. If I were in the city right now, John wouldn't be able to concentrate on his work. Not only does he need the distraction of work, his patients need him."

"And he needs you," Charley said.

"If I needed him close at hand he could take a leave but I'm so glad he hasn't. When he's hovering over me I feel so bad. I feel like because of me John has to be worried and sad."

"John's a strong man, don't worry about him. Worry about yourself."

"Charley, I am," she said. "This is what I wanted to do and it was the right thing. I'm at peace with everything. And this is good. It's everything I hoped it would be. Hell, it's more than I hoped. You bumped into Jake and now Andrea can get to know him. She can connect with her DNA, learn her biological family history. That wouldn't have happened if you hadn't come here. Have you told Michael?"

"I told him," she said. "He said, 'That's great.' But it wasn't convincing."

"I'm sorry. I think you should go home. Work things out with him."

"Easier said than done," she said.

Meg was quiet for a little while and Charley didn't speak. Finally, Meg said, "Listen, Charley, I hope it's not over between you and Michael. I love him and you two have been so good together. But whatever it is, end it on a high note. There's a lot to be said for letting go because it's complete and there's nothing more to do. Don't drag it out. Get it resolved. Put your affairs in order. Suffering sucks."

Charley wanted to ask Meg if she was suffering, if there was something they should talk about. Was Meg giving up?

But instead she said, "I'm fine. It's just easy to be lazy here, isn't it? But you're right—I'm going to write him a long letter. It's really not like us to be at odds. We've negotiated bigger things than this."

She looked at her sister and smiled. Then she thought, *Please don't leave me, Meg! Please!*

Jo asked Krista when her next day off was. "Great. I want you to get up nice and early and pack us a picnic lunch."

"Where will we have this picnic?" she asked.

"If no one objects, I thought we'd take the boat across the lake and find a quiet spot. Maybe an empty lot. We'll find something."

"Should I invite Meg and Charley?" she asked.

"Can it just be you and me? Just for a few hours."

"I'm sure that's okay. But are you staying over?"

"One night."

Krista wasn't overly curious about this invitation. When her mother visited they often found some excuse to get off by themselves to talk. There wasn't much either of them wished to hide from the other two women but there was so much catching up to do. Over the years their phone calls had been so short and their letters so guarded. Krista had tried opening up about her life at Chowchilla but she didn't want to say too much. So much of that life had been dirty and painful and she didn't want to see that pain reflected in Jo's eyes.

Pity. The main reason Krista didn't talk about prison life was because enduring anyone's pity was too difficult. Krista had so many adjustments yet to make. She would never be an ordinary, normal woman. She would always and forever be a woman who had spent hard time in a penitentiary.

When Jo arrived Charley and Meg wanted to know how Hope was getting along. "She's doing pretty well, I suppose," Jo said. "She's settled in a very nice rehab facility, but it's a hospital, not the Ritz. She's very clear on what's happening, but it's so amazing—she still slides into that old delusional way of thinking without so much as a comma in her sentence. She'll pop out something like, 'I wonder if Franklin will take time for a couple of weeks at the Cape with us.' And I just shake my head. She's depressed, of course. Her life as she sees it or wants it has been taken away. But the doctor said it would probably be like this for a while."

"Do you visit her a lot?" Charley asked.

"When I can," Jo said. "I admit, the whole scene depresses me, too! But if Hope will make an effort I'll support the effort."

"She's lucky to have you," Charley said. "You have such a forgiving nature. I don't know if I could be as forgiving."

"If it was your child, you could."

Their boat was a small fishing craft with a motor and oars in the event the motor ran out of gas or had some other problem. They settled in and Krista worked the motor. "Tell me when you see a spot you like," she told her mother.

After about fifteen minutes of puttering along Jo yelled her name and pointed. There was a spot with a short beach they could land the boat on. There didn't appear to be a house on the lot and above the beach was a grassy, shaded area. They pulled the lightweight aluminum boat up onto the beach. Jo spread a towel to put their picnic on, then settled herself on the grass beside it. "Let's see what you have here," she said.

"Tuna fish," Krista said. "With lettuce and pickles and chips and apples. I will never eat bologna again."

"Got enough of that, did you?"

"Almost every day," she said. "And I didn't like it that much before."

Jo popped the top on a canned lemonade. "We've had so much time together, you'd think we'd be all caught up. But things keep changing."

"With any luck things will stop changing all the time," Krista said.

"As a matter of fact, I'm making some changes, Krista. I think it will surprise you. I'm going to a part-time schedule at the flower shop for the next three weeks and then I'm retiring."

Krista gasped. "Can you afford that?"

"It turns out I can. I've been in secret talks with your aunt Lou. All these years I thought she was living in luxury—her own type of luxury—but in fact she's been putting money aside and saving for retirement."

"What do you mean?"

"Remember I told you back in the old days, when you were small, every time Roy and I needed to borrow, Lou would ask me to sign away a piece of my potential inheritance. Well, she said once Roy was gone and I was alone, she changed her mind. When the Grand Avenue house was sold so Grandma could go into assisted living and then the nursing home, Lou put the money in mutual funds and bonds, keeping it safe. Many of the more valuable keepsakes—art, crystal, silver, jewelry—she kept in her house." Jo laughed and shook her head. "You should see the place. Looks like a hoarder's dream. It's like a warehouse. When I asked her why, she said she didn't think I'd have anyone to take care of me in my old age and, typical of Lou, she didn't give me enough credit for trying to take care of myself. She was wrong. I was smart enough. I didn't have much of a job but I had it for a long time. I had a little IRA and I saved here and there. Plus, I lived lean. There wasn't anything I really needed that I denied myself, but I wasted nothing. It was a habit I formed when you girls were small and we seemed to always be on the brink of collapse." She took a bite of her sandwich.

"But you always sent me money!" Krista said.

"You needed a little to get you by," she said.

"Is that why you got rid of the car?" Krista asked.

"When the price of gas went a little crazy, I left it parked and made good use of the bus. Before long I decided it was crazy to keep a car I didn't drive when the bus worked just fine. Lots of people in my neighborhood used the bus. Lots of people in the neighborhood are now old like me," she added, laughing. "So, I'm retiring because there are things I want to do. I want to spend more time with you, I want to be sure Hope is getting what she needs and I'd like to see more of Beverly."

"Does this mean you and Lou are friends again?" Krista asked.

"You girls meeting at the lake for the summer made me realize how much our daughters need us, and need us to be sisters again. I guess we'll always squabble—we always have. But I'd like us to always make up, the way we used to. Our girls are slipping away from us. Literally."

"Meg."

"Lou rejected my comfort when Bunny died," Jo said. "Just in the way Lou has been secretly preparing to help me through retirement I've been trying to think of ways to reunite us. All of us. I'm afraid we might lose Meg. Lou and Charley have been bristling at each other for years. We have to pull together."

"Well, I hope you can if that's what you want," Krista said. "I don't know why it took you this long."

"Too much happened to us, Krista. I'm going to tell you about the week that Bunny died. About that summer before Bunny's death—but you can't write about it until we're dead."

Krista choked and turned it into a cough. "Write about it?" she croaked.

"I know what you're doing," Jo said. "Your questions and your hunger for detail lasted far longer than your therapy did. But you have to hold on to this last bit. We broke the law, Krista. And we're not really sure what the end of the story is."

Krista swallowed hard. "Go ahead, Ma. What did you do?"

Jo began with the sudden appearance of Ivan and Corky and how strange an occurrence that was. Krista remembered them, though vaguely. But she had known their visit was odd and the whole family was "off." She was not aware that Jo and Aunt Lou were being targeted. Jo explained that it was only a matter of weeks until Lou was convinced that Ivan truly cared for her and could also make her rich.

"You mean she was falling in love with him?" Krista asked.

"Probably not love," Jo said. "But he was seductive. And so handsome. And seemed so accomplished. He seemed sophisticated, talking about his favorite galleries in Europe, literature that moved him, famous people he knew. Lou found him captivating. And so different from Carl, who was kind and sweet and quite successful in his business, but didn't talk much and wasn't social. Ivan had traveled the world and Lou couldn't get Carl to go anywhere."

"We thought he was gross," Krista said.

"You didn't know the half of what was going on," Jo said.

"I was so afraid Lou was going to make a terrible mistake. And the worst of it was—I knew your father had something to do with it. He brought them, left them at the lake. Roy was in on the con, whatever it was. And Lou would never forgive us, never."

Jo told her the rest of the story, trying to emphasize how fast everything happened—her confrontation with Ivan in the boathouse, how terrified they were, how certain they were that Corky would freak out and tell the police they were murderers. And suddenly they'd done it. "And I was the one to sink that car," Jo said. "I saw his body float away."

"Holy shit," Krista said. "I almost hate to ask—what did you do with Corky?"

"Told her that Ivan had left her and put her on a bus. But that wasn't the end of it. A few days later we saw a small article in the paper—he was found and taken to the hospital with a head injury and amnesia. Then he wandered off. There was a picture asking if anyone had any information about him to contact the police. It was him."

"Then you didn't kill him!"

"I guess not but we also don't know if he survived. He might've wandered off and died from that head injury. Before we could even discuss if there was anything we should or could do, Bunny drowned and the whole world changed. Your father was long gone, Lou was in deep mourning and rage, Charley was pregnant. Oh, Krista, the whole family imploded."

"But, Ma, the last you knew of him, he was alive. Know what I think? I think he tricked you and everyone. He had himself a couple of hysterical women and if he wasn't dead you would've told the police everything—the scam, the con, his attack on you, everything. If they investigated him, they probably would've found a long trail of crimes. He tricked you, faked dead and disappeared."

"Well, I like that story. But I'm not sure the Winslett police were up to an investigation that complex even if we spilled the beans on him. It was more likely they'd have arrested us for assaulting him and trying to drown him." Jo looked down at her lemonade. "We got through it, somehow. And here we are, a family of women, picking up the pieces the best we can."

Krista lay back on the grass. "What the heck—you and Aunt Lou were bonded in crime! Why did you quit speaking?"

"Lou was never sure I wasn't in on it," Jo said. "She thought maybe I betrayed her. She thought I went along with Roy's scheme for money just so I could run away and be happy with Roy."

"Why in the world would she think that?"

"Because when your dad was at his absolute worst and I was ready to chuck it all, he'd find a way to convince me to give him one more chance. And one more and one more and I always did."

"You loved him so much," Krista said.

"I wish that were true. He was my addiction. And I was his enabler."

Krista was quiet for a long time, looking up at the sky. Finally, she said, "Do you suppose he's dead?"

Jo sighed. "God takes care of drunks and children, they say. He's probably out there somewhere."

"He hasn't been in touch?"

"He wouldn't dare, Krista. While Lou always accused me of being a sap for love and giving in to Roy, your father always accused me of being more loyal to my sister than to my own husband. Both of them were wrong." She smiled wanly. "See, you're not the only one who took the wrong path."

Charley wanted a fountain pen but she was going to make do with a black fine felt-tip. She wanted some of her personalized stationery but that would have felt phony. When was the last time she wrote a letter, in her own hand? Thank-you notes—she'd penned lots of those. But she usually composed email at her computer or tablet or even dictated into her phone.

She wasn't sure exactly what she was going to write but she knew what she wanted him to feel. That she was earnest, that she was vulnerable, that their relationship mattered to her, mattered more than anything. She treasured him. She wasn't saying no again; she was just going to ask him to give her time.

Darling Michael,

You can't possibly imagine how much I love you or how desperately I miss you. I reach for you in the night. Sometimes I catch a scent and think you're in the room. You're not just part of my heart but part of everything that is my being. I ache because we're in conflict, because we haven't been able to compromise. The one thing we've always been good at—talking a problem through—we've utterly botched.

This is undoubtedly my fault. I'm not my best self right now. Hell, I'm not even half myself. My job loss affected me so poorly and I realize I must have identified too much with that person, that talk show person. I wish I'd known there was a danger of that; I wish I'd been prepared for what it might do to us.

I write this to beg your forgiveness—I answered your

loving proposal with a kind of flippant dismissal when that wasn't what I was feeling. I was feeling shock. Not by the proposal but more by the fact there was something, no matter how big or small, that could come between us. I didn't think it was possible. I thought our commitment was for life. Mine was. No, mine is. I love you and I want to be with you forever. I'll do anything you ask. If marriage makes you feel safer and more comfortable, so be it. Anything you want. I love you and the thought of not having you in my life is torture. I've been in love with you for twenty-two wonderful years and I want more.

If you still want me.

Yours always,

Charley

A couple of days after Jo's visit Jake walked Krista home after work. It had become their habit to stop for a little while on that lot with the swing. Jake's lot.

"I love this space," she said.

He sat down on the soft grass and pulled her down beside him.

"You've been very quiet," she said. "You usually talk all the time, but the last couple of days…"

He gave a huff of laughter. "Have been very eventful. But you've been quiet, too. Did Charley's revelation shake you up?"

"No," she said. "I admit, it surprised me. But it all makes stupid sense—if she hadn't moved to California and made a life there, if she'd been around Minnesota, she might've found you. Do you wish you'd known sooner?"

"Of course. I don't know how I would have handled it as a younger man. I wasn't that great with my own kids but I love them and they love me. If I could have known her as a little girl, as a troublesome teenager, as a college coed... She called me," he said. "I talked to her last night. She has Charley's quick laugh and wit—she's hilarious. Telling me about her adoptive parents, her husband and kids—she had me laughing. I told my kids right away—I called Andy and Shanna. Shanna found it all completely romantic and asked if there was any possibility her real father might come forward and turn out to be a prince or movie star or something. I told her she was stuck with me."

"And what did Andy say?" she asked.

"He said he'd want to kill himself. He's twenty-three. I guess a twenty-three-year-old guy suddenly finding out he's a father would seem like the end of the world."

"You were pretty young when you started your family," she said. "I mean, the ones you had on purpose."

"Always in a hurry," he said. "Careless and eager, that was the younger me. It's such a relief to have grown up a little."

"What do you suppose Andy and Shanna will think when they find out you're seeing an ex-con?"

"They'll love you," he said.

"Oh, I'm not so sure about that," she said. "They might hide all the valuables."

He lay down on the grass and pulled her down, too. Then he rose over her and looked into her eyes. "And are you being quiet because suddenly I'm the father of your cousin's child?"

"Nah, that's nothing to me. Well, it is something, but you were pretty wonderful about the whole thing. Just the right amount of shock and remorse and happiness and willingness. I don't know much about men, you know. I mean, I just know about the wrong kind. I have a feeling you're special and I don't know why you like me."

"I told you why," he said. "I'm not going to keep feeding

you compliments and begging you to believe me. Just love me back."

She was startled for a second. "We were saying *like.*"

"I know. It's growing." He smiled at her. "Kiss me."

"You're not going to keep the truth about me from your kids, are you?"

He lowered his lips to hers and covered her mouth in a deep and delicious kiss. She lifted her arms to hold him, rubbing his back, her fingertips gliding up to his neck to thread into his hair. When the kiss was done for the moment he said, "I'm not going to worry about that now. But I won't lie to them. I've never lied to them." Then he kissed her some more.

Krista had never seen the possibility of this in her life. In fact, she hadn't imagined there would be a man in her life at all and certainly not one so wonderful. As for this kissing, she couldn't remember ever kissing like this. It made her insides all squishy and there was such wanting, a pulling, low in her belly. She held him tighter, opened her mouth for him, loved that he moaned.

"Are we almost very good friends?" she asked him.

"I think so, yes."

"Why are you waiting so long?" she asked.

"I want to go slow. I want us to last. I'm not playing around, Krista. I want you in my life."

"You understand, I'm probably going to be working through issues the rest of my life?"

"I probably am, too," he said. "I think I could be happy doing that with you." He sighed. "It's hard to be patient. I want the rest of my life to get here right now."

"And I want every day to last forty-eight hours," she said.

"I should get you home," he said. "I have a little work to do back at the lodge." He stood up and put out a hand to pull her to her feet. He kissed her forehead. "I'll see you early in the morning."

"I'll be there to bring you breakfast."

"What will you do tonight?"

"Oh, you know," she said. "We make dinner together. Relax. Talk. Read. Just the three of us tonight. Meg's husband will be here for the weekend."

"Was your visit with your mother good?" he asked.

"It's always good. We took the boat across the lake and had a picnic. We talk about old times. She's decided to stop working at the flower shop. She's managed the shop for years but she wants to spend more time with family." Krista enjoyed the feel of his arm around her shoulders. "She told me an interesting story about that last summer at the lake," she said on a whim. "I think I kind of remember it. She said there was a story of a man who drove his car into a lake around here and got hurt. There was a little piece in the newspaper—he couldn't remember who he was and they published his picture asking if anyone knew his identity. He went missing from the hospital and they were looking for him. She thought about that poor man wandering around, not knowing who he was, lost. But then Bunny was gone and we all left. You were here then, right?"

"I think I remember something about that," he said.

"Do you remember what happened?" she asked.

He stopped walking and turned her toward him. "Is it important to you to find out?" he asked.

She blanched, giving her head a quick shake. "It's not important. I was just curious."

"If it matters I can find out," he said. "I don't have to tell anyone why I'd be asking."

She almost laughed. That's how she ended up doing twenty-three. She was actually a lousy liar and her face showed too much emotion, too much of what she'd rather hide. "How could you ever find out now? It was so long ago!"

"I have a lot of family and friends around," he said with a shrug. "People who have been around my whole life. I even know a couple of guys who worked as cops around here. Remember, my brother and sister still live here with their families. By the way—I promised to take you to the farm. The next day off you have that your mother isn't coming, let's do that."

"Will I have to meet your family?" she asked.

He laughed. "Are you afraid to meet them?"

"Yes," she said. "What if they take one look at me and know I'm not good enough for you?"

"Oh, we better do this soon," he said. "You have to stop being afraid. You're too stubborn and strong to be afraid of a farmer and his wife, Krista!" They walked a little while. "That story," he said. "It's important to you, isn't it?"

"I wouldn't want anyone to know I was asking," she said. Then she felt her cheeks grow hot.

"Someday you'll tell me the whole story," he said.

"Maybe," she said. "I'm still figuring out my wayward life and how I ended up in prison."

"I can look it up anytime, remember?"

"Then why don't you?" she said. "Why don't you do that before you kiss me anymore?"

"Honey, I know as much as I need to know. And you know about me. I was a nineteen-year-old jerk who took advantage of some young girl, got her pregnant, ran away before she could even tell me… That wasn't even me at my worst. I was such a miserable idiot. I had a temper and got in fights. I resented responsibility, treated my family badly. I was jealous and thought the world owed me. I might not have gone to jail but I wasn't a very good person."

"And you just grew out of it?"

"Sort of. Kicking and screaming the whole way."

"What turned you around?" she asked.

"Church."

She stopped walking and looked at him. "Come again? You started going to church?"

"I was raised in the church. Not hellfire and brimstone, just a nice small-town Methodist church. When I was in my twenties and my wife was leaving me, a guy I worked with said, 'Jake, come on to church with me Sunday.' I said, 'No, thank you.' Long story short he kept asking and I finally went and found peaceful solutions to some of my problems. I found some answers and even more questions. Things started to be different then. Better."

She was surprised. Then again, it made sense. "So, you're religious."

"I guess I am. It works for me. Life just hasn't been as hard since. It was such a struggle." He shrugged.

"Oh, God," she said in a breath. "I'm never going to have sex, am I?"

He threw back his head and roared with laughter. "See how fun you are? I didn't take a vow of celibacy, so beware."

"Thank God for that," she said. "Hey! Am I a project?"

He frowned. "What kind of project?"

"You know—be nice to the poor ex-con. Save the bad lady."

"For Pete's sake, do you have to make everything about you? You don't need saving. But you could use a decent boyfriend. That's the only job I'm after. But I should be completely honest. I don't tell many people at the lodge. I'm actually an ordained nondenominational Christian minister. I don't work as a minister. Well, maybe I do a little bit—I teach a Sunday school class at my church."

Her mouth hung open. "Oh, God, I wanna die right now..."

"Let me guess, it's about you again."

"You're a fucking minister? Oh, Jesus, this isn't happening to me. How many times have I cursed since I've known you? Maybe not too many—you being my boss and everything." She ran a hand through her hair and spun around in a circle. "Dear God, I've been kissing and begging for sex with my boss and my boss is a secret minister!"

He laughed at her. "You'll get used to it. I'm not a bad guy. And I think I swear more than you do, especially during football season. Don't freak out on me—sex is definitely in your future."

"I bet it's not," she said. "I bet you're way too decent for me."

He put his arm around her shoulders again. "Come on, lighten up. I'm just a guy. Don't be so judgmental. You never suspected—that means I've just been a guy who, on the outside, seems normal and stable enough that you'd take a chance on me. And you're just a woman who is fun and pretty and sane enough that I'd want to be around you. You are, you know. It's kind of crazy that you're the most sane woman I've dated in the last twenty years. You shouldn't be. But you have this basic good sense. I watch it in the restaurant. You walk up to a table and know in ten seconds whether they're going to need a lot of attention or need to be left alone. And you're so good with the other employees."

"You learn to make the right friends where I came from," she said.

"That's what it is—street smarts. That's not a bad thing, you know. That just means a good survival instinct and common sense."

"You should have told me this minister thing before you kissed me!"

"And how would that have changed anything?" he asked.

"I might've kept my tongue in my mouth for one thing!"

He laughed so hard he was bent at the waist. He laughed so hard that when he tried to kiss her goodbye, it was just wet and sloppy.

"Hey! Is that proper behavior for a minister!"

"Yes, ma'am," he said, giving her a salute and walking off back toward the lodge. Laughing his cute butt off.

"Man, can I pick 'em," she said to no one.

Chapter Seventeen

Krista refilled Jake's coffee cup and he gave her free hand an affectionate pat. "After your shift, I'd like to take you for a ride."

"Oh?"

"To the farm," he said. "I'll give you a lift home to change and tell your cousins where we're going, make sure they don't need you for anything, then we'll go. It's not far."

"Did you ask your sister and brother-in-law if they mind?" she asked nervously.

"My sister is at work until dinnertime and my brother-in-law will be working around the farm. They won't mind." Unconsciously, she backed away. "Don't be nervous," he said. "They're very nice people. Very welcoming."

Of course there was no way Charley and Meg would ask her to miss a trip to the farm, not because it would be such a great new experience for her but because Jake was taking her. They were almost giddy with excitement.

It was a beautiful August day, the sun bright with just a few scattered clouds and enough of a breeze to keep her clothes from sticking to her. It was less than a thirty-minute drive to an old farmhouse surrounded by barns, outbuildings and what seemed like miles and miles of green fields. The corn was high, the wheat was thick and there were other growing things she couldn't identify. "Soybeans and sugar beets," Jake said.

Also, there were several trucks.

"How much of this does your brother-in-law farm?" she asked.

"Everything you can see. That house to the north—that's the Jaspers and they don't farm anymore. Richard leases their fields. That house to the west, that's Nicholls and they only have a small plot, mostly for their own personal use. There are a few other neighbors here and there but this is the biggest farm in the area."

"All the trucks?" she asked.

"Richard has hands. Day workers. Seasonal. He only keeps two year-round and usually has another four from planting to harvest."

"Look how vast," she said in an almost reverent breath. "What must it have been like to grow up here?"

He laughed and said, "I thought I was cursed. Lotta chores on a farm."

He parked and met a bunch of barking dogs in the yard. At first Krista stiffened nervously and counted—four. One blond, one black and white, one solid black and one chocolate brown. Jake good-naturedly talked to them all. One of them, the golden one, sat in front of her, waiting.

"That's Lucy," he said. "She'll sit there patiently until you pet her. The others all run around in excitement because they have company."

"They don't run away?"

"This is where their food is," Jake said. "Twice a day, morning and night. They have work to do—keep the wildlife away from the chickens and any unfriendlies away from the house. And if they ran off, I don't know who'd go looking for them."

Close to the house was a vegetable garden with tomatoes that were huge, melons nearly ripe, zucchini and yellow hook-neck squash. There was a row of lettuce and a large plot of cucumbers. "Zoe likes to can pickles," he explained. There were a couple of apple trees and Jake pulled two off, rubbed off the dust on his jeans until they shone deep red. He handed her one.

There was a swing set with two swings, a slide and hanging rings. Beside it, a sandbox. "The grandchildren," he said.

He showed her the chickens, kept in a modern coop that was heated in winter, their three horses in the pen and two miniature mules. There were two cows and an old bull in the pasture. "They're more of a hobby than anything. If Richard gets a calf, he usually just sells it. Once he had a Clydesdale—someone was mistreating the horse so Richard took him in until he could find a permanent home. It took him five years."

"Five years!"

"I suspect he was dragging his feet. It's an expensive horse to feed and take care of and Richard's Clydesdale didn't make beer commercials. But his kids were young then and loved that horse."

He walked her through the cornfield to a pond right on the property.

"Oh, my God, it's beautiful," she said. "Did you swim in it as a kid?"

"We did not," he said. "It's a swampy thing. The water's okay, but not as pleasant as the lake. We skated on it in winter."

She saw a virtual army of big green farm machines, learned that three generations had lived in that farmhouse, his sister was a nurse who worked for a doctor in Willet, their two kids were grown and they had two grandchildren. She met a little pack of new kittens in the barn, got chased by a rooster and Lucy followed her devotedly, leaning against her regularly for a pat.

"I don't know if I can leave this dog," she told him.

"She's a lover, isn't she? Lucy was my dad's dog. He passed six years ago."

"Do you ever wish you were still involved with the farm?"

"Nah, I'm not a farmer. I like to come out here on a nice day, though. There's nothing harder than running a farm but to a visitor like me it seems so peaceful and healthy. I don't have to think about an early freeze, a bad storm, a long winter, a flood..." He picked a few daisies from a border along the side of the house, handing them to her.

"I bet you had adventures here," she said.

He took her hand and led her through the yard toward the barn. "Adventures in weather," he said with a laugh. "Blizzards in winter, tornadoes in summer, floods in spring. There are two types of kids raised in rural Minnesota. The ones who can't be happy in the city—it's too loud, messy, crowded, dangerous. And the ones who can't wait to get off the farm. I was the latter."

"I bet there were fun times," she said.

"Like you and your cousins had," he said. "Fun times, hard times. Growing up isn't easy. Let's go in the hayloft. I want to talk about something."

"We've been talking the last couple of hours," she said. "All the way here, out to the pond, through the veggies..."

He pulled on her hand. "You like those veggies, don't you?"

"You have no idea what a luxury they are. Charley goes to the farmers' stands all the time." She looked around, saw the ladder to the loft. "I bet you got into a lot of trouble up there."

"Not me so much as the other kids. Up you go," he said.

"But what about Lucy?" she asked.

"I'm sure she'll be waiting for you."

"Why are we going up there?"

"Because after we're done talking, we'll want to be alone."

"Oh," she said. "I guess I get it now." She smiled over her shoulder. "More kissing, I assume."

"If you don't mind."

She stepped up onto the loft. There were a couple of hay bales, an old horse blanket and a pile of loose hay in the corner. There was also a big hatch, a window, that Jake opened to let in the breeze. He sat down on a bale and pulled her down beside him.

"Tell me how the summer usually ends for you and your cousins."

"What do you mean?" she asked.

"When do you close up the house and leave?"

"When we were kids we left in time to get home and ready for school. We had to get our school things—new shoes, clothes, notebooks and things. We usually left right before Labor Day weekend."

"And this year?"

"I don't know. So much depends on Meg. We might be able to stay through the holiday weekend but we can't stay after the temperatures drop. We've all avoided talking about it."

"It's August, Krista. We have to talk about it, you and me. What are you going to do?"

"I don't know," she said, her voice barely a whisper. "Go back to Saint Paul. Maybe to my mother's? Or maybe I'll rent a room, get a waitress job."

"What if I said I don't want you to go?" he asked.

"Careful, Jake," she said. "You don't want to bite off more than you can chew."

"I don't want you to go," he said. "I don't want to scare

you but I think I love you. I know you mean a lot to me, like nobody has. And I know I haven't felt this way in a long, long time. Together, we just hit all the right notes. I don't want you to go."

"Well, I might not have a choice," she said.

"If that lake house has to be closed up, I can find you a place."

"Winter will come," she said. "I don't have a car. I have appointments I have to keep."

"I'll make a commitment to get you around," he said. "Did you ever drive? Have a license?"

She shook her head. She had driven, many years ago, but never got her license. "I don't want to be dependent on anyone," she said.

"You're dependent on Charley," he pointed out.

"You know how different that is," she said. "I've known you for two months!"

"Let's think about where to go from here," he said. "Just suppose we find you a place nearby for after your cousins leave. Something decent and affordable, close to the lodge so you can work. Just let me know when you need transportation—I'll be glad to help with that. There will be cold, snowy days when you can't walk. There will be your appointments and I suppose you'll want to visit your mother. Let's try it, Krista, because if you leave..." He shook his head. "I'd hate that. I love having you here. I love being here with you."

"Just what are you suggesting?" she said.

"I don't know. I want to be a couple. I don't mean to rush you, I don't want to pressure you, but I want you to know what I'm willing to do and I wanted to talk about it before summer is over. Before I wake up one morning and you've gone and we haven't thought about what we could have been together."

"A couple?"

"I don't care what kind of couple as long as it boils down to me and you. Will you think about it? Talk to your cousins if you want to. Talk to you mother, maybe. I can't promise you'll be happy every day but I can promise I'll give you my best and anything you need. If I can deliver it, I will. Krista, I just want to be with you. That's all."

She touched his cheek. "I think you're a little crazy," she said. "Sweet, but a little crazy. I'm not sure I can agree to anything right now. I'm new at this."

"Then let's just stay like we are," he said. "We'll give it time, let it grow, see where we go. If there's a day you think it's not right, not good for you, you'll call your mom, you'll tell me you need a ride. But the wild card is, you have to be here if we're going to test it out. Take a chance on me, Krista."

"I want to think about this," she said.

"That's all I ask." He pulled her closer. "Now kiss me like the wild woman you are." He pulled her arms around his neck.

She met his lips willingly. "That's it. You're getting a little wild stuff, aren't you? I'm not wild anymore, Reverend McAllister. I want to be good."

He laughed. "You are and I love you just the way you are, you sassy little broad." He smothered her with a kiss that was hot and steamy. It never failed to melt her to the bone. She held on to him so tightly it was a wonder he could breathe.

He wants to be a couple. She wasn't even sure what that meant. For right now it meant kissing her senseless, leaning back against the hay with him, holding each other and letting their tongues tangle. She could hear his heartbeat; she could taste his desire; she could feel arousal in both of them. Maybe this would be the day.

"What does it mean to be a couple?" she asked him.

"That you're my girl and I'm your guy," he said. "It can mean anything you want it to mean. You want me to keep walking you home? Do you want to live together? Do you want to be engaged? Whatever it is that doesn't make you feel you're at risk. You can count on me, I promise."

There was a lot more kissing, leaving her feeling a little crazy and mushy inside. She had a wild urge to undress him. Instead, she broke away a little bit. "What if I only want you to walk me home sometimes? For the next year?" she asked him.

"As long as we're in the same town so we can do that—you get to call the shots. That's why I want you to think about staying here. I'll help make that possible any way I can."

"I shouldn't trust so fast," she said. "I'm inexperienced."

"Bullshit," he said. "You've had more experience than you can stand. I just want to be with you. But only if you want it, too."

"I'm not ready," she said.

"Just think about staying," he said. "Everything else—let it mellow till you're ready."

"It should be at least a year before I make any decisions that could affect me permanently. I have to adjust to this life. This life of being a regular citizen."

"Then stay a year," he said. "There are places to rent here just like the city."

"Aw, shit, let's just make out," she said.

"I'm down with that," he said.

"And don't try to be cool!"

Krista and Jake kissed themselves blind for about an hour. A little touching was added, a great deal of pushing and moving against each other, and she could sense the promise of how loving and satisfying making love with him could be.

But not today, not in his sister's hayloft. They reluctantly let go of each other, mostly because Krista needed a bathroom.

"You can use the house bathroom. The door is never locked."

"Really? Is that wise?"

"No problems so far. The dogs bark when there's company, remember."

"And here's dear Lucy," she said. "She waited!"

"Told you." He slid an arm around her waist and led her to the house. He opened the back door for her and she immediately jumped back.

"Hello?" Zoe said, turning from the sink.

"Hey, Zo," he said, smiling at his sister. "I didn't know you were home!" Then he went to her, kissing her cheek. She was almost as tall as him. She wore nurse's scrubs and white tennis shoes.

"I came home a little early. What are you doing here?"

"Just knocking around the farm. This is Krista, my girlfriend."

Zoe grinned and dried her hands on a dish towel. She stretched out a hand toward Krista, who had suddenly turned shy way down to her toes. "Girlfriend, is it?" she said with a chuckle. "How do you do!"

Krista muttered a greeting.

"We just came in to borrow the bathroom before heading back to Waseka," he said. "It's right around the corner," he told Krista, giving her a little shove in that direction. "Ladies first."

Krista didn't really have a chance to look around, so stunned was she at running right into Jake's sister. She hadn't even had a chance to prepare herself! And then to be called a girlfriend? It was all a little much.

It was an attractive little bathroom, decorated to look like a Victorian powder room. So pretty. And like new. From the outside it looked like a very old house. She'd barely glanced at the kitchen and it appeared new. Jake's sister must have remodeled.

She could hear them talking and laughing out there. Krista looked in the mirror. Her lips were ruby from kissing, her cheeks flushed. She had a six-inch stalk of hay in her hair. Dear God! She pulled it out and tossed it in the trash can. Then she plucked it out of the trash and tucked it into her pocket, hiding the evidence. Maybe Zoe hadn't seen it.

Back in the kitchen she found that Zoe had a large basket of vegetables she was washing in her big sink, setting them out to dry on a dish towel on the counter. Gloriously bright colored tomatoes, squash, green beans, cucumbers, scallions, peppers and a colander full of leafy greens.

"My turn," Jake said, leaving Krista in the kitchen.

"Your vegetable garden is beautiful," Krista said.

"Thank you. I cheat a little bit—Richard or one of the guys tends it more than I do. I'm pretty busy with work and the grandkids."

"I think you have everything growing out there. A real farmer's garden."

"I hope you'll stay for dinner. Most of it's coming out of the garden. I put a pork loin in the slow cooker with a couple of potatoes and onions. Richard needs his meat!"

"I'm sorry, I told my cousins I'd be back by dinner."

Jake was back so quickly it was like he'd never gone. "Krista's cousin has been battling cancer," he said. He dropped an arm over Krista's shoulders. "Is it okay to say that?" he asked a bit after the fact.

"Yes. Yes, sure. It's not a secret. Breast cancer," she said. "She's been fighting a long time—four years now. She's so happy to be at the lake house for the summer. She's looking a little better."

"You must be filled with hope," she said. "We'll add her to our prayers."

"Thank you," she said.

"Since you can't stay, will you at least raid the garden? It's all such good, tasty stuff. And here it is August! We only have another month or six weeks left before fall."

"I love the fall," Krista said. "I don't want summer to end but I can't wait to see the leaves change color."

"Where are you from, Krista?"

"Originally, Saint Paul. But I've spent the last twenty-three years in California."

"Well, fall in the Sierras is glorious but our falls are pretty amazing, too, if you remember. Jake, you have to take her to Stillwater! The changing leaves along the Saint Croix River beat everything." She pulled a grocery bag out of a drawer and handed it to her. "Let's go pick, should we?"

"That's very generous of you," she said.

"I'm happy to thin the garden a little. And tell your cousin it's all organic—no pesticides or fertilizer. We make our own mulch." She grabbed a big knife out of her drawer. "Come on—I think I saw a great big broccoli flower just begging to be cut."

Krista followed her, listening while she chattered away happily. She was a very attractive woman in her fifties, her close-cropped light brown hair streaked with blond. She had those same blue McAllister eyes and they danced happily; her slim arched brows were so expressive. Her smile was infectious.

"Here we go," she said, lopping off a couple of broccoli stalks. She handed Krista the knife and pulled a pair of scissors out of the pocket of her scrubs. "Bandage scissors will do—I don't want to go back inside and find a proper pair."

She cut about three inches off the top of leaf lettuce and romaine. "You need beans and tomatoes and scallions to finish a salad. And how about some of the yellow hook-neck squash? It's still young and so delicious. Jake? Get me another bag! You're not leaving here without at least two big zucchinis. Every day I see another one as big as a horse's leg. Steam it with a great big onion." She dug around and pulled one out of the ground. "Throw in some mushrooms and garlic—but you're on your own for that. I don't grow either. Would you like some flowers for your table?"

"That would be so nice..."

She walked over to the house where the flowers grew tall against the wall and began snipping them into a generous bouquet. "I don't remember the last time Jacob brought a girlfriend around," she said. "High school, maybe."

"It hasn't been that long," he said.

"Bet it has," she teased. "Here you go, carry these for Krista. Now, I want you to come back when you can stay a little while. We'll have dinner. Let's do it soon."

"Thank you," Krista said. "And thank you for all of this."

"It's a pleasure. I'm happy to share the garden with friends anytime. Now, you kids stay out of trouble," she said, then laughed very happily at her own joke.

Jake gave Zoe a kiss on the cheek, told her to say hello to Richard, then escorted Krista to the truck and proceeded to load all the vegetables behind the passenger seat. Then he helped her in, putting the flowers in her lap, talking all the time. She didn't hear a word he said.

She buckled up and watched the vast fields as they drove away. He was still talking. He was proud of Zoe, how friendly and generous she was. She was a nurse, had he mentioned that? So she would be sensitive to the fact that Krista's cousin was fighting cancer. He hadn't told Zoe and Richard about

Andrea yet, and really, he couldn't wait, but he was trying to be patient. He had a lot of explaining to do and wanted the time to do it.

"Hey," he said, slowing the truck and pulling over. "You're crying! Was something said that upset you?"

She shook her head.

"Then why?"

She turned her tear-filled eyes toward him. She hiccuped. "She's so nice. She liked me…"

He rubbed a knuckle down her cheek, wiping away a tear. "Everyone likes you," he said. "Know why? You're very likable."

She just dissolved into more tears. Sobs, really. *Man, this crying thing,* she thought. *Once you let go, it was never-ending.* Women who cried like this in prison were in for it. Someone took her aside that first week, covered her, protected her and told her to dry it up. Criers got beat up. But she was out now and the tears were freed.

Zoe was so nice. And Zoe liked her.

Jake put his arms around her while she cried into his shoulder.

Could it happen? Could it work? Could she live in the outside world among good people? People who didn't wish to do anyone harm? Could she live in the arms of a good man? A man who didn't want anything but her happiness? Could she? Could they?

"Good tears, I guess," Jake said. He stroked her back. "Aw, sweetheart, everything is going to be okay."

Jo didn't bother knocking on the screen door at the lake house. The inside door stood open and she could hear voices. "Good morning," she called, stepping into the house.

"Aunt Jo!" Charley and Meg both said.

"Ma!" Krista said. "What are you doing here? How did you get here?"

"I drove Aunt Lou's car. I'm sorry I didn't ask if it was all right—I thought it was time we all talked. I have some things to explain. How about a cup of coffee? If you can spare one?"

"Absolutely. I'll get it. Sit down. Tell us what's on your mind," Krista said.

"Well, you know I've been talking with Louise?"

"How's that been going?" Krista asked, passing the coffee.

"I went to see Lou and begged her to talk about it all, negotiate a truce, kiss and make up."

"And?" Charley asked.

Jo was momentarily distracted by Meg. She moved to her right slightly to press her cheek, giving her a little kiss. "How are you feeling, darling?"

"Pretty good actually. I know I don't look good, but that'll come. I have a good appetite, Charley can vouch for that."

"I so look forward to watching you blossom." She sipped her coffee. "So, Lou and I have been talking, resolving our differences. It was much easier than I expected, really. We're both to blame for our standoff. Without going into all the details, we were both angry about a lot of things. Lou feels afraid everyone blames her because she was the one to make the proclamation that the lake house was closed, forbidding anyone from coming back."

"Well, it *was* her," Charley said.

"And it was me who wouldn't try to reason with her or change her mind. Don't you think I could have come here anytime I wanted to? I was letting her simmer in her own juices. Her own lonely juices. I was withholding my affection and making myself emotionally unavailable because I was angry with her. It's Lou's way to lash out and let everyone know when she's angry. Not me. I'm passive-aggressive."

"Aunt Jo, you don't have to be so forgiving," Charley said. "Mother was hoarding all the booty from Grandma Berkey's house! She can be so selfish."

"Actually, she wasn't hoarding. She was storing. She was saving all the valuable stuff for our retirement. Both of us. She was pretty sure I wouldn't have anyone to take care of me and she intended to be sure I had the means. We're planning an estate sale." She shook her head. "She's lucky that house of hers didn't go up in flames. She's lucky she wasn't robbed. I fired her cleaning crew. We're moving ahead. Then we're getting rid of her house and my condo. We're looking around for the right arrangement—probably a duplex of some kind. We'll be very close neighbors but not roommates, if we can find something. We talked to an agent who says that should be easy."

"Really?" Charley said, astonished.

"We're both so relieved by this decision. Especially your mother. I didn't realize how lonely she's been. She has a lot of regrets and doesn't quite know how to go about mending her fences. She'll be the first to admit, she has a lot of foolish pride. I told her it would be easy—all she has to do is say that. Don't we all want to be a family again if we can?"

"Well...sure...but we're pretty busted up," Charley said.

"The three of you managed just fine and I do believe you're thriving. If this could be the first of many summers, wouldn't that be nice? I think it could be. I told Lou we had to come right away and talk to you, explain our reconciliation, our plans. We want to know if there's anything of Grandma's you have an eye for before it's all gone the way of the estate sale. There's a lot of old junk but there are some beautiful pieces and if there's anything... Well, we talked and talked and talked. I insisted we come right away. Putting it off makes no sense—the summer is almost over. But poor Lou. She's terrified. She thinks everyone hates her. Blames her for everything. I told her that wasn't true, that we're all just sick of her cranky, sourpuss attitude."

"You *told* her that?" Meg said.

Jo nodded. "Made her cry."

"Mother doesn't cry," Charley said.

"It's you she particularly wants to make amends with. When you were sixteen, when you were pregnant and she insisted you go away to have the baby, she wasn't in her right mind. She couldn't undo it and she believes you'll never forgive her."

"She might've tried saying she was sorry," Charley said.

"She might be in a better place to do that now," Jo said. "She's not all alone now."

"We'll see," Charley said. "When I see her next. I'll be sure to visit her before I leave Minnesota."

"You can visit with her right now," Jo said. "She's in the car."

"She's in the—"

"I got her in the car," Jo said. "I couldn't get her out. She said when you all turn her away, it will be too much. I told her she was a big baby and everything would be fine. She didn't believe me." She smiled weakly. "Twenty-seven years is a long time to nurse a grudge."

"She's in the car?" Meg said.

Jo nodded. "I've never seen her like this. Someone is going to have to go get her."

"I can go," Meg said.

"I think it should be Charley," Jo said. "You're the one she's most afraid will never forgive her, never give her a chance. Are you ready to help me tidy up this mess?"

"Why do I always get the hard jobs?" Charley said.

"Well, you're the strongest one," Jo said.

"Wish I felt like the strongest one," she muttered.

Chapter Eighteen

There were a dozen accusations Charley wanted to throw at her mother. Louise hadn't called her, sometimes for years. They only talked because Charley initiated the call, not so much trying to be a proper daughter but something much less fitting. Never let it be said that Charley prolonged or contributed to this rift between them. Louise didn't seem to care about her grandchildren—not the one she forced Charley to give away, not Eric, who Charley raised. Louise visited her in California twice and on both visits she didn't bother to see Krista; Krista could have used a visit. On those occasions she did see or talk to Louise it had been like a fight just waiting to happen. Louise was hostile.

Charley stood on the porch and looked at the car, parked behind hers in the drive. It didn't seem possible but Louise looked so small. Louise had never looked small.

Charley took a deep breath and decided to take one for the team. She walked out to Louise's car and slid into the front seat, the driver's side. "So, rumor has it you're afraid to come inside. And I drew the short straw."

Louise didn't look at her. "I suppose you have good reason to be angry," she said.

"And why is that, Mother?"

Louise gave a short laugh. "I guess I wasn't prepared for you to ask me to list my mistakes. I'm sorry about the baby, Charlene. I couldn't have kept you home and cared for your baby while you attended school, not so soon after losing Bunny. Things wouldn't have worked out as well for you if you'd tried to keep her and raise her yourself—I know that seems cruel, but it's true. If I'd been in a better place, maybe we could have found another solution. I'm sorry. That's all I can say. It was a terrible mistake. I'll apologize to Andrea if that would be appropriate."

"Forget it," Charley said. "Andrea always wanted to know her biological parents but was never unhappy with her adoptive parents."

"That's good."

"How are we to make up?" Charley asked. "We've been completely cold to each other since I was sixteen. Totally irritated and angry with each other. How do we change that?"

"I have no idea," Louise said, sounding a little tired. "I told Jo this wouldn't work."

"It hasn't failed yet," Charley said. "Want to try to contribute something here? A suggestion? An idea?"

"Here's an idea," Louise said. "You could forgive me. We could start there."

"You know, I hated you," Charley said. "I hated you so much. There were about a hundred times over the last twenty-seven years I needed you to be tender toward me. Loving. Like when Eric was born. Or when I got my show. Or when I *lost* my show. When I found my daughter! Mother!"

"Every one of those events I heard about from Meg," she said, her voice uncharacteristically soft. "Every one. It appears we had the same expectations of each other. You were angry that it seemed I didn't care—didn't care that you'd found yourself a nice man in Michael, that you'd had a son, that you were successful, that you found your lost daughter. I was angry that you never called to share those things with me. How much more anger do you suppose we can find to throw on this teeter-totter? I give up, Charlene. When Bunny drowned I realized I was not the strong one in the family. I never was. I was the hardy one. I could run and swim. Emotionally, my best was never good enough. I lost my temper. I hurt easily. I'll do whatever you want, Charlene. Charley. Whatever helps us put this hatred to rest and try to mend what's left of our family."

"Hatred," Charley said. "Mother, I don't really hate you. If I hated you, you wouldn't have mattered a damn. I loved you. I just wanted you to love me back."

"I always loved you," she said. "I just couldn't find a way to say it to your angry, disappointed face. But believe me when I tell you—I'll do whatever you want. I'm old now. I want to live to be much older. I don't want to spend the rest of my life without you in it."

I'll do whatever you want.

"I said something like that to Michael," Charley said softly. "A surrender."

"Exactly," Louise said. "We can make a list if you like—you can list all my transgressions and I'll apologize for each one."

"See how sarcastic… Ach! Stop. We're going to have to put up with each other, that's all."

"Sounds pleasant," Louise said. "Why did you say that to Michael?"

"Oh, it's nothing," Charley said.

"I hope it's nothing. You've been very happy with Michael."

"He's a wonderful man," Charley said, feeling the cloud of tears invade.

"Charlene, I'd like us to do a little better than put up with each other," Lou said. "I know I'm not an easy person. I'll try if you will."

"Aunt Jo said you were saving all that junk from Grandma Berkey's house to help her with her retirement."

"It's not junk," Louise said. "There's some very valuable stuff. Art. Jewelry. Antiques from Grandma's grandmother. Not to mention a trust. Grandma Berkey was an only child and her father was wealthy."

"But I thought you made Aunt Jo sign all that away," Charley said.

"Who told you that?" Louise asked.

"I think Jo told Krista, who told us."

"Hmph. That was a different time. Roy was so damned irresponsible but your father was bound to help him, anyway. And Jo's pride was hurt every time they had to ask for help, yet she wouldn't give up on him. We had to do something to try to stop him from wringing us dry. It wasn't legal. It couldn't supersede a will."

"You said there wasn't that much," Charley reminded her.

"I lied," Lou said. "There's plenty."

"Jesus, don't tell Hope," Charley said. "She's been planning on an inheritance for a long time. And on top of that, she's nuts!"

Louise burst out laughing. "Don't worry, by the time it gets down to Hope, she'll be old like we are. Besides, we might do a couple of things. I've always wanted to go on a cruise. I could talk Jo into that. We could spend it all."

Charley found herself smiling. "Are you a little relieved that Jo made you come? That we're trying to mend things in the family?"

"I suppose I am," Lou said.

"Well, for God's sake, don't let it show!"

"I'm never going to meet your expectations as a perfect mother, Charley. Another twenty years and I'll be as cranky and obnoxious as Grandma Berkey. So just worry about what kind of mother you're going to be."

"I found Andrea's father," she said suddenly. "Or maybe I didn't find him exactly. Krista has been working as a waitress at the lodge and the hotel manager—he's the guy. We had a little summer fling and... Well, it was quite a surprise because Krista is actually dating him and she brought him to the house to introduce him to us and voilà! We recognized each other."

Louise gasped and covered her open mouth.

"See, Mother? You miss a lot by not hanging out with us."

"Did you tell her?"

"Right away. I gather they've talked. When I told him, he was so shocked I thought he was going to faint."

"Did you want to just kill him?"

Charley laughed. "He's very nice. We were stupid kids, that's all."

"Have you told Michael you reconnected with him?"

Charley was shocked. Louise might not even realize it but this was a whole new behavior. She didn't often ask many questions. She usually acted like she couldn't care less. "I haven't talked to Michael just lately."

"Why?"

Charley didn't answer. "You have to come in the house now, Mother. You have to see Meg and Krista. There's not that much lake time left. This is what Meg wants—family. You're going to have to hang out awhile. John will be here tomorrow night for the weekend. You have to stay. Meg and Krista have questions about the family history and the family trouble. I don't actually give a shit, but if there are answers, I'd like to hear them, too."

"How much of this family trouble am I going to have to swallow?" Lou asked.

"Probably about four cups or so. Don't worry, I have liquor."

"You are a good child," she said.

And she actually smiled.

Meg was the only one to cry sentimental tears when Lou came inside. This was what she had wanted—that her mother and her aunt Jo would reconcile and be each other's strength again, like they were when the girls were young. They spent hours telling stories about the early days at the lake house, stretching all the way back to when Jo and Lou were girls and *they* snuck out for little flings with boys from the lodge.

"I should've known," Charley said. "The apple never falls far from the tree."

They spent only that one night at Lake Waseka, then promised to be back in a few days. They had things to do in the cities, not to mention Jo's need to check in on Hope and make sure she was doing all right.

When Krista got home from work the next day, Jo and Lou had gone. John was due to arrive in late afternoon or early evening and so for a brief space of time it was just the three of them again. Meg was dozing in the bedroom.

"Was having your mother here upsetting to you?" Krista asked softly.

"No. I might still be in shock but Meg was right. Part of putting this family back together is putting *them* back together." Charley looked at her phone. "My mother is so much easier to take when Aunt Jo is around."

"And my mother is so much happier. So what is it?"

"What do you mean?" Charley asked.

"You've grown moodier every day and you've checked your phone about a hundred times."

"It's nothing, really…"

"Oh, it's something. Wanna talk about it?"

Charley sighed. "It's probably going to sound completely stupid. I'm not even sure how it happened. It's Michael. Michael and me, probably mostly me. I lost my job. When you lose a job in television the defeat is so public. And there was no warning. I never even sensed it was coming and I was so wounded. I was shattered. I felt like I had a rock in my gut and sandpaper in my throat. I wanted to scream and cry and I couldn't. At the very same time Meg was getting ready for her cell transplant, one last-ditch effort at getting her beyond metastasized cancer. Her odds of surviving were not great. And Michael's reaction? He decided it was a good time to get married!"

Krista's eyebrows shot up.

"After twenty-two years and what anyone would call a successful relationship, he thought he could cure my joblessness and my sister's disease by marrying me." She shrugged. "So we fought. And fought. Men—they're fixers, you know. He wasn't listening to me. He wasn't thinking about what was happening to me. He said he was fifty-four and he didn't want to die and leave behind a girlfriend. It made no sense and his timing couldn't have been worse."

"When was this?" Krista asked.

"My show was canceled in March. Megan was having her bone marrow transplant at about the same time. I was so brokenhearted and angry, I said I'd go to Minnesota to stay with Meg, that maybe we needed some time apart. And he said, 'Maybe we do.'"

"But you've talked to him, haven't you?"

"Sure. And to Eric. But so often when I talked to Michael we'd argue. No, it was worse than arguing. He kept asking if I'd reconsidered. Or maybe he wouldn't and so I'd say, 'At least you didn't ask if I'd reconsidered,' and he would say, 'Why bother? You've made yourself clear.' And it would crash from there."

"Man, it sounds kind of silly," Krista said.

"Thanks," Charley said.

"You've been with him twenty-two years, you have a kid together… When he asked you to get married did you by any chance say, 'What's the rush?'"

"It wasn't that I was offended by his proposal. It was the way he did it. I said I felt like my life was over and he said, 'We might as well get married, then.' Don't you see—it was my crisis and he made it about him."

"He probably stupidly thought knowing he wanted to make an even bigger commitment might make you feel better."

"Yeah, maybe he did."

"What an idiot," Krista said.

"You understand?"

"No, I don't understand!" she said loudly. "Look, I don't know anything about relationships, especially boy-girl relationships, but you probably should have tabled the conversation for a while. Instead of saying no, you probably should have asked for a little time to get over the current crisis before thinking about a wedding. I mean, it's not likely you'd say no, is it? After this many years?"

"As a matter of fact, I wrote him a letter. A real written letter and not a text or an email, and I said I'd do whatever he wanted. If he still wanted me."

"Wow. I bet that just melted him."

"Krista!"

"Seriously? You said, 'Okay, whatever you want.' Did you add, 'Even though it'll kill me,' just like your mother did with my mother about going to the lake? Really, your side of the family has some serious sticks up your asses. My side is nuts but your side? Do you have to have everything your way?" She shook her head. "You wouldn't do well in prison. You know why I love you, Charley? You're one of the most generous, loving people I know. You're commitment driven as long as you feel in control. But you're a tad inflexible."

"He hasn't called me. He would have gotten the letter a few days ago and he hasn't called." She looked at her phone again. "Or anything."

"Well, thanks, you just helped me think through a kind of heavy issue of my own. Jake has asked me to consider staying at Lake Waseka after you all have closed up the house and gone. He offered to help me find something small and close to rent. He doesn't exactly have his own place—he stays at the lodge. He gets his room and meals on the company so there's no point in him wasting his money on rent. He's saving to build a house here, but *when* is the mystery. Anyway, I said I thought it was too soon to make any kind of commitment—we've only known each other about two and a half months. But now I think maybe we should try that. He promised to help me with my transportation issues so I can make appointments, run errands and, on cold, snowy days, have a ride to work. I think, yes, I should see if what I believe about him is true—that he's a very fine man. He treats people very well. I have that red flag thing down. I'm not missing anything. And what's the worst thing that can happen? I can ask him for a ride to the bus and go to my mother's." She rolled her eyes upward. "Oh, please, God, don't let Hope be living with our mother! That would make this whole idea a miserable failure."

Charley just watched her with her mouth hanging open. "Krista, do you love him?"

"Probably," she said. "I haven't had a lot of practice with

that, you know." She became wistful. "He's so kind to people. Sometimes they don't even know it. One of the waitresses has two special-needs kids at home. She and her husband have to work opposite shifts so one of them is always home and Jake keeps an eye on her because sometimes she's real tired. You know, if she has a hard night with the kids. He tries to make it look like he's just a good manager but it's more than that. He's kind. You can't get away with that in prison. If you're soft, you're history. I don't think I ever was, you know—soft. But boy, did I get hard in prison. Being around Jake—it gives me back some of that. You can be soft around Jake and be safe."

"That's so lovely," Charley said.

"I usually try to stay out of people's business but I think you should try to find a way to patch things up with your Michael."

"Yes," she said. "But I did ask him to forgive me. In that letter that he should have gotten by now."

"Maybe he hasn't even checked the mail, Charley."

She shook her head. "He's obsessive about the mail."

"You're going to have to do something. Maybe you should go home. At least call him."

"I'm a little afraid to," she said. "What if he's over me? We were both pretty angry."

"Huh. I thought you were fearless."

"Me? I'm afraid of a lot of things."

"Then why do you act so damn tough?" Krista shook her head. "You girls on the outside, you can sure get yourselves worked up over meaningless bullshit. This thing with your man? I'm sure it hit you wrong, but if you look at the whole thing, it's not even a thing. You hurt each other's feelings. That's all." She jutted her chin toward the bedroom where Meg was sleeping. "Now that's a thing."

They were both respectfully quiet for a moment.

"You don't have to rent anything, Krista," Charley said. "You can use this house as long as you want. You can walk across the lake when it freezes. Just wait till the ice fishermen put up their fishing shacks to be sure. When you see the trucks drive on the ice, you'll know it's safe."

"I don't want to abuse my welcome. I want to try to pay my way."

"On a waitress's salary? That's going to be tough. But this house was paid for decades ago. And with someone here watching over it, we can visit it in winter if we want to. We can make sure the heater is serviced before it gets too cold."

"I'll have to ask the board of directors," Krista said. "Louise and Josephine."

Three days later, on Krista's day off, the three women were barely finished with breakfast when someone tooted a horn. Krista went to the porch.

"Oh, you're not going to believe this," she yelled into the house, bringing the other two out.

Jo and Lou were helping someone out of the car. They had brought Grandma Berkey to the lake. She was focused on the ground in front of her, watching her steps carefully, though Jo and Lou each held an arm. Krista's first thought was that she was so tiny. She must be no more than a hundred pounds. She was only a little hunched. Her hair was an interesting shade of pink and quite thin.

"Surprise," Jo said when they got to the porch steps. "Careful, Mother," she coached.

"Grandma!" Charley said. "Have you been kidnapped?"

"'Bout time someone got me out of that hellhole."

"Don't worry, we'll only be staying a few hours," Jo said. "We thought you might enjoy asking Grandma about the good old days."

"They weren't all that good," Grandma said. "You got any coffee? I hadn't hardly had my coffee when they snatched me."

Krista held the screen door open while Lou and Jo shepherded her into the house. Grandma paused and patted Krista's cheek. "So they let you out, did they?"

"Yes, ma'am."

"And I guess they taught you some manners in there. Well, they kept you way too long. A tragedy." She came up to Krista's chin. "You look none the worse for it."

"Thank you. I guess."

"So this old place didn't fall down while we were away?" She shook her daughters off her arms and took little shuffling steps to the chair in the living room. She looked around. "Looks just like it did."

"Do you want cream and sugar, Grandma?" Charley asked.

"Yes, please," she said.

"Add a little water to her coffee so it's not too strong. And not too much sugar," Lou said.

"I like it strong!" the old lady barked. "I'm Swedish—we like it strong! And don't spare the sugar! We used to give you girls coffee in your milk when you were toddlers. That's what the Swedes do!"

"Her hearing seems fine," Krista said.

"Damn right, it is. Everything is fine. I don't know why I'm locked up in that snake pit."

"Mother, it's the best facility in Saint Paul. There's a waiting list!"

"I don't care! I hate it. I miss my house. My parents bought me that house!"

Krista went and sat close, sensing her best chance at information at hand. "You must have loved the house," she said.

"I loved it once the judge was gone," she said. "It was a

good place to raise my daughters. A good house. My parents bought me that house."

"As a wedding gift?" Krista asked.

"That's right."

"And the lake house?" she asked.

"The judge," she snorted. "Once he got his hands on some of my money, he did as he pleased. With caution," she added with a cackle. "He was not a good judge, you know. He was a mean judge, that's what. My father wasn't unhappy about that, if you want to know the truth, because even though my father was in Chicago and the judge in Saint Paul, my father knew his price, the old bastard."

"Your father?" Krista asked. "Your father was an old bastard?"

"No, my father was a businessman! The judge was for sale!"

There was an "Ohhh" from the gallery.

"He couldn't get his hands on all my family money so he found a way. But he had to be very careful because if I had to call my father, there would be a firm talking-to. The kind that leave marks! And this cabin? I hated this cabin."

The girls looked between each other.

Grandma chose to sip her coffee and hum quietly to herself. She sipped again. "Very good, Louise," she said, looking right at Charley. "It's strong and sweet." She sipped some more, hummed some more.

"Grandma, why did you hate the lake house? It was the finest lake house here," Meg asked.

"Well," she said, putting down her cup. "I don't have any proof of this, but the lake house idea came at the same time as a new court reporter. She was a very buxom blonde. The judge thought sending me and the girls to the lake for the summer was a good idea." She shook her head. "He was always unfaithful. Always. But he didn't hit me after that first year. Because my father would have killed him. My father wasn't in the mob in Chicago but he wasn't opposed to doing business with them. They had a thing about justice. I think the only man the judge was ever afraid of was my father."

"Jesus," Charley said. "You should write an autobiography!"

"You'll never know how much of it is fiction," Lou whispered.

"I heard that! You calling me a liar?"

"Tell them about your betrothal and wedding, Mother," Jo said.

Grandma Berkey smacked her lips and began a story of society parties, bridal showers, bridesmaids, 1950s fashion, pastel gowns, flowers and champagne. She wanted Bobby Darin to sing at the reception but that didn't work out. The wedding and reception was attended by three hundred, they honeymooned in Miami Beach and her mother met her at her new house in Saint Paul to help her get organized. There were friends of friends who lived in Saint Paul to call on and the right country club had to be found.

Meanwhile, Robert Leonard Berkey, later known only as the judge, was ten years her senior and a junior lawyer in the prosecutor's office. If not for Grandma's money, he wouldn't have been able to so much as take her out to a nice dinner. But thanks to generous campaign contributions from her family to key politicians in Saint Paul, Robert's rise was pretty quick. Grandma had women friends who were also newly wed; their children came along. She was endlessly busy with social events. Her schedule was packed! And she had a very well-trained household staff. Only four, but they were good. There was the nanny, the cook, the housekeeper, the maid.

"We were so busy," she said, laughing. "We had such a good time."

"It sounds like you were happy," Krista said.

"There were happy times," she said, sipping her coffee again.

"So marriage to the judge had its positive side?" Krista asked.

"That old buzzard?" she asked. "He managed to make me hate him in no time at all."

"Forgive me, Grandma, but you never acted like you hated him," Charley said. "You grieved horribly after he died."

"I slept more peacefully when he was gone than I ever had before. I grieved when Mama died, that's when I grieved. Thank God I had my girls." She hummed and picked up her coffee again.

Charley looked at Lou. "I never heard a cross word between them."

"We did, growing up. But nothing worse than our friends' parents."

"When did all this start? She's really hostile!" Charley said.

"I heard that!" Grandma snapped. "You'd be hostile, too, if someone took you out of your home and stuck you in some snake pit!"

A few more stories were told, Grandma Berkey taking center stage with many more stories from her youth than from her married years. She had fancied another boy as her future husband but he wasn't a professional and her father had in mind a doctor or lawyer. When she met the judge, he was so respectful to her parents she thought it would be fine. She looked right at Charley and called her Louise three times.

Then, right in the middle of a sentence, she nodded off. Her head bobbed, her chin on her chest.

Jo and Lou exchanged glances and softly chuckled.

"We'll have a small bite of lunch, if you'd be so generous, then we'll take her back to the snake pit," Jo whispered.

"You're welcome to stay," Charley said.

"No, we can't," Lou said. "Mother wanders at night. A bit of sundowning. Her snake pit is also a memory care facility. She has Alzheimer's. I'm sure I told you that. She gets medication and she's doing very well."

"When did all this business about hating the judge start?"

"She's always had her complaints but, you know, she's very proud and wants to maintain her good reputation in society. She wouldn't want her friends at the club, for instance, to think she didn't have a perfect marriage—though I'm sure none of them did, either. Back in Mother's day men were typically disrespectful to women in general."

"Was Daddy?" Charley asked.

Lou shook her head. "Your father was a sweet man. Quiet and awfully boring at times, but he treated me well."

"Roy wasn't a chauvinist or abuser," Jo said. "He was a hopeless alcoholic. If I'd known then what I know now…"

"Once we took her to the nursing home, she stopped worrying about her reputation and began referring to the judge as 'that old bastard.' I don't know how much of it is real or a by-product of the disease. She was never so angry before."

"She might've been and didn't show it," Jo said. "I know the judge sure made me angry."

"He was widely known as a hanging judge. He didn't seem to have mercy for anyone."

"I'm proof of that," Krista said, remembering what happened when she had begged for his help.

After waking, Grandma Berkey stuck to her script. She hated her husband.

"I wonder, Grandma, why didn't you divorce him?" Charley asked.

"My parents died, the money was left to me in a trust and the judge would have never let me get away with anything. In those days only the desperate or notorious dared to get divorced. In the '50s and '60s none of us were happy. It wasn't fashionable to be happy. Now all anybody wants is to be stupidly happy every second whether they deserve to be or not."

Krista made a face. "A philosopher," she said.

Chapter Nineteen

If there was ever a single event that could be at once hilarious, depressing and exhausting, the visit from Grandma Berkey was definitely it. She wore them out. And while her tales were completely plausible, she was clearly not playing with a full deck. She mixed up Krista and Meg, called Charley Louise and asked Jo to fetch her walker—she wanted to go to the sunroom.

It wore Meg out completely and she ate a little something, then went to her room to rest. Charley cleaned up the kitchen and went down to the dock with her phone. Krista opened her laptop on the breakfast bar, looking out the window. She was worried about both of them. Charley seemed to be crumbling under the weight of a broken heart, and Meg, it could not be denied any longer, was not getting better. No matter how many times you asked her how she felt and no matter how many times she answered, "Pretty good actually," she was dwindling. Her eyes were rarely bright, her coloring sometimes became grayish and she was moving so slowly, so cautiously.

Krista sat before the laptop, trying to decide what to do next because, it appeared, in defiance of all reason, she was the most together member of their merry little group. She had Jake and what resembled a future, even if that was assuming a lot. She glanced down toward the dock to see Charley sitting cross-legged there, staring at her phone. It was an ominous future, she thought, if two people who loved each other could become estranged when exactly the right thing was not spoken in exactly the right way.

She felt grateful. She had health, something prison should have squashed like a bug. She had freedom. And she had a clear mind.

Meg was growing weaker. She would not be taken away from the lake now, Krista knew that. It was late August, Labor Day was almost upon them and the summer and Meg would be finished at about the same time. *Poor Charley*, Krista thought. *Her losses keep growing.*

And then a car pulled into the drive, parking behind Charley's rented SUV. And Krista smiled.

Charley escaped to the dock the second Meg took to her bed. The three women had gone to their separate corners rather than doing a postmortem on their grandmother's visit. Old age must be a great deal of work, she found herself thinking. Blessed few live to be beyond eighty-eight with a sound mind and strong body. At the moment she wondered if Grandma's body was too strong. She needed help to physically get through the day—the simple tasks of washing and making her own food had left her several years ago. Stuck in that big old Grand Avenue manse full of stairs, she'd have fallen to her death in no time. She'd started in assisted living with a part-time nurse, and when she began to wander at night, she was transferred into memory care. Charley had visited a few times when she was home to see Meg. Louise was right—it was a very stylish, comfortable and bright facility while that old Grand Avenue manse had grown moldy and dark.

Charley kept staring at her phone, checking her email and her texts and her voice mail. Could Michael really leave her after all these years? Now? While Meg was so ill? While she was feeling so vulnerable and in such need of his—

She lifted her head at the sound of a vehicle. She hoped her mother and Jo weren't bringing Grandma back. She turned around and gulped back tears. Michael got out of the car and walked toward her. She stood. She covered her mouth with her hand and she let go, let herself cry. One thing had not changed in twenty-two years. He was the most handsome man she knew.

Her tears came in gulps and her steps were slow and unsteady. He wouldn't come to tell her goodbye, not Michael. He wasn't that kind of man. She approached the end of the dock when he stopped, smiled at her and opened his arms. With a cry, she ran to him and filled his arms. She buried her face in his neck and he held her, her feet leaving the ground.

He rubbed her back. "Hey, baby," he said gently. "Having a bad day?"

"Michael," she sobbed. "I needed you so much."

"I'm here," he said. "I love you."

"Oh, Michael, are you here to stay?" she asked through her sobs.

He set her down. "No, honey. Just a couple of weeks. I still have a commitment in England. But I'll be back. This long separation is much too long to be apart."

She made a sound, a joyful sound, and covered his mouth in a searing kiss, their lips wet from her tears. He chuckled against her lips, held her tighter and returned the kiss. He devoured her like a starving man. When at long last they parted, he whispered, "I can't remember when I last saw you cry."

"I thought you were leaving me!" she said with a hiccup of emotion.

"I told you I was in forever, not just until I didn't get my way."

"Oh, God," she said, tears flowing again. "Why didn't you tell me you were coming?"

"Now, why would I do that?" he said with a little laugh.

"I wrote you a letter!"

"I know. I got it three days ago. I had to close up my office and the house and make travel arrangements and—" He shook his head disapprovingly. "Really, Charley? A letter? When did we stop talking?"

"I think it was about April," she said.

He wiped her cheeks. "We've talked a hundred times since then."

"But we argued so much! I didn't want to argue anymore."

"But a letter? You could have told me your feelings."

"I was doing that so badly."

"Me, too. So I decided to come to you instead of calling or writing you a letter. We're not going to do that anymore. We've always known where we stood with each other. You're the only woman I've ever loved. I'm not giving you up that easily."

She put her head on his shoulder and cried again. He held her close and kissed her tears away. "Is there somewhere we can be alone?" he asked her.

"The boathouse," she said in a breath.

"I mean, really alone," he clarified.

"There's a lock on the door."

He gently wiped away her tears. "I need some reassurance."

She laughed through her tears. "Me falling apart isn't reassurance enough?"

"It's a good start," he said. "Your sister and cousin? Will they miss us?"

"Meg is napping. Krista was on her computer. I have so much to tell you."

"Maybe we can talk a little later. Right now I think my body needs your body."

She took him by the hand and led him up the stairs to the little room above the boathouse. What a stroke of brilliance it was, finishing this space. Before the door was closed she decided they would stay here together while Michael was visiting. Away from the others, listening to the water.

The beauty of a long, committed and loving relationship is the satisfaction of intimacy between two people, each wanting to please the other. They had many inventive ways of showing each other that pleasure, but none of those would work today. They'd been apart too long, aching for each other too long. Charley laughed as Michael tried to get her out of her clothes without tearing them off her.

Once they were down to bare skin, their hands all over each other, Charley fell back on the bed. Foreplay was completely out of the question and unnecessary; their mutual hunger drove them full speed ahead. "This isn't going to last nearly long enough," Michael said. "Charley, it was so hard without you."

"Let's not do that again. Whose idea was that? Don't answer. Just kiss me."

He spread her thighs and nestled inside her. That stopped him. He didn't move for a moment, luxuriating in the sensation. "Home," he said softly. He brushed back her hair and kissed her softly. "This is where I belong."

"Yes, it is," she agreed. Her hands on his shoulders, she caressed his beautiful arms and back and chest. And he'd barely begun to move before she exploded into pleasure so lovely her eyes filled with tears yet again.

He kissed her eyelids. "No more crying," he said. "Just loving. We can steal an hour of just loving."

"This might kick off a marathon," she said. "You've always been so good at that."

"You're good, that's why," he said. "Damn, I missed you."

He started to pull away but she held him. "Not yet," she said. "Stay a little while longer."

"I'm heavy," he said.

"Nah, you're just right. Wow, that was such a good idea." She smiled into his eyes. "Makeup sex is my specialty."

"I think you've got it down," he said. "Want to make up one more time before we go to the house?"

Krista thought she heard Meg in the bedroom. She leaned her ear against the door to listen and there was a soft moan coming from inside. She tapped on the door and opened it. Meg was rolling her head back and forth, gritting her teeth. She glistened with sweat.

Krista sat on the side of the bed. "You're in pain," she said.

"A little bit," she said. "I have some pain medication in my top drawer. Do you mind?"

"I'll get it. Just one?"

"I think I'll throw caution to the wind and have two."

"Is that all right?" Krista asked. Meg just laughed, though there was little humor in it.

She fetched the pills and a glass of water. She had to help Meg to sit up to take the pills. She fixed a pillow behind her back. Meg leaned back and closed her eyes, breathing steadily.

"How long has this been going on?" Krista asked.

"Oh, it comes and goes."

"How long, then?"

"A couple of weeks. Maybe a month."

"How in the world did you manage to hide it?"

"Oxy. Powerful stuff."

"And you're getting weaker," Krista said.

"My balance is off, that's all," she said. "I heard a car..."

"Michael is here," she said. "They hugged and kissed and disappeared into the boathouse. I think they'll leave us alone for a while."

"Tell me a story? Tell me what happened that summer. I know you know."

"In just a minute. Will you excuse me just a minute and I'll come right back? May I use your phone?"

"Please don't do anything stupid," Meg begged. "Please don't sound the alarm! I'm okay."

"I'm not going to sound any alarm," Krista said. "I'm going to get you more pain medication."

"Oh," she said, relaxing. "I guess that wouldn't hurt."

Krista took the phone and left the room. Although she knew it was prying, she went through Megan's texts for that day—all from John.

How are you feeling?

I'm fine—stop worrying.

Your appetite?

Excellent. Leave me alone and get back to work. What are you doing today?

ER today, so it will move fast. ILY.

ILY, too. To the moon and back.

Krista fought tears. She sniffed them back bravely. She dialed John. Of course she knew he would answer immediately as the call was coming from Meg's phone. "Hi, babe," he said.

"It's Krista," she said. "I just gave Meg two pain pills. She was hurting. I think she takes them more than she admits. She's weak and unsteady and she lied about her appetite—it's not great. She is eating, though. A little."

"I'll come," he said.

"John, pack for a long visit. And bring some good drugs."

She heard him sigh into the phone. "Okay."

Then she took the phone back to Meg. Krista could tell the pills were already kicking in. Meg gave a wan smile. "I heard you," she said.

"No, you didn't," Krista said. "Why didn't you tell us it was getting bad? You can trust us."

"I didn't want the focus to be on me, on my cancer. I wanted you all to focus on getting back on track. Together. Making a family."

"You're family, sweetheart. And you're sick."

"I'm not leaving," Meg said. "Damn it, I wanted to see fall. The colors around the lake are so beautiful."

"Who says you won't?" Krista asked.

"It's better if this doesn't drag out. I have it on good authority that the other side is excellent. I'm not afraid. I have only one fear, really. I hope it's a silly fear. I hope they have it all worked out. I'm just afraid I'll miss the people I love, but I bet they have that all worked out."

"It'll be okay," Krista promised. "Anyone who can come up with heaven can figure out the missing people glitch."

Meg closed her eyes softly. "I thought heaven was right here," she said. "Even the adventure with Hope." She opened her eyes. "I guess you should let everyone know what's happening."

"Maybe later," Krista said. "You said you wanted me to tell you the story of that summer. You aren't going to believe what happened…"

John slid onto the bed beside Meg, threading his arm under her head. She roused slowly. "Hmm, hello, darling man."

"Sleeping off the pain pills?" he asked softly, cradling her in his arms.

"They're very good," she said sleepily.

"How's the pain right now?" he asked.

"Muted. I'll get up for dinner."

He brushed her fuzzy cap of hair back. "Did you think you were fooling me?"

"Nah. You've looked into the eyes of too many patients. I'm glad you're here. I've been thinking about something."

"What's that?"

"You should remarry. You're young. It would be such a waste if you didn't. But she must be just slightly less wonderful than me. Can we agree on that?"

He kissed her temple. "There will never be anyone as wonderful as you."

"I know, but if you make an effort, you might get close." She kissed his chin. "John, I'm sorry. You were the best reason to live. I let you down."

"No, Meg. No."

"I've learned that dying well can be a lifetime job." She sighed. "It's harder than it looks."

"I'll do whatever I can," he said. "I'm very proud of you. I admire you, Meg. You're the strongest person I know."

"I hope you're ready," she said. "I did everything I could think of to help you get ready. I'd rather it be any other way."

"I know," he said. "Me, too."

"Have I told you how desperately I love you?" she asked.

"God, yes. If there's one thing we've always had, it was the greatest love. I'll carry it in my heart forever."

She patted his cheek. "Good. Then do your physician's magic and make all the little children feel better."

"I wish I could make you feel better," he said.

"I'll be feeling better soon…"

Chapter Twenty

October 2016

Meg passed away very quietly at the lake house the first week in September. She was right, Krista thought—the leaves around the lake were breathtaking. Krista believed Meg probably had a very good view of them now. If ever there was a person who was going to achieve lofty heights after passing, it was Meg, the most beautiful person in their family.

She passed in the arms of her husband, with her mother holding her hand, her sister close by and her beloved cousin telling her a story. It was painful and beautiful. And so fitting.

Krista was so relieved that Meg didn't linger in pain for terribly long because some very important things happened before she died. Beverly and her family came to the lake when they learned Meg was dying. Meg was able to meet Beverly's husband, her two children and two of her foster kids. Krista was able to renew the relationship with her sister and they promised to stay in touch.

Andrea and her family came primarily to meet Jake, but as luck would have it, Eric had come to the lake so Charley's whole family was able to spend a little time together. Andrea's small children were positively adorable, but also typical little ones—wild and crazy. They didn't spend too much time at the lake house—Jake had a cabin at the lodge for them. Krista was able to leave the lake house for a little while to spend time with them; Krista was Andrea's aunt and, Jake said hopefully, would also be her stepmother.

Josephine brought Hope to the lake house for one afternoon for a very pleasant and very brief visit. Hope was amazingly calm and seemed remarkably sane. "Isn't medication the best invention?" Meg said.

After Meg's passing, Jo and Lou were able to find and move into identical condos in the same development. It was more upscale than anything Jo had had in the past and she was very proud of it. As for Louise, she happily welcomed the smaller and less cluttered living arrangements, so both were fulfilled.

Other matters were being worked out. Frank Griffin was monitoring the sale of Hope's house and that, along with alimony, would be her income. Jo held a power of attorney so that Hope wouldn't run through her windfall irresponsibly. Hope was living in the same condo complex as Jo and was in therapy. Her goal was to get a job and support herself, which there was every reason to believe she could do.

Before Meg passed, Jake was able to bring the news that the mystery man Lou had whacked with an oar had not really had amnesia, though he had had a concussion. His name was Clyde Bannon, about as far from being Russian as he could be. The Winslett police department had found him and began an investigation that uncovered a series of scams and frauds and he went to jail. Whether he actually stood trial or went to prison, Jake didn't know. He knew what he did because an old uncle of his was a police officer in Winslett thirty years ago and they considered Clyde a big catch.

So the notorious Berkey sisters, while at times dangerous, were not murderesses, after all.

Krista was waiting tables at the lodge and living in a very fine home—the lake house. Her boyfriend often spent the night and she had a feeling of peace and tranquility she hadn't expected to enjoy in her lifetime. Jake had talked with the owners of the lodge and expressed an interest in staying on in a permanent capacity as the manager; the answer wasn't in, but they seemed interested. There was a very good chance they would stay and build that house on the lot with the swing. She still enjoyed reading and writing but no longer felt a compelling need to tell the story of the Berkey family.

Today, on this late October day when the leaves were bright with color, the fall colors Meg had so wanted to see, many of them were coming back. Jo and Lou, certainly, though out of kindness they left Grandma Berkey behind. Hope was there, practicing empathy. John, of course, along with a few friends of Meg's from the city. Beverly came without her husband this time; he was still deep in the harvest. Charley, flying solo—she'd left her husband and son hard at work at the University of Cambridge in England and would be returning to them right away. They'd gotten married the moment Charley arrived in Cambridge.

Together they would sprinkle Meg's ashes on the still waters of Lake Waseka, where they'd had so many joyous years growing up. Jake would provide a brief service. They would all hold hands, bow their heads, give thanks for all the summers that were.

And for Meg, who brought them together again.

★ ★ ★ ★ ★